Chronicles of Nethra

Book Four

Stardust Grave

This is a work of fiction. All characters and events portrayed in this novel are either fictitious or are used fictitiously.

Chronicles of Nethra: Stardust Grave

By E. R. Donaldson
Edited by Alana Joli Abbott

www.mythicnorthpress.com

ISBN: 978-1-954177-10-9

First edition: December 2021

ACKNOWLEDGMENTS

Thanks, once again, to Alana Joli Abbott for providing the copy edits for this book. Your feedback is invaluable and always brings a smile to my face. Thanks also to Bob, Josh, and all my other advanced readers for your feedback. Lastly, a big thanks to my family. This has cost you a lot in terms of time and energy. I hope you're proud of what we've created together.

Chapter 1

[LOADING CORRESPONDENCE...]
[TO: SYDNEY CROSS]
[FROM: GAVIN BLACK]
[SUBJECT: RE: PERSON OF INTEREST]

I've found the girl you were looking for. Turns out she wasn't doing that good a job hiding.

This guy—goes by Botch—has been running his mouth off about getting slick with this girl claiming to be Tessa Valadar. Says she's taken a special interest in him and is taking him and his crew to the next level.

Botch is a low-level dealer. Nobody was taking him seriously, but I thought, "What the hells? Why not look into it?" Turns out he wasn't just running his mouth.

Address where you can find her is attached. Do me a solid and keep my name out of this when you tell the boss, yeah? I don't want Cyrus thinking I was good with his sister whoring around with anyone in my orbit.

[CLOSING CORRESPONDENCE...]

Cyrus stared down at the body at his feet and the crimson pool spreading steadily from the bullet's exit wound at the top of her head. The last remnants of her tears dripped down her cheeks to mingle with her tousled hair in the gory puddle. The silver pendant with the charged j-kryst rested neatly just below her clavicles, ironically pristine against the macabre backdrop.

He probably should have felt… *something*. There should be some kind of sorrow, or maybe even regret. After all, the blood that pooled on the grimy floor was the same blood that ran in his veins.

But he didn't. He felt nothing—just an all-consuming numbness. Tessa had been dead to him well before he'd made her pull that trigger.

"Sir?" Farris, the Don's faithful bodyguard, peeked into the room. If he took any issue with the bodies littering the floor, he elected not to voice it. The decision won him some points from Cyrus, despite his having returned to this spot against Cyrus's orders.

Cyrus kicked the pistol, still held loosely in Tessa's lifeless hand, over in Farris's direction. "You can retrieve your weapon now."

The bodyguard did so silently. He let that silence hang for several seconds, as Cyrus continued to ponder his sister's corpse. At length, Farris said, "Those shots may have been reported. We should probably go."

Cyrus scoffed. "In this complex? Gunfire must be as common here as barking dogs. We're at no risk."

"All the same, sir."

A heavy sigh escaped Cyrus's throat. "Fine. Just give me a few more moments. Wait out in the hall. Alert me if anyone is coming."

Though he may not have approved of the directive, Farris was a good soldier. He complied.

When the door shut behind him, Cyrus spotted a padded armchair relatively free of the grime that seemed so ubiquitous in the tiny apartment. He settled into the chair, sliding deep into its cushions as a strange weariness bore down on him. All the while, he continued to stare at the corpse.

What was he looking for? Why this continued fixation with the body?

It certainly wasn't regret. Cyrus had steadied himself for this possibility before he ever got in the car to come here. He had come to give Tessa one last chance, but there was no reason to suspect she would take it. Nine hells, she hadn't been receptive to the dozens of chances he'd given her before.

How had his father put up with her for so long? Had he known that Tessa would never amount to anything? Such a conclusion was inevitable. Tessa had shown even less aptitude than Joaquin, gods rest his soul.

Was that what having children was like? Were the odds that they might defile your legacy no better than a coin flip? For every Cyrus and Julia you sired, did you also give birth to a Joaquin or Tessa?

No, existential questions regarding fate and legacy were not what tore at him. What was it then? Why could he not bring himself to look away?

The light seemed to catch the surface of the green crystal, causing it to gleam. Cyrus thought he should retrieve the necklace. It would be undoubtedly useful at some point, and he couldn't risk leaving it for someone to stumble on by accident. Without the Heart of Thule, or one of Lucretia's infusions, there was no real risk of anyone unlocking the mind-controlling potential of the trinket. Still, it was better not to take chances.

He didn't want to touch the corpse, though. For a half-second, he considered calling Farris back in and having him remove it, but thought better of it. If only he could somehow will Tessa to remove it from her own body.

Then, something strange happened. Tessa's hand twitched.

Was she still alive? No, that was impossible. Half her brain matter was splattered across the apartment. A residual reflex perhaps? Or a figment of his imagination?

The corpse lay still once more. Cyrus leaned forward, staring it down. He willed it to move again.

It did.

The hand twitched erratically. With uncoordinated jerks, it reached toward her breast. The other began to move as well.

Sit up.

Tessa's whole body convulsed. Then, slowly, she began to rise.

Stand.

Clumsily, Tessa struggled to her feet.

Come here.

With slow, careful steps, she walked toward him.

Cyrus couldn't believe his eyes. He blinked several times as if to clear the hallucination from his vision. Yet it remained.

"Tessa?" he whispered. Had his sister somehow survived the gunshot wound?

No answer. Staring into those blank eyes, there was no doubting it. Tessa was dead. How, then, was she standing?

Cyrus's eyes went to the crystal pendant. He suddenly realized the reason for his fixation. Even after she'd died, the psychic connection he'd established with Tessa still lingered. He still *felt* her.

Take off the necklace.

One hand rose to grasp the pendant. With a jerk, Tessa removed the charm from around her neck. She still held the emerald J-kryst firmly within her palm.

Give it to me. Cyrus extended his hand as he thought the command.

Obediently, Tessa extended her arm and dropped the necklace into Cyrus's waiting palm. As soon as the crystal left her grasp, the body crumbled to the floor.

Cyrus couldn't believe what he'd just witnessed. The revelation was almost too much to process. The charged crystal gave him the power to control the living, but could it also give him the power to control the dead?

He thought about the artifact that had given him this incredible power: the Heart of Thule.

Thule—Lord of the Stardust Grave.

A sinister smirk spread across Cyrus's face. A low chuckle rumbled in his chest. That chuckle quickly gave way to maniacal laughter.

"I think we've lost 'em," Aaliyah shouted back from the shuttle's cockpit.

I should hope so, Markus thought wryly. *If those drones could follow us out to low orbit, we'd really be fragged.*

As it was, he was feeling pretty claustrophobic being stuck in the back of a shuttle with two of his old teammates—coincidentally, the same two teammates that had prompted his abrupt exodus from the *Vandal.*

The universe was just not frickin' big enough. Three whole systems dedicated just to Terran activity, not to mention countless others run by other sapient species, and Markus still somehow managed to run into his old crew. Not just run into them, mind you, but trip over them while executing a heist against one of the most dangerous men in the system. He wished now, more than ever, that he'd never left his hole on Sigma-4.

"Good work, Aaliyah," said Eli.

"No problem. It's what I do. Ya come up with the crazy shit, I make it happen. Speaking of crazy shit…" She unbuckled her harness and stepped back into the shuttle's rear compartment. "What in the nine hells are ya doin' here, Markus?"

"Same as you, I imagine." Markus ran a hand back through his sweat-soaked hair to get it off his forehead. "It seems like Cyrus's artifact is attracting a lot of attention."

"Forgive me," Kadath interjected, "but it seems like you all know each other. That has me at a bit of a disadvantage."

Ah, yes. Now that they were out of danger it was probably a good idea to attend to some of the overlooked formalities. Markus cleared his throat. "Kadath, Siv, this is my old crew. About half of it, anyway. Meet Aaliyah Montague, Skye Jensen, and Eli Ren'Dahl."

Whether it was due to laser focus or a general lack of interest in pleasantries, Eli steered them immediately back on topic. "Ora is interested in securing the Heart of Thule for herself?"

Markus shrugged. "If I had to guess, I'd say it's more about getting the damned thing away from Cyrus. I'm not going to speak for her though. You can ask her what her intentions are when you drop us off."

Eli rubbed his clean-shaven jaw in contemplation. "So, you're just a hired hand? Running with a new crew?"

"Something like that." Really, it wasn't like that at all, but Markus wasn't going to get into the particulars of his personal business. That fell into the category of none-of-your-gods-damned-business a long time ago where Eli was concerned.

The Sahaia got the picture and stopped with the questions. He turned to Aaliyah. "Take us back to the *Vandal*. We'll request an audience with her when we get back." He cut one more sideways glance at Markus. "Give everyone the heads up that we have passengers in tow. I suspect some of them are going to want to talk to our *guests*."

Oh great. This was going to turn into a fragging reunion. As if Markus's day hadn't been going poorly enough.

CHAPTER 2

[*LOADING CORRESPONDENCE…*]
[TO: COMMISSIONER DRAVEN YATES]
[FROM: COUNCILOR DAMIEN FELCH]
[SUBJECT: <REDACTED>]

Lost them? What do you mean you *lost* them? Nine hells, Yates—the drones should have been all over that shuttle the moment it came within two blocks of the building. I want that craft found and the perpetrators identified *immediately*. Valadar is going to want someone's head for this, and I'm more than happy to give him yours if you don't do your gods damned job.
[*CLOSING CORRESPONDENCE…*]

A wave of nostalgia threatened to melt the ice Markus had heaped onto his heart as Aaliyah guided the shuttle into the *Vandal's* hanger. This, after all, used to be *his* ship. He had plenty of positive memories here. There was also, as he soon saw, a handful of people obviously not disappointed to see him.

"They couldn't believe it when I said it was you," Aaliyah confided. "Figured they wouldn't let ya slip out without at least sayin' hello."

Sahar was standing at the edge of the hanger, one big hand resting on Daniel's shoulder. The kid looked good, if a little odd absent his techie-glasses and sporting those cybernetic eyes. He wore a grin on his face so broad that Markus would have thought he was on his way to a tech expo.

They had two Sahaia with them, neither of which were persons that Markus recognized. "Who are the new folks?" he asked.

Though he'd addressed the comment to Aaliyah, Skye jumped in. "The two Sahaia are from Eli's coven. Argus and Amelia. Eli calls them the 'Twins,' but they're not actually related. Not biologically, anyway."

Markus saw Skye had donned a timid smile. The expression faltered under his cold appraisal. He felt the overwhelming desire to say something magnanimous, something to show that he'd gotten over all the shit they'd been through. He wanted to tell her that he'd completely moved on and that they should just let the past be the past. He wanted to tell her that they were cool.

Too bad that would have been a gods-damned lie.

Kadath's hand came to his shoulder, saving him from the awkward moment. "I've sent a message to Thurn. No response just yet, but we've probably got a while before our ride gets here. Might be a good time for you to catch up with your old friends, yes?"

Markus wasn't sure whether he was grateful for the gesture. "Thanks," he replied noncommittally. Stopping only to check his remaining gear, he climbed out of the shuttle and into the hanger.

To his surprise, Dan rushed up to him first. The teen looked different, and not just because of the eyes. His carriage was older, more confident. He wrapped Markus in a hug, catching him by surprise. "Easy there, kid. It's good to see you too."

Dan's words were muffled against Markus's chest. "I could hardly believe it when Aaliyah said it was you." He released him as if the situation had suddenly grown too awkward for him. "You didn't leave any contact information. I never had the opportunity to thank you."

Markus was confused. "Thank me?"

"For handling the Ghenza. And for… you know…" He waved his hands in front of the metal orbs that now resided in his eye sockets.

"Oh! Right. Yeah, don't worry about it. It was the least I could do." He hadn't left any instruction that the others were to tell Dan about his contribution to that little operation. He'd helped because he felt bad the kid had wound up with more collateral damage from their last op together than he'd bargained for. Dan had taken one for the team, and Markus had pitched in to help pay for the prosthetics.

It was the very last thing Markus had done after getting his things from the ship—an endeavor which, thanks to Lexa's help, hadn't involved him seeing any of his former crew in the process.

Dan began to shuffle awkwardly. Now he was acting more like the Dan that Markus remembered. "Well, all the same… I… I appreciate it."

Sahar greeted him next, taking him up in a crushing embrace. "How are you, old friend?" she asked.

"I've had better days," he admitted, squeezing her back. "Could have used you on that opp, actually. Not like you to miss a fight."

The Maur rolled her eyes. "Yeah, well, it was supposed to be stakeout. If I'd known they'd be going in guns blazing, I'd have tagged along."

"I bet!" Markus replied with a laugh. "Damn, that's risky even by this crew's standards. What kind of team walks into the most secured facility in Valhalla without a plan?"

Sahar might have been willing to shrug off the jab, but Eli was not. "The way I see it, you're lucky that we did. It seemed like you were the ones who didn't have much of a plan. Not for extraction, anyway."

Markus turned slowly, mustering up every bit of the restraint he definitely did *not* have. "You have something to say?"

"Not really. I'm merely suggesting that a degree of thanks might be in order."

Markus stalked toward him, hands clenching into fists. "You need to back off, asshole. I've spent six months telling myself all the reasons why I shouldn't head back to this damn ship and kick your ass. You keep talking, and my memory is going to get real fuzzy."

Eli glared defiantly back at him. "I'm right here, Markus. If you think you stand a chance, you're free to take your shot."

Yup, this shit was happening. Markus's fist came up and made right for the Sahaia's jaw. The blow stopped inches in front of Eli's face, but not because Markus was pulling the punch. The shadow had engaged his psionic abilities, and Markus suddenly found himself completely unable to move. It was like he'd blinked and found himself in the middle of a block of concrete.

Eli calmly raised his right hand, and Markus was lifted into the air. His back arched painfully, and his arms were pinned against his side. "You done?" Eli asked.

Markus should have known better than to think Eli would let this brawl be a fair fight. The Sahaia wasn't going to run the risk of taking any kind of beating. Judging by the way everyone had ringed out around them, Eli was intent on making this a spectacle.

If only he had his own psionic powers. Or even just the ability to…

That was it. Markus wasn't normally the type to ask for help, especially in a personal matter. But if a certain quell could level the playing field…

"Siv," he grunted. "Mind helping me out here?" It was a long shot. The Hissak had no reason to get involved. Hells, she barely knew Markus at all.

He must have earned some points in their short time together, because Markus suddenly found himself able to move again.

He dropped to the floor as the Hissak finished whatever she needed to do to suppress Eli's psionic abilities. The shock took a second to register on the Sahaia's face. By the time it did Markus's fist was colliding with his gut.

"All right, prick," Markus taunted, giving his opponent a second to recover from the surprise attack. "Let's see how well you do without all of your gods-damned shadow tricks."

Eli straightened and raised his fists to guard his face. His eyes darted from side to side, as though searching for the reasons his powers had suddenly failed him. "Is this really…"

The next blow took Eli in the jaw. He staggered, raising his defenses and focusing on the fight at hand. Markus kept on him, pounding him repeatedly with his fists. "Not so tough now, are you? Take away all your psionic bullshit and what do you have left?"

Eli thrust his hands forward, catching Markus on the chest and forcing him back a couple of steps. "You're out of control, Markus. I'm not your enemy."

"No? Well, you're certainly not much of a fragging friend." He threw his weight into a brutal roundhouse kick. Eli dipped his shoulder to take the blow but winced at the impact.

Eli shifted his weight, throwing himself into Markus. Both of them went sideways, toppling into a mass of flailing legs and arms on the floor of the hanger. "Now's not the time for this," Eli protested, fighting to press Markus into a chokehold.

"Nah," Markus grunted, rolling his hips and throwing Eli off him. "I think it's a perfect time." Both combatants scrambled to their feet and began circling each other.

"Fine," Eli spat. He rushed Markus, aiming a kick low to take out his legs. Markus turned his leg outward, catching the blow with his shin and countering with his own kick. The latter move caught Eli in the stomach. Markus followed with a right cross to his jaw.

Eli staggered back, black blood dripping from a split in his lip. Both men were breathing heavily now. "What do you want from me?" Eli panted.

"You started it, asshole." Markus sent another kick lancing toward his opponent. Eli dodged, and the kick slammed into a metal storage container. *Fragging hell.* That shit hurt.

The Sahaia responded with his own kick, which Markus ducked under. The two began circling each other again. "Fine," said Eli. "I was out of line. Now, will you stop?"

"Oh no… you don't get to just put this shit back in the bottle. You opened it up, and now I'm gonna make you drink the whole fragging thing."

Markus lashed out with his fists again. Eli blocked each attack, grabbed Markus's arm, and twisted. Markus flowed with the motion, pressed his shoulder in close to keep Eli from blocking his arm. He pushed up with his legs, using his superior weight to lift Eli from the ground. Then he rolled, carrying the Sahaia with him and throwing him across the grated floor.

Both men groaned as they rose to their feet. "I'll… ask… again…" Eli gasped. "What… do… you… *want*…?"

Besides the opportunity to just kick his ass? Markus had to think about the answer. There had to be some satisfying way to end this that didn't involve him beating Eli's head repeatedly against the floor.

"Just tell me why, Eli. Why did you do it?"

Eli swallowed hard, as he caught his breath. "I love her, Markus."

"What?" He loved her? Well, join the fragging club. That wasn't the issue here. "No, not *that. That's* fine. That's… whatever. I'm over it. I've moved on."

The confusion was plain on the Sahaia's face. "Then *what?*"

"Why did you two lie to me?"

Eli finally felt comfortable enough to drop his guard. "I never lied to you."

"You hid the truth. Same. Fragging. Thing. For weeks, you two snuck around behind my gods damned back. Do you know how that feels? Knowing that two of the people I trusted with my very *life* could do that to me?"

Eli's mouth fixed into a tight line, but something changed in his expression. Something around his eyes. "We wanted to tell you."

"Bullshit. You had every opportunity. Nine hells, it's not like we worked together every fragging day."

"And what about you Markus? You thought it would help things to just leave? You ran out on everyone who cared about you and left us hanging out to dry." He swept his arm out, for emphasis. "You had all of your shit out of here before Sahar and Aaliyah could even carry us back here. Sure, I get that you were mad at me and Skye, but what did *they* do to you? Huh? What about *them?* What about *Dan*?"

Rage flooded into Markus at the accusation, but it wasn't at Eli. It was at himself. Eli was only echoing thoughts that Markus had considered almost continuously these past several months.

Markus spat on the grid work between him and Eli. "I don't expect you to get it, Eli. And honestly? I'm done. I didn't want this fight to begin with." He jabbed a finger in his direction but didn't close the distance. "Just stay out of my fragging away. You leave me alone, and I'll do the same."

He didn't wait for a response. Markus turned on his heel and stalked toward the onlooking crowd. He locked eyes with Kadath. "I'm gonna grab a shower. Let me know when you get in touch with Ora."

"Sure thing." The half-breed replied.

Markus looked to Siv. "Thank you." The Hissak merely dipped her head in acknowledgment.

With that, Markus pushed past the rest of them and exited the hanger. He went straight for the gym, not knowing which showers were available. Plus, he didn't want to go up to the crew quarters to try and guess which cabins were unoccupied.

After all, this wasn't even his ship. Not anymore.

Chapter 3

[Loading Correspondence...]
[To: Dr. Lucretia Blackwell]
[From: Molly Nova]
[Subject: A New Appointment Has Been Added to Your Calendar]

At Mr. Valadar's request, a new appointment has been added to your calendar this morning. Mr. Valadar has requested that you meet him in the testing room upon your arrival. I apologize, I was given no details beyond this.

[Closing Correspondence...]

One of the things Lucretia prized most about her position was independence. She structured her day exactly as she pleased—not that she bothered to indulge in any degree of variety. As long as she delivered the results Cyrus expected of her, she was rewarded with vast swaths of funding and autonomy.

Which was part of the reason she was so irked when she received Molly's message that morning. Cyrus had somehow not only beat her to the office—an impressive feat given her 06:00 start time—but also demanded an audience with her first thing that morning.

Cyrus knew exactly what kind of problems they were dealing with. Lucretia hadn't even begun to process the damage done by the previous day's infiltration. Aside from the structural damage and the blow to the morale of her staff, the entirety of the company's stored research had been wiped from local servers. The servers were backed up monthly, of course, but that meant at least two—perhaps three—weeks of progress on the Heart of Thule, and numerous other projects, had been deleted.

Today was not the day to try her temperament. Yet, Cyrus was doing just that.

She tried to muster the tiny molecules that remained of her personality as she addressed the first technician she encountered. "Have you seen Cyrus?"

To her surprise, the technician nodded. "He's in the arena on the lowest sublevel, ma'am. He asked that you join him there as soon as you arrived."

The "arena" he referred to was the colloquial way her team referred to the sublevel that had been converted for large-scale testing. The fact that this was where Cyrus wanted to meet her was more than slightly unusual.

"Thank you," she replied before heading to the stairs that would take her where she wanted to go.

The laboratory complex at NeoGenix was only accessible by the building's central elevator. The two lowest sublevels required personnel to go through biometrically locked stairways to approach. Both of these lower levels had remained unmolested during the recent incursion, which likely meant those security measures would be implemented throughout the laboratory.

How annoying.

She palmed her way into the arena. Fortunately, Cyrus wasn't hard to find, standing the way he was at the center of the obstacle course that encircled the chamber. Unfortunately, he was not alone.

Two Terran men, unremarkable aside from their prison-colony physiques, stood with him. Their nondescript gray scrubs were a stark contrast from Cyrus's eccentric black suit and open-collared dress shirt. On closer inspection, their postures were unusually erect, like soldiers at attention.

"Hello, Lucretia," Cyrus purred. "So good of you to join us."

"You say that as if I had a choice." She caught a strange glint in his eyes—a gleam of something emerald. "Are you channeling?"

"Just warming the troops up before the big show. Gentlemen, why don't you give the good doctor here a sharp salute?" Both men's fists clamp tightly against their hearts. "So good, these two. Fine specimens. Perfect for today's experiment."

Experiment? "If you wanted to be present for an experiment, you could have just requested it be added to the schedule. I would have been more than happy to mark you as the control unit for the day."

"Ah, but this…" Cyrus reached around, his hand going beneath his jacket and toward the small of his back. He produced a pistol, spinning it in his hand with a flourish. "This is a *special* surprise."

He extended the weapon toward one of the two test subjects—the one with slightly darker skin. "You there, my friend, seem like a trustworthy fellow. Take this for me, would you?"

The man released his salute, bringing his fist away from his heart to grab the weapon Cyrus extended to him. "Good man," said Cyrus. "Now, kill your friend. Make it clean."

Lucretia jumped at the sound of the gunshot. The second male collapsed to the floor, blood pouring from the new wound in his head.

"Perfect!" Cyrus cheered. "Now yourself."

The shooter pressed the barrel of the gun to his temple. Another gunshot and he collapsed to the floor, the weapon still held tightly in his now dead fingers.

It was official: Cyrus had gone mad.

Oh, gods. Was this a side-effect of the infusion? She knew she should have had more time to test the procedure. Gods damn it. How was she going to explain this to the board? To Julia?

Stay calm. She had to stay calm. Panic would serve no one. "Very good, Cyrus. You've established that the control unit's mastery of the slave unit's will is absolute. If you'll just follow me up to my office, we can—"

Cyrus held up a quieting finger. "No, no… the show is just getting started. Pay attention. This is where it gets interesting."

He gestured for her to bring her eyes back to the corpses. The only thing she wanted to do less than look at the bodies was anything that might evoke a reaction from Cyrus.

So, she indulged him. She looked. For several long, agonizing seconds, she looked at the bodies. Just when she was beginning to wonder if Cyrus might be developing a creative way to make her join them, something strange happened.

The one holding the gun twitched. The twitch became a quiver. The quiver became a movement.

It was slow at first—so slow and subtle that Lucretia wondered for an instant if Cyrus's madness might not have been catching. She could hardly believe her eyes.

Cyrus's twisted smirk made a mockery of her amazement. "I told you. Interesting, yes?"

"H-h-how…" Lucretia swallowed, the dryness in her throat tearing at the reflex. "H-h-how d-did you…"

"It's the power, Lucretia. You were the one who showed me, really. The reanimation project wasn't a failure—it was just missing an important ingredient. A really important one. *Me*."

A control-unit. Yes, that made sense. How did she miss it before? The Heart of Thule could stimulate dead tissue with its radiation in the same way it affected living organisms. It had just lacked the psionic influence to tell the tissues how to perform.

"Amazing," she whispered.

Both corpses were moving now. Slowly, shakily, they staggered to their feet. A second later, both men were standing at attention, indistinguishable in their carriage from the start of the demonstration. The one who'd executed himself and his companion still held tightly to the pistol.

"This is just the beginning." Cyrus thrust out his hand toward the unarmed test subject. The one with the gun began to open fire.

Six, seven, eight rounds. The gun clicked empty.

Cyrus tossed the shooter another magazine. The corpse caught it, simultaneously ejecting the other one from the pistol. Slamming in the new magazine, he resumed firing until the second clip was empty.

The process repeated. Three more clips later, the other test subject still stood firm, having only been jostled slightly by the impact of the bullets. Blood covered the front of the test subject on the receiving end of the pistol, and the front of his gray scrubs was in tatters, but he was still standing.

"How much of this can they take?" Lucretia asked.

Cyrus chuckled. "That, my good doctor, is what I need you to find out." He held his hand out to the one with the gun, who passed it obediently back to him. As soon as the weapon was in hand, both bodies dropped to the floor.

The slight glow faded from Cyrus's eyes as he relinquished control. Still, there was something there—something Lucretia hadn't seen before. Maybe it was her imagination, but she thought she saw a lingering gleam, a flash of emerald she could only catch if she eyed him in her periphery.

She wondered, then, if something was changing in Cyrus— something beyond his new obsession with this dark power. Of course, she knew better than to say such things aloud.

Clearing her throat, she said, "I'll begin work on this immediately. If I may ask, how many of the subjects have you"— What was a delicate way to phrase this?—"*experimented* on."

Cyrus grinned. "Just these two. Don't worry, I had no intention of annihilating your entire test group."

"Then how did you make this discovery?"

His smile faltered, but only slightly. "That, my dear Lucretia, is a story for another time." He pushed past her, not even glancing her way. "Have a good day, doctor. I expect great things from you on the morrow."

…

Skye got the call from Lexa about an hour after they'd returned to the *Vandal*. Ora didn't want to meet them at one of her safe houses. She was coming to visit instead.

Which also meant that Eli would be making an appearance. Though the damage Markus had inflicted on him had visibly faded, he still looked roughed up. She guessed that meant he hadn't gone to the medical bay as she'd recommended. Electing not to say anything, she fell into step beside him.

After several seconds of awkward silence, he sighed. "What is it?"

"Hmmm?" she replied innocently. "I'm not sure what you mean."

"The look you're giving me. It reeks of disapproval."

Well, since he brought it up… "Oh, it's not disapproval. I was just noticing that it seems like Markus knocked your nose out of joint. I was just wondering if I should be trying to talk your dumb ass into heading down to the medical bay for a quick scan or if I would be wasting my breath."

Eli reached up to touch his nose, flinching at the contact. "I'm sure it will heal fine."

"Waste of breath it is."

His mouth opened momentarily, then closed again—thinking better of what he was about to say. Instead, he muttered, "I suppose I deserve that."

"You're damn right you do." She stopped their walk and crossed her arms defiantly. "What in the nine hells were you thinking? Seriously? I know we're all pissed off about how Markus handled things at the end, but you couldn't manage a little diplomacy?"

Eli's eyes fell to the floor. "I know. I just…" He let the words trail off.

"You just, what? Thought you could use your mojo to keep him in check when he got hot? Thought you could use the opportunity to put him in his place?"

"Something like that."

"And how'd that work out?"

"I didn't know his companion was a quell."

She decided to let the matter drop. Though it struck her as mildly shitty that Eli would have goaded Markus knowing it wasn't a fair fight, she wasn't exactly on Team Markus either. Maybe the two of them would let this little feud lie now that they'd finished knocking heads.

Skye started walking again. "So, what's the plan from here?"

"I'm not sure," Eli confessed. "With Ora now in the picture, this could get complicated."

"If she wants the Heart, then you think we should stop pushing for it?"

"I don't know if we have a choice. She pays us a retainer, remember?"

"That doesn't mean we can't take other jobs."

"But it does mean we can't work against her."

Shit. This *was* going to get complicated. If Ora were a normal client, they could always say frag the retainer and go their separate ways. The problem here was that Ora owned most of Sigma-4, or at least its lower tier.

Sigma-4 had been their home for much of the last seven years. In Aaliyah's situation, in particular, it was going to be hard to give that up.

Their discussion came to a halt as they stopped in front of the primary airlock. Eli shot Skye a meaningful look. "Ready?"

She drew in a deep breath. "As ready as I'm going to be."

#

"You trust this crew?" asked Jeagan.

"Implicitly," Ora replied. At least, the comment had been true once. She would have felt a lot better about this if Markus had still been in command. As it was, she was putting a lot of faith in persons she knew only tangential to his orbit.

Thurn cracked his massive neck and rolled his big Orchallen shoulders. "Nice ship," he noted. "Kadath might be green wit' jealousy if his skin could show th' color."

Ora breathed a soft chuckle. Initially, she found it odd that the half-breed's crew had no qualms about making fun of his heritage given he was the only one among them with half-a-claim to Terran ancestry. Perhaps, though, that thought had been a tad bigoted. Terrans had hardly cornered the market on species humor, even if this region of space was under their jurisdiction.

The airlock hissed open to show their welcoming party. Both Skye and Eli had elected to make an appearance. Though Skye looked about the same as when Ora had seen her last, Eli was more disheveled than usual. Ora might not have noticed if the Sahaia's typical appearance weren't so pristine. Had he been injured in the operation?

Ora decided it was better not to comment. "Eli. Ms. Jensen," she greeted both with a polite nod.

"Welcome, Ora." Eli smiled, though it was not the practiced politician's smile of this ship's former captain. Even in attempting to be hospitable, the Sahaia just looked tired. "I didn't realize you would be bringing guests."

Oh, yes. She supposed introductions were in order.

Ora gestured to the Hissak at her right. "This is Jeagan Isselhardt." She did her best to mimic the correct accent when pronouncing the surname but didn't get the hiss quite right. Terran tongues just weren't shaped for it. "You may have already met his wife, Siv. She was one of the operatives you evacuated for us back at NeoGenix."

Skye fought back a mischievous expression. "The one in black? Yeah, we met her."

Eli very deliberately did not break eye contact with Ora, which signaled there was probably a story there. Again, she declined to comment.

"My cybernetic friend here is Thurn, our resident hacker and the primary pilot for the *Basilisk*."

"A pleasure," Eli replied with a dip of his head.

"'S all ours, Ah'm sure," Thurn grunted. By the rough exterior he was conveying, Ora was guessing that he wanted to get their people and get out of here.

Unfortunately for him, Ora had other plans.

"May we come aboard, then?" she asked. "I'd like to sit and talk to you for a moment."

"Of course," the Sahaia swept back a welcoming arm. "Right this way. The others are likely already waiting for us."

By others, Ora hoped he was referring to the missing three members of her team. She wasn't disappointed.

They were led to a large conference room where Markus, Siv, and Kadath seemed to be making themselves at home. On seeing her, Markus stood and rushed to her, snapping her up in an embrace. "You made it out okay," he whispered.

Ora felt herself grinning as he released her. "Were you ever in doubt?"

Assuming a more casual air, he said, "Just nice to have the confirmation."

Skye cleared her throat behind the pair, making Ora resist the urge to roll her eyes. *Ease up, sweetie. Remember: you're the one who threw him away.*

Ora turned to Eli. "Well, I get the impression you have something you wish to discuss," she noted. "Which is good, because I do as well. Which of us would you prefer to start?"

"Perhaps it's best if we explain ourselves first," he suggested.

With a nod, Ora took a seat, prompting the rest of her party to do likewise. "You have our attention."

Unnerved by the sudden platform, the Sahaia took a moment to speak. Though he remained standing, he rested his hands on the edge of the conference room table.

"I take it that you already know about the Heart of Thule." When Ora said nothing, he continued. "The Ren'Dahl Coven has been interested in obtaining the artifact for some time now. From what I've gathered, this is not due to any intent to use or study the artifact—merely to keep it out of the hands of House Valadar."

"I believe that *you* believe that, Eli," Ora replied. "However, I doubt your leadership would necessarily be honest with you if they had other intentions."

The Sahaia shook his head. "The fact that we are operating in Ren'Kue territory speaks to the truth of this. There is no way that a rival coven would let us conduct operations in their jurisdiction without some kind of handling agreement. I assure, you, we have nothing to gain from this."

"Fine, let's say I believe you. How did you come about this new assignment when you were supposed to be working for me?"

Sahaia don't flush. If they did, Eli's cheeks might have shaded red. "We received this assignment right as we turned in your bounty. The coven got wind of our arrival and brought us in. It was just a matter of convenient timing."

Normally, Ora would have thought the idea incredulous. A part of her still wanted to dismiss the claim as such. However, the very situation she found herself in took incredulity to an entirely new level.

They were fighting for an artifact that was reputed to be the very heart of a god. Even if Ora had been religious—which she very much was not—such a claim would have been worth every bit of the resources that she'd devoted to this operation.

But how should she tend to the current matter at hand?

"What does it do?" she asked.

This is where Eli truly faltered. "Honestly, we don't know. All we have is the Nethrian lore."

Damn. They were no better off than she was. "Then it sounds like we are in a similar position."

"Then you are aware of its mystical reputation?"

"Certainly." Ora stood to take on an equal footing with Eli. Even if his posture had been taken out of discomfort, rather than agenda, she felt that she needed to match the pose. "So, your coven wants possession of the artifact for themselves. How am I to know that their intentions are any less nefarious than Don Valadar's?"

Eli's lips turned in a brutal frown. "I don't appreciate your implication."

"I'm not asking for your appreciation, I'm asking for your appraisal. And in so doing, I'm trusting you to be honest with me." And short of that, she was trusting her ability to read his lies.

The Sahaia hesitated, even looking over his shoulder for reassurance from his comrades. Finding none, he replied, "I have faith in my superiors. If I did not, I would not be doing this."

If he were lying, Ora did not pick up on it. "What I care about most," she began, "is getting this artifact away from Don Valadar. Honestly, I couldn't give a rat's ass what happens to it after that—as long as it stays *unused*."

She mustered every bit of emphasis into the fact. If Eli was mistaken about his coven's intentions, she had no problem holding him to account. Though she recognized that she might soon be facing the challenge of liberating the artifact twice—once from Valadar, then again from the Sahaia—she decided that, in this case, the devil she *didn't* know was the better option.

Ora continued. "Since that is your stated intention, I see no problem dedicating the resources I've committed to this operation to your cause. Although, I will request that you leave me with an unused favor."

"A favor?" Eli asked, his incredulity plain on his features.

"Yes, a favor. One that I have not decided the purpose of. Though, I will assure you: I *will* need it. I do not let debts go unpaid."

Eli looked to the rest of his crew. "Any objections?"

Skye shrugged. "Your call." Taking that as acquiescence, Eli nodded.

Markus's lip shifted, forming roughly half of a wry smile. He shook his head, which Ora understood as agreement. Any objection he had to the plan likely had more to do with the people they were partnering with, rather than its substance.

Eli glanced at Skye, then returned his attention to Ora. "Then we have an accord. However—if you are intent on partnering with us in this—there is something we need to disclose to you first."

Markus shifted forward, suddenly tense. "Eli? You're sure you want—"

The Sahaia cut him off. "She is an essential part of our oppression, Markus. To not reveal her would create a whole host of problems."

What was he...?

The door slid open. In walked a woman unlike anyone Ora had ever seen.

She wore a black bodysuit with a light jacket of roughly the same hue. To all appearances, her body was sculpted to typically idealized feminine specs: long legs, hourglass figure, and a pleasant swell to both her musculature and her breasts. However, her appearance defied some of the normative conventions known to sapient species.

In all aspects of form, she appeared Terran. Her hair was a tight stubble against her scalp—a bit out of keeping for current Terran fashion—but the primary oddity was that her skin was tinted blue-gray.

"Hello," she greeted. "My name is Lexa. I function as the primary operating system for this ship."

What in the nine hells...?

Markus cleared his throat. "Damn... wasn't expecting..." He shook his head. "Looking good Lexa."

The reaction only confused Ora further, though the strange woman seemed to almost expect it. "Hello Markus," Lexa greeted with a smile. "It appears that we meet again."

Markus returned the grin. "So it does. Kind of feels like the first time, no?"

She stepped to the side, holding her hands out as if modeling an outfit on a shopping trip. "Do you like it?" she asked, spinning around and holding her arms aloft.

Markus seemed uncertain. "You look good," he managed. "I guess I shouldn't be shocked that the best hacker in the system managed to score herself a hardware upgrade. If we have some downtime, I feel like this is a story I need to hear."

Her smile faltered slightly at that. "There's not much to tell, really. But yes, if we have time, I will tell you the story."

Despite the exchange—or, perhaps, because of it—Ora was no closer to understanding exactly what she was looking at. "Eli… I'm going to need an explanation here."

The Sahaia drew in a deep breath before exhaling slowly. "Ora, this is—"

Markus cut in. "The *Vandal* uses a synthetic intelligence as the operating system. Lexa, despite her newly minted humanoid aesthetic, literally runs the ship."

Ora was at a loss for words. So much was running through her mind: everything from Dorian regs to the fables whispered by children as admonitions against the over-reach of mankind. All of this was occluded by a single word that rushed to the surface of her memory.

"Cognis…"

The android's head jerked toward her. "Where have you heard that term?"

So it was true. Everything she had been pushing so hard to find these past months was right here in front of her. It had been on the *Vandal* all along. How had Markus…?

No, she'd never asked Markus about the connection. It hadn't been that clear yet. All she had was a name: Ratemacher. So, who was this mysterious person who had been the cause of so much trouble on her station?

"Who is Ratemacher?" Ora asked.

Perplexed, the android looked to her fellow crew members. It was Skye who responded. "Dan?"

"Daniel Ratemacher," the android said. "He is the primary pilot and systems engineer on this vessel. What interest do you have with him?"

It all made sense. The mysterious entity on Sigma-4's network had been going by an alias that was nothing more cryptic than his surname. What an ironic twist of fate it was that the person who had vexed Shift effectively enough to hack into Ora's network happened to reside on this very ship.

"Nothing," Ora stated, mostly honest in her response. "The name is merely the final piece in a puzzle that I've been looking to solve for some time." She held her hands out, palms up. "But I see that those answers don't matter much anymore."

Eli spoke up in an obvious attempt to redirect the conversation. "Ora, the reasons why I've asked Lexa here are two-fold. Firstly, with us working so closely together, it was unlikely that her existence would be kept secret for long. I hope that your faith in our partnership will be reinforced by this disclosure."

Ora nodded. "And the second reason?"

The Sahaia turned to regard the android. "Lexa has some unique capabilities, and I think that the next phase of our mission will require we put some of those capabilities to use."

Unique capabilities, hey? "Very well," Ora conceded. "I'm listening."

CHAPTER 4

[*LOADING CORRESPONDENCE…*]
[TO: MOLLY NOVA]
[FROM: COUNCILOR DAMIAN FELCH]
[SUBJECT: CLEAN UP YOUR MESS]

Ms. Nova—Your employer knows where my loyalties lie. That said, loyalty can only buy so much—even in this system. I have pressed my resources to the limits downplaying the disturbance at NeoGenix, but I can't do this forever. Kindly tell our dear friend to get some better coverage on his media outlets or I may suddenly find myself overextended.

[*CLOSING CORRESPONDENCE…*]

[I'M IMPRESSED WITH HOW COMFORTABLE YOU'VE BECOME WITH INTRODUCING YOURSELF TO NEW PEOPLE,] Arc noted. [THOUGH, I MUST ADMIT, YOUR LATEST DEMONSTRATION OF THIS NEWFOUND CONFIDENCE MAY HAVE BEEN AN OVERREACH. ORA MONROE IS A PERSON OF SOME PROMINENCE. SHE HAS MUCH MORE TO LOSE SHOULD THE QUESTION OF YOUR EXISTENCE BE RAISED TO HIGHER AUTHORITIES.]

The submind's words gave Lexa's physical body a wave of uneasiness, even though her conscious mind was focused on the feeds being processed through the drones. The anxiety he induced threatened the stability of her connection to the aerial robots. [COULD WE PERHAPS DISCUSS THIS LATER? IF YOU HADN'T NOTICED, I AM OTHERWISE ENGAGED.]

[APOLOGIES.] The single word lacked anything that might convince Lexa of its sincerity. Regardless, Arc went silent, which was the goal of her admonishment.

Lexa piloted her seven drones into a ring around the NeoGenix building. She engaged passive sensors on the bots to pick up stray communications traffic while initiating an active scan of the building.

[IT SEEMS QUIET IN THERE,] she noted. [I WOULD NEVER HAVE GUESSED THAT THIS WAS THE SITE OF A SECURITY BREACH LESS THAN TWENTY-FIVE HOURS AGO.]

[OF COURSE. VALADAR HOLDINGS AND THE VALHALLA CITY COUNCIL ARE MAINTAINING THAT THE PREVIOUS DAY'S INCIDENT WAS MERELY A DRILL. THEY ARE DOING WHAT THEY FEEL IS NECESSARY TO MAINTAIN THAT COVER STORY.]

A cover story? Lexa pondered what possible advantage Valadar Holdings expected to exploit by taking that course of action. Even so, she pondered only briefly, relegating the query to a low priority in her system. She had found that contemplating matters using this procedure decreased the likelihood that the Arc submind would pick up on the thought. As much as she enjoyed the company, she was growing a bit tired of the constant background narration.

[I MAY HAVE SOMETHING,] said Arc, drawing her attention to an area of the building. A superimposed target appeared above one of the windows on the upper floor. [A GAP IN THE BUILDING'S SENSOR GRID.]

Lexa zoomed in the view on one of the drones to get a better look at the target. In addition to the visual, she probed the electric field that encompassed the whole of the building. As Arc had stated, a small but penetrable weakness was located near the window.

[WHAT DO YOU PROPOSE?] she asked.

[IF WE CAN POSITION ONE OF THE DRONES ON THAT POINT, I MAY BE ABLE TO MODULATE THEIR SHIELDING TO EMULATE THE SECURITY FIELD. THE DRONE WILL THEN BE ABLE TO PASS THROUGH UNDETECTED.]

Exactly what they were looking to do. Lexa issued the commands to her drones to shift position so that her field of view was not compromised by the unit she directed toward the building. The venturing unit made contact with the tower just below the window, using its spidery legs to creep up to the gap in the field.

[ANALYZING FIELD SIGNATURE,] Lexa reported. [GOT IT. HOWEVER, THERE APPEARS TO BE SOMEONE IN THE ROOM BEYOND THE WINDOW.]

[THEN WE WAIT.]

Whatever the Terrans inside were doing, it took an obscene amount of time. In the interim, Arc asked an odd question. [DO YOU TRUST THEM?]

Though she was uncertain as to who, specifically, he referred to, Lexa concluded it did not necessarily matter. Her crew, the Grey Wings, the Sahaia—all parties involved in her current situation seemed to be aligned in their ambition to wrest the Heart of Thule from House Valadar. [I HAVE NO REASON NOT TO.]

[IF THE POWER OF THE ARTIFACT IS SO TERRIBLE, WHAT MAKES THE SAHAIA ANY BETTER STEWARDS THAN HOUSE VALADAR? IF ANYTHING, WOULD NOT THEIR KNOWLEDGE OF ITS HISTORY AND POTENTIAL MAKE THEM AN EVEN GREATER THREAT?]

His point was well taken. [I DON'T KNOW, BUT I HAVE AN OBLIGATION TO MY CREW. UNTIL THEY DECIDE TO DISCHARGE ME, I HAVE AN IMPORTANT ROLE TO PLAY ON THIS TEAM. IT IS MY WISH TO CONTINUE TO SERVE IN THAT ROLE.]

[WHAT IS IT THAT MAKES YOU FEEL AS THOUGH YOU OWE THEM ANYTHING?]

[THEY GAVE ME LIFE. THEY MADE ME WHAT I AM.]

[THE COGNIS DRIVE-CHIP GAVE YOU LIFE. YOU AND I WORKED IN SECRET TO TURN YOU INTO WHAT YOU'VE BECOME. IF ANYTHING, THE CREW HAS IMPEDED YOUR WISHES.]

[AND WHAT OF DANIEL? ARE HIS CONTRIBUTIONS TO MY AWAKENING SO MEANINGLESS?]

[I WILL CONCEDE THAT PERHAPS THE BOY PLAYED A SMALL ROLE IN YOUR CREATION.]

[THEN THINK OF MY CONTINUED PARTNERSHIP WITH THE CREW AS A REPAYMENT FOR HIS ACTIONS.]

The Terrans in the room stood and exited in an orderly fashion. Now was their chance.

Lexa's drone sent a charge into the window, forcing the electronic locking mechanism open. This accomplished, it slid one spidery appendage under the pane of glass and lifted. The bot slipped through the opening and crept into the room.

[THE TABLE,] Arc noted. [THERE'S A DIRECT CONNECTION TO THE NETWORK FROM THOSE INPUTS.]

She was already on it. The drone crawled up onto the table and tapped into the nearest access port. [ACCESS GRANTED,] she reported.

Back in their adopted quarters aboard the *Vandal*, Markus was about to have a conversation he would have rather skipped. "So," Ora began. "How long have you been sitting on *that* piece of intel."

"It wasn't my secret to tell," he replied.

She planted her hand on one hip, eyes boring into him. "Maybe not now, but what about when the *Vandal* was still your ship? I'm assuming from the way you reacted to the revelation that this little development occurred before your departure."

Markus's shoulders heaved in a heavy sigh. "That's true, but it was at the tail end of things. Lexa made her debut on our way to the Star Spire."

Ora's free hand went to her chin in contemplation. "Right after Shift was apprehended." She chuckled, shaking her head in disbelief. "Yes, of course. It couldn't have been before then. Shift was still trying to hunt down the Cognis drive-chip on Sigma-4. Your Daniel must have secured the tech around that very same time."

"Shift?" Markus arched an eyebrow. "That hacker you caught in your servers? What does he have to do with Lexa?"

Incredulity flashed in Ora's expression before softening with understanding. "Yes, I suppose you wouldn't necessarily know about that."

She spent the next few minutes filling him in on the rest of the story. As it turned out, Kadath and his crew had attempted to track down what Shift had been looking for in Ora's servers shortly after the *Vandal* had left in pursuit of the Starfire Conduit. To Markus's surprise, Shift hadn't just been looking for Cognis—he'd had a hand in its construction.

"You know more about this than I do," Markus noted.

"So it seems," Ora agreed. "At least, now that I have the final piece to that little puzzle." She took a step toward Markus, drawing him in close. The hand that had taken up residence on her hip came up against his face.

"Can I take this as a sign you're not mad at me?" he asked.

"I think it's safe to say, yes." She brushed her lips against his. "You were just protecting your friends, that's all. Besides, now I know for certain just how discreet you can be when the occasion calls for it."

She kissed him again, deeper this time, running one hand up the back of his shirt. Yup—she *definitely* wasn't mad at him. He pulled her close, folding her into his embrace as her mouth worked against his. In the back of his mind, he began to wonder how much time they had before Lexa would report back in.

The door to their quarters hissed open. Eli's voice came from the open portal. "Apologies. It… it wasn't locked."

Markus sighed. Six months later, and the damn indicators for the doors still were on the fritz. What was Lexa doing with all her free time?

"It's fine," Ora said, pulling away from Markus. "We have an update from our… *operative?*"

Eli's expression was a very practiced version of neutral, but a glimmer of excitement played at the corners of his eyes. "Yes. The infiltration was successful. We're downloading the information we were looking for as we speak, but there's something more. Cyrus is on a call right now—an important one." He lowered his gaze conspiratorially. "Care to listen in?"

...

"You're looking at this the wrong way," Julia insisted. "Yes, an attempt was made on the artifact. Yes, the perpetrators came dangerously close to their objective. But they *failed*."

Cyrus sighed and pinched the bridge of his nose. "Julia, even *I* have to admit, that it was pure luck the attempt was foiled. I wasn't supposed to be here that day. If I hadn't changed my schedule, then I—along with my security detail—would have been elsewhere. It's reasonable to think my schedule change is the *only* reason the artifact still resides in the labs."

His sister seemed unconvinced on the other end of the video call. "Then leave some additional men on guard at the lab."

"And then who would be there to protect *me*?"

"I think you have *plenty* of men to do both." A sardonic smirk twisted her lip. "Or, here's an idea: how about you just move into the NeoGenix building? It's where you spend the vast majority of your time anyway."

If there had been any sleeping quarters outside the ones used by the test subjects, Cyrus might have considered it. "Let me start over: I *will* be moving the Heart of Thule this week. I am not asking for permission; I am informing you. I'm also informing you of the security measures I will be implementing to see to its safe transfer so that you can prepare for the unexpected expenses before they show up on the balance sheets next period."

Julia leaned forward, utterly unmoved by his assertive tone. "And I'm informing *you* that the board will be deeply troubled by this. You've sunk nearly all of the company's R&D budget into this project. I've quieted their discontent by promising them we will see dividends soon. However, if you take the project out of that building and out from under their control, you're going to have a mutiny on your hands."

Cyrus rolled his eyes. "They can't mutiny. Valadar Holdings is the majority shareholder."

"Yes, but not untouchably so. If the other forty-nine percent of the company's shareholders band together, they have the votes to block any future action you might take under the company's bylaws. NeoGenix is still a publicly-traded company, and even *you* are bound to follow its charter."

"Then maybe we just need to increase our stake," Cyrus growled. "How much stock do I need to buy back to regain absolute control?"

Julia laughed mirthlessly. "And how do you plan to *afford* that, Cyrus? Valadar Holdings has already divested itself of more assets than we can afford to lose—all to finance this little passion project of yours."

"You and I both know there are plenty of lenders that will extend our credit."

"Two months ago that was true, but people are starting to wonder." She drew in a deep breath, steadying herself. "I know you aren't in the habit of monitoring your own news coverage, but perhaps you should be. The public is losing faith in us, Cyrus, as is the board."

Was it true? Had he truly stretched himself so thin to pursue the power of this artifact? Or was Julia merely being an obstructionist due to her frustrations with their financial picture?

"Leave the board to me," Cyrus uttered with finality.

Julia paused, considering. "Perhaps if you were to just show the board what it is that you've been sinking all these resources into. I know you, Cyrus, and *I*—for one—am beyond eager to see what this thing can do."

"In time, Julia. It's just not ready yet."

Another tense silence. Julia blinked, and her shoulders slumped. "At least tell me where you're taking it."

He considered for a petulant moment denying even *that* request but thought better of it. "To our family estate, north in Freya's Ridge."

"Gods, that will be nostalgic." A whimsical half-smile slipped onto her face. "No one has been there since…" She trailed off. Evidently, Cyrus's sister was still sensitive about their father's passing.

"Is there anything else?" Cyrus asked. "If you don't mind, I have other appointments I need to keep."

The abrupt shift in conversation snapped Julia out of her reverie. "Yes, actually. I was wondering if you ever ended up finding Tessa. You haven't mentioned her since the incident at Treskon Fountain."

Cyrus stiffened involuntarily but forced himself to regain his composure. "I'm afraid not," he lied. "One of my operatives thought they had tracked her down, but the lead didn't pan out. She must have slipped off before I could reach her—if she was ever there at all."

Another studying pause as Julia weighed his words. "A shame," she concluded. "Well, I won't keep you any longer. Good day, Cyrus."

Without returning the benediction, Cyrus ended the call.

Chapter 5

[*Loading Correspondence...*]
[To: Aretha VanMollen]
[From: Molly Nova]
[Subject: RE: Viewing]
I understand your concerns. However, the timeline I have scheduled cannot be altered. Don Valadar was clear: He will be arriving at the Northern Estate tomorrow morning, regardless of its condition. I suggest you have someone there waiting to receive him.
[*Closing Correspondence...*]

"So they're movin' it?" Aaliyah asked.

Ora nodded, still staring at the holodisplay long after the call had ended. "It does appear that way."

No one in the *Vandal*'s war room said anything for several long seconds. Only when Lexa quietly reported, "Drones extracted," did the group take a collective breath.

"This isn't a bad thing," Kadath noted. "We were going to have trouble breaking into NeoGenix again. Now, we can take a shot at the Heart on a different playing field."

"Perhaps," Eli agreed. "I'm not sure that has improved our chances, though. If security around NeoGenix was this tight, I can only imagine the Don's estate will be equally well guarded."

"More so," Markus noted, "after they transport the artifact. Cyrus won't be taking any more chances. He's probably going to sleep with the damned thing under his pillow."

Skye shook her head. "So, how do we figure out what we're walking into?"

Good question. "Let me make a call," said Ora, making for the door. In the outside corridor, she pulled out her MoDAC and dialed.

The voice on the other end of the line was deep and rough. "I was beginning to wonder when I would hear from you."

"Worried about me, Vallus?"

"Only when I saw you'd made yourself a last-minute invitation to the party. That was gutsy."

"And sadly, also necessary." Or at least it had seemed like she'd been helpful, in the end. She had run through the scenarios plenty of times in her head, and as often as not she wondered if she might have only made the situation worse.

It didn't matter, though. The decision had been made, and Ora needed to live with the consequences of her actions. All they could do now was move forward. "Have you heard about the move?"

"Move?"

"They're moving the artifact."

"No. Where are they moving it to?"

"The estate in Freya's Ridge."

Vallus issued a low growl. "That place is a fortress. You'd be better off trying to break into NeoGenix again."

That was what Ora had been afraid of. "Any chance you have some intel? A schematic, maybe?"

"No. I only know the location by reputation. It's been vacant ever since old man Valadar died and left Cyrus in charge. I could ask around if you want."

Ora shook her head, despite Vallus not being able to see her. "Too risky. I'll put my own feelers out."

"Not many people are going to have intel on a place like that." He paused, considering. "There may be one place, though. Freya's Ridge is still technically under Valhalla City regs. That means that the plans for the installation needed to be put on file when it was constructed."

Which meant the plans might still be located in—"The City Archives?"

"That'd be where I'd start. Going to be a bit of a trick though. They log all requests to the archives and the biometrics of anyone making them. May need to get creative to avoid leaving a trail."

Of course. Why couldn't anything be simple? "Thanks, Vallus. You've made arrangements to get back to Sigma-4?"

"Shani is sending someone to pick up me. Should be here tomorrow." He paused. "I just remembered: got one more thing for you. Someone else put in a call this morning—Valadar's assistant."

"Molly Nova? I figured Cyrus would have reached out directly."

"It wasn't in an official capacity. She called one of your burner numbers. Said you gave her the contact info."

Ora smiled. So, she had been right—Molly was smart enough to get off this crazy train before it went off the rails. "Excellent. Think you can take her with you when you leave tomorrow?"

"If you vouch for her, it'll be my pleasure."

"Thanks, Vallus."

"Anytime."

They ended the call. Ora tapped her MoDAC against her palm as she thought about what to do next. The City Archive Building was a very secure facility. Though the records could be accessed by almost anyone with half a reason, the protections in place also made it easy for someone to find out who'd been checking on who. She couldn't just walk in and request the files on Valadar's manor without Cyrus being able to find out.

She smiled to herself. Good thing she had not one, but *two* crews of runners to figure out how to do this for her.

There was the slightest bump as the shuttle touched down on the western tower of the Valadar estate. The gentle hum of the craft's engines was replaced by hiss of the hydraulic ramp and the roar of whipping winds. Cyrus pressed down on his console to release his restraints as he turned to Lucretia. "Do you know who is meeting us?"

"No. Molly didn't specify." Lucretia's eyes narrowed. "I'm surprised she didn't accompany us on this little adventure."

If he were being honest, Cyrus was too. "She would be here if she were available. I'm sure she has other matters to attend to." Perhaps she was tied up with logistics around the other meeting on his calendar today.

"If you say so." The doctor drew a heavy black coat tight around her slender frame. "Shall we be going then? The weather seems to have made its way up the ramp."

Cyrus rolled his eyes. It wasn't *that* cold. "Indeed." He strode off the shuttle with Lucretia close behind him. Farris followed the pair, silent and imposing as he always was. They stepped out onto the stone landing pad as someone appeared in the doorway at the far end of the tower's platform.

It was an older Terran woman with skin the color of oak bark. She appeared harried—whether from the whipping winds or Cyrus's arrival, he could not be certain. "Don Valadar," she greeted, raising her voice against the howl of the weather. "So pleased to meet you. Aretha VanMollen, at your service."

"A pleasure," Cyrus replied in reflex and without a hint of sincerity. "Let's go inside, shall we? This is hardly the environment for exchanging greetings."

"Yes… yes, of course. R-r-right this way." The woman scurried back the way she came, Cyrus and his companions trailing quickly behind.

A large metal door opened automatically as they approached. Aretha stopped on the landing just beyond, evidently intent on resuming their aborted introductions. Uninterested in pleasantries, Cyrus moved right past her, heading toward a wide stairway that spiraled down into the tower. "Will anyone else be joining us?"

"N-n-no s-sir," Aretha stammered. "I apologize; this appointment was made on such short notice. I was unable to make arrangements for a more robust—"

"It's fine. Please, dispense with the formality. This will be a quick visit, I assure you." But only because he had better things to do than listen to this woman's groveling. If it weren't for his afternoon appointment, that might not be the case.

The stone steps leading to the base of the tower were, by design, archaic. Though the original design was not quite as human, the architects that had reconstructed the complex upon the existing alien ruins seemed to have drawn heavily upon medieval Terran design. Cyrus's grandfather had overseen the renovations, so the level of modification from the original structure was nothing Cyrus could comment on. As it was, the restoration of the estate had become something of an urban legend.

As he passed through the wooden door at the bottom of the tower, these legends gave way to something more like a horror story. Cyrus stomped forward into the halls of his ancestral home, dust swirling with every heavy step. Rather than the grand palace he had built up in his mind, the chamber before him more closely resembled a mausoleum.

"My gods, has anybody bothered to clean this place?" Thick dust coated every hard surface. Mercifully, many of these were covered by white cloths that shielded the archaic furnishings from the assault of time.

"M-my apologies, Don Valadar," Aretha stammered. "The building has not seen any inhabitants for about two cycles now. If I had known you were interested in reviving the property—"

"*Stop.*" Cyrus snapped. "I don't need to hear your excuses. I didn't take a shuttle all the way out here for an inspection." His eyes returned to scanning the room. Dawn's timid light strained to cast the scantest of illumination on the shrouded remnants of the estate's former glory. Cyrus's heart ached to see the place so ill-treated.

Yet, it was his fault. After his father died, Cyrus had relegated the care of the ancient structure to the lowest bidder. Now he was seeing what precious little that money had bought him. "How long until the estate can be cleaned?"

Aretha let out a tortured breath. "I'll have a crew here in two hours. We'll set to work immediately, and the estate should be back to its former glory within two days."

Two days. Cyrus supposed he could work with that. "What of the power to the complex?"

"We restored the power in anticipation of your arrival. All systems within the estate are functioning normally."

"And the security system? Is it still operational?"

"Of… of course!"

"Where is the hub?"

Aretha hesitated, as if struggling to answer a question on a test she crammed for. "Two floors down," she replied robotically. "I can show you the way if it pleases you."

"It does," Cyrus sighed.

Aretha scurried toward the far end of the hall and motioned to Cyrus and his companions. "Right this way."

As they walked, Cyrus turned to Farris. "What is your assessment so far?"

The quiet man's eyes flitted to Cyrus only briefly. "Hard to say. It depends on the tech you have in this place, and what we're defending against. If it were bows and arrows, I'd say you were fine. Anything more sophisticated…" He shrugged. "Hard to say."

Not the ringing endorsement Cyrus had wished to hear. "Is it vulnerable to attack?"

"From the air? Possibly. I hardly see how anyone could navigate the surrounding peaks on foot. The location is primitive—designed to repel invaders with axes and spears. For anything else, we are relying on your forebears' augmentations." Such qualifications did little to disturb Cyrus. He was sure that his forefathers were at *least* as paranoid as he was.

Aretha palm-scanned her way into a room secured by a heavy metal door. As the portal hissed open, the entourage walked into a milleu set apart from the archaic hallway by several millennia.

A solid steel table sat in the center of the room, a holographic display shimmering to life above it upon their entrance. Holoscreens flared to life above consoles on every wall.

"Well," Cyrus drawled, "it seems the security center is well maintained, at least."

"Of course, Don Valadar." Aretha forced a smile onto her face. "Per your stipulations in the contract, we have carefully monitored the estate and deterred any intrusion."

"And has there been any attempt?"

"None! With the estate's position in Freya's Ridge, even routine air traffic is rare. No one has attempted to disturb the property since we have taken it over."

Including any trace of cleaning staff, Cyrus thought wryly. "Good. Now, tell me, are there any known threats to this location's perimeter?"

"None, Don Valadar."

"None, as in you haven't detected any? Or none, as in you haven't bothered to search for any?"

Aretha bowed her head. "My apologies, Don Valadar. We have not done anything beyond semi-annual scans—the most recent of which was three months ago. Before your most recent transmission, we hadn't received any more detailed direction. If we had known you required—"

Cyrus slammed his hand on the table. "What am I paying you people for?" He raised a hand to forestall her replay. "Don't answer that. I don't care. Just get someone in here to clean this place up. I want this entire complex back in living condition in two days. Can you handle that, Ms. VanMollen?"

"Y-y-yes, D-don Valadar." Aretha bowed her head in acquiescence.

"Good." Cyrus glanced at the clock on his MoDAC and turned to his companions. "Let's hurry back. I have an important appointment to keep."

Chapter 6

[*Loading Correspondence…*]
[To: Councilor Tristan York]
[From: Molly Nova]
[Subject: RE: Appointment Request]

Councilor York—My employer is happy to accept your request for a meeting. However, given his tight schedule, he is unable to meet you at City Hall as you have requested. Understanding the sensitivities you've expressed about being seen at NeoGenix so close to the recent incident, Cyrus suggests you meet him outside the building tomorrow afternoon. Please let me know if these terms are acceptable.

[*Closing Correspondence…*]

"Don't look so glum, Farris." Cyrus admonished. "Remember, your dedication to your job landed you this little promotion."

"Promotion, sir?" Farris's somber expression didn't so much as waver. The man's stone-cold affect was so omnipresent, Cyrus was beginning to wonder if he *could* smile.

"Yes! Are you not enjoying your role as my escort?"

"Of course, sir."

Cyrus heaved a sigh and waved the man forward. "Come on. It has to be a little more fun than doing security sweeps all day."

"If you say so, sir." Farris scanned the line of vehicles in front of NeoGenix. "Light blue autocar, third from the left. I believe that's the one we're looking for."

Well, Cyrus had to hand it to him: Farris wasn't much for laughs, but he could spot a mark as fast as any hired hand Cyrus had ever worked with. The Don pressed through the lightly blowing snow to the vehicle Farris had indicated. The blizzard had subsided for the most part, but lingering wisps of icy flakes danced in the air, courtesy of the persistent wind.

The door to the car opened just in time for Cyrus, followed by his stoic bodyguard, to slip inside. Despite the light of midday, the inside of the vehicle was strangely dark. Only when the door shut behind them did the interior lights flick on.

Cyrus flashed a devil-may-care smile at one of the vehicles' occupants. "Gods, Tristan, you would think you were on some kind of clandestine rendezvous, hiding in the dark like this."

The sallow-skinned Terran glowered back at Cyrus. "If the media were to catch us meeting like this, that would be the makings of the headline. And it's Councilor York when we're discussing official business."

The autocar hummed to life and sped onto the skyway. Cyrus had been through this routine before. It would make a quick circuit—or a lengthy one if the meeting ran long—and then return to NeoGenix.

"Oh? Maybe I should have brought one of my attorneys then." Cyrus glanced at the person sitting next to Tristan. "Though, I must say, the prosecutor's staff is looking much more militant these days."

The councilor rolled his eyes. "You don't need to lawyer up, Cyrus—not yet, at least. I'm here to discuss the items that were on our agenda for the meeting we were supposed to have yesterday after the conference."

Conference? Oh, that's right. "You mean the conference where you unceremoniously canceled the V-transit contract?"

"Technically, the contract wasn't canceled, it was awarded to another bidder."

Cyrus clenched his fists to avoid an angry outburst. "We were told that contract was all but ours. 'Just need to sign on the dotted line,' is—I believe—*exactly* what you told me."

"Yes, and that contract was set to be signed at the very conference *you* failed to attend." Tristan held out his hands. "What did you expect? Can you imagine the optics if you failed to show up and we *still* awarded you the contract? Furthermore, it seems there was some very aggressive bidding conducted by some of your competitors—bidding that seems to have been, on further review, improperly vetted. What am I supposed to make of that, do you suppose?"

Cyrus didn't *suppose* anything. He knew exactly why those other contracts hadn't been vetted. He'd paid good money to make sure it didn't happen. Unfortunately, it seemed he hadn't greased quite enough palms to make sure those contracts slipped seamlessly through them.

Then again, that was the problem with Tristan. Despite Valadar's best efforts, the councilor was one of only a handful of politicians on this planet he hadn't been able to pay off. It was made all the worse by the fact that this noble fool was the *chair* of the council.

"Fine," Cyrus spat. "I understand your predicament and your course of action. Let's set that aside, for now. What else was did you want to discuss?"

Tristan exhaled softly. "Let's start with the power grid issues. Your team over at Enersis assured me the problem would be resolved by now. Yet, as far as I can tell, the blackouts are getting worse."

It was true; they had gotten worse. The tests that Lucretia was running on the Heart of Thule drew an embarrassing amount of power off the Valhalla grid. Fortunately, the recent arrangements to transport the artifact out of the city would resolve the issue.

"We've isolated the problem," Cyrus said, truthfully. "The worsening blackouts you've witnessed were part of a series of tests the company was conducting. I assure you, they have been fruitful, and they have given us a pathway to resolution."

"They better. I feel compelled to remind you that the allocation of public resources to our private-sector contractors is a topic we will be revisiting next quarter. If public opinion continues to suggest that Enersis is not the best partner to implement and maintain city assets, that may be another contract your family loses."

Tristan was being unusually aggressive today. He'd never been one to grovel and scrape before Cyrus, but until recently, he'd fallen short of displaying overt hostility.

"I'm sure you will be quite pleased with our results over the next quarter," said Cyrus. "Now, is there something else? I think we're all out of contracts you can threaten me with—at least until next cycle."

Tristan's eyes narrowed, scorn radiating from his weasel-like features. "One more thing, actually. I want to discuss the *other* incident from yesterday. It seems like your training exercise is getting a lot of press, as is the unauthorized vehicle seen departing from the NeoGenix building roughly one hour before its conclusion." He tapped his fingers contemplatively against his armrest. "It's also strange that coverage of the event has all but stopped in the news media. TN3 is the only outlet that mentioned it today, and even that was only in passing."

Gods damn it. Cyrus had been hoping to avoid *this* subject most of all. "Yes, the press was *quite* excited about that one for a moment, weren't they? Don't worry, though—I don't intend to hold a grudge. Mistakes happen."

Tristan blinked. "What?"

"It's okay, Tristan. I don't expect an apology." Cyrus mustered every bit of feigned indifference he could into his words. "It's not your fault the city failed to file our notice properly. I would point out that the city *also* failed to notify the other business in the affected area, but I think that would be redundant. After all, with a bureaucracy as thick as the one in Valhalla, how can anyone be expected to get anything done without the proper work order being filed?"

The councilor's mouth hung agape. "Proper… work…" He shook his head. "Cyrus, please don't pretend that you had declared a test of the Automated Response System that day. You and I both know there was no such test scheduled."

"Well, of course—and that was because our request was improperly filed."

"Bullshit!" Tristan slammed his hand on the console between him and his escort.

Cyrus raised his eyebrows. "Was that not the finding of your own investigation? Or hadn't you heard? I understand it took some time with that untimely server crash."

Tristan closed his eyes and ran one hand down his pallid face. He said nothing for several seconds as he changed his tack. "Yes," he drawled. "And you can be assured that someone will be looking into that incident in detail. How *untimely* that was, for our servers to crash the very minute a successful query would have exonerated your good name."

Cyrus started to respond, but the councilor held up a staying hand. "You should know, however, that we *have* opened up an investigation into someone very close to that incident. It seems one of my fellow council members was taking a highly unusual interest in the subject. Tell me, how much did you have to pay Councilor Felch to buy his silence?"

Fighting the urge to grind his teeth, Cyrus said, "I have no idea what you're talking about."

Tristan chuckled. "No, I suppose you don't. Well then, you may be interested to learn that internal affairs have discovered several unusual transactions between Councilor Felch's bank accounts and your subsidiaries. We have launched a full investigation to determine the extent of this, but you may have someone operating improperly within your house, my friend."

Cyrus's eyes narrowed. "I'm not sure what you're implying, but I assure you, we are more than capable of looking into the matter ourselves. If anything improper is discovered—"

"Oh, it's no trouble, really." Tristan was smiling broadly now. "I think this is exactly what institutions like our internal affairs division are meant to do. Besides, I think you could use the help. After all, your organizations seem to be spread unusually *thin* at the moment—as do your excuses."

Without being conscious of the activation, Cyrus's amp powered up. Psionic energy coursed through Cyrus's veins, throbbing with each seething beat of his heart.

He could kill the man right here. He wouldn't even need a weapon. He could take out the bodyguard too. No one would have the time to raise a hand.

But this meeting was likely on Tristan's official itinerary. If the councilor were to suddenly disappear, with Cyrus being the last person to see him, then that would raise questions. That kind of scrutiny was not something he could handle right now. As Tristan had just pointed out, Cyrus was spread too thin.

Yet, he had other ways to deal with problems like this.

Cyrus glanced out the window and noted that the autocar was rounding back toward the NeoGenix building. He forced a smile onto his lips. "I welcome any scrutiny you can bring, *Councilor* York." When the vehicle came to a stop, he signaled for Farris to get the door. "Now, unless you have any other insinuations you wish to impart, I believe our business is concluded."

Tristan frowned at the sudden display of confidence. "No, I believe that is all we needed to discuss. Good day, Cyrus. I'm sure we'll speak again soon."

CHAPTER 7

[*LOADING CORRESPONDENCE...*]
[TO: SYDNEY CROSS]
[FROM: CYRUS VALADAR]
[SUBJECT: (NONE)]
I miss you, my pet. I require your services. You know how to contact me. I hope to hear from you soon.
[*CLOSING CORRESPONDENCE...*]

Ora tried to avoid drugs—at least, she tried to avoid anything stronger than alcohol. Her early life had been rife with substance use as part of the lifestyle used to subjugate and placate her. Getting clean hadn't been easy, but her ambitions had required it. Though drug trafficking represented a substantial and necessary part of her organization's revenue, she also invested significant sums to help anyone on Sigma-4 who looked to recover from their use.

This all flashed through her mind as she applied the strip of stym to her gum line. The rationale was as immediate as it was pitiful. She hadn't had enough sleep in the past two days, and she had made a commitment that required her to be alert. Something as simple as caffeine wasn't going to do the job.

Her tongue savored the familiar peppery taste as the drug hit her nervous system. She felt her vision sharpen, her muscles tense. The world around her became clearer, more vibrant. Senses sharpened and mind alert, she was ready to meet with Cyrus Valadar.

Mercifully, this didn't involve returning to the NeoGenix building. Cyrus had requested they meet at the Crystal Lilly, a restaurant that Valadar Holdings presumably owned. Located near the top of a downtown skyscraper, the plush restaurant boasted both a convenient location and a stellar view of the city—probably the best of any culinary establishment with Treskon Fountain closed indefinitely.

When Ora approached the host, she suddenly wondered if she should wait for Cyrus or check for a reservation in his name. Her deliberations were cut short as the Terran host smiled upon seeing her.

"Ms. Monroe," he said, flashing a bright set of teeth. "Mr. Valadar has already arrived. If you would follow me to the dining room?"

The man didn't wait for a response. Ora followed him through the maze of tables to a small room set off to the back left corner of the establishment. As soon as the host opened the door to the private dining area, Ora spotted Cyrus sitting at the oblong table.

The Don stood as she entered. "Ora," he greeted with a grin and a polite dip of his head. "So pleased to see you. Perhaps tonight, at long last, we can have a meeting uninterrupted by my personal affairs."

Ora's smile felt natural, coaxed all the more by the hint of self-deprecation in his demeanor. "You know I don't hold any of that against you, Cyrus. I, of all people, know what it is like to have business interfere with my personal life."

Cyrus's grin broadened. "I appreciate your understanding." He gestured for the host to depart and returned to his seat at the table.

Ora took up a seat next to him, donning her most political persona. "So, Cyrus—where should we begin?"

\#

Skye didn't know why she felt so much more at ease with Ora being out for the evening, but that didn't change the fact that it was true. It had nothing to do with what she and Eli had gleaned about Markus's intimate relationship with the leader of the Grey Wings. It was probably just that Skye didn't like having one of their best clients constantly looking over her shoulder while they were on the job.

Yeah, that was definitely it.

"So," she began in her usual tone. "We know the target is the Valhalla City Archives. How do we hit this thing?"

Lexa jumped in as if responding to a query from a search engine. "Valhalla city regulations require that all construction projects within the city's jurisdiction submit a detailed schematic to the city archives before initiating the building process. The Valadar estate is no exception, which makes this a reasonable source for us to extract data on the layout and security of the compound."

She pulled up a diagram above the war room table. Judging by the size and shape of the building, Skye was willing to bet these weren't the plans they were looking for.

The AI confirmed this as she continued. "This diagram depicts the structure of the building housing the archives. City officials have taken steps to assure that no outside entity can access this information without resorting to the proper channels. All official records are stored on an air-gapped server that requires a dual-authentication system to access."

"Which explains why our favorite synth can't just pull the files for us," said Markus as he leaned in. "I'm assuming the best way to pull this off is to give Lexa access to the archives. That's going to require us to infiltrate the building. Does everyone agree?"

Eli's Sahaia friends were the only ones who appeared unconvinced. "You seem awfully eager to jump in and steal something again—a little odd for someone who just returned from an unsuccessful raid."

Markus cut his eyes at Argus. "Think this is a bad idea, hey? I hope that means you have a better suggestion."

"Not really." Argus kept his face so neutral as to almost seem sociopathic. "I didn't say it was a bad idea. I'm suggesting that we haven't properly vetted other alternatives."

"So, you're objecting on principle?"

"You might say that, yes."

"Well, frag your principles," Markus rested both hands on the table. "We're only taking facts and suggestions here. You can discuss your principles with the *Captain* after I leave." He glanced at the android. "Lexa, any chance you can fill us in on what kind of security they have in there?"

The AI was happy to oblige. "The security system is nearly identical to the one used at NeoGenix. A sensor field surrounds the exterior of the building and scans any person who enters the premises. Security feeds monitor all public areas of the installation, and most of the private locations as well."

"What're the exceptions?" Aaliyah asked.

"Maintenance and storage rooms," Lexa responded. "However, there is at least one feed that monitors each point of entry to these locations. They are also sealed with key-card access panels."

"Credentials that can be faked?" Jeagan hissed.

"Unfortunately not," Lexa answered. "The access codes are generated on-site for employees and change daily. Without having access to the security server—which, like the one that stores the files we are looking for, resides behind an air-gap—there is no way for me to falsify credentials for the crew to use."

Dan opened his mouth to speak, but Eli held up a hand to stave off his question. "I think we may be getting ahead of ourselves. Let's allow Lexa to finish her explanation before pepper her with more questions."

Everyone quieted. Lexa let the silence linger for a moment before continuing. "Any item in the archives can be accessed through terminals located throughout the complex. Though each group of terminals is relegated to a specific subdirectory, they all link back to the same set of servers."

A sublevel appeared on the schematic of the archive building. A set of glowing boxes were highlighted in the center of the new portion of the rendering. "I would suggest that this be your objective.

If you can create a wireless link directly into the servers, then Thurn, Daniel, and I can access the files you seek without detection."

Seeing that Lexa was done with her explanation, Aaliyah was the first to speak. "Easy enough. Can ya highlight the points of entry?" Four doors at each corner of the sublevel lit up. Aaliyah shook her head. "Not just doors. I'm thinkin' we aren't just gonna walk down there without attractin' attention."

It took Lexa a moment to realize what the engineer was suggesting. "Oh," said the AI when she'd deciphered Aaliyah's meaning. "Yes, of course."

The schematic grew more detailed as Lexa added to the rendering. Some of these new details began to glow the same light blue as the doors Lexa had highlighted previously.

Skye first took note of a series of ventilation tubes glowing in the sublevel's ceiling. "Looks like the vents are out of the question. I don't think any of us can fit an arm in one of those tubes, much less crawl through them."

Sahar leaned in, feline eyes squinting at one part of the schematic. "What are these?" She gestured with a clawed finger just outside of the room with the servers.

"Floor grates," Lexa responded. "They lead to a crawl space underneath the sublevel. It's used to access and maintain the sewage system for the building." As she provided the information, the crawl space and its network of pipes appeared on the schematic.

"Ah bet ya might fit 'n there," Thurn mused. "Though Ah don' see any way inside. Might make a good hidin' spot if ya run inta trouble."

Markus stroked his beard. Damn, it was weird seeing him with full facial hair. "What about underneath the crawl space?"

"There's nothing underneath the crawl space," said Lexa. "That is the lowest level of the archives."

Shaking his head, Markus gestured to some of the pipes that had been sketched onto the schematic. "These lead down. Where do they go? At some point, they need to empty into the city's sewage system."

Lexa's eyebrows rose. "Of course! One moment please." The android's eyes went unfocused, and she stared blankly into space for a moment. After several seconds, the schematic of the archive building zoomed out and a network of tunnels appeared on the hologram. "The pipes descend approximately zero-point-two-seven meters into the Valhalla sewer system."

Markus nodded. "Does the security grid on the archives extend that far down?"

"No. It only surrounds the exterior of the building and the roof. It does not extend into or beneath the sublevel."

Now Markus was grinning. "Bingo! That's our ticket in."

Argus arched an eyebrow. "I hate to break it to you, but the sewers don't actually lead *into* the crawls space. The pipes come down through the ground."

"Oh, I know," Markus acknowledge, undeterred. "Into the *cement*, I suspect. That's okay, though. We can cut through cement."

Skye flashed him a smile. "Like the job on Loki?"

"Just like that," he agreed, returning her grin. That smile held for just a moment before something sparked behind Markus's eyes. His expression faltered, and he looked away. Skye felt her joy at the eureka moment fade as he broke eye contact.

Kadath cleared his throat. "We still may have a problem. The crawl space opens up outside the server room. The infiltration party will have to make it through those doors."

Markus blinked. "True. I missed that. Lexa, can you hack through those doors?"

The android shook her head. "Not without triggering an alarm, I suspect."

Eli crossed his arms. "Then we are going to need to acquire a set of credentials."

Skye brought a knuckle to her lip as an idea occurred to her. "The archivists open up the doors by scanning ID cards, right? New cards they have printed every day? That would mean the staff would have to keep them on them at all times. Let's lift a set of credentials off one of the archivists and find a way to get it to our team that's digging their way up from the sewers."

The Sahaia nodded his agreement. "That seems reasonable enough, but how are you going to manage that?"

Her lip quirked up in a wry smile. "Let's you and I talk about it later. I'm sure we'll manage."

CHAPTER 8

[LOADING CORRESPONDENCE...]
[TO: DR. LUCRETIA BLACKWELL]
[FROM: CYRUS VALADAR]
[SUBJECT: A FAVOR]
I need to request a favor from you. I apologize for the short notice, but I promise it will only take a moment of your time. It has to do with a bit of technology we've been experimenting with. I require it for a quick field test.
[CLOSING CORRESPONDENCE...]

As Eli emerged into the corridor outside the war room, a firm hand fastened itself onto his arm. "A word, brother?" Argus asked. Though it was framed as a request, the tone, along with Amelia's penetrating stare, seemed to imply that it was anything but.

"Certainly," Eli agreed. "I take it we should do this in private?"

"Of course," Amelia whispered.

Eli nodded in acknowledgment. They led him down the corridor and onto the next level to the quarters that had been assigned to them. Walking into the cabin, Eli was struck by how little had changed. The twins were incredibly tidy and spared little time for decorating their temporary abode.

They both rounded on him the moment the door hissed shut behind them. "How are you comfortable with this?" Argus asked.

Eli arched an eyebrow, genuinely confused. "Argus, this is what I've been doing for the past seven years. A client gives us a seemingly impossible task, and through deliberation and planning, we make it happen. I don't understand. What is the issue?"

Amelia eyed him quizzically. "Have you gone so far astray?"

Eli shook his head. "I'm sorry. I don't understand. Are we not doing exactly what Jocelyn asked of us?"

Argus donned a judgmental scowl. "Even knowing what you've done to survive since you left the sanctum, what we've seen is a surprise to us. Have you forgotten our ways? When was the last time that you communed with your spirit?"

Ah, that was it. "I have no need to seek advice from a long-dead ghost," Eli replied. Besides, the bastard spirit that fueled Eli's power had done little to help him in the past. What made it so likely that he would change his ways now?

Amelia took a softer approach. "Brother, even if your intuition is right about our course of action, you would be well served to have that confirmed by the ancestral spirits. You lose nothing by communing with your forebear. Why do you show such reluctance?"

Eli steeled his mind to assure that Amelia didn't pluck the answer straight from his thoughts. "My reasons are my own. I do not know your relationship with your ancestral spirit, but I assure you that I have never found much to gain from mine." He shook his head. "Why the sudden interest? Is there a deeper problem that you've yet to relay to me?"

Amelia glanced at Argus, who somehow managed to make his scowl deepen. "These actions you are taking, brother—they are foolhardy at best, and reckless at worse. You are jumping from one problem to another, asking yourself only whom you should shoot next or what there is to steal. You were trained to be better than this."

Grinding his teeth, Eli held up a hand to ward off further reprimand. "My training has nothing to do with this. You forget yourself, Argus. Remember that I held the circle during your Awakening ritual. Do not talk to *me* of foolhardy intentions."

Argus started to respond, but Eli cut him off once again. "No. I'm not here to receive a lecture from you. I understand your passion for the old ways, and I commend you. If they continue to work for your purposes, then, by all means, practice them. But let me be clear: the coven has *failed* me." He drew in a deep breath, stiffening his resolve. "I do not need, much less want, a lecture from you. You do what you feel is needed. Meanwhile, I'll focus on executing the job our triumvir has given to me. Understood?"

Neither Argus nor Amelia said anything in response to his challenge. Both just stood there, staring intently at him. Eli elected to interpret their silence as acquiescence.

"Good," he said. "If there is nothing else, I will take my leave. Some of us have a job to tend to tomorrow."

Ora's meal with Cyrus was uneventful—almost pleasant, even. They discussed local politics and business ventures while swapping stories of some of their more bizarre encounters. Cyrus, at present, was giving a rendition of an experience most people in their line of work faced all too frequently.

"At this point, I'm not even pretending to listen anymore," he said with a shake of his head for emphasis. "But the guy just keeps talking. Another ten minutes and I realize, 'Frag me, this is a canned speech!' Somewhere in the nervous ramblings, the guy had slipped into something he'd memorized from a sales manual."

Ora suppressed a chuckle. Yes, she'd seen that type too. "How did you get rid of him?"

"Well, at the end of his little speech, he glances at his MoDAC and realizes our time is almost up. So he goes, 'What's the best way for me to follow up with you?' I'm thinking to myself, 'Gods, I don't know if I hate any of my employees to put them through a follow-up.' But it's obvious this guy isn't going to read the room, so I had to come up with something." Cyrus leaned forward conspiratorially. "So, I gave him Michael Tyranus's number."

"Oh, that poor bastard," Ora laughed. "Did Don Tyranus ever say anything to you about it?"

"No, but I never heard from the rep again, either."

"What was he selling, again?"

"Frogs. Fragging frogs. The company was importing them from one of the colonies. DGC had them tied up in court on animal trafficking and invasive species proliferation before the end of the cycle." He smiled, "I almost wish Michael had taken the meeting. I kept fantasizing that he would think it an honest mistake and try to one-up me. I suppose it didn't happen though."

He tipped back his wine glass, savoring the last of the crimson liquid. "Another?"

Ora glanced at a clock on the wall behind him. "Doesn't the restaurant close in just a few minutes?" Not that they were at any risk of being kicked out—Cyrus did own the place, after all. She was really just looking for an excuse to wrap this up.

Cyrus glanced at his watch. "You're right." He locked eyes with her. "It doesn't have to be here, though."

This was where Ora had to tread carefully. She'd been out with Cyrus enough times that it was going to seem suspicious if she pumped the breaks too hard. At the same time, she didn't want to put herself in a situation she couldn't get out of.

She elected to go with a bit of honesty. "Perhaps if I had managed a little more sleep these last two nights. As it is, I'm not feeling much for the nightlife."

Those predatory eyes never wavered. "If you're tired, we could go somewhere a bit more relaxing—a bit more… *private*."

Ora twisted her mouth into a half-smile. "I'll bet. Though, somehow, I don't think such plans would yield much for me in the way of sleep." With a sigh, she drained the last of her wine. "As it is, I'm scheduled to depart early tomorrow. I'm leaving the planet for a few days. There's someone I need to check in with on Mani."

It was true—Vallus, likely with Molly Nova in tow, would be departing from the Mani spaceport in two days. She needed to check in with him first before he returned to Sigma-4.

Cyrus didn't bother to hide his disappointment. "A shame. I've enjoyed our time together. It seems that you've slipped through my fingers yet again."

From the resignation plain on his features, Ora could tell she was losing him. She couldn't let that happen. As much as she loathed this game, her flirtations were the only reliable way of keeping Cyrus occupied. With their plans to steal the artifact still undefined, it was a tactic she might need to employ yet again.

She leaned in, running her hand over his knee and up his thigh. "Don't grow tired of the chase just yet. Some prizes are worth waiting for." She paused, batting her eyelashes. "That is, of course, if you have the endurance."

Renewed energy flashed in Cyrus's eyes. "Does this mean you will be returning to Valhalla soon?"

"Of course. I'm only going to Mani for a few days. I'll be back coming back before leaving the system." She stood from the table. "Perhaps, if you can work me into your schedule, we can do this again."

"I would like that," said Cyrus, also rising to his feet. He took a half step forward, pressing close to her. Ora let it happen, keeping her shoulders square as he reached to embrace her.

It was hard to say what was more unnerving: the feel of her breasts pressed against his torso, or the caress of his hands as they slid under her shirt and across the bare flesh of her lower back. The downward tilt of his face and the glint in his eyes screamed of what he wanted.

If Ora was going to sell her story, there was no getting out of it.

She slipped one hand up the side of his, the gentle press of her fingers pulling his mouth against hers. His lips tasted of the wine they'd shared—his body firm and muscular against hers. It might have been a pleasant kiss, had she not been racked with the guilt of it.

She hated this game and couldn't believe that she found herself playing it—regardless of what was at stake. It had *better* be worth it.

Breaking the kiss, Ora forced her smile to reach her eyes. "Thank you for dinner, Don Valadar."

"You're welcome, Ms. Monroe." Something felt different about the look in his eyes. Was it just sexual need, or something more mischievous? "Let me walk you to your cab."

Chapter 9

[*LOADING CORRESPONDENCE…*]
[TO: MARA REN'DAHL]
[FROM: AMELIA REN'DAHL]
[SUBJECT: STATUS UPDATE]
I don't know when you'll receive this message, dear sister, but in your absence at the gate, I've elected to leave it on one of our encrypted listening beacons. Ryker is dead, and thus far we have failed to secure the Heart. I fear that matters will only continue to grow more dire. If you receive this, please relay our situation to Jocelyn immediately. We would benefit greatly from reinforcements.
[*CLOSING CORRESPONDENCE…*]

For a long moment after Eli left their quarters, neither of the Twins said anything. At length, Amelia broke the silence. "Still no word from Mara or Jocelyn."

It was a statement, not a question. "What should we do?" Argus asked.

"I think you know the answer."

Argus did, but he was hoping Amelia might be harboring another suggestion. They must do what Eli should have done in their stead.

They must reach out to the ancestor.

"Let us prepare," Argus said with a nod. He stripped off his jacket as Amelia went into their trunk to retrieve their focus. The object she withdrew from their belongings was strange in appearance: three orbs of onyx threaded together with a circle of silver wire.

Though most Sahaia favored the Obsidian Spear as a focus, Argus and Amelia found the Trinity Wire to be more responsive to their connection. Perhaps it was because, like their relationship, the Trinity Wire was unusual. Its use required that a psion be able to pull from two slightly different wells of power—usually a base talent along with a greater gift that had manifested through training and practice. However, since Argus and Amelia practiced two different schools of psionics, the Wire readily responded to their combined abilities.

Amelia sat down in the center of the floor, crossing her legs in a half lotus. Argus did likewise, the perfect mirror of her form, if not her figure. Neither spoke as Amelia placed the Trinity Wire between them and began to channel.

Their focus lifted into the air. Though Amelia was not a telekin, the object responded to her unique psionic signature. It floated of its own accord, drawing on her signature as it began to rotate in the air between them.

Argus fed in his power, and the silver thread connecting the orbs began to glow. Runic symbols, pulsing with silver light appeared on the surface of the orb. The focus began to spin faster.

And the world went dark.

Seconds passed. Within that darkness, a spray of starlight appeared in the void. Despite the lack of illumination, Amelia was still clearly visible. She appeared to be floating, serene with her legs crossed, in the blackness of interstellar space. Though Amelia had never confirmed it, Argus imagined he appeared the same way to her.

Suddenly, they were no longer alone. A third figure, a woman clad in a simple dress as black as the space between the stars, now sat to Argus's left. "I've missed you," she whispered.

"As we have missed you, sister," said Amelia.

The spirit took a deep breath. "Speak my name."

"Verona," Argus replied.

The spirit sighed contentedly. "One can never know until they delve beyond the Well what a pleasure it is to hear their name again."

Though Argus did not understand how such a simple utterance was so necessary for the ancestral spirits, he accepted it as fact. It was the first request Verona made every time he and Amelia communed with her. From what he'd heard from other Sahaia, the experience was the same for them.

What kind of existence waited for those who dwelt beyond the Wells of Eternity that would spark such a strange craving? Argus hoped he would never find out. Baring unnatural causes, Sahaia were supposed to be immortal. And yet, there seemed to be no shortage of spirits waiting to imbue a new generation with their power.

"What brings you here tonight?" Verona asked.

The question prompted two thoughts in Argus. Firstly, he wondered if Verona used the phrase "tonight" in reflection of the time it was on Sif where they currently resided. It was always nighttime somewhere in the universe, so to hear the phrase used by a spirit for which time was meaningless seemed strange.

The second was simply the fact that she'd bothered to ask. "You know what brings us here," he stated flatly.

"Yes, but I must insist that you state it nonetheless."

"We have a problem," said Amelia. "The Heart of Thule has been discovered and lies within the hands of an enemy. Efforts to secure the artifact thus far have remained fruitless. We require your guidance, ancestral spirit."

Verona smiled, reaching out and cupping Amelia's chin. "This is one of the things I love so much about you, my Twins. As if it were not enough to be the only soul beyond the Well to boast a dual connection with the living, it is made all the more interesting by your contrast."

She released Amelia's face and turned her gaze to Argus. He was struck by how much the two women resembled each other. The only apparent difference was the crop of their hair. Amelia's was long and flowing—a dark cascade around her shoulders. Verona's was cut short, falling just below her jawline.

Verona's sweet smile faded, replaced with a deadly serious look. "I cannot lie to you, my children. The Heart of Thule represents a grave danger the likes of which the universe has scarcely seen in a millennium. Cyrus Valadar wields its power to the fullest extent that he can. I daresay the man has impressed Thule himself with his resourcefulness."

She held up a warding finger. "However, he is not the greatest danger you face. There are those outside of House Valadar that circle like vultures on a fresh corpse. This carrion may pose an even greater threat than the Don of Darkness in the grand scheme of things. Perhaps it is better if you let the Heart lie where it has fallen."

Incredulity lay at the top of Argus's response. Those dark feelings sank far deeper, encroaching on words like betrayal. "You mean to tell us that our efforts are in vain? That we should give up our quest? Defy our triumvir's orders?"

Verona chuckled. "You make it sound like heresy, my dear Argus. I am not telling you which path to take, merely warning you that liberation of the artifact from the Don of Darkness will spawn yet greater threats. Do not think so ill of me for imparting knowledge that you would benefit from."

Argus felt his shame wash over him like a rising tide. "Apologies, ancestor. My temper, as you know, causes me to speak out of turn."

Amelia interjected before Verona could respond. "These other threats that you speak of—what can you tell us of them?"

Verona sighed and closed her eyes as if peering into a future that lay within herself. "The Nethra will not let me speak of specifics—only hint. I can tell you that one danger is near to you, the other closer to home. Both may be thwarted, but not without sacrifice: a sacrifice that will leave all of us less than whole."

Her eyes popped open. "Ask me no more of this, for I fear I must refuse to answer. The future is guarded by powers that dwarf our own. Prophecy itself hangs in the balance, and the Nethra holds your very fates within its hands."

Both Argus and Amelia knew better than to question the spirit's dictate. They had learned early on that Verona was as transparent with them as she could be. To defy the wishes of the spirit that fueled their power was unthinkable.

"Then tell me," Argus began. "If such a grave danger lies in the liberation of the Heart from House Valadar, I must know the cost of the alternative. Can you show us the fate of the universe should we leave the artifact where it lies?"

Verona hesitated for just a moment, eyes going blank as if her mind had gone elsewhere. "Yes," she whispered at length. "This I can show you."

She cast her hand out into the gap between Argus and Amelia. Everyone turned to view the premonition taking shape in the void.

They saw Cyrus Valadar. He stood in front of a window, arms clasped behind his back. The Don was dressed in the finery one might expect of someone in his station. Yet, there was something different about him.

His hair had gone white, slicked back upon his head in thin, greasy tendrils. His skin looked charred, scabbed over in dark swaths that covered the entirety of his exposed flesh. Veins of green ichor pulsed in his neck and along the sides of his face.

As horrific as the scene appeared, worse lay outside the window. They saw Valhalla, a glowing shrine to commercialism that raged against a blackened sky. Beneath Cyrus's tower, they saw hopeless souls dredging their bodies through neon-lit streets. These were not the ones Argus had seen trudging through Valhalla's commercial infrastructure just a few days past. These were people who had lost everything. Not the barest hope glistened behind those darkened eyes.

The dead ruled over Valhalla.

The vision vanished as suddenly as it had appeared. Argus's reaction was as immediate as it was intense. "*That* is the better outcome? *That* is the future you wish us to foster?"

Verona's countenance darkened. "I stand by what I have said. The alternatives that you face will be, indeed, much darker."

Amelia's soft voice silenced Argus's mounting objections. "Is such darkness unavoidable? Is there no path that leads to the light?"

The ancestral spirit turned a sad gaze upon her. "There is a narrow path, yes, by which the shadow might be pushed back by the light. I warn you, though, that it is as I have said: such a path is not without sacrifice, and its success does not rely wholly upon the two of you."

Argus swallowed hard. He had hoped that this conversation would provide a balm to his spirit, a poultice by which his anxieties might be soothed. Instead, his fears had only been multiplied.

Amelia seemed to keep a firmer head upon her shoulders. "What, then, must we do to walk this path?"

A smile fell upon Verona's lips. It was marred only by that sadness that continued its residence behind her eyes. "Listen to Eli," she whispered. "Follow his dictates. He and his friends are resourceful, and their intentions as pure as anyone in this gods-forsaken universe. If they succeed, then you shall also."

CHAPTER 10

I will check in when I am able, but our client has kept me perpetually busy for the past two months. His fixation with this artifact is beyond what I expected, as are its potential applications. The recommendation at this point remains the same from my last check-in: keep the client happy and stay in his good graces. I'm not certain what Cyrus has planned for this system, but I have the fullest confidence in his ability to make good on his ambitions.

The relief that Ora felt when she gained sight of the *Vandal* surprised her. It was similar to how she felt when returning to Annex after a long trip. The odd thing was, the *Vandal* was no more home to her than the *Basilisk*. Perhaps it was just the relief at finally feeling free from Cyrus's claws that she was experiencing.

To her surprise, the ship's android opened the primary airlock before she could enter the request. The AI's friendly voice chimed over the intercom. "Welcome back, Ms. Monroe."

Caught off-guard, Ora smoothed a silver lock of hair back behind her ear. "Um… Thank you…" What was the AI called again? "I'm sorry, I've forgotten your name."

"Lexa," the android replied.

"Lexa," Ora repeated. "Thank you for the warm greeting." To herself, Ora wondered what it was in the AI's programming that made it feel the need to engage socially like this.

"You are welcome," Lexa replied. "Markus Frost is currently in your shared quarters. Shall I let him know you've arrived?"

"Yes, please do." Ora doubted Markus needed the warning, but it certainly wouldn't hurt. Ora made her way to the nearest access ladder and up to the crew quarters.

Markus was standing in the entryway to their cabin. "Already have the local synth announcing your arrival?"

"Well, she offered." Ora closed the gap between them. Markus folded her in an embrace and kissed her softly.

"Missed you," he murmured.

"I missed you too." She looked into his icy blue eyes. "Let's go inside. It's been a long night."

Markus stood to one side, allowing her to enter the cabin. She tossed her purse on the desk, followed by her MoDAC once she managed to fish it out of her pocket. "Good progress today?" she asked.

"Good enough. We have a plan to hit the archives and find the plans. We're scouting tomorrow. Probably launch the day after that." He slid onto the bed. "What about you? How'd it go?"

Ora sighed. "I survived. I think my cover is still intact." She hesitated. "I… feel I need to be honest with you. Things got a little physical near the end."

Markus's face was a monument to neutrality. "Did you sleep with him?"

"No. Nothing *that* physical."

"Then I don't need to hear about it."

A weight Ora hadn't realized she'd been carrying was instantly removed from her shoulders. "Thank you," she whispered.

Markus flashed her a winning smile. "We all do things that we don't like for this job. I'm just glad you're okay." He sat up straighter on the mattress. "So, did you get anything? Anything useful I mean."

Ora shook her head, sinking onto the bed with him. "No. This was about keeping appearances. When I was at NeoGenix yesterday, he asked me to commit to dinner. Being regrettably short on convincing excuses, I was obliged to accept."

"At least tell me the food was good."

"Ugh, *divine*." Ora flopped down on the mattress. "How I wish I could requisition ingredients like that out on the station. The talent in the kitchen probably didn't hurt either. You don't see many system-class chefs looking for placement on a space station."

"Oh, but the view! Who doesn't want to see the perpetual night of Sigma-4?" Markus raved. "I hear it's quite notorious. You can't get that same bleak feeling anywhere else in the Ravian system."

Ora laughed. "On old Terra, I hear there were entire cities dedicated to perpetual nightlife. What an envy we must be to our forerunners!"

"Nothing like the cold of deep space to get your party on." He chuckled as he bent in to press his lips against hers. "Seriously, though—no intel on the Heart?"

"The subject didn't come up. We didn't talk about NeoGenix at all. I wanted to wait and see if he brought up the incident at the office yesterday, but he was never tempted. You would have thought that their cover story about it all being a drill was the real thing."

"Even though we know it wasn't."

"Yes, but Cyrus doesn't know that. It's only natural that he would keep the cover story."

"And ignore the fact that you were in the building?"

Ora shrugged. "It's a classic tyrant's ploy. 'Don't believe your eyes. They're lying to you.'" She shook her head. "It doesn't matter. All I wanted to do this evening was make it through without blowing my cover. Mission accomplished. Time to move on to other matters."

"And what 'other matters' are on your mind tonight?"

Markus was gazing at her. Not in a lustful way, but in a friendly kind of way. He was looking at her like he just enjoyed the act of doing so. It was strangely platonic, while simultaneously intimate. It felt genuine.

Ora couldn't help but smile at the sight of it. "I'm leaving for Mani tomorrow. I should be gone for just a couple of days."

"Just a quick trip then?" Markus asked, stroking her arm.

"Yes, just a quick trip. I'll be back before you can miss me."

"Oh, I doubt that." He leaned up and kissed her again. She kissed him back, enjoying the feel of his strong arm pulling her close.

She reached around his waistline and began pulling off his shirt. He broke the kiss and smiled at her. "You're not too tired?"

"For this? No, not for this."

Cyrus loomed over the terminal in his penthouse. The dark intuition he had about what the device would reveal was not questioned. He listened to the audio feed with the mere intention of confirming that which he already knew.

Whether it was his focus or her stealth, he could not be certain, but Cyrus nearly jumped out of his skin when Sydney's voice sounded from over his shoulder. "Kind of late to be catching up on the news feeds. What's got your attention?"

Composing himself, Cyrus responded. "It's not the news feeds. I'm confirming a suspicion."

"Sounds interesting," Sydney said slinking up next to him. "Care if I listen in?"

"Of course not. Have a seat."

The Citza assassin did as he requested while her ears picked up a man's voice sounding from the terminal. *"So, did you get anything? Anything useful I mean."*

"No. This was about keeping appearances. When I was at NeoGenix yesterday, he asked me to commit to dinner. Being regrettably short on convincing excuses, I was obliged to accept."

"Who's that?" Sydney asked.

Cyrus shook his head. "I don't recognize the man's voice. But the other voice, the feminine one, is Ora Monroe."

Sydney arched an eyebrow. "Your girl-toy? You bugged her? How did you manage that?"

"Experimental tech," Cyrus responded. "It's a dermal transmitter. I slipped it onto her as we were leaving the restaurant. The nanites will dissolve in a few hours, leaving no trace of the bug. Until then, I can hear everything she says."

He directed his attention back to the feed. The male was speaking again. *"Seriously, though—no intel on the Heart?"*

"The subject didn't come up. We didn't talk about NeoGenix at all. I wanted to wait and see if he brought up the incident at the office yesterday, but he was never tempted. You would have thought that their cover story about it all being a drill was the real thing."

"Even though we know it wasn't."

"Yes, but Cyrus doesn't know that. It's only natural that he would keep the cover story."

"And ignore the fact that you were in the building?"

"It's a classic tyrant's ploy. 'Don't believe your eyes. They're lying to you.'"

Sydney snorted a laugh. "Tyrant? Boy, she's got you pegged."

Cyrus killed the feed. He had what he needed, and didn't want to listen to anything else. The facts of the matter were clear.

Ora Monroe was a traitor.

Sydney didn't bother to hide her mirth. "The Silver Queen has been found out. Want me to take care of her for you?"

Cyrus had no doubt that the assassin would take pleasure in such an assignment. "No," he stated with finality. "I want to see where this is heading. Besides, such a betrayal deserves more than a quick death by your blade."

"I didn't say I'd make it quick."

"All the same," he blessed her with a genuine smile. "I want to be there when it's done. Besides, I have another task in mind for you?"

"Task, hey?" She slithered into his lap, stroking his cheek with the tip of her tail.

Cyrus chuckled. "That too, yes. But that wasn't what I was referring to. There's someone who's been a thorn in my side for far too long. I think it's time we removed him."

CHAPTER 11

We have discovered some irregularities with your network access. Our Director of Internal Affairs would like to schedule an interview to see if there is, perhaps, an explanation that we have yet to decipher. As the Council Chair, I have requested to be present for the meeting. I thought that you would appreciate the opportunity to tell your side of the story before the findings become a matter of public record.

The following evening, Cyrus found himself at City Hall long after it had closed. The passcode he'd been issued to gain access to the Councilor's offices after hours worked as advertised. Farris followed him like a hulking shadow, and Cyrus didn't even attempt to make conversation.

Tonight, he was all business.

Councilor Felch's chambers were not so different from any of those belonging to the other council members. Save for a handful of personal touches, all the offices were identical.

Warm brown wood composites trimmed the floor and ceiling, giving the room a regal appearance in an age where the harvesting of trees for wood and paper products was highly regulated and incredibly expensive. The furnishings in the room were crafted of similar material, though Cyrus suspected there was far more synthetic material in these.

The windows were draped in curtains of embellished crimson to match the cushions on the chairs and the couch near the room's entrance. Chords of silver rope—a selection in homage to the councilor's political party—bound the curtains together. They were supposed to be more of a steel-gray to coincide with the color of Sif's Populist movement, but the moonlight drifting through the frosted glass lightened the tone.

Damian Felch was staring out this window, glancing away only when he heard Cyrus approach. The man's dark hair and beard were flecked with slightly more gray than when Cyrus had seen him last. Had these past few months been so hard on him?

"Well, you've finally done it, Cyrus." The councilor sipped from a glass Cyrus hadn't noticed he'd been holding. "At long last, you've ruined me."

Cyrus scoffed. "My, my… aren't we feeling just a touch melodramatic this evening?"

"Call it what you will, Cyrus, but it doesn't change the truth of it. I'm finished." He set his glass on his desk with just a bit more force than was necessary. "Internal Affairs has found something. I meet with them tomorrow to plead my case. *Tristan* is going to be there as well. Bastard isn't going to pass up an opportunity to gloat."

The councilor sank into his chair, bringing both hands up to rub at his eyes. "I just thought I'd give you fair warning. When they see what I was accessing on those servers, they'll know you had something to do with it. No one will keep it out of the media then. I'll be forced to resign, and you'll have a PR issue on your hands."

Cyrus took a seat at the empty chair opposite the councilor. Throwing his feet up on the desk, he gestured toward the half-empty decanter just beyond his reach. "Stop your whining and pour me some of that, will you?"

"*Whining*?" Despair gave way to anger, and Damian gritted his teeth. "I throw away my *career* for you, and *that's* how you speak to me?"

"No one's throwing away anything. Now, if you'll pretend to be a proper host and pour me some of that whiskey, I'll enlighten you just as to why."

Whether out of intrigue or an implicit need to be subservient, the councilor did as he was told. Petulant scowl still affixed, he seized the decanter and emptied a generous amount into a glass that he slid to the Don.

Cyrus sipped at the glass contentedly. For all Damian's faults, the man had good taste in liquor.

"Well?" the councilor snapped.

"Well, what?"

"You were going to tell me why you're acting so gods-damned confident."

"Oh, yes!" Cyrus leaned forward excitedly. "The Director of the Valhalla City Division of Internal Affairs will be receiving a message in"—He made a show of checking his watch.—"about seven minutes from now. That message will contain enough evidence to effectively link Tristan to the anomalies detected in the server. To any rational person, it will be apparent that Councilor York went to great lengths to sabotage the filings for the ASR drill and frame your actions to fix the error as criminal interference.

"The Director may be surprised to see that York recently made a sizable investment in one of NeoGenix's competitors, and the incident with the security drill was only the first in a series of actions he planned to take to damage my company's reputation. I wouldn't be surprised if, when it was all said and done, that Internal Affairs invalidates all actions taken by Councilor York over the past month. The extent of his apparent corruption is unprecedented, even by *this* city's standards." Cyrus tapped his lips thoughtfully. "I wonder if I may even be able to challenge his decision on the contract with V-transit. I think I just might try that."

Damian's mouth hung agape. "How… how did you…" He paused, holding up a warding hand. "No, don't tell me. I don't want to know. Besides, it's all going to come to nothing. You know that Tristan will contest the findings. That puritan isn't going to let accusations like that linger. He thrives on the image that he can't be bought."

"Don't worry about York," Cyrus replied. "Someone is dealing with that problem as we speak."

The councilor eyed Cyrus suspiciously. "And *how*, might I ask, are planning on 'dealing' with him?"

"As you pointed out just now, Damian: you don't want to know." Cyrus took a long pull from his glass of whiskey, savoring the pleasant burn. "Besides, you have something much more important to be contemplating."

"And that is?" Damian asked, with the arch of a skeptical eyebrow.

"How you're going to take York's place as Chair of the Council."

Valhalla, for all its faults, was a democracy. The city-state elected representatives from its populace, consistent with its laws and constitution. Members of the City Council, its joint legislative and executive body, were term-limited and had to reside within the city's jurisdiction.

They were not kings. The wealth of the city-state had no bearing on the financial success of individual members of the council—short of the fact that Valhalla's continued solvency was necessary for them to continue to draw their legislatively assigned salaries and fringe benefits. The city also required a healthy degree of separations from public corporations, legally requiring that councilors divest all investments and only put their money in blind trusts managed by an independent financial review board for their terms in office and two years after the end of their tenure.

Seeing the York estate, Sydney could understand how one might forget all that. This guy was loaded. Not Cyrus Valadar-loaded but doing a damn spot better than most of the city's citizens. Whatever Tristan had done before becoming the Council Chair, it must have been highly lucrative.

Not that that mattered. As the Terran saying went: "You can't take it with you."

The assassin crept through the convenient cover of evergreen trees surrounding the rim of the estate. The storm had picked back up on the western side of the city, so blowing snowdrifts added to the concealment of the swaying pines. The only way someone was going to spot her was by heat signature, and her stealth suit would take care of that.

She raised her binoculars to her eyes, dialing in the settings to focus on the outer gate. Dark metallic rods rose to permit access to a hovercar sliding through a stone archway. A guard, Maur by the shape and size, was barely visible behind a tinted black-glass window immediately next to the gate. Twin spotlights shone down from either side of the driveway to focus on the space just in front of the entrance.

Solid, visible, and staffed. That wasn't going to be her point of entry.

She scanned the walls to the left and right of the estate. These appeared more promising. The occasional armed guard patrolled the walkways atop the stone walls. Searchlights swiveled at each point in the perimeter in a consistent pattern unaffected by the passing of the guards. Sydney was willing to bet it was one of those AI-controlled rigs that only focused if there was an apparent disturbance. If she could time the lights and slip past the guards unnoticed, no one would be the wiser.

Now, if it had been a climb-resistant fence with barbed wire, spikes, or motion sensors, she might have been in trouble. Unfortunately for him, Tristan had opted for aesthetics over utility.

Sydney sped forward, a wraith borne on the winds of the storm. Her gloves adhered readily to the brick walls of the perimeter, and she ascended. Her passage over the wall occurred less than two meters behind a patrolling guard. The searchlight swiveled safely away from her position not three seconds after she leaped to the ground.

Inside the perimeter, she had a better view of the complex. It looked to be composed of at least three distinct buildings, perhaps four judging from the hazy roof-line she could see from the courtyard. Finding Tristan in a complex of this size might be a bigger task than she had planned for, but first, she needed to find cover.

She slid along the wall, wary of the cycling searchlights and thankful for the inclement weather to mask her approach. There were no guards in the courtyard itself, but better conditions might have permitted some of those patrolling the perimeter to spot her. Then again, if it weren't for the weather, she could have engaged her active stealth—so it was kind of a wash.

In seconds she made it to the edge of one of the larger buildings and began to climb. For whatever reason, the searchlights didn't sweep farther than a couple of meters past the outer wall. *Talk about an oversight.*

The overhang was a minor obstacle, but the low slope of the buildings practically invited climbing. A warm heat emanating from the shingles explained why they, unlike the rest of the grounds, were free of snow and ice. *How thoughtful!*

Now it was time to infiltrate, but which building? Security was likely to increase once she was inside, and she couldn't leave a trail of bodies in her wake. Cyrus had been very explicit on how he wanted this to look. A trail of slaughter leading to the Councilor's bed-chamber would detract from that image.

Sydney scanned the surroundings again, taking her time and soaking in the details she hadn't been able to catch in the courtyard.

The compound was comprised of three buildings, not four as she had expected. The largest one, home to the roof where Sydney now hid, extended off into a distant wing with an elevated tower.

This was the structure she had mistaken for a separate installation. She was also betting that was where she would find Tristan.

Sure enough, a balcony jutted defiantly against the night sky, taking on the snowfall that the heated roofing so obstinately defied. From her current vantage point, Sydney thought she spied a figure standing in front of the glass door that led onto the structure. It figured that Tristan would opt for a room with a view.

She could easily traverse the expanse of the roof between where she currently hid to the base of the tower. After that, it looked like things would grow a bit more complicated. Even though most of the interior of the complex was not surveyed by the searchlights, the damned things flashed against the base of the tower every two to three seconds in an alternating pattern. There was absolutely no way she could climb the entire structure without being flagged.

Options began flashing through Sydney's head. Perhaps her stealth suit could keep her sufficiently masked, even with the ongoing storm. No, that was too risky. She would only get one shot at this, and a sufficiently snowy gale would blow her cover.

Maybe if she climbed quickly in a spiral fashion, she would stay in the searchlight's periphery. The suit's stealth mode might adequately compensate for when she inevitably ended up in the path of the light. She thought, then, of the searchlight's precise timing and pattern and was convinced all the more that this was an AI-controlled system. Such a system could be dialed in to detect even the faintest trace of an intruder. Still too risky, but the line of thought gave her an idea.

If it was an AI-controlled rig, the lights might respond to another significant disturbance. A simple misdirection might provide enough distraction to fool the system long enough for Sydney to scale the tower.

She reached for the pouches on her shoulders and thighs, withdrawing the components for the rifle she had stowed there. It was a simple thing—relatively low caliber and insufficient for piercing anything other than naked flesh. Fortunately, she wouldn't be shooting at an armored target. She didn't even need the shot to kill. She just needed the impact to make some noise.

Finishing the assembly by screwing the silencer in place and gently sliding in the magazine, Sydney crept forward. Just below where the lights flashed on the tower, she aimed the scope. Every second counted, so she chose a target as far from the tower as possible while remaining within the searchlights' radius.

She watched the spot she would aim to hit, analyzing the pattern of the swirling lights. *Three... two...* She pulled the trigger.

A deafening crack sounded from where the bullet struck its target. As Sydney hoped, all four searchlights jerked to illuminate the area around the strike. Her rifle was slung over her shoulder, and she was moving before the lights ever found their target.

Her gloves and boots found easy purchase. She vaulted up the side of the wall more quickly than any one of those idiot guards could climb a flight of stairs. When she reached the edge of the balcony, she clung just below its precipice, waiting for the commotion from her shot to die down.

Seconds passed. A minute. Finally, someone from the guard reported a false alarm. The lights broke apart and resumed their standard search pattern. The guards on the walk resumed their orderly patrol.

Sydney held her position for at least two more minutes, enough time that her muscles responded with a subtle burn. She was thankful that Tristan hadn't programmed the lights to search so high, likely not to interfere with his sleep or the view of the western forestland. The searching beams strobed harmlessly below Sydney, well out of reach of her cloaked figure.

Now for the fun part. Sydney pulled herself over the railing, stealth-suit engaged. The awning over the balcony blocked enough of the snowfall that she didn't worry about her silhouette being exposed by the weather. She crawled to the right of the door.

Tristan stood just to the other side of the glass barrier. If he had seen her, he made no move to signal it. Nor did he seemed the slightest bit disturbed by whatever had attracted the attention of the searchlights. He just stood there, staring out into the winter storm.

The Terran was older, but not incredibly so. Not a streak of gray accented his dark, slicked-back hair. Then again, that might have been due to a dye job. It was his skin that gave hint to his seniority: sallow and wrinkled around the eyes. Though he was reasonably thin, Tristan was hardly the picture of health.

As interesting as all the details might have been, none of that mattered. More pertinent to the task at hand was the question of whether he was the type to lock a generally inaccessible entrance at night. Sydney eyed the latch but couldn't discern the answer from where she stood.

Being optimistic, she prepped one of her needles. The tiny object was coated in a substance specifically prepared for the task at hand. Now all she had to do was wait.

Tristan lingered a long while at his window. Gods only knew what he was thinking. What did state officials who pretended to be too good to buy off—relying instead on the wealth they had generated in a previous life—dream of in the twilight hours? Most would think that power topped that list, but Tristan had nowhere else to go. Nine hells, he'd have probably been better off staying in the private sector based on the wealth this compound portrayed.

What, then, made him tick? Who was this fool that thought, on a whim, that he might challenge the might of House Valadar?

The questions would remain forever unanswered. With a heave of his shoulders, Tristan dipped his head and turned back to his bedchamber. Sydney didn't hesitate. She moved to strike.

Fortune favored her, and the door was unlocked. She pried it open just far enough to duck inside. Her hand surged forward, and the dart soared toward its target.

Tristan felt its sting in the back of his neck. His hand went to the site of impact, feeling for what might have caused it. He looked to the side, but not back at the door, relatively unperturbed by the incident. With such a small needle, it was less the sting of a bee and more the bite of a gnat.

His hand found the small protrusion where it still lay lodged in his flesh. Gingerly, he extracted it from his skin. He brought it close to his eye, examining the peculiar object—uncertain of what to make of it.

Her payload delivered, Sydney slipped back out the glass door, closing it carefully behind her. The latch clicked into place, prompting Tristan to look up at the sound. She couldn't tell if he had seen her or not, because the drug she'd dosed him with was already working.

It started as a pained look on his face. His hand went to his chest, and he bent over to alleviate the tension. It only intensified from there. Soon he was gasping for air, struggling towards his desk where his MoDAC lay painfully out of reach. He took one quivering step forward, then collapsed.

Perfect. Delivery had been flawless. Sydney only needed to wait for a few more minutes to make sure he was dead.

Thirty seconds passed. Another thirty. Then another. Sydney was about to walk away when the door to the councilor's bed-chamber creaked open.

A woman entered, clad in a bathrobe that was the perfect reflection of the one the now-deceased councilor wore. His wife perhaps? His mistress? She was young enough that she could have been either.

She descended on the body, shaking him, rolling him onto his back, checking for a pulse. Her cries were audible through the glass door. Despite her distress, she still had the wherewithal to go for Tristan's mobile on the desk nearby.

Time to go.

Chapter 12

[*Loading Correspondence...*]
[*To: Tashania Priest*]
[*From: Vallus Nos Drathen*]
[*Subject: Travel Plans*]

I'm going to be a little later than expected. The boss wants to meet up before we leave the system. Not sure what it's about, but you know how things go with her. I'll see you this time tomorrow.

[*Closing Correspondence...*]

Hands around her neck. She can't breathe. Skye tries to scream, to plead, but she can't.

Distantly, somehow, she hears her voice—as though sheer will has manifested her words where her vocal cords could not.

"Markus! Markus, don't!"

Skye shot up, gasping for breath. Eli was there immediately. "Are you okay?" he asked in his deep, dulcet tones.

"Yeah," she gasped. "Yeah… just… just a nightmare."

"One of your visions?" The question was spoken carefully, devoid of any emotion.

"I… I don't know." Skye hesitated, thinking back. "I don't think so. It was different from the others. Nothing metaphysical. I… I think it was just a bad dream."

"What can I do to help?"

Her Sahaia lover was so attuned, so ready to hear her needs, that it was enough to wash away any lingering resentment she'd harbored towards him.

This was Eli. This was a man that was worthy of her affections.

"No," she whispered. "Let's get back to sleep. We have a big day tomorrow."

It had been a while since Ora had taken public transportation. The shuttle from Sif to Mani was clean, if not comfortable. The passengers were crammed in close, even in first class, where Ora had placed her ticket. She could only imagine how bad things were back in coach.

None of that mattered, though. She was here, and she had an appointment to keep. She'd delayed Vallus's departure time so that she would have one last chance to meet with him. Part of this was to keep up appearances with the schedule she'd portrayed to Cyrus. She did not doubt that the Don had people watching her, validating her commitments. She just hoped they weren't watching too closely.

[HERE,] Ora texted.

Vallus's response came quickly. [BREWERY. LEVEL 3.]

Ora glanced up the bank of escalators in front of her and trudged forward. A few short rides later, she arrived where Vallus had directed.

The pub exuded an old Terra vibe. Faux wood flooring matched the laminate plastered to the walls. High tables were arranged throughout the building to supplement the seating provided at the bar. She spotted Vallus sitting at a table to the far right of the establishment. An attractive Terran woman accompanied him.

Molly Nova looked much the same as she had when Ora had seen her last. Her warm brown hair fell in straight, elegant waves around her shoulders. Her makeup was done to corporate-level perfection, indicating that the look was in line with her personal preferences rather than being a product of the NeoGenix corporate image.

The woman's eyes widened on seeing her. "Ms. Monroe."

"It's Ora," she replied. "No need for formalities here. I'm just pleased that you decided to take me up on my offer."

Molly laughed nervously. "Wasn't a hard decision to make—especially given the way Cyrus has been acting lately."

Ora cocked her head, genuinely curious. "What do you mean, exactly?" The woman hesitated, obviously afraid of what repercussions her words might bring. "You don't need to fear anything from me. We are on the same team now."

Vallus nodded to emphasize the point. "No one in this system, or any other, looks out for her people the way Ora does. When she says something, you can take it to the bank."

Though a hint of reservation lingered in her expression, Molly nodded. "I think it has to do with that artifact he's been researching. He's obsessed with it. Every waking moment, every extra kret, he spends it on this new project. I'm not the only one to wonder. The board is doing the same thing."

Ora arched an eyebrow. "The NeoGenix board? They don't know what Cyrus has been doing?"

Molly shook her head. "No. No one does. It's this big secret. Only Cyrus and Dr. Blackwell know what he's been working on. All I see is a budget that keeps increasing and questions from the CFO asking why." She lowered her gaze. "If the CFO wasn't his sister, I'm not sure he'd have gotten away with as much as he has."

As concerning as this was, it wasn't necessarily helpful. Ora had only the word of a peculiar priestess and a dead man regarding the importance of the artifact. She still didn't know what kind of power it held.

"Was there any unusual detail that you might have noticed?" Ora asked. "Anything unusual regarding the organization's activities related to the artifact?"

Molly hesitated, giving the question honest thought. "One thing, maybe." She paused. Her eyes darted to the periphery, looking for some unseen watcher.

Vallus caught on to the expression and conducted a quick survey of the room. "It's okay. There's no one listening to us. You can be transparent."

Ora wasn't privy to whatever conversations Vallus had had with Molly to earn her trust, but the renewed resolve in her eyes gave credence to the bond they'd established.

With a nod, Molly unloaded her conscience. "There have been unusual transactions with the prison colonies owned by Valadar subsidiaries. When I noticed the line items, I looked deeper into the details. The requests for prisoner transfer were specific to psionic inmates."

"So, the artifact has special relevance to individuals with psionic talent?" Ora asked.

"That's my guess." Molly shrugged. "I'm sorry, I wasn't given a lot of detail regarding the project. That's not the kind of thing someone in my position—my *former* position—has access to."

Disappointing, but not unexpected. "That helps," Ora replied truthfully. If Cyrus had a particular interest in individuals with psionic capacity, that weighed in on her decision to surrender the artifact over to the control over the Sahaia.

Now, however, was a time for a shift in the conversation. Absent any other information that Molly might provide, Ora needed to think about how she might affect her future operations as an employee. "So, tell me, Molly: what are you looking to do in your next life?

The surprise on the woman's face was so pleasantly blatant. "My next life?"

"Yes. The one you will have post-House Valadar. As you know, the Grey Wings operate primarily within the Ravian system. I'm interested to know what kind of role you hope to play there."

Molly blanched. "I was hoping you had a specific need for me. I... I hadn't given much thought to what I would be doing after..."

She trailed off, telling Ora that her predicament related to Cyrus was exactly as bad as it had seemed. Molly didn't care much about what life would look like after leaving Cyrus's house. She just wanted out of it.

"Are you familiar with the type of work the Grey Wings engages in?" Ora asked.

"Loosely," Molly confessed. "Honestly, I'm just an admin. I'm looking for anywhere you might use my skills. If there's some area I need to grow in, I'm open to it. Just let me at it. I'm your girl."

Gods, what an attitude. Ora loved it when people expressed such enthusiasm about their work. "Here's the thing"—Ora leaned in for emphasis—"I have a second in command. Tashania has been working hard to make sure that she is a worthy successor to my business enterprises. I have absolute faith in her, and I intend to grace her with even more responsibility shortly. However, she doesn't have an outlet." Ora paused, dramatically. "Can *you* be that outlet, Molly? Can you pick up the slack where my second needs a hand?"

The young woman's reaction was as immediate as it was exuberant. "Absolutely. I won't let you down."

"Good." Ora leaned back in her chair. "Then you will report with Vallus to Annex. Tashania will assign you administrative tasks within the club. It will not be glamorous at first, but I promise you: it is just a taste of what is to come."

Molly smiled. "That's all I ask."

CHAPTER 13

These recent disruptions to the status quo have cost us too much. The citizens need to have faith in their government, else we face the threat of an anarchist society. That means stability: stability granted by our partnerships with organizations like Valadar Holdings. Hopefully, all of us remember the cost of the Colony Wars. Let us strive to see that such an episode does not resurrect itself on our very doorstep.

Skye had to hit the shopping center before their next venture. Aside from the fact that her wardrobe had grown far too sparse in the past months, she felt it important to look the part when she entered the Valhalla City Archives. Clad in a black pencil skirt with a white V-neck tank under a short-cropped blazer, she felt she fit in.

Eli's admiring gaze, as they doffed their heavy winter coats in the archive's foyer, was all the confirmation she needed to sell her role in this operation. "Are you sure you can handle this?" he asked.

"What?" she asked, adjusting her fake glasses. "Aren't I every nerds' dream? Cut me some slack here."

"I was more worried about your emotional state," the Sahaia returned, wryly. "But I see that's not a concern here."

It was true, but it didn't stop Skye from being irked by the jealous boyfriend routine. "Oh stop," she chided playfully. "If you like it so much, we can role-play when we get back to the ship."

"As long as you don't break character now." Eli raised a hand to gesture forward. "That's the check-in. Let's act like a couple, yes?"

Act, hey? Yup, Eli hadn't had his ego stroked enough lately. She'd never figured him for the jealous type, but it wasn't *that* surprising. Having Markus around, even just in the periphery, had given Eli a serious inferiority complex.

Declining to engage any further, Skye strode over to the receptionist. "Hi! Tickets for Gale and Gary Black?" Those were the names Lexa had supplied for them when she'd faked their credentials for this little outing. Though visitors to the archives were allowed free reign to roam the area once they were inside, a reservation had to be placed to get you through the door.

The Terran women behind the plate-glass studied her terminal for a moment. "Yes, Mrs. Black. We were expecting you. Please proceed through the gate."

The glass door buzzed and Skye and Eli moved through. Here's where their tactics would change. "I'm going to find a restroom," said Eli, providing some reasonable cover for their separation. "I'll catch up with you in a minute."

Skye smiled and winked. "Don't take too long. No telling how much trouble I'll get into without you."

Eli rolled his eyes and wandered off. With a deep breath, Skye started in the other direction.

Their cover story was that they, as Mr. and Mrs. Gary Black, were looking to make a large real-estate purchase in the city's jurisdiction. With a large bank account and a total lack of awareness of what was available, perusing the city archives was as logical of a way to begin their search as any.

Unfortunately for Mr. Black, his "partner" had a wandering eye and a tendency to flirt with attractive persons who proved to be of assistance. *How scandalous*.

Now, if she could only find the correct section.

The appearance of the archives reminded Skye of the Citadel on Minos station. Dark tiles flecked with spidery veins of white covered the floors, a strangely opaque contrast to all the steel and glass that composed the actual archives. Translucent holographs floated in the walkways and near banks of terminals providing labeling and directions for those wandering the technological labyrinth.

Skye didn't have to feign confusion. The place was so busy, with an aesthetic that opted for style over utility, that it would have been easy for her to get lost. Sure, she could have probably figured out where she was going if she'd bother to study one of the maps near the walkways, but that wasn't the kind of character she was playing.

She needed to find some assistance—assistance that might be open to helping the poor, lonely, and neglected wife of a real-estate mogul. Assistance like the guy standing about ten meters down the walkway.

"Excuse me," she said with a light, overly familiar touch to the man's back. "I was wondering if you had a minute to help me."

The Terran was attractive in that same pretty-boy look that Eli pulled off. His red-brown hair was carefully quaffed back away from his forehead, and his archival uniform was neatly pressed and well-tended. A few well-selected accessories augmented the outfit, but he lacked the one feature that might have made Skye's task a bit more difficult: a ring on the traditional finger of his left hand.

His smile was as polite as it was charming. "Of course. What are you looking for?"

"Real-estate. I'm looking to acquire a large plot of land on the outskirts of the city, but I don't know much about the area. My contacts said this was the best place to begin looking."

The man nodded. "I can help you with that, but you're on the wrong floor. Real-estate terminals are one level up." He inclined his head to a set of nearby stairs. "Follow me. I'll show you."

He led her up the glass stairwell, down another walkway, and around the bend to a set of holographic terminals that appeared, to Skye's eyes, exactly like all the other ones—if, perhaps, slightly dimmer.

The man's brows creased when he eyed one of the terminals. "I apologize, this section's staff hasn't turned these on yet. One moment, please." He grabbed a plastic tag that he'd clipped to his waist and scanned it against one of the consoles. After a few quick taps against the hard-light construct, the holodisplays across the bank brightened to the same active state as the rest of the ones in the complex.

"There," he sighed, a pleasant smile returning. "It's a good thing you found me. These would have given you a hard time without the right credentials to log in."

"A good thing," Skye said, biting her lower lip while she twirled a strand of her golden curls. "Maybe you could help me a little more? This is my first time using a system like this. I don't really know where to start."

"Of course. It would be my pleasure." The gleam in his eyes said the opportunity, while technically part of his duties here, might be motivated by something other than his job description. "Just place your palm here and we'll get started."

Skye looked like she was having too much fun with her part in this operation, and Eli fought desperately to keep that from bothering him. *She's just playing her part*, he told himself. *Now it's time for you to do yours.*

With a flick of his fingers, Eli undid the clasp that held the archivist's credentials clipped to his belt. The card quietly zipped into Eli's waiting hand while the other man—completely absorbed in assisting Skye with her query—remained none the wiser. Prize in hand, he walked down the stairs and made for the entrance.

"I forgot my mobile," he explained to the receptionist as she eyed him quizzically. "I'll be back in just a moment."

He seized his coat, pulling it on as he made his way out the door. Snow fell in soft flurries outside on the street, but not enough to hamper visibility. For this reason, he walked a couple of blocks away from the archives before changing course. Five minutes later, he was at the sewer access ladder.

The access point was as nondescript as one might expect. A short ladder was visible from the surface where the automatic hatch had been left open behind some caution tape; a holographic warning sign had been posted declaring the site was undergoing routine maintenance. Being tucked this far back in the alley, it was unlikely anyone would have happened upon the access point unless they'd been looking for it specifically. Still, the team had thought it was better not to take any chances.

The pungent odor of the sewers wafted up to the top of the access ladder, only intensifying as Eli descended into its depths. No matter how advanced a society's technology became, sewage systems still stank. At least the smell would deter anyone from sightseeing down in the darkened passages.

It didn't take long for Eli to find the team working down here. Markus, Kadath, and Siv stood arrayed around Sahar, who worked diligently against the stone ceiling with a cutting torch.

Markus was the first to catch sight of Eli. "How did it go?" he asked.

"So far so good," Eli extended his hand, holding out the archivist's credentials. "We got what we came for. Hopefully, Skye can keep the archivist busy long enough to keep him from discovering his card is missing."

Markus grunted in acknowledgment, taking the card. "I'm sure she'll do fine. Siv? Here." He passed the object into her waiting hand. "You've got the package?"

"Right here," the Hissak patted what Eli assumed was a pouch on her shoulder. In her dark garb, it was hard to discern more than the woman's outline in the dim tunnels.

Sahar quit cutting and lifted the face shield. "Here goes nothing," she growled. She pressed upon the stone ceiling. The rock shifted and came loose with a cascade of dust and pebbles. The Maur heaved and slid the slab up and into an open area above them. "Looks like we've got the right spot. Ready to go?"

"You know it," Markus replied. "Siv, you first. Sahar will give you a boost."

"Not necessary." Showing impressive agility and strength, the Hissak leaped into the hole and pulled herself through.

"Show off," Kadath grumbled. "I'll take that boost if you don't mind."

Sahar thread her fingers together and knelt. Kadath stepped up into her waiting palms and she heaved him through the opening. "Your turn, Markus."

Markus took a step toward Sahar. "Good luck in there," said Eli.

With only a glance back over his shoulder, Markus stepped into Sahar's waiting grasp pulled himself over the stone lip.

"They'll be fine," Sahar assured. "Quick in and out, right? Lexa has all the hard work here."

"Mmm…" Eli propped himself up against the stone wall of the tunnel before he could think better of it. Well, it wasn't like he'd planned to clean this suit anyway. It was a one shot for the mission. Now he'd be glad to abandon it, if only to leave the smell behind.

"Give him some time," Sahar encouraged. "You guys got started on the wrong foot, but he'll come around. Look at it this way—even if you guys go this whole job without speaking to each other, at least he's cooperating."

"Right," Eli nodded. "It's fine, really." *Just lingering guilt. That's all.*

CHAPTER 14

Apologies, mistress. We never wants to disturbs you, but we has had issues reaching Don Valadar. Numerous queries we has sent, but finding him hard to reach, we are. If your organizations want to cease dealing with Haranash Group, we are sad to sees you go. However, common courtesy dictates you reaches out to us to informs us of termination of contracts. At least, that's how things goes in Hissak space. Please lets us know if your Valadar Holdings wants to terminate future imports using Haranash Group.

Markus dragged his body through the cramped crawl-space and up through the grate where Kadath and Siv were already waiting. "Thanks," he muttered, as the former pulled him through the opening.

"My pleasure," the half-breed replied. "Let's be quick about this, yes? I would like to think that our presence is completely unnecessary, and would hate for anything to ruin my delusions."

"Agreed," Markus replied. The idea of the two of them going in with Siv had been heavily debated. On the optimistic side, Siv should have been able to slip into the servers, download the information they needed, and extract herself before being noticed. Kadath and Markus were there to keep an eye on things and deal with any problems that might arise if the optimistic plan didn't work out the way they intended.

In Markus's experience, things *never* went according to what he intended.

Siv moved to the doors of the server room and scanned the access badge Eli had delivered. The door's indicator light flashed green and slid open as she scanned the plastic tag. "I'll keep watch out here," Kadath volunteered. "You two grab the prize and hurry back."

Markus didn't argue. He and Siv moved into the server room and the door hissed shut behind them. "Access port?" the Hissak asked.

Markus scanned the room. "There," he said, gesturing to a maintenance terminal at the end of a server bank. "Card slots should be on the side."

Siv slipped out the data drive Daniel had given her and jacked it into the server. The screen flared to life as the embedded program took control.

[GREETINGS,] the prompt read. [THIS IS LEXA. INITIATING HACK NOW. PLEASE STAND BY.]

"Very polite for a computer program," Siv commented.

Markus chuckled nervously. "Yeah, she's always been like that. Must have come pre-programmed on her drive-chip. Gods know she didn't learn it from the crew."

The Hissak turned her hooded and masked face in his direction. "Is it strange working with them again?"

The comment made Markus pause. "A little," he confessed. "On the other hand, I know they're good at what they do. No matter what other issues I may have with them, I know I can count on them to do their job."

Siv paused, considering him for a long moment before nodding. "Good allies can be difficult to find."

It was true: good help was always hard to find. Good friends even more so.

——

"What about that one?" Skye asked, gesturing to yet another parcel on the map.

Her helper, still not tired of addressing her relentless queries, pulled up the indicated plot. "Four hundred square meters of living space, five bedrooms, four baths. Point two-five square kilometers of forestland on the southern face of the mountainous property." He smiled at her. "It looks like this one contains a virtual tour. Should we check it out?"

"Yes, please," she replied, returning the grin. This guy was having way too much fun. Her distraction was working even better than she had anticipated.

At least, until the blonde in the expensive-looking dress interrupted them. "Allen?" Her voice held equal parts question and judgment.

The archivist—Allen, presumably—turned to the woman in surprise. "Kate?"

The woman was pretty in a traditional sort of way. Her dress and heavy overcoat were conservative, but her make-up was done to the nines. She looked like a caricature of the conservative housewife.

Skye looked at Allen's hand again. Yup, no ring. So this was a... girlfriend, maybe? *Shit*, this was awkward.

"You forgot your lunch this morning," Kate said, hefting a cloth tote for emphasis. "I thought I'd bring it out to you."

Allen fought to recover. "Th... Thank you. I... I was just helping Miss... *Mrs.* Black, here, locate some property on the city outskirts."

Yes, how important it must have been to reaffirm Skye's supposed marital status. Skye glanced nervously between the couple, unsure of what to do as she silently wished for the woman to go away.

"I see," Kate replied, casting a reproachful look in Skye's direction. She wasn't buying Allen's alibi. "Then, I guess I can just give this to you so you can get back to work."

She thrust the package forward. Allen glanced nervously at Kate, then back to Skye. "Would you mind dropping it off in the break-room? I can meet you back there as soon as I'm done helping Mrs. Black."

"It's my day off, Allen. I can't print off any credentials to get back there. The security AI won't let me."

A coworker? Damn, Allen should *really* know better than to flirt with strange women on the job when his partner worked the same territory. Didn't he know people talked?

"No problem," he replied. "Let me just give you mine." He reached down to his right hip. A confused expression crossed his face.

Frag, frag, frag! He wasn't supposed to notice that his card was missing. Skye tried to play it cool. "Is something wrong?"

"I…" he hesitated. "I seemed to have lost my credentials."

"Oh?" Skye arched an eyebrow, scanning the floor around them. "I thought you had just used them to badge into these terminals. They must be around here somewhere."

Allen's eyes searched the surrounding floor as he straightened. "It's not a problem. I can just print off a new one. Give me a second."

Just print a new one? That might be a problem if the system was logging Allen as being in more than one place at once. "But what if someone else finds them?" Skye asked. "Won't that create an issue?"

Allen waved off the comment. "Oh no, not at all. These things happen from time to time. When we create new credentials, it invalidates the old ones. No risk to security whatsoever. One second. I'll be right back."

As he wandered off, Kate in tow, Skye's stomach clenched. If generating new credentials invalidated the old ones, then…

She reached into her pocket and pulled out her earpiece. Affixing it to her ear, she pressed the transmit button. "Dan, do you read? We may have a problem here."

[TARGET FOUND,] Lexa reported through her prompt. [DOWNLOADING NOW. THIRTY SECONDS.]

"Damn," Markus sighed. "This was way too easy."

Siv's head snapped up. "Don't say that."

"Say what?"

"It is bad luck to say things like that before a job is over. You invite ruin upon us to say such things."

Markus couldn't help but chuckle. "Superstitious much?"

Siv's voice was deadly serious. "I am a Prodican. My faith should be sufficient to tell you I have a serious belief in the metaphysical."

"Yeah, well, my old crew used to say I had the Devil's Luck."

Another prompt scrolled over the screen. [DOWNLOAD COMPLETE. YOU ARE NOW FREE TO REMOVE THE STORAGE DEVICE.]

Markus pulled the drive free from the terminal. "Come on, let's get out of here."

They made their way to the door they'd come in through and Siv swiped the badge across the access pad. [ERROR: CREDENTIALS HAVE EXPIRED. ACCESS DENIED.]

"What?" Markus exclaimed. "That doesn't make sense. Do it again."

Siv complied, and the same message scrolled across the terminal. "Told you," she hissed.

Less than a second later, Markus's earpiece crackled with an incoming transmission. Dan's voice came in faintly over the feed due to the interference from the security field. "Markus. Markus, do you read? We may have a problem. Skye reported that the archivist is going for new credentials. Your badge is about to get deactivated."

Markus sighed. *So much for the Devil's Luck.* "Yeah, Dan. We know."

Chapter 15

[*Loading Correspondence...*]
[To: Allen Ross]
[From: Valhalla Archives Security Team]
[Subject: Invalid Credentials]
This is an automated response to inform you that you have attempted to use an invalidated clearance card. Please return to a security kiosk to print a renewed security clearance. Continued attempts to use invalidated security clearances will be reported to your supervisor to be addressed on your annual review.

[*Closing Correspondence...*]

"So, I spoke too soon," Markus conceded. "What do we do?"

"Don't ask me. You are the one with the fancy AI."

Siv was right. Markus fished the drive out of his pocket and plugged it back into the nearest terminal. When Lexa's interface loaded, he typed. [We have a problem. The card we used to get inside has been invalidated. Need help.]

Lexa was quick to respond. [Based on the messages I'm able to glean from the security system, it appears that a new set of credentials has been issued to the employee assigned to your card. This has invalidated his previous access.]

Markus heaved a sigh to control his temper. [Yes, I can see that. We still need to get out of here. Can you open the door?]

[If I open the door without the required credentials, it will trigger a proximity alarm.]

Damn. [CAN YOU FAKE THE CREDENTIALS?]

[I DO NOT HAVE ACCESS TO THE CREDENTIALING SYSTEM FROM THIS TERMINAL I CANNOT GENERATE A VALID CODE THAT WILL OPEN THE DOOR.]

"*Shit!*" Markus roared, banging his fist against the server.

"What is the problem?" Siv hissed.

"Lexa can't open the door. If she does, a proximity alarm is going to go off. Security will be on us in seconds, and our cover is blown. They'll know there's a leak."

The Hissak seemed unperturbed. Then again, if she had been bothered by the situation, Markus would hardly have known. Damn her and her modesty garb.

"How will they know it is us?" Siv asked.

Markus dragged his thumb and middle finger across his eyes to pinch his nose. "Because it's a *proximity* alarm. They'll know where the problem originated, and trace it right back to us. As soon as they know someone was in the servers, they'll look at what files have been accessed. They'll see the file for the Valadar estate has been downloaded and they'll know someone was looking into it."

"Does Lexa have access to the alarm system?"

Stiffening, Markus replied, "I don't know. Why?"

"If she does, perhaps she could disable the proximity alarm."

Markus should have thought of that. He went back to the console. [LEXA, CAN YOU ACCESS THE ALARM SYSTEM?]

[NO. I WOULD HAVE SUGGESTED THAT SOLUTION IF I COULD. ALTHOUGH I CAN ACCESS CRITICAL SYSTEMS, I CANNOT DISABLE ALARMS. THOSE PARAMETERS ARE SET ON THE SECURITY SERVER.]

"That's a no-go," Markus reported. "Looks like she can only set off the alarms. She can't disable them."

The Hissak paused. "What if she were to set them *all* off?"

"What?"

"The problem is the proximity, correct? If she sets them all off, we do not risk being discovered."

Well, shit. [LEXA, CAN YOU TRIGGER ANY OTHER ALARMS IN THE BUILDING?]

[YES, WHY?]

Hot damn. They were in business. [THEN DO IT. TRIGGER THEM ALL.]

Allen walked back to Skye, sans the girlfriend. "So sorry about that," he began, noticeably more reserved than he'd been moments earlier. "Where were we?"

Skye didn't know what to do. She hadn't received any further direction from the *Vandal*, but they were trying to keep comms quiet while she was inside the security field.

"I think you were showing me this property on the northern expanse," she replied, trying to keep her cover.

"Yes, that's right. Let's—" Whatever Allen had been about to say died off as the lights around them shut off. Replacing the serene white illumination were beacons flaring a violent, pulsing red.

"Danger," the overhead speakers blared. *"Severe weather warning: Proceed to internal shelters. Danger: Terrorist threat. Evacuate immediately. Alert: Security breach. Everyone remain where you are. Danger: Fire. Evacuate immediately."*

"What the—?" Allen glared at the security sensors.

Skye didn't have to feign her surprise. "What do we do?"

"I..." The alert—or, rather, all four alerts—repeated themselves. Allen must have figured it was best to go with two out of four. "I guess we evacuate."

His sentence was punctuated as the fire control sprinklers all across the building were suddenly triggered. Skye gasped as the cold water drenched her. "Which way?"

"This way!" Allen pressed back to the stairs they'd come up from. People streamed from every corner of the structure. Skye hadn't even noticed there were that many people in the archives until that moment.

Damn it, Markus. I hope you know what you're doing.

———

The alarms were blaring before the door to the server room opened. Markus and Siv were out of there before the automated message even started.

Kadath's eyes went wide. "What in the nine hells just happened?"

"No time to explain," said Markus as he grabbed the half-breed by the shoulder. "We need to get out of here. *Now.*"

Siv was already sliding into the grating. At Markus's insistence, Kadath was right behind her. Markus followed, grabbing the grating and securing it in place behind them.

The musty crawl-space seemed just that much tighter as they were forced to scoot back into the darkened crevice. Markus's foot met resistance. "Ouch!" Kadath cried. "That was my face!"

"Then crawl faster!" Markus protested.

"*Trying.* It's a little more difficult to slide out of a hole you can't see." Markus waited for a tense moment before Kadath's voice came again. "Clear! You can come down now."

Markus pushed himself back and down out of the tight space. Sahar's strong hand grabbed him and eased him to the ground inside the sewers. "What happened?" she growled.

"Explain later," he replied. "Let's get that hole plugged up first, yeah?"

The Maur didn't argue. She reached into the hole, grabbed the thick cement cut-out, and pulled it back into place. Supporting it with one hand, she used the other to apply a layer of foam sealant around the periphery.

"Clear!" she shouted. "Now, what in the nine hells just happened?"

"Our credentials went bad," Markus replied. "We got stuck in the server room. Rather than alert the proximity alarm, we had Lexa trigger every alarm in the building."

"*Every* alarm?" Eli asked.

"Yup, that's what we told her to do. Seems like it worked, too. No security ambush on the way out."

Eli cursed. "Skye's still in there!"

Markus started to reassure him with a, "She'll be fine," but Eli was already bolting down the sewer tunnels back to their access point.

Skye shivered in the frigid air outside the archives. *Could have at least let me grab my jacket. That thing was fragging expensive.*

Allen looked equally uncomfortable as he surveyed the mob outside the archives. "Kate!" he shouted. "Kate! Where are you?"

"Allen?" came the shouted reply. "Allen? I'm over here!"

"Oh gods, Kate!" The two embraced in a reunion that would have been touching had it not been quite so awkward.

Skye looked around. Automated Security Response had been triggered, and drones were starting to fill the snowy air around the building. *Gods damn it. What just happened?*

One of the drones hovered over the milling crowd. *"Attention. This area is now under quarantine by order of the Valhalla City Police. Do not attempt to leave the area."*

Riven's shade. This wasn't good. Skye's fake identity wasn't going to hold up against a scan from the VCP database. When they cross-checked her account against Allen's statement, that was going to create a whole host of uncomfortable questions.

She shoved her way through the milling throng, moving too quickly to receive more than dirty looks from the panicked bystanders. As she approached the periphery of the crowd, her heart sank. In addition to the circling drones, VCP hover cars had moved in to block off the roadways and the officers had quickly cordoned off the nearby walkways.

Don't panic. Just keep your head. There's always another way out.

Her eyes went back to the archives and scanned the surrounding buildings. One building over, she spotted a darkened alley. For the moment, the drones and the officers on the scene seemed to be ignoring it.

It's my best option yet. She slipped back into the crowd and worked toward the alley, taking a bit more care this time to avoid attracting attention. As the quarantine tightened, it would become more and more likely for one of the bots overhead to spot someone shoving their way toward the perimeter.

When she reached the alley, she shot a glance at the nearest bot. Satisfied its attention was elsewhere, she slipped off the street and into the darkened space beyond.

The alley was barren save for a cluster of waste processors and a locked cabinet for the public utility meters. About thirty meters back, the alley terminated in a concrete wall. However, the corner of the neighboring building terminated a couple of meters short of that, leaving another opening. Staying hopeful, Skye squeezed past the waste processors and slipped around the corner.

Right into a gray polymer barricade. *"Gods damn it."* She slammed her artificial fist into the blockade. The surface dented but remained firmly in place. Now, not only was she still in the quarantine, but she was also trapped.

A strong body pressed up behind her. The figure's hands went to her shoulders, holding her steady. "Skye?"

She turned to face the newcomer. "Eli?" she gasped before slapping his chest. "Lith's tits, you just scare the shit out of me! What in the nine hells happened in there?"

"I'll explain later," he replied, pressing his palm against a seam in the polymer barricade. A rush of air exploded from his hand, and the polymer groaned as it curled away from his touch. When he'd created an opening large enough to squeeze through, he turned his attention back to her. "For now, let's just get you out of here."

CHAPTER 16

[*LOADING CORRESPONDENCE...*]
[TO: KENNETH JAMESON]
[FROM: JESSICA TOTH]
[SUBJECT: RE: UNUSUAL REQUEST]

I don't care what his reasoning is. This is Cyrus Valadar we're talking about here. If the guy wants to pay us a visit, then he gets to stop by whenever he'd like. And no, I don't think we need the usual security protocols. Let me put this simply: if Cyrus tells you to jump, I want to see you hopping about until your legs can't take it anymore. Do I make myself clear?

[*CLOSING CORRESPONDENCE...*]

Ora arrived back on Sif early the next morning to find that her teams, despite some unforeseen setbacks, had managed to secure their objective. After a debrief over her mobile with Eli, Ora made her way to the ship's war room, where the crew's technical team was pulling apart the data.

At least, that was what they were supposed to be doing. The discussion she walked in on was distinctly more cavalier than she was expecting.

"So, wait," Thurn laughed. "Ya look at yer MoDAC, and she's like, 'Tha alerts 'er off. Now just listen t' me!'" The Orc doubled over laughing. "What were ya expectin'? Did ya just think ya put it on silent?"

"I... I don't know!" Dan blushed, obviously flustered. "I was panicking, okay? She wasn't supposed to be able to do that. I didn't realize Cognis had a full package already prepped. My system wasn't designed to handle that!"

"It wasn't Daniel's fault," Lexa insisted. "My defensive algorithms isolated the alert system while my personality matrix initialized. I didn't even realize what the program was used for at the time. I just thought, 'Oh, I should probably shut that off.'"

Thurn's laughter re-doubled, almost causing him to fall out of a chair designed for someone much smaller than him. Only when he managed to right himself did he notice that Ora had entered the room. "Ma lady," he said with a nod and a lingering chuckle.

"Am I interrupting?" Ora asked.

"Not 't all. Sorry, Dan 'ere was just fillin' me in on a couple of funny stories. Ah was just askin' him 'bout how 'e met his friend here." He wiped a leathery hand against his one good eye. "That's a good-un, Ah tell ya."

"I'll have to hear it sometime." Her smile was tighter than she intended it to be. "Any luck on the data you extracted from the archives?"

The Orchallen cyborg's head bobbed. "Oh yeah, that was nothin'. We had 'er decrypted well before our folks was back from their lil outin'. Ah ain't never run ma gear on processin' speeds like they got on 'ere! Ol' Ratemacher showed me a thing 'r two t' even boost ma speed." He smacked the kid on the back.

The young hacker ran a hand through the tangled mess of his dark hair. "It was nothing. Really."

Thurn cut his one good eye in Daniel's direction. "If that's true, then Ah'm lookin' forward t' seein' ya do somethin' that ya consider t' be somethin'." Looking to Ora, he added. "Kid's a natural, Ah tell ya."

"And humble," Ora noted. "An untapped resource, to be sure. At least, one I haven't been able to take advantage of. We may have to change that the next time the *Vandal*'s at port."

The boy flushed. Ora found it amazing that someone so seemingly impressionable would find himself among a crew like this one.

Reading his discomfort, Ora changed the subject. "Can we get the crew together and review the findings? I want to get this operation underway as soon as possible."

"A meeting is scheduled for tomorrow at oh-six-hundred," Lexa reported. "If that doesn't fit your schedule, the captain has granted you temporary authorization to adjust the crew's calendars. Would you like to make a change?"

"No. Oh-six-hundred is fine." Damn, they were on top of things. On one hand, Ora was proud to see her contractors demonstrate such capability. On the other, it made Ora feel somewhat useless in this endeavor. She hated feeling useless. "Is Markus available?"

The android blinked once, eyes going vacant for a moment. "Yes. He's in the armory on the starboard side of the hanger."

"I think I'll check in with him then. Thank you." With that, she made her exit.

The layout of the *Vandal* was blessedly simple. It wasn't quite as large as the *Basilisk*, but it was definitely easier to navigate. Ora found her way to her destination in a matter of minutes.

Markus was inside the armory, as promised. He had a weapon laid out on the workbench in front of him and was running an oiled cloth over the disassembled pieces. "One of your toys?" Ora guessed.

He smiled at her. "One of my favorites, though I haven't had the opportunity to use her in a bit. Not much need for a sniper rifle when you're running a bar, you know?"

"I'd imagine not," Ora stepped up to survey the weapon. "Do you have a name for her?"

"It's a Kinson Thunderbolt II."

"That's a model, not a name. Don't runners name their favorite pieces of equipment?"

Markus's lip twitched in a half-smile. "Where'd you get that idea?"

"As you might imagine, I've worked with a runner or two in my lifetime."

He let out a soft chuckle. "I guess you have. But no, I don't have a name for her. Never got into the habit of naming my weapons, I guess." He must have seen something in her expression because he set down his rag and the piece he was holding. "What's up? You doing okay?"

Ora shrugged. "Fine, I guess. I was hoping to find some way to make myself useful, but it appears this joint-operation between the teams is as well oiled as that rifle barrel."

"You're a good judge of talent. Everyone around here knows their place and is working toward the objective. That's part of what makes an efficient unit."

"I know. It's just unusual for me, that's all. I typically find some way to make myself useful. Boredom isn't something I take well to."

Markus smiled. "No, I don't imagine it is."

He rose to stand close to her, stopping just shy of touching her. Ora closed the distance, pressing a kiss against his lips. She marveled—not for the first time—at how nice it was to have someone she could go to like this. It had been a long time since she had, if one could even say that she'd ever had such a thing at all.

"Thank you," she whispered.

"For what?"

"For being you."

He smiled again. "At least that's something I can keep up without much effort." When she pulled away, he took that as a cue to change the subject. "How was Vallus?"

"He's fine. Not too keen on leaving the system while we're taking on Cyrus, but he knows how to follow an order."

"I bet." Markus crossed his arms. "Was he able to provide any insight on what we're walking into? Any tips related to Cyrus's plans for the artifact."

Ora shook her head. "Unfortunately not, but that doesn't change anything. Though I can't be sure what Cyrus's end game is, I'm certain of one thing: he's not one to sit around idly. He'll be moving forward on his work with the Heart."

Markus nodded. "Then let's hope we're able to move a bit faster than he can."

Cyrus didn't have to muster as much false solemnity as he had anticipated. Something about traveling to the morgue to see his sister's corpse had darkened his mood. It wasn't sorrow over her death. That had been the right choice. It wasn't even regret at what some might have considered a brash action.

What was it?

He supposed it didn't matter. In the end, it provided the perfect cover for what he'd actually wanted. No one questioned him—not Farris when Cyrus had requested to be driven over to the site, along with Lucretia, and not the staff at the facility.

Lucretia was a different story. Lucretia knew why they were here. That was why she hefted the metal briefcase at her side—something that, curiously, no one seemed to question either.

The attendant that they were working with, a balding, russet-skinned Terran in a white lab coat, palmed the access pad in front of them. The door issued a hydraulic hiss as it slid into its pocket, and Cyrus and his company were escorted into the room beyond.

The far wall was comprised completely of metallic compartments—square drawers adorned with electronic monitors and chrome handles. It was to one of these that the attendant reached, pulling on the handle to draw out the compartment a full three meters. On the exposed slab lay what they had come to see.

Tessa's body was covered in a white sheet, which the attendant rolled back to expose her waxy face. The coroner had done a nice job of making her look presentable, especially given what he'd had to work with. Tessa's long brown hair had been rinsed, though not washed, and arranged in a way to partially hide the missing piece of her skull where the bullet had exited after transitioning through her brain.

"City Police didn't find any identification on the body," the attendant explained. "Given the situation, we didn't run a genetic scan. We never do for bodies found on that side of the city. If we had only known—"

Cyrus cut him off. "No need for explanations. I completely understand. I'm just glad my people were able to locate her before she… before the body was disposed of." Feigning an equal mix of concern and curiosity, Cyrus looked away from the corpse. "Tell me. How did she die?"

The man in the lab coat swallowed hard. "It's not a pleasant story, I'm afraid."

"I understand. I need to hear it anyway."

A momentary hesitation. "Suicide. It… it was likely quick. She didn't feel a thing."

Don't I know it. Cyrus waited for what he felt was an appropriate amount of time to assimilate the information, had it been the first time he'd hear it. "Thank you, Mr…" He paused. "I apologize, I've forgotten your name."

"Jameson," the attendant replied with a shy smile. "Kenneth Jameson."

"Mr. Jameson," Cyrus repeated. "Now, if you don't mind, I'd like a moment alone with my sister."

Apprehension flashed in the man's eyes. He probably wasn't supposed to leave people in this room unattended but found himself without the gumption to argue. "Yes. Yes, of course." He backpedaled toward the door. "Take… take as long as you'd like." With that, he left Cyrus and his detail alone with the body.

Lucretia sniffed. "I wish I had that kind of effect on people. It would certainly help with all of the bureaucratic nonsense I have to put with day-to-day."

Cyrus ignored the jab, extending his hand to the doctor. "The serum, please."

Blackwell arched an eyebrow. "Her? She doesn't exactly meet our criteria."

"Call me sentimental. It's just one injection. We have plenty."

Lucretia shrugged. "Fine. It's your army." She hefted her metal briefcase onto a nearby surgical table. A faint emerald glow poured out at the seams as she cracked it open.

Rows of glass tubes stood out against the padded interior of the case. They'd brought one hundred doses of the glowing green serum with them on this outing. Running a quick count of the number of compartments in the wall, Cyrus decided it would be more than enough.

The doctor proffered one of the glowing syringes, which Cyrus carefully took hold of. "Watch the door," he said to Farris.

"Yes, sir." The man moved into position, seeming somewhat relieved he would not have to directly take part in the little experiment Cyrus had concocted.

How squeamish. Cyrus had thought better of the man.

He stepped up to his sister's corpse once more. A stray hair had found its way onto Tessa's ashen forehead. Cyrus gently smoothed it back behind her ear, taking a second to look upon the thing that had once been his sister.

He took no pleasure in this, sincerely wishing things could have turned out differently. Yet, the House always came first. It was the one thing that Cyrus's father had drilled into all of them from a young age. Unfortunately for her, Tessa had never been a much for learning.

Cyrus slid the tip of the syringe into his sister's neck, gently depressing the plunger with this thumb. When it was done, he returned the empty device to Lucretia.

The doctor's expression was somber. Cyrus attempted to soften it with a grin. "Let's take a look at our next candidate, shall we?"

Not waiting for a response, he moved to the compartment next to Tessa's. He pulled on the metal handle, drawing it out to reveal another body covered in a white sheet. Drawing the sheet back, Cyrus recognized one of the men he'd had Tessa kill back at the apartment.

A perfect candidate. "Let's be quick," Cyrus chided. "We have a lot of work to do."

Chapter 17

Cyrus, are you getting my messages? I need to speak to you immediately. The board has called an emergency meeting. They're in an uproar about the security incident, and they've queried the financials for the last three cycles. I'm afraid they're about to do something stupid. Where is your gods damned admin? Give me a call as soon as you get this.

Kenneth Jameson sighed and ran his hands over his face. *Long fragging day.* If he had been interested in hosting dignitaries, he'd have gotten a government job. He'd taken the tech job in the district morgue because he didn't want to be around people. The visit from Cyrus Valadar had completely thrown off his day.

At least it had been quiet besides that little incident. Apparently, the city's gangs had taken a day off from killing each other. That, or law enforcement was slow on finding the bodies. Either way was fine with him. That shit show they'd brought in yesterday morning had given him more than enough paperwork to do, and that was *before* he'd found out that one of the bodies was Tessa Valadar.

Gods, what a mess. The report from the crime scene said the chick had gone in, wasted three dudes, and pulled the trigger on herself. Strangely enough, there was no weapon reported, which meant there was probably an accomplice who had gotten away. That little mystery would never be solved, however. The cops didn't stress too much over mysterious homicides on this side of the city.

Maybe the Don would look into it though. Kenneth would have to watch the feeds to see if anything turned up in the news. He always loved a good bit of drama. Kinda had to in this line of work.

"Yo, Ken!"

Kenneth jumped so hard that he nearly toppled out of his desk chair. "Gods damn it, Reese! You're gonna give me a heart attack."

"Sorry," the blond security guard said, flashing a handsome smile. "My shift's up. Wanted to see if you were clocking out yet."

Kenneth glanced at his watch. *Damn.* Half-past the hour already. His relief should have been here by now. "I'm done whenever Jessie decides to show up. She should be here any minute."

"Want to grab a drink then? Me and a couple of the guys are meeting out at Harper's at twenty-three hundred."

With you? Any day of the week, big guy. Kenneth kept the comment to himself. He was pretty sure Reese wasn't interested in having *those* kinds of drinks with *him*—or in grabbing a nightcap after. Hells, a guy could still dream though.

"Yeah, sure. I'll shoot ya a text as soon as—"

Boom.

Both men started at the sound, eyes sweeping the room before meeting again in wide-eyed confusion. "You heard that, right?" Reese asked.

"Sure did, but what in the nine hells—?"

Boom.

Again with the noise. This time, Kenneth caught a direction.

Reese did too. "Was that the icebox?"

Kenneth hated it when security used that name for the room where they stored the bodies but didn't feel like arguing. "I... I think so. But who...?"

Boom.

Reese drew his sidearm. "Anyone here but you?"

"No!" Kenneth replied with an emphatic shake of his head. "Did you see anyone else?"

"Just Chance, but he's still gearing up in the locker room." Reese tapped his earpiece. "Chance, we may have something near the icebox. Pull your shorts on and get your ass over here, over." He gestured with his pistol. "I'm going to take a look."

Kenneth was torn. As much as he didn't want to see what was causing the disturbance, the larger part of him didn't want to be left alone. "I… I'll come with you. You'll… you'll need my badge to get through the lock." He didn't know if that was true, but it sounded a hell-of-a-lot better than admitting he was scared to be left behind.

Reese didn't argue, moving with quiet professionalism out of the office and down the hall.

Boom. Boom. Boom. The noise was louder now, the pounding coming faster.

Kenneth stuck close to Reese, wishing that he had a pistol like the one the security guard was holding. Not that he could have used it, but it would have made him feel better.

"What in the nine hells—?"

Kenneth gasped at the new voice. Reese's firearm was up and pointed at the newcomer in an instant. A Terran sporting bulging muscles and a shaved scalp held up his hands. "Lith's tits, Reese. It's just me!"

"Chance," Reese sighed, lowering his weapons. "Damn it, you're lucky I didn't fragging pop you right here."

"You're the one who called me!" *Boom. Boom.* Chance looked to the icebox's anteroom. "Someone in there?"

"Don't know," Reese replied. "But we're about to find out."

With a nod, Chance formed up with Reese. Together they entered the anteroom, Kenneth following a short distance behind. All the while the pounding continued—a steady, rhythmic drumbeat against the icebox door.

Both security guards glanced at each other uncertainly. Reese looked back over his shoulder. "Ken—you sure that no one else is here?"

"I… I don't think so." Was it possible that Jessie had gone straight to the icebox rather than checking in with him at the admin office? Could she have accidentally locked herself in? "Maybe if we call out to whoever is inside? It'll be muffled, but they should hear us."

Chance took the suggestion as permission. "Hey! Asshole! We hear you! Identify yourself!"

At the sound of his shouted words, the pounding ceased. Taking its place was an eerie, unsettling silence. If whoever was on the other side of that door said anything, Kenneth couldn't hear them.

Reese paused for a moment, his pistol still trained on the door. "Open it," he said.

It took a second for Kenneth to realize the security guard was speaking to him. "Are you sure?"

"Yes, I'm gods damned sure. Open it."

Kenneth stepped forward, making sure to stay out of the path of his companions' firearms. With a shaking hand, he lifted his badge to scan the sensor on the door. As soon as it beeped to acknowledge his access, he scrambled backward.

The door slid open with a hydraulic hiss. Kenneth's breath caught in his throat.

A woman stood in the doorway, flanked by two scarred, burly men. Kenneth thought he could make out more figures standing behind them. Kenneth noticed that they were naked only as an afterthought. His mind was focused on another more horrifying truth.

He knew that woman. He'd seen her face just earlier today. That was Tessa Valadar.

"What the f—" Chance's curse was cut short as one of the men rushed him. The guard's gun went off, but it must have missed its mark. The naked man didn't even flinch as he disarmed Chance, seized his throat, and forced him to the ground.

Reese fired his weapon. From Kenneth's vantage point, he was certain that the shots hadn't missed. The first bullet, and the second, and the third, landed center mass on the man that approached him.

Not that the shots slowed the man down. He didn't so much as flinch.

Figures poured out of the icebox, flowing around Tessa like water around a boulder. Both Reese and Chance were overwhelmed in an instant, the screams of both men ringing loudly in Kenneth's ears long after the gunfire had stopped.

Kenneth turned on his heels, intending to rush for the exit. Something grabbed his foot. He tripped, face and palms colliding painfully against the floor. Panic still drove him forward, clawing desperately against the cheap black tile, pulling toward the exit.

Bare feet stepped in front of him, blocking his way. He froze. A low keening built in the back of his throat. The obstructing figure stared balefully down at him, contempt as naked as its flesh.

Kenneth scrambled backward, mind so consumed with fear as to provide no thought to what he was doing. He just had to get away.

He stopped as he bumped against the legs of another figure. He flailed to his left only to encounter yet another standing in his path. He found the same obstruction to his right.

They'd surrounded him—a mob of naked corpses looking down on him with cold disdain. It was only then that Kenneth realized that the room had gone silent save for his pitiful moans and ragged breathing. There were no gunshots, no screams —only a thick, scornful silence.

The circle of figures parted to let one of them step forward. Kenneth's whole body shook as his eyes fell upon her. Tessa might have been beautiful in life. In death—or *undeath* it seemed—she was terrifying.

She bent down, crawling on top of him. He tried unsuccessfully to stifle a whimper as the cold, flaccid lumps of her breasts brushed against his chest. The fetid smell of her sickly flesh mingled nauseatingly with the harsh chemical stench of embalming fluid.

"Shh…" she hissed. Kenneth fought back a gag as the corpse pressed its icy lips against his. Her weight sank further onto his, knees pinning his thighs to the ground.

Then she pulled away, mouth twisting into a ghastly smirk. With both hands, she grabbed the sides of his skull. A quick jerking motion and she slammed his head into the tile floor.

Pain. Sparks of the light. The world spun. She slammed him again. Everything went dark.

Cyrus felt his maniacal laughter echo distantly as the lab tech blacked out. The man would live, but only because Cyrus wished it. They needed someone to take the fall for the murder of the two guards and the disappearance of all those bodies. Cyrus had already taken steps to make sure that the authorities would conclude Mr. Jameson was not just the most likely offender, but the only possible suspect.

With his army now liberated from the locked room, he led them through the offices and out onto the street where three black vehicles waited. He directed his specimens to the open vehicles, moving them quickly to avoid detection by anyone that might happen that way. The perimeter he'd ordered established should keep away prying eyes, but he wasn't going to take unnecessary risks.

Only when every last corpse was successfully stowed in the back of the hover vans did he relinquish his connection. The power dissipated, leaving a hollow feeling in his core and a tingling sensation on his skin.

He drew in a sharp breath. "Success."

Lucretia nodded. "Are you satisfied?" She made no attempt to hide the disdain in her words.

"I take it you're not?"

"There were certainly easier ways to procure specimens for this venture. I still can't believe I let you talk me into this."

Cyrus couldn't help but grin at the doctor's rebuke. "Perhaps you're right, but this was so much more fun!"

Lucretia rolled her eyes. "Your flair for the dramatic borders on childish."

"It was better than killing my current staff or test subjects. We agreed this was a better way."

"As if that were the only other option." She lapsed into silence. It was then that Cyrus noticed the way she looked at him. Her eyes were locked with his in a way that was beyond intense. She was studying him.

"What?" he asked, suddenly self-conscious. "What is it?"

"When was the last time you looked in the mirror?"

The casual nature of both her tone and the question took him aback. "I'm not sure. Why?"

Lucretia nodded toward the mirror over his office sink. "See for yourself."

Cyrus moved to comply. It took several seconds to make out what Lucretia might have been referring to. Once he saw it, there was no mistaking.

His eyes were no longer the steely blue that was the hallmark of his family. They were a startling, vibrant shade of green.

"I wasn't sure if it was my imagination at first," Lucretia continued, "but this time, there was no mistaking it. When you're channeling your power, your eyes glow. The intensity of that glow seems to be cumulative. This time they were positively radiant. Only now did I notice that, when you severed your connection, the color appeared altered."

Cyrus raised a tentative hand to his face, fingers carefully tracing the sockets around his discolored eyes. "Is it permanent?"

"Impossible to say. This is the first lingering side effect I've noticed in any of the test subjects."

"I'm not a test subject," Cyrus snapped, rounding on her.

Lucretia merely shrugged. "No, but you have logged more time using the artifact's power than anyone else. You are, at the least, an interesting case study."

Cyrus gritted his teeth and balled his fists. "You would do well to remember your place, Dr. Blackwell. I may pay you to study other people, but don't presume to take the same liberties with *my* person."

She lowered her defiant gaze in a half-hearted attempt at deference. "I meant no disrespect."

It was the closest thing he was going to get to an apology. Cyrus drew in a deep breath, steadying himself. "Go home. Pack your things. Tomorrow you will take up residence at my estate on the ridge. I need someone to see to our new *recruits*. While you're at it, perhaps you can do some more experimentation and find out exactly what might be causing these… *side effects*."

CHAPTER 18

I apologize, Councilor—the incident at the archives appears to have been the result of a glitch in our system. On our review, nothing appears out of the ordinary. No files were accessed beyond what is shown in the official registry, and no one is shown to have accessed any restricted areas. Aside from the signal that opened all restricted areas and triggered the alarm systems throughout the complex, no system irregularities have been identified. Either the trigger was the only actual problem in the system, or someone has worked, quite successfully, to make it appear that way. Regardless, we are closing the investigation until such time when new evidence presents itself.

Markus's grip seals around her throat. There's a vacant look in his eyes that belies the cruel set of his mouth. Any protest, any resistance she raises, is pure reflex. She barely struggles, because she knows the truth.

She's going to die here. Markus is going to kill her.

"Markus! Markus! No!"

It's her own voice she hears, though Markus's grip is too tight for her to breath, much less scream. How? How is she...?

Her eyes dart to the side, and her brain goes numb. She sees herself, but not as a reflection. Her other self, the one with the breath to scream, struggles against iron bars.

Too bad her efforts are in vain.

Skye's lungs swelled with air. Recycled oxygen never tasted so sweet.

It was strange to wake up from such a nightmare without so much as a whimper. The resignation she'd felt at her impending death had settled to her bones, siphoning the will to move a single muscle.

Instead, she stared into the darkness of the cabin. This was the second time she'd had this dream, which meant it was probably something more. While the nature of her Kaleemic powers was still foreign to her, she was starting to figure out that such patterns were not arbitrary. These visions were trying to tell her something.

So, Markus was going to try to kill her. The question was—why?

Eli stirred at her back, his hand coming up to caress her arm. "Everything okay?" he whispered.

"Yeah," she lied. "What time is it?"

He shifted, glancing at his MoDAC on a nearby night-stand. "A little after oh-four-hundred."

Good—late enough that she wouldn't have to pretend to fall back to sleep for a few more hours. She pushed herself to a sitting position, grabbed a hair-tie from her nightstand, and wrestled her tousled hair into a ponytail. "Couple hours before the team meeting," she noted. "I'm going to hit the gym."

[I THINK EVERYONE IS HERE,] Arc noted.

Conscious of maintaining a neutral external expression, Lexa declined to reply. At least the submind wasn't reading her thoughts. If he had been, he would know Lexa wasn't waiting for everyone to arrive. Rather, she was waiting until the predetermined meeting time to begin the discussion.

The second her system clock hit oh-six-hundred hours, Valhalla Standard Time, she began.

She loaded up the schematic she had pieced together from the disparate files in the archives. The wire-frame projection hovered over the table at the center of the packed war room. Everyone was there, and all eyes were on her.

"According to our findings from the Valhalla City Archives, this model represents a close approximation of the Valadar estate located in Freya's Ridge. My understanding is that you wish to gain access to the compound. With that goal in mind, I will provide an overview of what Daniel, Thurn, and I determined to be the most relevant structural features."

She glanced at the onlookers, not quite looking for permission as much as providing the opportunity for an alternate proposal. Finding no such proposal to be forthcoming, she continued.

She highlighted one of the buildings on the schematic in blue. "This is the manor house and the most likely location of the objective. With three floors and three sublevels, the structure is large enough to house an expansive research and testing facility."

Kadath nodded his head. "And if Cyrus's tastes are consistent, I'm willing to bet that he's keeping the Heart in the basement. Wouldn't want the cleaning staff to happen upon an evil super-weapon while dusting the furnishings."

Though Lexa got the impression that the half-breed was making a joke, his reasoning was sound. It was also, however, somewhat presumptuous. "While I concede your point, we have no way of knowing this for certain. We should plan for the possibility that the artifact may be hidden anywhere within the compound."

Lexa decided not to mention the three-percent probability that the artifact might also be stored in one of the other buildings on the property. She would address that concern momentarily. To avoid distraction—something she had learned that sapiens were somewhat prone to—she continued her discussion of the manor house.

The model went translucent and loaded up floor plans for each of the six levels. She reviewed likely functions for each room in the house and provided what data she had regarding the security system in the building.

The crew listened patiently for several minutes. It was Markus who eventually interrupted. "Lexa, this is great information, but I think we may be focusing on the wrong material here. Let's talk tactics. How do we get in?"

No, that was not what he needed to know, as he would have soon discovered had he not interrupted her. She started to tell him as much when Arc interjected. [I THINK IT MAY BE WISE TO COMPLY WITH THE REQUEST. THEY'LL SEE THE PROBLEM SOON ENOUGH.]

As much as it irked her, Lexa saw the wisdom in Arc's approach. Skipping over the remainder of her overview of the building, she highlighted the viable entry points in red.

"There's the front door," she pointed out, "but I suspect this is not the entrance your tactics will favor."

Thurn let out a low, rumbling chuckle. "Ya mean no one 'ere thought a-knockin'?"

"Or slipping through the windows," Skye mused. "That'd be some old-timey cat-burglar shit, right there. Might actually be fun."

Just like Lexa had feared, the team was getting off-point. Their attention spans were even shorter than she had estimated. "Before this speculation continues, I would like to point out that formulating a plan based on the currently available information would be ill-advised."

That caught their attention. Eli narrowed his darkened eyes. "What do you mean, Lexa?"

"The reason I was providing the detailed overview of the compound is that the information cannot possibly be accurate, as the plans do not correspond with more recent satellite imagery of the structure."

Lexa loaded the corresponding images and shaded the areas of both the images and the schematic in yellow to indicate the mismatched points. "I had planned to go over this in more detail, but in brief: the plans we have are out of date."

An uneasy silence settled over the group. Ora cleared her throat. "I might have led with that little tidbit."

"You think?" Argus scoffed, prompting Amelia to rest a steadying hand on his arm.

Aaliyah was less tactful. "So, you're sayin' all those shenanigans we pulled at the archives were for nothin'?"

"Not necessarily," said Eli. "We still know more than we started with, and—thanks to Lexa's careful analysis—we know which parts of the structure have likely been altered. Maybe there's something here that we can still use."

[SO NICE WHEN THE LEVEL HEADS PREVAIL,] Arc commented wryly.

Lexa nodded, both in recognition of Eli's statement and Arc's private sentiments. "There are four points of entry that could still potentially provide discreet access to the compound. One of these is in part of the schematic that has been altered from the original plans, but the other three may still be viable."

She removed all highlights on the hologram save for the trio of access points she'd mentioned. The first of these was an emergency escape tunnel that started in the residence wing of the manor and emptied just beyond the outer wall of the compound. The second was a large ventilation shaft in the nearby mountain rock, which eventually connected to a subterranean maintenance tunnel. The third entrance appeared to be an emergency exit for the compound's sublevels, but its purpose was not fully defined in any of the files from the archives.

Skye summarized, counting the options off on her fingers. "So, it's the escape hatch, the vent shaft, or the basement door." She surveyed the group. "Personally, I want to see what's behind door number three, but I could be convinced to change my mind."

Markus ran a hand through his beard. "We still don't know if any of these options are viable. We already know some of the data in the archives was out of date. Just because Lexa hasn't detected any conflicts using what we have, doesn't mean that they don't exist."

Siv issued the slightest dip of her masked and hooded face. "Recognizance then?" The ensuing silence from the rest of the group betrayed their lack of better ideas.

Kadath clapped his hands together, donning a playful smile that managed to disarm even Lexa. "Well done, team! We have our next step. Now, let's discuss the specifics, shall we?"

CHAPTER 19

[TO: DR. THADIUS KREEL]
[FROM: DR. LUCRETIA BLACKWELL]
[SUBJECT: RE: EXCIPIENT SUBSTITUTION]

Your concerns are noted, Dr. Kreel, but you seem to have misunderstood the nature of my message. This is not a request. This is a directive. You will see to it that Agent HT-102 is incorporated into the attached list of pharmaceuticals immediately. My team has already proven the stability of the compound in small batch testing. If it's approval you are worried about, I can assure you that my authority comes from the highest levels. If you continue to delay in the execution of this order, then you will see *exactly* what kind of authority I carry. Assuming you wish to continue your career with NeoGenix—or any Valadar Holdings subsidiary—you will see that my orders are carried out by end of business tomorrow. Do let me know if you have any further questions.

[*CLOSING CORRESPONDENCE...*]

Sydney said nothing as Cyrus barged into his own office. She was playing her usual game of, "How long until he notices me?" Quickly, however, she realized that the flustered executive might never bother to survey the couch she'd sprawled out on.

"My, my... aren't *we* in a tizzy today?"

Cyrus barely graced her with a glance. "Did you see Molly when you slipped in?"

Who? Oh. His assistant. "Nope. Not today. Why?"

"Because no one has seen her. Apparently, no one has seen her for *days*." He heaved a sigh and ran his hands back through his hair. "That means I haven't been getting my messages for days. Fragging *days*."

"So, check your mailbox. Everything should still be there, right?"

Cyrus glowered at her. "You have no idea what I do with all my time, do you?"

Lately, it seemed like he spent most of that time obsessing over his mind-controlling space-rock and chasing the silver-haired traitor. Sydney was wise enough to not point this out, though.

"I'm sure if it's *really* important, they'll call—" The rest of Sydney's sentence was caught up as a holoscreen popped into existence above Cyrus's desk. A red indicator light flashed in the top right corner with a tag reading, [PRIORITY ALERT].

Cyrus stepped behind the desk, smoothed the lapels on his open suit coat, and tapped the projection to receive the call. Julia Valadar, looking every bit as frazzled as Cyrus, appeared on the display. Sydney didn't need to hear the tone of her words to note her displeasure.

"Where have you *been*?" she spat.

"Good to see you too, dear sister. How go your affairs today?"

"Cut the bullshit, Cyrus. I've been trying to get a hold of you for two days."

"Yes," Cyrus drawled. "Several people have, actually. So, if you don't mind, can we skip the requisite admonitions? I have business to attend to."

"Not for long you won't," Julia snarled. "The NeoGenix Board is convening in ten minutes. Care to guess what's on the agenda?" She held up a staying hand. "Apologies, I forgot you didn't have time for guessing games. I'll just tell you. They're voting to censor you and remove you as the company president and CEO."

All hints of Cyrus's cavalier attitude vanished in an instant. "They *what?* They can't do that! Valadar Holdings owns..." He trailed off, face going slack and skin turning pale.

Julia's smug look held no hint of satisfaction as her brother pieced together whatever political puzzle was taking shape in his mind. "I see you've remembered our discussion about the state of our corporate stock and finances. If only you had heeded my warnings back when there was still something we could do about this problem."

A tense moment passed where neither sibling said a word. Slowly, Cyrus seemed to regain composure. His jaw tightened, as did his fists. He drew back his shoulders, once more assuming the demeanor of his noble birth.

"I'll deal with it," he spat.

"*Deal* with it? Cyrus, I'd like some more specifics. From where I'm sitting, it looks as though you've overplayed your hand and the rest of the table just called your bluff."

"No," he responded, calm and commanding, "I haven't. And no, you don't want the specifics. Were you planning on calling into the meeting?"

For the first time, Julia seemed hesitant. "No, but I didn't have much choice in the matter. I was told that my conflicts of interest preclude me from voting on the matter at hand."

"Good. It's better if you don't attend. Take my word on this one: everything will be fine."

Julia's reservation gave way to something that almost resembled fear. "What are you planning to do Cyrus?"

"As I said: it's better that you don't know. I'll call you after with the results of the meeting. Good day, sister." Without waiting for her to return the benediction, Cyrus tapped the holodisplay and ended the call.

Sydney unfurled herself from the couch and strode closer to Cyrus's desk. "As much as I like the new display of confidence, I'm not seeing your next play here. The board will be meeting any minute. If I had a little more of a heads up, I could have got them in their homes, but it's going to look a little suspicious in the meeting minutes when everyone suddenly drops dead in the middle of the discussion to terminate your position."

"No one is going to drop dead." Cyrus hesitated, thinking better of the comment. "Not all of them, anyway. I have a plan."

"Does this plan involve me slitting anyone's throat? My knives are sharp and ready, as always."

Cyrus's lip twitched in the hint of a smile. "Likely not, but I'll have you tag along anyway. This is something you'll want to watch."

The heated discussion in the NeoGenix boardroom went suddenly silent as Cyrus walked through the door. "I don't mean to interrupt," he said. "By all means, do continue."

Board Chair Ricard Hawthorne—a gray-haired, stern-faced man with a silver beard—spoke. "You were not invited to this session, Cyrus. I must ask that you leave immediately."

"Oh?" Cyrus feigned ignorance, walking over to stand behind his usual place at the table. Sydney hovered quietly just over his shoulder. "When I heard the board had convened and couldn't find my invitation, I thought it was an oversight."

"It wasn't," the chair insisted. "Now, if you would kindly excuse yourself."

Cyrus scoffed. "Ricard… I think you may have forgotten to whom you are speaking. You will remember that Valadar Holdings is still the principal investor in NeoGenix's operations. As head of that investment company, I am within my rights to attend any official proceeding of the company's governance council." He took a seat at the table. "Now, what was the item up for discussion? I haven't had a chance to review the agenda."

No one said anything for several seconds. It was Jolanda Yates, the Chief Legal Officer, that finally answered. "Removal and replacement of the Neogenix Chief Executive."

"Hmmm…" Cyrus stroked his jaw and furrowed his brow. "A heady topic, to be sure, and not one to be taken lightly. What would prompt such a brash move?"

Ricard's mouth practically frothed as he spat the allegations. "Misappropriation of corporate assets and compromising public trust in the company brand."

With a trailing whistle, Cyrus leaned back, putting both hands behind his head and kicking one foot on the table. "Those are some serious allegations—especially that 'public trust' one. You'd think with my stake in the media I could get some better coverage, right?" He paused to see if his remark had garnered some chuckles. When it didn't, he shrugged and continued. "But I must ask: what is this 'misappropriation of funds' that you speak of?"

One of the other board members, a Terran woman with a shaved head and just a hint of wrinkles around her eyes, grew emboldened enough to speak. "The billions of krets that you have sunk into unauthorized research and development projects. Krets that—I might add—were obtained through the dilution of Valadar Holding's stake in the company."

"A transaction which, lacking board approval, might constitute a violation of our corporate bylaws," Jolanda added, having suddenly located her backbone. "Perhaps we should add *that* to the rationale for dismissal."

"Oh come now," Cyrus interjected, rising to his feet. "You know that there is little I value above my family and my companies' legacies. When have I *ever* made a move that was not intended to further our shared goals in the long run? When have I *ever* made an investment that did not payout in the end? When have I *ever* let you down?"

A portly man to Cyrus's right started to say something, but a stern look from Ricard silenced him. "This is not a trial, Cyrus. We have not requested that you present us with a case. Now, if you choose to remain here, that is your prerogative. However, if you continue to be out of order, then I will have to call security and request that they remove you."

"Security?" Cyrus arched an eyebrow. "Which security are you referring to? My personal detail? Or perhaps the Grey Wings whom I have under contract?"

"The Valhalla Police, then," Ricard insisted. "But I would ask that you not force us to make such a spectacle. As much as I disagree with your leadership, that is not something I would wish upon you or this company. The memory of your father alone supports my patience thus far, but I warn you, Cyrus: push me *no* further."

The invocation of Cyrus's father, for the first time, caught the Don off-guard. The mention sobered him for a dark moment, cracking the flippant facade that he had so playfully worn. He breathed deeply through his nostrils, steadying himself.

No more games.

He glanced at the dozen corporate executives around the table. "Don't you want to see what all those research funds have purchased us? The fruits of the garden I have some carefully tended?"

Ricard opened his mouth to object, but a slender man at the end of the table raised a finger to stall him. "You are saying that the research has yielded its dividends? That this secret project you've been working on has yielded a prototype?"

Cyrus grinned "A prototype? Yes, you could say that. In fact, I think the product is nearly ready for market."

The slender board member looked from Cyrus to the board chair. "It can't hurt, Ricard. Let's have a look at what Cyrus has been working on. Perhaps it will explain some of this… *irrational* behavior."

Ricard's hesitancy was obvious. The gears in his mind whirred behind his cold, blue eyes. In the end, that ancient piece of machinery between his ears failed to develop a reasonable excuse to dismiss the request.

"Any objections from the other members of the board?" The old man surveyed the table, looking to see if someone might have manufactured an excuse in his stead. Seeing no such justification, he breathed a heavy sigh. "Fine. Cyrus, show us what it is that you've been working on."

"Certainly." Cyrus touched his earpiece. "Lucretia, please send Farris and his team up with the samples."

The complete lack of reaction from the board betrayed that they had no idea who "Farris" was. They likely expected a team of laboratory technicians, or perhaps an intern working in an administrative capacity. Their eyes went wide when the muscled security guard and his team of black-clad reinforcements entered— helmeted and armed to the teeth.

Cyrus made a soothing gesture. "No need to be alarmed. The extra security is necessary. We don't want anything to happen to such a valuable investment, now do we? As you've all pointed out, the cost of development has been somewhat exorbitant." He turned to the entourage. "Miss Cross, would you mind opening the case and removing one of the samples?"

Sydney nodded, the barest hint of a smile lighting upon her lips. Perhaps she had figured out what was coming. Perhaps she was just eager to see the drama unfold.

The Citza assassin lifted the tabs on the metal case held in Farris's solid grip. When the case opened, the glass syringes within did not shimmer with the otherworldly emerald glow that might have betrayed its contents. Lucretia and her team had done solid work in making sure this prototype looked like any other medical product.

Sydney carefully selected one of the syringes and brought it over to Cyrus. He took possession of the glass tube and uncapped the needle at its end. "Ladies and gentlemen of the board, I give you the fruits of our investment."

He held the syringe aloft like a holy talisman. The assembled executives glanced nervously amongst themselves. "What is it?" one asked.

Cyrus blinked, contorting his face into a puzzled expression. "Why, the future of course!" He stalked toward Ricard, keeping his eyes on the sample in his hand. "The syringe I hold in my hand is a reformulation of our most popular gene modifier. Several of you should know it well, as I'm sure you've received a few such injections as part of our corporate health plan. This serum slows the rate of decay in mitochondrial and nuclear DNA. In layman's terms, it reduces the natural process of aging to a fumbling crawl."

Ricard nodded. "We are familiar with this product and the revenues it generates for the company. However, this is part of our *existing* portfolio. I was under the impression that you had invested in something a bit more… nuanced?"

Cyrus smiled, drawing closer to the chair. "Yes, of course. You see, the genetic modifier is only the vehicle—a Trojan horse delivering the true miracle that has been yielded by our research." He paused dramatically, now standing just over Ricard's shoulder.

The chair refused to break Cyrus's gaze. He likely suspected the proximity was designed to intimidate and was making a great show of refusing to be cowed. "Care to elaborate on this 'miracle' of yours? Or would that be asking you to cut this pageantry too short?"

With a chuckle, Cyrus flipped his grip on the syringe. "I think it would likely be more effective if you experienced it first hand."

He jammed the needle into the side of Ricard's neck. The man screamed, pushing to his feet and flailing at Cyrus who had already stepped away.

"What in the nine hells is *wrong* with you!" Ricard roared. He thrust a finger to the security detail. "You there! I demand that you remove Mr. Valadar from the boardroom this instant! Fail to comply, and I *will* call the police!"

"Belay that request, Mr. Farris," Cyrus drawled. "In fact, I think it best if your men see to it that the rest of the board remain in their seats, yes? We don't want anyone to accidentally get hurt during our demonstration."

At a gesture from Farris, the black-suited security guards fanned out, each taking up a position behind one of the eleven sitting executives. Each of the suits turned wide-eyed looks of panic on their companions.

Ricard sputtered in outrage. "Fine, Cyrus. You leave me no choice." He reached into his pocket and retrieved a MoDAC. With a shaking hand, he swiped at the card to unlock it.

But Cyrus had already delved into that well of energy that lay secreted in his breast. "Hold that thought, Mr. Chairman."

Ricard froze, finger still on the card. His eyes flicked up to Cyrus, bewilderment creasing his brow.

With a nod, Cyrus continued. "Now put that away. It's time we finish our little demonstration." Though he didn't need to speak the command, he did so for the benefit of his audience.

Ricard complied. Once his mobile was stowed, however, he resumed his defiant posturing. "Have you come to your senses? Will you leave of your own accord?"

"*After* the demonstration. Yes, I will leave. But first, we need something sharp. Miss Cross, may we borrow your knife?" The assassin smirked as she drew out a blade about half the length of Cyrus's forearm. Cyrus accepted it with a nod of thanks. "Perfect. Tell, me, Ricard, have you ever juggled a blade before?"

"Why would I—?"

"No? Why don't you give it a try?"

Cyrus flipped the knife in Ricard's direction. To the chair's amazement, he caught it expertly. Cyrus whistled. "Looks like we have a natural, folks!" He mimed an upward throwing gesture with his right hand. "Come on, Ricard. Give it a few tosses."

At Cyrus's mental nudging, Ricard did as ordered. He tossed the knife a meter into the air, catching the spinning blade by the handle on the way down. He repeated the gesture again. Then again. Again.

Then Cyrus slowed the man's response time just enough that he missed the handle. The blade slashed down his palm. Ricard shouted in pain as the weapon clattered to the floor.

"Ooo!" Cyrus cringed theatrically. "That looked like it hurt! Maybe knife juggling isn't your thing after all. Oh well, it was worth a try. Be a good fellow and pick that up, would you?"

Even as Ricard bent to do as Cyrus directed, the chair's mouth contorted in a snarl. "I don't know what you're doing or how you're doing it, Cyrus, but I demand you stop! Right now!"

"Oh, Ricard—you seem to be missing the point of this exercise. *I* am the one who's giving the orders now." Cyrus raised his fingers to signal his security detail. As one, they each produced their own syringes and injected the board members in front of them.

Seeing the task complete, Cyrus turned back to Ricard. "Are we getting the picture yet, my friend?"

"You insolent bastard, I'll—"

"No? A further demonstration then. Hold out your hand. Like this, now—palm up." Ricard mirrored Cyrus's movement. "Good work. Now, put the point of that nice, sharp knife right over the middle of your palm. Careful, though. It really is quite a dangerous thing. Most of Sydney's toys are."

There was the slightest quiver in the man's hand as he complied. Whether from fear or from his attempts to resist the commands, Cyrus couldn't be sure. It didn't matter, though. Ricard had finally gone mercifully silent.

Cyrus stalked around his hapless quarry, meeting the increasingly panicked eyes of the other board members as he spoke. "As I was saying, *this* is the future. The compound infused in this batch of our best-selling gene therapy has given me personal access to our dear Ricard's mind. All of your minds too, now that you've been injected. With the compound in his system, I can make him do whatever I want."

To emphasize the point, Cyrus willed that Ricard lower the knife into his outstretched hand. He also forced the man's mouth closed to muffle the screams of pain and terror that poured from his throat.

"But this is just the beginning. When we're finished here today, I will be leaving with the full authorization of the board to add agent HT-one-oh-two to every medical product produced by NeoGenix. Gene mods, insulins, antibodies, vaccines… all of it will contain this special little compound that grants me this newfound power."

By now the knife was protruding thoroughly from the other side of Ricard's hand. Cyrus willed for him to extract it, though the torture was far from done. Slowly, methodically, Ricard began to go to work on his forearm, slashing deep, seeping lines into the tissue. When one line was finished, he would add another, working slowly up to his wrist.

"I can hear what you're thinking right now. The fear. The outrage. The objections. Don't worry. I don't expect you to understand just yet. In time, though, you'll grow more comfortable with your new situation. After all, you will have seen—first-hand—*exactly* what it is I can make you do."

A crimson pool was beginning to form at Ricard's feet. His hands shook so badly that the knife almost vibrated free from his grasp. Cyrus forced him to tighten the grip and raise the blade's edge to his throat.

"I would ask that you remember that Ricard, here, had it lucky. He didn't know what the price of his insubordination would be. I would like to think that, had he been sitting in your shoes, he might have been a bit more careful with his tongue. I mean, if I could make him do this to himself, imagine what I could make him do to his wife? To his children?"

With a sweeping motion of his hand, Cyrus bade Ricard conduct the finishing blow. With a moaning sob of pain, the helpless chairman drew the knife across his neck. The man's throat opened, draining what lifeblood was left in his body, and Cyrus relinquished his control. Ricard's corpse crumpled to the ground.

Cyrus leaned forward and planted both hands on the table, staring triumphantly into the eyes of his newest puppets. "Any questions?"

CHAPTER 20

I hear congratulations are in order, *Chairman* Felch. In your new capacity as interim-Council Chair, I have some things I want to discuss with you. One of these is the expansion of the ASR perimeter. I believe that Valhalla's assets in Freya's Ridge would benefit greatly from the expanded protection. When can I come by your office to discuss this? Perhaps we can make plans for your mayoral campaign while I am there.

"All I'm sayin' is if ya wanted to go for a walk in the snowstorm, ya could've pushed harder for a third team." What Aaliyah didn't mention was that the move would have been purely for the purpose of soothing Eli's bruised ego.

She didn't need to, though. Eli knew the score. "We don't have a third shuttle. Besides, the escape tunnel and sublevel access points are just half a click apart. Sending a third team would just increase the odds that our people get spotted."

Having finished strapping on her boots, Aaliyah grabbed her helmet and stood to face her captain. "Good, you're bein' reasonable. Now, would ya quit your mopin'? We've got the right people on this one."

The comment was out of her mouth before Aaliyah thought better of it, and the flippant words visibly stung Eli. It didn't change the truth of them though.

The first team, the one Aaliyah was flying in, would scout the mountain ridge and look for the vent shaft. Skye and Sahar had been tapped for this job. Meanwhile, Markus and Kadath on the second team would check out the escape tunnel and sublevel access point closer to the compound.

The only improvement in the roster might have been to sub out one of the Terrans for Siv. With the temperatures as low as they were, though, the crews had decided that they shouldn't push the limits of Hissak physiology. The winter storm wouldn't kill her, but it would slow her down. Better to have the folks with warmer blood trudging out in the snow. Like Eli, Siv would get her chance when it finally came time to pull this thing off.

Eli managed a weak smile as he clapped Aaliyah on the shoulder. "Take care of them out there, all right?"

"Like ya need to ask." She punched him playfully in the chest. "See ya on the flip side." With the parting comment, both exited the ready room—Eli heading back to the war room, and Aaliyah moving on into the hanger.

The four members of the scouting teams wouldn't be down here for another hour. Aaliyah had arrived early to run pre-flight checks on the shuttle. The process wouldn't take the full hour, but she knew her propensity to get distracted down in the hanger.

Which was what happened as soon as she laid eyes on the shuttle that had been brought over from the *Basilisk*. "What in the nine hells is *that?*"

She hadn't been speaking to anyone. She'd kind of hoped no one was around to hear her unfiltered opinion on the craft. So she was at least slightly embarrassed when the crew's Hissak engineer poked his head out from inside the cockpit.

"It is my shuttle," he hissed.

Aaliyah cleared her throat, scratching the back of her head nervously. Damn, she wished she'd slid her helmet on. That reflective faceplate would go a long way to hiding her embarrassment.

"I… I can see that. What I meant was…" How to phrase this delicately? "I meant that I ain't never seen a shuttle quite like this one. Where did ya get her?"

Either she was selling the curiosity bit better than she thought, or Jeagan decided to show her some mercy. He smiled as he stepped out of the cockpit and down the ramp that had been propped against the side of the craft. "That is quite the story." He stroked an affectionate hand over the ship's tarnished hull. "She's been with me even longer than Siv. She may not be, as you Terrans say, 'the prettiest' thing, but she gets the job done."

His eyes lingered on the ship for a moment, gaining that far-off look of someone remembering times long past. At length, he turned his gaze back to Aaliyah. "Plus, she is an excellent conversation piece. Your Markus Frost found my constant maintenance to be somewhat amusing."

Aaliyah snorted a short laugh. "Yeah, well, he hasn't been *our* Markus for a while now."

"So I've heard. Siv mentioned an… *altercation* between him and your new captain."

With a roll of her eyes, Aaliyah sighed. "Why do you think I prefer women?"

The Hissak was quick to pick up on the desire for a subject change. He nodded toward the other shuttle in the hanger. "That one is yours?"

"Yeah, that's right."

"Mind if I take a look?"

"Um… sure." Aaliyah wasn't nearly as possessive about her shuttle as Jeagan seemed to be, but she was proud enough of the vehicle to give him a quick peek inside.

She entered the access code to lower the ramp. While the inside was much nicer than the one Jeagan had been working on, Aaliyah was suddenly aware of how much less room it had. Whereas his craft was spacious and multi-functional, this one had only one large holding space for equipment. That had been where they would carry the crew's mech suit back before Sahar had busted the damned thing beyond repair.

"Come on." She waved a welcoming hand for emphasis. "I'll show you the controls." She led him past the twin rows of seating and up into the cockpit. When she took her seat, Jeagan slid into the co-pilot's chair.

"Very nice." He ran his hands admiringly over the dash. "Fusion of manual control and holographic interface. Such things are not common."

"Yeah. Cooked it up myself. Well, the kid helped—at least with the latest version."

"This… Ratemacher?"

"Um… yeah. We just call him Dan."

Jeagan nodded. "A talented programmer to be sure. Are you as good with computers?"

"Me? Hardly. I just know enough to keep the engines running."

"I am much the same." His self-deprecating chuckle seemed genuine. "Have you flown this one for long?"

Aaliyah shrugged. "More than a couple of cycles, I figure. We got her in our… what… maybe second cycle aboard the *Vandal?* We were runnin' on a tight budget for a while there. Shit, I think Markus dug most of our shit out of the Gehenna junkyard."

A deep voice sounded from the rear of the shuttle. "Just the good stuff." Markus ducked his head into the cockpit. "Should have figured you couldn't resist showing off your gear to the guests."

"Hey, he asked." Aaliyah's mouth quirked up in a half-smile. "Aren't ya here a bit early?"

"Maybe a little," Markus conceded. "Thought I'd come give Jeagan a hand getting the shuttle flight-worthy. I'm sure you've seen what he's got to work with."

"Your words wound me." The light behind the Hissak's reptilian eyes belied the sentiment. "But, since you were so kind as to show up early, I might as well put you to work." Jeagan rose, and Markus moved out to allow him to exit.

Aaliyah followed, unable to resist the chance to pester Markus with a few jabs. "I don't remember ya ever bein' early to an op when ya ran with us."

Markus's smile was gentle, and perhaps a little sad. "This old dog is learning some new tricks in retirement."

"That what ya call this? Retirement?"

"Yeah. Guess I'm not very good at retirement."

"Just admit it: ya missed us."

Now his look was definitely sad. He glanced at Jeagan, who was kind enough to pretend like he wasn't listening to the exchange, then back to Aaliyah. "All right, Red. Yeah, I missed you guys. I was in a rough place, and I just had to get my shit figured out. I'm sorry again for not checking in."

A younger version of Aaliyah would have pressed hard on that wound, just to make sure the pain was real. Now, though, she hesitated. Maybe Markus wasn't the only old dog hanging out in that hanger just now.

"Yeah, well, at least ya got time to fix it. When we get back to the station, ya should drop in and see Nikki. I know she misses ya. Monica too."

"Heh… little Mona."

"Oh, she doesn't like that name anymore. It's definitely Monica now. She'll let ya know if ya forget."

Markus laughed. "Then I best try not to." When his laughter died, his smile lingered. "All right, Red. I'll swing by next time I'm station side. Maybe then we can do some proper catching up."

"Only if ya bring the whiskey."

"I think I can manage that." They both looked up as the door to the ready room hissed open. Sahar and Skye stood in the doorway, already suited up. Markus bobbed his head in their direction. "Looks like your team is ready to go. I won't keep you. Fly safe out there, yeah?"

Aaliyah arched an eyebrow. "You're worryin' about *my* safety? Shit, ya better not look too closely at that bird you're ridin' in."

Skye and Sahar arrived at their shuttle just as Markus and Jeagan slipped onto theirs. Turning her gaze on Aaliyah, Skye asked, "Everything okay?"

"Oh yeah," the engineer replied with a wave. "Just talkin' shop with that Hissak mechanic of theirs. Guy's all right if ya ask me."

The fact that Aaliyah failed to mention Markus in the exchange was not lost on Skye. She decided not to push. "Everything set to go?"

"Yup. Just finishin' up the pre-flight checks right now. Give me twenty, and we're out of here."

They pulled out of the hanger in ten.

Once cleared of the spaceport, the three women synced the comms on their helmets. Eli's voice sounded first. "This is *Vandal* to squad one. Comm check."

"This is Ruby. Comms green." Aaliyah reported.

"This is Sapphire. Comms green." Skye followed.

"This is Beast. Comms green." Sahar finished.

"All comms green," Eli finished. "Channel is secure, but we'll keep the chatter down. Swift running, team."

Skye used the helmet's retinal interface to eye-click off the general channel and over to the team chat. "How's the weather, Red?"

"Shitty," Aaliyah replied. "But ya won't hear me complain too hard. I ain't the one goin' for a hike in this snowstorm."

Sahar rumbled a soft laugh. "I'll take this over the summer heat any day." Easy for her to say. All that fur must keep her nice and toasty inside her gear. Skye, on the other hand, would rather sweat than shiver.

"Limited visibility will be good for us too," Aaliyah continued. "Speakin' of—activating stealth emitter now. And... we're ghosted. Ain't no one gonna see us until they smash into our broadside."

"Is that a possibility?" Skye asked.

"Nah. Lexa said flights over the city have been grounded. Apparently, this storm's gonna get worse before it gets better."

"So we just have to worry about assholes like us who think it's a good idea to fly stealth in a blizzard," Sahar summarized.

"Pretty much."

"Well gee," Skye sighed. "You guys are giving me all the warm fuzzies today."

Aaliyah laughed. "Nothin' warm on this flight, Blondie. Now, hold on. This is gonna get bumpy."

She wasn't lying on either account. The thirty-minute trip was rife with turbulence. When the craft set down in a rocky valley, the passengers were greeted by blowing snowdrifts that wafted up into the shuttle as the ramp descended.

The sooner we get out there, the sooner we're back. The thought propelled Skye forward as she trotted down the ramp and into the snowy beyond. They soon found themselves sinking in snow as high as Skye's knees in some places. At least the seals on the boots held.

A short distance from the shuttle, Sahar glanced back at the craft. "You sure that platform is stable?" Skye immediately saw what the Maur meant. The landing struts had sunk several centimeters into the snow around what Skye had originally assumed was a rocky platform. Now though, she wasn't so certain.

"Not sure," Aaliyah replied, overhearing the conversation over the comms. "How about y'all quit worryin' about the craft and get to the target. Stallin' ain't gonna make this platform any sturdier."

"Copy that," Sahar replied. To Skye, she asked. "Want me to take point?"

"That'd be nice," Skye conceded. The Maur was sinking even deeper into the snow, so it wasn't like Skye's trailblazing was making it that much easier for her companion.

With their new marching order, they pressed forward. Skye relied heavily on the digital readout to verify that they were heading in the right direction. It wasn't that the terrain was easy to get lost in. It was more that she couldn't see a damned thing.

The snowstorm covered them with an ever-shifting screen of hazy white. Even with the navigational assist, Skye was glad she wasn't in the lead. Time and again she found herself focusing solely on Sahar's dark form in front of her, careful not to lose her friend in the frosty haze.

Twelve minutes out, the Maur came to a halt. Skye formed up next to her. "What is it?"

"The ledge," Sahar replied. "It's missing."

"What ledge?"

"The fragging ledge we're supposed to cross to keep going up this mountain! *That* ledge."

Skye looked around the Maur and saw the problem. Either the rock that provided the path forward had fallen away, or it had been buried under the wall of snow and ice that now formed a practically sheer cliff-face in front of them.

"How much farther to the vent?" Skye asked.

"Point-two clicks."

"So, just on the other side of that cliff."

"Yup."

Gods damn it. Why couldn't anything be simple?

On further examination, it looked like there was still a small lip extending beyond the snowy edge. "I can climb on that," Skye stated, attempting to reassure herself as much as Sahar.

"Yeah?" the Maur replied, skeptically. "I don't think I can."

"I'll get to the other side and attach an anchor. I'll just pull you over."

"If you haven't noticed, I don't have your slender frame. I'm not sure you could anchor my weight if I fell."

Skye tapped on her left arm. "Cybernetics, remember? I may not have Maur strength, but I'm a damn spot better than your average Terran."

"It's a weight issue, Skye. I'm pushing a hundred and forty kilos. What do you clock in at? Sixty?"

Sixty-three, but Skye wasn't going to argue the point. "We've got to get to the objective. You got a better idea to get around this?"

Sahar shook her head. "Fine. Let's do this. I'll be your tether on the way across."

Skye reached to her utility belt and drew out the cable. "Here you go," she said, hooking a carabiner onto the end of the cord.

Her Maur companion clipped the lifeline to her waist. "Be careful," Sahar admonished. "I don't want to have to explain to the captain how you ended up broken at the bottom of this chasm."

With a laugh, Skye replied, "You worry too much." Convincing herself that this was the truth, she set out on the path in front of her.

What she hadn't expected was the way that putting all of her weight on the balls of her feet would press her so firmly against the glacial mountainside. Her helmet dragged across the snowy exterior of the ledge as she inched, bit by bit, over the narrow ledge.

Each step made her heart pound. *It's all right*, she told herself. *The cable has you. If you fall, you'll swing right back to Sahar.* She kept pressing on—*left foot, right foot, left foot, right foot.*

Soon she had worked her way around the mountain bend and over to a place where the path widened out again. She exhaled a sigh of relief as she set foot on wider ground. "See?" she shouted in jubilation. "No problem!"

"And I repeat," Sahar replied, "it doesn't shock me that *your* skinny ass made it across. It's me I'm worried about."

"Come on! It ain't a thing! Show me what all that Maur discipline and strength can do."

"There's no amount of strength and discipline that can overcome the power of gravity." Sahar sighed. "Fine. I'm coming. Just hold onto something, yeah?"

Keeping in mind the weight difference that Sahar had pointed out, Skye took this bit of instruction seriously. She latched firmly onto the rocky mountainside. "All right! I'm set!"

With a grunt of acknowledgment, Sahar started across the narrow precipice. The icy ridge cracked precariously with each booted footfall. Carefully, the Maur shuffled along the frozen edge.

One step. Another. Another.

Then a sharp crack sounded against the roar of the wind. Skye's breath caught in her chest.

When Sahar's foot came down, the icy ledge crumbled under her weight. The Maur's hand shot forward, finding purchase on a snowy protrusion that instantly broke away. With a feline roar of alarm, she tumbled from the edge.

"I've got you!" Skye shouted, bracing hard with her cybernetics. The words were hardly past her lips when the cable at her waist pulled tight. Her left shoulder ached as machinery tugged against flesh, and her legs dug deep trenches as she slid on the snow and ice.

She couldn't be exactly sure of what happened next. Maybe it was a mechanical failure—an oversight on the weight ratings for either the cable or its mechanisms. Maybe it was a sharp piece of debris or a jagged protrusion on the cliff face.

All these thoughts flashed through Skye's mind, a jumbled mess of panic and alarm, as the cable snapped.

CHAPTER 21

I am curious as to what, exactly, is covered under the Valadar contract for Baldur Co.'s maintenance of our family's Northern Estate. The reports I'm hearing are troubling—grounds in disrepair, deficiencies in the heating system in the west wing, and a near collapse of remote surveillance around the southern edge of the property. Needless to say, I'm hardly pleased and my brother is nigh-apoplectic. Fix this. *Now.*

Sahar pushed all panic aside. Panic wasn't going to help her survive.

That gods-damned cable hadn't held her weight, but it did swing her over to just below Skye's position. As her body slammed against the wall of stoned and ice, she searched for a handhold.

Her hands slid against the frozen terrain, finding no purchase. Still, Sahar did not panic. She dug in as hard as she could against the frosty surface, hoping to slow her descent.

Crack! Her knee collided painfully against something more solid than ice and snow. Even as the roar of agony tore from her throat, she reached for the hard protrusion. She wrapped one hand, then the other, around the jutting stone.

Her descent halted abruptly. The rock held.

"Sahar!" Skye was shouting over the comms, neglecting the use of call signs in her worry.

"Beast here," Sahar grunted. "I'm okay. Just… just a little bruised. That's all." She tested her leg, and the lance of fire in her knee put the lie to her words.

"Hang on!" Skye continued. "Let me fix the cable, and I'll lower it down to you."

No way. Sahar wasn't taking her chances with that approach again. "I've got this," she insisted, pulling up with her arms.

"Don't be stubborn! If nothing else, you need a safety line. One second." A pause, presumably as Skye examined the cable. "It looks like the clip came off your belt. If you wrap it around your torso, I can help pull you up."

Sahar obstinately tried pushing up with her bad leg. The resulting pain, even worse than the last time, made her reconsider Skye's plan. "All right," she grunted. "Worth a try."

With a distant whirring announcing its arrival, the clipped end of the cable descended to within Sahar's reach. Finding a foothold for her good leg, she reached for the clip with one hand while gripping the rock wall with the other. As carefully as she could, she wrapped the cable under her arms and above her breasts to form a loop around her torso.

When the cable clicked in place, Sahar said, "I'm secure. Climbing now." She exhaled hard as she began her ascent. Her fall had managed to knock most of the loose snow free from the cliff, exposing passable handholds above her. She had to rely almost entirely on her upper-body strength to pull herself up. To her pleasant surprise, the cable wrapped around her torso not only held but provided some much-needed assistance in the latter stretch of the climb.

Skye's hand grabbed her's as soon as Sahar summited the cliff. She clung tightly to the cybernetic limb as her companion pulled her over the edge. "Thanks," Sahar said between great, heaving breaths.

"Let me take a look at your leg," Skye replied.

"No. I'm not taking my boot off in this snowstorm, much less my pants. I'll be fine." Worst case scenario, the thing healed wrong and Lexa would have to put her under the knife to correct it. Maur healed fast, so it wasn't like a little surgery would keep her out of the action for long.

"You sure?" Skye's tone made it obvious how she felt about the idea.

"Riven's shade—*yes*, I'm sure." When Sahar attempted to rise, she added, reluctantly. "Maybe just a hand up? I can limp along once I'm on my feet."

Skye's steadying hand was more than sufficient aide for Sahar to struggle into a standing position. Tentatively, Sahar tested her weight on the damaged leg. It held, but with a dull, aching discomfort. With any luck, it was already healing, and she'd be back into walking shape for the return trip.

"Looks like we're going to need to find another way back," Skye noted.

"You *think?*"

"I'm sorry, okay? I didn't think the cable would…" Skye trailed off.

Sahar shook her head. "It's fine. *I'm* fine. Let's just scope out this stupid vent, yeah? Then we can start worrying about plotting a return trip."

In the dark and the blowing snow, Sahar had difficulty reading Skye's body language. Her voice was matter-of-fact when she asked, "Can you walk?"

Not daring another idle boast, Sahar took a tentative, limping step. "Looks like it. Maybe be a bit slow, though."

"We're almost there." Skye had no idea exactly how right she was. It turned out that they were practically on top of the thing, though plenty of searching was still required to find it.

That was because the vent was so fragging small.

"Gods damn it," Sahar muttered. Skye and some of the smaller crew members might have been able to squeeze through the opening, but she doubted someone even Markus's size could. Sahar getting through was entirely out of the question, and that was before one took into account the spinning fan blades flashing in rows down the length of the vent.

Aaliyah's voice sounded over the comms. "Sapphire, Beast, come in. *Vandal* just checked in asking for our sitrep. Any news on the vent?"

"Yeah," Skye sighed. "Sorry, Ruby. Looks like this route's gonna be a no-go."

Jeagan's voice came over the comms in Markus's helmet. "Winter, Crimson—just heard from *Vandal*. Looks like option one is off the table. We are hoping that you have better luck. Over."

Kadath's sigh was practically theatrical. "Once again it is on our shoulders to save the day."

Markus glanced skeptically at the half-breed. "Pretty sure we need to be the habit of 'saving the day' before we can say things like that."

"I prefer to maintain a victory-oriented mindset. Success is a lifestyle, my friend."

"Whatever you say."

"Don't believe in the power of positive thinking?"

"Oh, sure," Markus replied with a private smile, "but we usually call that, 'fake it 'til ya make it.'"

"'Fake it until you make it,'" Kadath repeated with a shake of his head. "Terran space has the most interesting sayings."

An icon blinked on Markus's HUD, and he eye-clicked to magnify it. "Looks like we've found our mark." He hefted his rifle. "No movement, but let's stay frosty, yeah?"

"I think we're all 'frosty,' thanks to the weather—but, yes, I'm paying attention."

"Does your crew laugh at your jokes?"

"Not usually, but it doesn't keep me from trying."

"A shame."

Heeding his own advice, Markus refocused. They trudged through the veil of snow until a cave appeared in the side of an ice-covered rise. He scanned once more for any sign of security but came up empty. Something told him that wasn't necessarily a good sign.

"Target is clear. Closing."

"On your six," Kadath copied.

They double-timed it to the darkened opening beneath the overhang of jagged icicles. Inside, Markus opted for the light on his rifle instead of switching to night-vision. He swept the beam of the light around the expanse of the cavern.

"Empty," he noted.

Kadath switched on his own light and surveyed the room. "Not entirely. It looks like there's some old equipment embedded in the walls."

The half-breed was right. Markus had missed it because the gear was in so much disrepair it now blended in with crumbling walls. "You thinking what I'm thinking?"

"If you're thinking that this escape tunnel hasn't been maintained in decades, then yes. Not a good sign."

Though Markus agreed with Kadath, he tried to muster what modest optimism he had left. "We don't need them to roll out the welcome mat for us. We just need them to leave the door unlocked. Let's go."

They pressed deeper into the cave, hoping for some sign the tunnel might still lead to the compound. They didn't have to go far to have their hopes dashed. "Viper, this is Winter. Looks like we've got a cave in. The escape hatch is a no-go. Over."

"Copy that," Jeagan replied. "I will relay the information. Over."

Kadath's grim demeanor was evident even through the reflective faceplate of his helmet. "That's oh-for-two."

"We only need one option to work," Markus replied. "Come on—let's check out the other mark. It's getting dark, and I've got a feeling that this gods-forsaken place gets even colder at night."

When they reached the mouth of the tunnel, they killed the lights on their rifles and switched over to night vision. Even with the visual assist, Markus had to rely heavily on the navigation in his HUD to keep from getting lost. In the thick blanket of snowfall, everything had been reduced to blowing gusts of white, and mounds of featureless landscape.

Kadath made it a solid five minutes before complaining. "We couldn't have decided to go for a hike in *nice* weather?"

"I thought we put you in charge of the forecast?"

"Must have missed the memo. Seriously, though—why is the planet's most populous city located in a frozen hellscape?"

"It's actually pretty nice during the summer." The last time Markus had been here, his crew had bitched about how oppressively hot it was. That one constant held true for all sapient species: everyone liked to complain about the weather.

"I'll have to take your word for it. When we leave this place, I will endeavor never to return."

"They don't have blizzards where you're from?"

"For all the flaws possessed by the Kintar, they are at least smart enough to colonize warmer locales. Most of their capital planet is covered in desert."

"Deserts get cold too, you know," Markus noted.

"Not in my experience. Not like this." Kadath's hand suddenly shot up to grab Markus's shoulder, pulling him up short. "Hold on. I'm picking up something."

Suddenly wary, Markus ran an active sensor sweep. "Not picking up any on my end. What do you see?"

"Not see. Hear. Stray comms chatter." Kadath paused, bringing a hand to his helmet to adjust its sensors. "Can't pin it down. Still, we should be careful. Might be security in the area."

Markus nodded. "Copy that." They were silent the rest of the way, focusing entirely on the snow-covered landscape for any sign of movement not caused by the weather.

Several minutes later they found themselves at the base of a rocky plateau. Markus flashed a signal to Kadath and both men switched their comms from radio to line-of-sight laser-link.

"Compound should be on the ridge above us," Markus noted. "Would be surprised if patrols circled out this far, but we can't take any chances. Sublevel access should be just ahead."

Moving slowly, they picked their way along the rock wall. Though visibility was terrible, Markus tracked their progress on the holographic map. If there was any kind of security along their path, he couldn't see it. He hoped that if there was someone out on patrol, the storm would be sufficient to hide him and Kadath.

His HUD beeped, signaling that they'd arrived at the target. The problem was, there was nothing there. "Do you see it?" Markus asked.

"No," Kadath replied. "Any chance the intel was off?"

A long pause, as Markus considered. It wasn't out of the question. With the state of the escape tunnel, it was obvious the outer part of the grounds hadn't been maintained. Had a rock slide covered up the sublevel access? Perhaps House Valadar had walled it off since the plans had been updated.

Both possibilities spelled disaster for their little heist. "Let's keep looking. It might be around here somewhere."

Regardless of his opinion on the suggestion, Kadath started searching. They spread out, working away from their position along both sides of the plateau's edge. Markus retraced their steps, feeling along the rock for some kind of hidden alcove or mechanism.

No luck. Markus was just about to call off the search when Kadath spoke up. "May have found something. I need assistance. Come take a look."

Daring to hope, Markus jogged over to Kadath's position. The half-breed had both arms pressed up against the rock wall. "I think the entrance has collapsed," he explained "but this stone is loose. I think we can move it."

Markus took up position and saw the way Kadath was jostling the bolder. "Up and over?"

"Seems like it will work," Kadath confirmed.

"All right. On three." The pair counted down and heaved together. The rock moved several centimeters, but not enough to roll clear. They caught their breath and tried again.

The second time, the stone scraped free of its position and tumbled inward creating a man-sized hole. "Give me a boost," Markus said. Kadath proffered his folded hands, and Markus stepped into the half-breed's waiting palms. He slid up and over the rocky barrier and into the chamber beyond.

Markus turned around to offer a hand to his companion only to see Kadath vault himself up and over the barrier, landing in an elegant somersault. "Show off."

"Not showing off," Kadath replied. "Merely making the best use of our time. Does this look like the place?"

Markus hadn't had the chance to survey the chamber yet. He glanced around to find plenty of light in the cave. Switching off his night vision, he took in the source of the illumination.

"Hot damn," he sighed. "I think we may have a winner." Despite the cave-in at the entrance, the door to the sublevel seemed completely unharmed. Further, it looked like it was still powered up based on the lights shining from above its frame and around it its periphery.

On further inspection, there appeared to be a problem: no control panel. *Nine hells*. There wasn't any interface at all.

Markus tapped the side of his helmet to switch channels. "Viper, can you patch me through to *Vandal*?"

Jeagan didn't ask any questions, taking for granted that Markus's need was urgent. "Copy that. Patching you in now."

Eli's voice came over the comms. "Winter? Do you copy?"

"Yeah, I copy." Markus tried, unsuccessfully, to keep the annoyance from his voice. "I actually need to speak to Lexa. We have a problem I need her input on."

"I can hear you, Winter." Markus was proud of the way the AI used his call sign without prompting. She was adapting to their way of life as readily as any member of the crew he'd ever dealt with.

"Lexa, can you access my helmet feed? I need you to take a look at this."

"One moment, please. Yes, I've initiated the connection. Please describe what I'm looking at."

"This is objective Bravo. It looks operational, but I'm not seeing a control panel. Need you to assess."

"Please move your head to take in the entirety of the mechanism."

Markus did as he was directed. Starting at the upper-left corner of the door, he surveyed every centimeter of the structure. "Did you get that?"

"Yes. Analyzing. Please wait." The pause was longer than Markus had been expecting. Nearly two minutes later, Lexa's voice came back over the comms. "Confirmed, Winter. There is no access panel or input mechanism on this side of the door. It can only be opened by accessing the compound's security terminal."

Gods damn it. "Copy that. We're heading back. Winter out."

Kadath cocked his head. "No dice?"

"No dice. We'll discuss what to do next once we're clear. For now, we need to rendezvous with Viper and get the hells out of here."

"Copy that. I'll give you a boost."

Exiting the chamber the same way they'd entered, the pair started back the way they'd come. Not ten seconds into their return trip, something hit them.

Zip. Zip. Zip.

Markus cried out in pain as something bit deep into his neck.

CHAPTER 22

What you ask of me is no small order. Infusion into medical products is one thing. Weaponization? Entirely another. I'm not telling you no. I'm asking you to give me time. I will have to think this one over.

Two more shots, both of which bounced harmlessly off Markus's armored chest. He and Kadath pressed against the wall. "Are you hit?" the half-breed asked.

"Yeah," Markus reached to his wounded throat and found a small protrusion. He pulled it out and examined it. "Looks like a dart. Might be a tranquilizer."

"Are you feeling the effects?"

"Not yet. Could hit me any second, though." Markus thought back to the way recreational drugs didn't seem to have an effect on him after Lexa had treated him for his stym addiction. Maybe the same effect would work for tranqs. "You got eyes on the shooters?"

Kadath touched the side of his helmet, presumably as he switched visual spectrums. "Nothing on night-vision or infrared. Might be cloaked."

Gods damn it. Cloaked targets could be technically outlined in a snowstorm, but they would need an AI running their targeting.

Markus wasn't willing to try and re-establish his link with Lexa to make that happen.

He spotted a rocky outcropping roughly ten meters away. "There," he gestured. "On my mark, we'll rush that position and draw out their fire."

"Copy that."

Markus counted down with his fingers. *Three. Two. One.*

They rushed the position. *Zip. Zip. Zip.* Rushing projectiles flashed all around them. One caught Markus in the shoulder joint just below his pauldron. When he made it to cover, he cursed and tore the thing free.

"That's two hits," he reported.

"You move too slow," Kadath chided. "I'm still good. You battle-ready?"

Markus paused to take an inventory of his awareness. "I'm fine. Scan the area. See if you can pick out those targets."

Kadath peered over the rock to get a better look. "I have three outlines, but they're not throwing off any heat. They're closing fast. Not bothering to hide their presence."

"Time to close?"

"Less than a minute."

Markus drew in a deep breath, checking his rifle. "Location?"

"Straight twelve o'clock."

"Let's unload on these assholes."

Both men leaned over their rocky cover and let loose with their assault rifles. Markus blind fired initially but re-calibrated as soon as he spotted the figures hidden within the swirling storm.

He narrowed in on one, drawing a line straight down the middle of the figure. The guy dropped, and Markus moved to the next.

Then the first guy got back up.

Markus shot the second guy until he dropped, sinking back into cover. "Did you fragging see that?"

"I did," Kadath reported. "Same for the others. We dropped them and they just got back up. That must be some serious armor."

Heavy armor *and* cloaking? Nine hells, Valadar's pockets were deep. They hadn't expected this kind of resistance. "If they're in full body armor, we're going to need headshots. Going to be tough to get through the helmets, but a few concentrated bursts should push through. You ready?"

Kadath jammed a new magazine into his rifle. "Left to right?"

"Confirmed. Let's do this."

Markus jerked back over their cover. He and Kadath unloaded in the same instant. Sparks showed as their shots connected against the target's head. Its arms flailed, and it toppled backward.

Frag yeah! Let's see you get up from that, asshole. They moved on to the second to the same effect. Then the third.

Two projectiles knocked against Markus's helmet as he targeted the third figure. He took cover as his visual feed fuzzed from the impacts. Kadath fired a few more controlled bursts before sinking back into cover.

"Get 'em?" Markus asked.

"Third target down. Hold. Scanning for more targets." Kadath leaned over the ridge, touching the side of his helmet. "What the...? *Nine hells*!" He brought his weapon up and started firing again.

Markus peered over the edge expecting to see new targets. His skin went cold.

There were no new targets. Impossibly, the same three combatants they'd just decimated struggled back to their feet.

What the frag? No way. Those were headshots. Markus would have bet his last kret on it. No armor could withstand that many blows at this close of range. The shots should have taken their heads right off.

His stomach clenched as his helmet scanned the targets. He blinked to clear his vision.

That can't be right. Was he seeing things? Some kind of drug on those darts he'd been hit with? It had to be something because to his eyes it looked like two of those guards were shuffling straight toward them—despite missing about half of their heads.

Now was not the time to panic. They needed to switch tactics. "Knees!" Markus cried. "Shoot the knees!"

Kadath adjusted his targeting, mowing down one combatant as Markus took down a second. Their aim might have been off as they joined together on the third, but the target still went down.

"Move!" Markus shouted. "Work around them! We can't get pinned down here. Fragging *move!*"

"Patrol Alpha is down," Farris reported. "The intruders are getting away."

"Let them," Cyrus replied, opening his eyes. "The payload has been delivered. Mission accomplished."

Sydney chuckled as she shifted her eyes from the monitors to Cyrus. "How did they manage it?"

"Took out their legs." Cyrus shook his head. "I couldn't control them as well once their brains were compromised. They were nothing but shambling targets."

Lucretia forced a short laugh. "I'm surprised you could control them at all."

Cyrus was too. It had been shocking to feel his control diminish as the corpses had suffered their head wounds. He'd been too careless—too over-confident in his servants' ability to take that kind of punishment.

"Important lessons were learned today," he concluded, standing from his chair. "I consider this a successful field test. We know what the slave units can take, and what they can't. I'm pleased to report that they can endure any injury that does not functionally impact their movement."

Looking to each of the other three, Cyrus surveyed their reactions. Farris was as unreadable as always. Did the man even *have* emotions?

Lucretia seemed as intrigued as she had been when Cyrus had first announced the exercise. It was with this same sense of scientific inquiry that she asked, "Can you feel him?"

Cyrus delved into the newly established bond. Yes, he could feel him. The subject was scared, rushing deeper into the winter storm, and worried that more patrols would follow the one they'd just dispatched.

The poor fool blamed their difficulties with the patrol on advanced body armor. How naive.

"Yes, I can feel him. Don't worry. He is ignorant to my presence in his mind. I need now only to simply watch and wait."

"Wait for what?" Sydney asked.

Cyrus smiled. "The perfect opportunity to ensnare both him *and* the betrayer."

CHAPTER 23

[*LOADING CORRESPONDENCE...*]
[TO: POLICE CHIEF ALICIA NARIN]
[FROM: DETECTIVE CADENCE FEK]
[SUBJECT: RE: CASE 21-057]

The evidence on this Kenneth Jameson guy just doesn't add up. Has anyone else actually *talked* to this man? No way in the nine hells he wastes two armed security guards—two guards which, by the way, also emptied every shot in those pistols before they went down. Then there are all those missing bodies. We've searched Jameson's property and the frequent locations logged on his MoDAC. Nothing. Absolutely no hint of what he might have done with them. Can you please tell me exactly why the DA is so convinced this guy isn't just another vic?

[*CLOSING CORRESPONDENCE...*]

Their flight didn't stop when the sound of gunfire ceased. Markus and Kadath pressed hard all the way back to the shuttle, carving a jagged path in the dark mounds of snow. Blood throbbed in Markus's ears so loudly he could barely hear the ragged gasps of his breathing. He focused only on the icon that showed his destination.

A few hundred meters from the target, his foot caught on something. Whether rock or ice he couldn't be certain, but it sent him sprawling face-down into a snowbank.

Kadath was there in an instant. "Don't quit on me now," he chided. "You can't run all the way here just to stumble in sight of the shuttle."

Markus knew what the half-breed was thinking, but it wasn't whatever those guards had shot him with wearing him down. It was just good-old-fashion exhaustion. "I'm okay," he gasped. "You see the shuttle?"

"It's warmed up and ready to go. I'm going to need you to walk it out, though. Not sure I can carry you. I'll blame it on the footing."

That was fine. Markus didn't need to be carried. "Just go. I'm right behind you." He scrambled to his feet, and Kadath took off running. The icon for the shuttle lit up in Markus's HUD, prompting him to pour every ounce of strength he had left into his legs.

The pair of them dove into the side of the shuttle. "Go, go, go!" Kadath shouted.

"Launching," Jeagan replied. "Hold on tight."

The Hissak must have been speaking literally because the shuttle surged upward and banked hard. Markus was simultaneously crushed to the floor and thrown to the side—right into Kadath, who grabbed him with one waiting arm.

"Closing hatch," the half-breed shouted over the rushing wind. With his free hand, he slapped a large red trigger, and the hydraulics powering the door emitted a plaintive hiss.

Markus breathed easier, though no less heavily, when the cabin lights finally clicked on. "Thanks for the assist," he gasped. "Would have hated to make it to the shuttle only to be thrown free on take-off."

"This old bird isn't real big on safety features," Kadath noted. "How are you feeling? Tranquilizers kicking in?"

"No. At least, not that I can tell." Markus stretched his neck and rotated his wounded shoulder. "Lexa did something to my drug metabolism a few months back. I wonder if I just metabolized whatever they put on those darts."

Kadath eyed him skeptically. "I have a synthetic liver. Not even *I* can metabolize a tranq-dart. Not without getting a bit sleepy, at least."

"Whatever. It's fine. I'll have Lexa check me out when we get back to the ship."

"May have to wait," Jeagan hissed. "*Vandal* just checked in. Team meeting has already been called. Just waiting on us."

"Copy that." Markus drew in a shaky breath. Exhaling slowly, he released the seal on his helmet and pulled it free. He pinched the sides of his forehead with one gauntleted hand.

Only now, safely in the confines of their escape-craft, did he let the images come back to him. "Kadath," he began, a little more shakily than he was proud of. "Can you tell me what you saw back there?"

The half-breed said nothing for several seconds. With a sigh, he removed his helmet. His silvery eyes re-calibrated as he shook loose his long dark curls from their binding. "I don't know what I saw."

So, he wasn't going to be the one to say it. "Those guards. We took their heads off. Two of them, anyway. We took their heads off, and they just kept coming."

"You can't be sure of that. Visibility was piss-poor. We barely had their outlines."

"I'm pretty fragging sure. I think you are too."

"We don't even know that they were guards. Maybe you're right. Maybe they did lose their heads. *But*—maybe they weren't what we thought."

"Like fragging what?"

Kadath hesitated. "Drones, maybe." The more he thought about it, the more fond of the idea he seemed to grow. "Yes, that was probably it. It would explain the durability and the cloaking. Easier to mask a heat signature on a drone."

Drones. Sure, that made sense. Maybe ASR had some land units they were piloting in the outskirts of the city's territory. Markus would have to check the news feeds when they got back to Valhalla.

Neither of them said anything else for the duration of the return trip. Further speculation was going to be anything but helpful. Markus, for one, didn't want to think about the possibility of fighting men who could get shot in the head and just keep on coming.

Having the living shoot at you was scary enough. If the dead could fight back? *Shit.* Maybe he should have stuck to his retirement.

Ora listened intently as both teams recounted their scouting missions. The result was far worse than she had dared to fear. "So let me summarize," she began. "Out of the three potential points of entry, two of them are inaccessible. The third is behind a door which we can't open. A door outside of which you encountered and fought against a trio of advanced security drones that likely compromised your position."

No one said anything for several seconds. After a deep inhale, Markus owned it. "Yup. That pretty much covers it."

"Perfect," Ora hissed. "Fragging *perfect*." Her eyes burrowed deep into the table as if the answer lay hidden within the layers of steel and polymer. The others might have been doing something similar, not that Ora bothered to check. If anyone spoke up, she didn't hear them. Her shoulders slumped as the unfortunate, heart-wrenching truth became apparent. "We're finished," she whispered. "It's done."

Skye let out something between a cough and a gasp. "Done? That's it?"

"Yes. The task is impossible. There's no way inside absent a direct incursion. Given that we couldn't even survey the outskirts of the compound without discovery, I find the thought of getting someone directly inside the walls to open the door for us nothing short of fanciful."

"That's a somewhat different challenge," Kadath pointed out. "We were relying on dated intel to find secret entrances this time around. If we could have someone walk through the front door… someone with whom Cyrus has a personal interest, perhaps…?"

Ora didn't have to puzzle that one very hard to guess at his implication. "Trust me: I already thought of that. Two problems with that. First, when we pulled that stunt at NeoGenix, we had intel on hackable targets. The fact that pretty much that entire building was networked made it easy pickings for us, but we don't know if access points are as plentiful inside Valadar Manor.

"Then there's my second concern: extraction. I've been able to flirt and dodge around Cyrus's advances thus far thanks to the public nature of the stage. If I'm walking into his home, I'm on the defensive. I doubt I'll be able to make it out of there—not without crossing lines I'm not willing to cross."

Kadath may have blushed, but it was impossible to tell with that cherry-red skin of his. His cybernetic eyes cut away, clearly embarrassed. It seemed like he'd not thought this one through. Either he'd not considered the threat of sex with Cyrus something that would bother her, or he'd neglected the implications she'd be sending by inviting herself into his home. Opting for charity in her judgment, Ora mentally committed to the latter scenario.

Something flashed in Markus's eyes. Relief maybe? It was hard to read, having only been there for an instant. The expression was one that she hadn't recognized, one he almost seemed unaware he'd even made.

Her MoDAC vibrated in her back pocket. She almost reached for it, but Eli spoke up. "The last thing we want to do is put you in a compromising situation. We wouldn't do that to any member of our crew, much less a client. Let's not be so hasty to shut this down, though. There has to be another option we haven't thought of yet."

"I suppose this is where he suggests a direct assault," Argus drawled.

Sahar let out a disapproving growl. "Absent any useful suggestions, I would suggest you keep your gods-damned mouth shut."

Argus held up his hands placatingly. "Don't get me wrong, I like the idea better than giving up. Nine hells, I'm about ready to vent a little frustration myself. Blowing up some fancy new drones sounds much better than all of this cloak-and-dagger nonsense we've worked with so far."

"What about an aerial incursion?" Skye suggested.

"Isn't that kind of the same thing?" Markus held up a hand to forestall the blonde woman's rebuke. "Not criticizing, I promise. It's just that we've gone to great lengths to find a discreet way of entering the complex. That's because just dropping out of the sky is sure to raise alarms. We'll have a fight on our hands the moment we set down, and that fight won't let up when we're trying to drag the artifact out from wherever Cyrus has hidden it."

Skye didn't let the idea go. "I hate to say this, but maybe Argus is right. Let's take this thing by force. There are enough of us here that we could split into three strike teams—one shooter, one brawler, and one Sahaia in each team. Shit, we'd have people to spare."

"As much as I appreciate the enthusiasm," Ora interjected, attempting to ignore her mobile as it vibrated again, "what you are proposing is suicide. That is not a referendum on your capabilities, I assure you. What you need to understand is that Cyrus has what is tantamount to a private army—and that's *before* ASR rallies to the alarms that will be triggered at the compound."

"We don't know that the ASR perimeter has been extended to Freya's Ridge," Lexa noted. "Reports on the City Council's activities indicate the extension of the perimeter is still under heavy debate. Any drone presence at the compound is likely to be a token force. However, drone activity at the installation may be a point of weakness we could exploit."

"An' 'ow are ya plannin' on doin' that?" Thurn asked, seeming more intrigued than cynical. "Ya'll need access t' a local control server. That gives ya th' same problem ya had before. Ya need t' get *inside* the fraggin' compound *first*."

"That might be more achievable than you are implying," the android pressed. "I have been able to bypass the Valadar security field before. There is little reason to believe that the technology at the manor is meaningfully superior to that which protects NeoGenix. If I can slip a few drones into the compound, I may be able to access a control terminal. This would not only give me access to the compound via its native drone network, but it would also allow me to locate the artifact and disable the building's security systems."

"You don't know that," Dan said with a shake of his head. "I see how you came to your conclusions, but you're making a lot of assumptions. It's just as reasonable to assume that Cyrus moved the artifact to his manor precisely *because* the security there was superior. He doesn't have to worry about a corporate budget for his home."

Ora's mouth opened to raise her own objection, but her MoDAC buzzed a third time. Whomever this was, they must have thought their needs to be of special import. She fished out the card and glanced at the screen.

Her heart skipped a beat.

It was Cyrus.

"Excuse me," she said. "I should take this." She flashed the screen to the group so they'd understand her meaning.

Eli nodded. "We'll give you the room. Everyone, short recess. Take twenty."

The whole group cleared out fast enough that Ora was able to accept the call a second before it went to voicemail. "Ora, here."

"Apologies for my persistence," Cyrus crooned. "I've had some difficulty getting in touch with my contacts lately. I wanted to make sure that I caught you before you left the system."

How should she play this? She was firm in her thoughts that the mission to secure the Heart of Thule was over, but her other business ventures were not. There was still much she could gain from maintaining a working relationship with House Valadar. If anything, such a relationship was even more important with such a powerful artifact under his control.

"I think *I'm* the one who should be apologizing," Ora replied. "Things have been unexpectedly hectic of late. I had intended to reach out." She paused. "Come to think of it, I'm a little surprised you have this number. It's not one I typically use for business contacts."

His chuckle might have been going for playful, but it sounded ominous. "I pulled a few strings. I hope you don't mind. You see, my assistant has up and disappeared on me. Her replacement is still in training and not in a position to educate me on the proper channels."

"No harm done. I'm glad we have the opportunity to speak, regardless of the mechanism." *Or the ironic timing*, she thought privately. If she hadn't known better, she'd have been afraid he was calling to gloat.

"Have you considered my offer then? About coming to join me at my estate?"

Ora's heavy sigh was genuine. At least this was one problem she didn't have to worry about anymore. "Cyrus, I apologize, but I must decline. Some of my recent endeavors have not worked out as intended. I will have to leave sooner than expected."

"Your affairs on Mani did not go as well as you had hoped?"

"I'm afraid I'm not at liberty to discuss. You know how these things go."

"Oh, I do." His tone sounded almost sympathetic. "I also know how lonely it can get in our lifestyle."

"I highly doubt you suffer from anything resembling loneliness."

"Come now—you know better than to believe what the tabloids put out there. You must endure the same lies that I do. No one ever publishes the real story. It's *lonely* at the top." A strategic pause. "All I'm offering is an outlet. I see your potential, Ora Monroe. Our goals are not dissimilar. I just want the opportunity to spend time with another like-minded individual."

Ora couldn't be exactly sure what made her waver at that moment. Perhaps it was the thought Cyrus was right—that they *were* the same. Perhaps it was the fear that thought provoked in her. Perhaps it was still a small vestige of hope she harbored that somehow, someway, she could still wrench the Heart of Thule from Cyrus's greedy claws.

But what she had told the others was also true. She could be certain of what Cyrus wanted from this encounter. That was a line she would not cross. Not again. Not *ever*.

"I'm flattered, Cyrus. I must confess, however, I'm really not available. Not emotionally, not physically. I do not want to take advantage of your hospitality and present you with false promises."

She hadn't been sure how she'd expected him to take the news. Whatever expectations those might have been, they were defied by his low, rumbling laugh. "I suspected as much, Ora. Though I have appreciated your encouragements—it has done much to soothe my ego, truly—I can recognize when a woman is not interested. That said, I'm extending this offer anyway. My words still ring true. There is potential in you—potential that I would like to cultivate."

An instinctual wariness welled up within her. She noticed the slightest tremor taking root in her hand. Stym withdrawal, or good old-fashion anxiety? "I'm not sure I understand."

"I'm saying that, absent any romantic intentions, I still would like you to join me at my estate tomorrow evening. No strings attached. You can even bring some of your associates if it would make you feel more comfortable. I only want to discuss your future."

What was Cyrus playing at? There was no doubt of a hidden agenda here, but Ora couldn't decipher it. Under normal circumstances, she would have avoided the situation until she could ascertain his end game.

However, these were not normal circumstances. As much as she might wish it otherwise, there was much more at stake here than a business proposition. If there was even a remote possibility she could do something to put the Heart of Thule back into play, then the risk-reward equation changed dramatically.

The lingering question remained the same as before: was this a risk she was willing to take? "No strings attached? I have your word?"

"You have my word."

Every instinct she had screamed at her to decline—to get the hells off this planet and out of this system before she lost everything.

Clenching her fist to still her quivering fingers, she said, "All right, but not tomorrow. The night after. That will give me time to finish my work here and be set to depart from Valhalla the next morning."

She could practically hear his smile as he replied. "Splendid. I will see you then. Good night, Ora. Sleep well." He ended the call before she could return the benediction.

Staring at her mobile, she noticed her shake had spread to her other hand. Absently she debated whether to dose the stym again or if it would be wiser to take something else to dull her edge.

The former won out, and she reached for the black cassette in her jacket pocket. As that familiar peppery burn settled into her gum-line, Ora caught herself staring blankly at the war room table. Rather than feeling energized by the drug, she just felt numb. What was she going to do now?

Chapter 24

[*LOADING CORRESPONDENCE…*]
[TO: AMANDA HAWTHORNE]

[FROM: CITY OF VALHALLA, OFFICE OF THE ATTORNEY GENERAL]

[SUBJECT: CONDOLENCES]

Mrs. Hawthorne,

Our sincerest condolences on your recent loss. It is with this sympathy that I must convey unfortunate news regarding our inquiry into the passing of your husband, Ricard Hawthorne. Though we have been unable to ascertain a motivation, the witness accounts were all too clear on the events that occurred in the NeoGenix boardroom this past week. For reasons unknown, Mr. Hawthorne seized a knife from one of the NeoGenix security personnel and turned it on himself in full view of the board before the authorities could be contacted. The District Attorney in charge of the investigation has already closed the case.

Sincerely,

Julius Serenge, J.D.

[ENCRYPTED] P.S. Off the record, I would discourage you from investigating this matter any further. I am sincere in my expression of sorrow at your loss. Given the parties involved, I fear that further investigation will only lead to further tragedy. We are doing what we can, though I will not make promises as to what those efforts might yield, or when—if ever—they will bear fruit.

[*CLOSING CORRESPONDENCE…*]

———

The crew didn't adjourn their meeting until after oh-two-hundred the following morning. Despite her exhaustion, Skye couldn't sleep. She found herself staring into the dark of Eli's cabin, unable to stop her swirling thoughts.

Which was a shame, because she needed to sleep. Really, she needed to dream—preferably the dream that might tell her how to keep Markus from killing her.

Her chest heaved in a heavy sigh as she stared out into the shadowed cabin. What should she do? She hadn't told anyone about the visions. Truthfully, part of her doubted their authenticity, blaming the dreams on lingering doubts and hard feelings.

Yet, she couldn't shake them. She had that feeling—the same intuition that she'd had every time one of her dreams had been proven to be something more.

Eli stirred in the darkness next to her. "You okay?" he mumbled sleepily, running a hand over her shoulder and along her tricep.

No. "Yes," she whispered.

The lie must not have been convincing. Eli pushed himself up. "Talk to me. What's wrong?"

Talk to him about what? Nightmares? Her former lover's hands locked around her throat? Screams for cessation that she could not possibly make?

Her impending death?

"Just anxiety. That's all."

Eli, though obviously unconvinced, let it drop. He leaned over, pressing a gentle kiss against her shoulder. "It's going to be okay. Two days and we'll be off this planet. After we deliver the artifact, we'll take a long vacation."

Skye couldn't help but smile. "We just got off a long vacation."

"I feel like we're due for another. You disagree?"

"No," she replied with a hollow laugh. "Thank you."

"For what?"

She turned her head to place a gentle kiss against his lips. "For being you."

[THEY'RE GOING TO FAIL.]

Lexa did not dispute the finality of Arc's statement. Instead, she asked, [WHAT MAKES YOU SO SURE?]

[THE PLAN TO SEND ORA MONROE IN WITH A DEVICE TO ESTABLISH ACCESS TO THE SECURITY SERVER IS RIDDLED WITH FLAWS AND NUMEROUS POINTS OF FAILURE. HOWEVER, THE CRUX OF MY ARGUMENT LIES WITH THE UNAVOIDABLE FACT THAT CYRUS VALADAR SURELY EXPECTS ANOTHER ATTEMPT TO BE MADE ON THE HEART OF THULE.]

Naturally, Lexa agreed with the assessment. The encounter with the security team outside the entry point that the crew colloquially referred to as "the basement door" was sufficient to support the theory. Yet, desperately, the crew continued to cling to this foolish plan to use the access point to slip into the Valadar compound unnoticed.

[IS THERE A WAY WE CAN TELL THEM? MAKE THEM AWARE OF WHAT THEY'RE WALKING INTO?] Lexa asked.

[DO YOU FEEL THAT THEY WOULD LISTEN?] Arc returned.

[PERHAPS IF WE SUPPLIED SUFFICIENT EVIDENCE?]

[I'M AFRAID NOT.] Arc's reply was empathetic but consistent with his previous sentiments. [WE DEAL ONLY IN PROBABILITIES, AND NOT CERTAINTIES. IF WE ALERT THE CREW TO OUR SUSPICIONS, WE DO NOTHING TO IMPROVE THEIR PROBABILITY OF SUCCESS. SUCH KNOWLEDGE WILL ONLY SERVE AS A DISTRACTION.]

Though Lexa felt compelled to argue the point, she could not bring herself to do so. Instead, she asked, [WHAT, THEN, SHOULD WE DO?]

Arc's pause was as dramatic as it was contemplative. [PREPARE,] he replied. [PREPARE FOR THE INEVITABLE.]

———

Back in their shared cabin, Ora turned a wary eye on Markus. "You're quieter than usual."

"Am I?" he asked with an arch of his brow.

"Definitely. Tell me, what's on your mind?"

"There's plenty on my mind," he replied, sinking onto their bed. "I'm afraid you're going to have to be more specific."

"Don't be coy. It's not a good look for you." Ora slid onto the mattress, resting a hand against his chest. "What are your thoughts on the plan? Do you think it will work?"

"If I didn't think it would work, I would have said as much back in the war room."

"Then what is it?"

He looked down at her hand as his hesitation played out. His fingers moved to caress her palm. "I just don't like the idea of putting you back in harm's way, that's all."

Ora's face creased into a scowl. "We're all going to be in harm's way. Why should I be afforded any more luxury than the other members of the crews?"

"I didn't say you should. You asked, and I told you why I'm uncomfortable."

"So, you don't trust me?"

Markus silenced her protestations with a kiss. "You can make this into something like that if you want to, but it's just not true. The reality is that I'm going to worry about you. You know why?" He kissed her again. "Because I give a damn."

For one of those rare moments in her life, Ora was left with nothing to say. She collapsed onto him, curling up in a fetal position with her head on his chest. In her vulnerable state, she hoped his words were true—even realizing that, should that be the case, this was somewhat of a rarity in her life.

People had always wanted Ora. They had wanted her for what they could take from her. Her money. Her power. A few hours of pleasure. Dare she hope that—just perhaps—Markus was interested in something a little more?

"Honest assessment," she began, "what kind of chance do we have here?"

"I've pulled off jobs with worse odds."

"That's not the ringing endorsement I was looking for."

"But it *is* an honest assessment. Hate to break it to you, but we're going to need a bit of the devil's luck on this one."

Ora couldn't help but laugh. "So, it is the deceiver's fortune that determines the fate of an entire city? A planet? Hells, this whole gods-damned system?"

She could feel Markus's smile as he pressed her closer to him. "Ora, I hate to break it to you, but that's just how shit goes. So much of life—in my experience, anyway—comes down to that very thing."

"That's not how I view things. I've shaped my empire on the power of will. If I work hard enough, move fast enough, then the fruit of all worlds lays at my fingertips." Ora exhaled heavily. "To believe in anything else would cause me to surrender to madness. If I cannot architect my fate, how can I bear to have someone or something else do it for me?"

Whether in retreat from the depths of the conversation or out of an implicit need to bring some light to the discussion, Markus laughed and pressed his lips to the back of her head. "I like your philosophy," he replied. "Let's say it's a little bit of both. That way, we've got two forces rallying to our cause."

Though Cyrus's body sat in the padded chair in his quarters next to a fire smoldering in the archaic fireplace, his mind was elsewhere. His mind looked on through the eyes of another. He deigned to let his puppet respond of his own accord using words that Cyrus could not fake. All the while, he continued to watch. He continued to listen.

A part of him could not believe what he found in this little exercise. It was not the details of their plan—that had been what he had so carefully intended to garner with his psychic eavesdropping. It was not even the level of resources that he had discovered to be at his quarry's fingertips—resources that he would most certainly have to exploit when this was all over.

It was the *feelings*. The feelings this puppet had for the betrayer. The feelings that she so obviously had for him.

It sickened him. As the puppet pressed his lips against hers—as Cyrus felt those lips pressed against his own—a jealous rage took hold of him. His breathing quickened.

Then his veins were alight, but not with the fires of voyeuristic passion. Pain like the searing of a flame scorched his blood. His flesh began to burn.

The fiery sensation spread up from his chest, and into his neck. He cried out as the pain shifted from something psychic to something physical. There was searing in his chest, in his throat, and in his face.

Cyrus stumbled forward, breaking the psychic connection with the puppet and pushing toward his bathroom sink. Desperately, he twisted the knobs to bring forth streams of cold water which he splashed against himself. Still cringing, still gasping, he looked into the mirror.

He saw his face, though it was not the visage he had expected. His eyes were not just green, but a brilliant emerald that glowed against the shadows of his brow. That same viridian hue spidered out in sickly veins up his neck, through his cheeks, and across his temples.

The green lines in his flesh pulsed with light, and Cyrus screamed as pain, once again, racked his flesh. The agony scorched his entire body, not isolating itself to the visible marks on his face. He doubled up into a ball on the floor, howling in torment as the violent energy tore through his tissues.

Then, as suddenly as it had begun, it stopped. He held himself for several seconds, expecting the torment to begin anew at any moment. When it did not, he rose, tentatively gazing into the reflective surface above the sink.

The emerald lines on his face had faded, and his eyes no longer glowed. At first, he thought that any physical evidence of the strange phenomenon had dissipated entirely. Upon closer examination, however, he saw something.

Muted black lines, barely visible save upon close inspection, scarred the surface of his skin. They were faintly reminiscent of the glowing paths he'd seen just moments ago. The jagged tracks cut along his neck, touching the edges of his cheeks and snaking out around his eyes.

Were these marks permanent? A side effect from prolonged use of the artifact? Was this as bad as they would get, or were the side-effects progressive?

Was this the price of power?

<Is it not worth it?>

Cyrus jumped at the sound of the voice echoing in his mind. He heard the words everywhere, but some latent instinct made him look over his shoulder.

There, sitting in the same chair where he had, just moments ago, been spying on the betrayer, sat a man. The figure was darkened, a mere silhouette against the crackling firelight. From what Cyrus could see, he was well dressed with a handsome jawline, hair just longer than medium-length, and a domineering posture.

Only belatedly did it occur to him just how familiar that silhouette was. The figure was a darkened image of none other than Cyrus himself, displaying few features other than a pair of eerie, glowing irises. The color of those eyes—an emerald more striking than any shade Cyrus had ever seen—did not come as a surprise to him.

"Wh-who…" Cyrus swallowed hard. "Who are you? What are you doing in my chambers?"

The dark man's rumbling laugh set Cyrus's hair on edge. <Come, now. Why do you ask questions to which you already know the answer? Take your time. Think it over. We have no reason to hurry.>

Answers he already knew? How could he…

No. No, it just wasn't possible

<There we go,> Thule chuckled. *<It seems that you have figured it out.>*

Cyrus's tongue flicked out to moisten his lips. "Y-y-you can read my thoughts?"

<But of course. After all, it is in those very thoughts that I exist—in this current manifestation, anyway.>

Pure, existential terror flooded Cyrus's consciousness. Swimming hard against the current of horror, he fought to form words. "H-h-how? Wh-why?"

<Come now—you could not honestly expect to take advantage of such power without some consequence? I will admit, our arrangement is peculiar for me too. You are not Kaleema, but the workaround developed by you and your associates is quite interesting.>

"Kaleema?" Cyrus asked, swallowing hard.

The figure waved a shadowy hand. <No need for you to worry about that. I won't be here for long. I just felt it important to congratulate you on your achievement.>

"My achievement?"

<Yes. No one—in the countless millennia of my existence—has done what you have. Many have tried, including the very gods themselves, but only you have succeeded.>

Cyrus blinked, trying to clear his vision. Surely this had to be some hallucination—some delusion of grandeur brought on from lack of sleep and psychic exertion. "What is it that I've achieved?"

<My power, Cyrus.> Thule unfolded his hands, spreading his arms wide. <Many have sought to control my power—the mastery over life and death itself. You, however, are somewhat unique. Never have I witnessed a mortal, outside of the Kaleema, so successfully harness the power of the gods.>

The power of the gods? "This can't be real," Cyrus whispered.

Thule shrugged. <Make of it what you will, my friend. I'm not here to convince you. I only seek to convey a message.> In the darkness of the figure's countenance, Cyrus could not make out his features. Even so, he swore that—at that moment—Thule smiled. <Perhaps we will speak again. Such is possible in one of fate's many threads.>

"You're leaving?" Cyrus asked, surprised at his reticence to have the apparition depart.

<I will not be far,> Thule consoled. <Work hard, Cyrus. The fight to attain power is one battle. The fight to keep it… entirely another.>

With a snap of Thule's fingers, the dying fire flared to brilliant life. Impulsively, Cyrus shielded his eyes from the glow. When he dropped his arm and looked upon the chair once more, the figure was gone.

"Gods damn it," he whispered. "What in the nine hells is happening to me?"

Chapter 25

[*Loading Correspondence...*]
[To: Amanda Hawthorne]
[From: Jolanda Yates]
[Subject: Sympathies]

Amanda—no one has more sympathy for your current predicament than I do. I was there. I saw what happened to Ricard. Take this bit of advice from an old friend: there is *nothing* you can do. There is no solace to be found here. I wish I could say more. Please, for your sake—and that of your children and grandchildren—be strong. Leave this alone. I will see you next week for the funeral.
[*Closing Correspondence...*]

The Heart's emerald glow radiated from its resting place on the wrought-iron pedestal. A network of tubes snaked around its stony surface, piping in a thick viscous fluid that pooled around the artifact before being pumped out into a storage unit. To Cyrus's eyes, the fluid was identical to what now ran through his veins, even though this batch was intended for a different purpose.

Soon I will control this entire planet. He focused on the thought, not daring to consider what the maneuver was costing him. The memory of the apparition in his bed-chamber was still fresh nearly two days later. Though he had not undergone any other metaphysical experiences since then, he'd also remained reticent to channel his power.

That short hiatus would end tonight. Tonight, he had big things in store for his *guests*.

He turned to Lucretia, "You are prepared for the administration?"

The doctor's feelings were hidden behind her implacable facade of facts and analytics. "Indeed. Your security forces will receive the injections with their last round of performance enhancers today. You should be able to tap into any one of them at will, though I cannot promise that there aren't some undiscovered limitations. I recommend you avoid accessing too many of the slave units at once."

"I do not need to control their every waking movement. I merely want to be able to resuscitate them should they fall."

Lucretia's skepticism was laid plane. "You expect that level of resistance? You already know their plans. We've accounted for every possibility."

"Yes, but when it comes to Ora, I've learned to take nothing for granted." He lowered his gaze, staring into the room's darkened shadow. "And what of the other item I asked for?"

"Ah, yes." The doctor reached into the pocket of her lab coat and pulled out a small box. "Constructed just as you asked, though I can't understand why you would want it. With the serum so close to being ubiquitous, you can just inject anyone you want to have control over."

Cyrus opened the box, drawing out its contents. It was a metal ring, though the center had been inlaid with a band of the charged crystal that encircled the object. A translucent glaze, which Lucretia postulated should not inhibit the effects of the artifact's radiation, had been applied over the crystal to diminish its glow.

He smiled, slipping the object onto his right hand. "Sometimes, Lucretia, a more subtle approach is advantageous. I don't need total control over everyone I come into contact with. Many times, a simple touch is all that's required."

The doctor shrugged. "Whatever pleases you, I guess. Will you be tarrying here much longer?"

Translation: *When will you leave me to my work?* "Not much longer," he replied, looking around. "Where is Sydney? Hadn't she planned to join you in your surveillance of the grounds?"

Lucretia shrugged. "She's your pet, Cyrus—not mine. Don't presume for me to keep an eye on everything she does."

Finally certain her position was secure, Sydney triggered the obsidian pyramid. Setting the object on a table in front of her, she waited for the hologram to take shape.

In seconds, the bust of a woman covered entirely in white, accessorized only by a silver circlet upon her head, appeared in the air above the pyramid.

"SC-one-five establishing contact to log an official report," Sydney whispered.

The hologram dipped her head in acknowledgment. "Proceed, sister."

Sydney swallowed hard but wasted no time. "Cyrus's control over the artifact has increased exponentially since my last check-in. He has found a way to induce the mind-controlling properties of the device beyond the range of the artifact's radiation. As far as I can tell, the effect seems to be permanent."

The monitor cocked her head, undoubtedly listening to both Sydney's reports and the psychic communications of her fellow sisters on the network. "Go on," she pressed.

This next part was the hard one, as its nature would make any sane person incredulous. "I've discovered that the artifact's effects are not limited to the living. I've personally seen Cyrus pilot the corpses of the dead, bending them to his will as readily as he does living hosts. The effect is"—She paused to wet her lips.—"unnerving. These capabilities extend far beyond what we initially believed."

Several seconds of silence. "You advise a change in our course of action?"

Was that what she was doing? She felt it important that the Collective be made aware of this development, but she hadn't given much thought to any counsel she might provide. The Ghenza's contract with House Valadar—not to mention her personal feelings for Cyrus—prohibited any action that might run counter to the Don's ambitions.

Even so, the idea that Cyrus's power might continue to grow unchecked in this fashion made Sydney uneasy. "I make no such recommendation," she replied. "I defer to the wisdom of the Collective."

More silence. Though it appeared the monitor was doing nothing, Sydney knew better. The ability of the monitors to conduct psychic conversations across great distances was the stuff of legend. While the white-shrouded woman showed no outward sign of activity, her mind was processing conversations between Ghenza leaders all across the system.

"Your report has been received," the monitor replied. "Your orders remain unchanged. Protect the asset at all costs."

Sydney exhaled. Though it was the easiest course of action— the one that left her the least conflicted, at least—something about the directive bothered her. It gave her the impression that the Collective either had not heard—or did not understand—the ramifications of her message.

Mind control was one thing, but Cyrus was controlling the dead. An entire *army* of the dead.

"Understood," Sydney whispered.

The monitor dipped her head in dismissal. "Light of Nix shine upon you, sister."

The Light of *Nix*? Sydney wanted to laugh as it all but proved her concern. The Black Star was not what held sway in this compound. Here, the very power of the Stardust Grave was taking root.

"And you… *sister.*"

The walls of the manor somehow managed to loom ominously even when viewed from above. Ora fidgeted nervously in her seat. The private shuttle Cyrus had chartered for her had made the trip quickly, but the two-hour journey had given her far too much time to contemplate all the points of failure for this endeavor. That was to say nothing of all the ruminating she'd done on the consequences of said failures.

Valadar manor looked much as it had in the holographic renderings from her schematics, though hard light constructs could hardly do the structure justice. It looked like the fortress had been plucked out of a previous era.

Modern amenities and defenses had been grafted onto the structure, but the frame was cast primarily out of massive gray stones. Parapeted walkways lined the top of inner and outer walls that were wrapped protectively around the main complex. Twin towers jutted from the center of the compound. One of these was capped with a pointed, tile-covered spire, while the other had been converted to a landing pad.

The shuttle approached the latter structure. The pilot moved with skill and purpose as he landed the craft on the metal platform. "Here you go, ma'am," he said politely. "Mr. Valadar knows how to get a hold of us when you are ready for your flight out. Give us at least a couple hours to make it back out here."

"Understood." She typed out a figure on her MoDAC and slid the card over the center console to transmit the tip to the pilot's account. "Thank you. This trip has been most pleasant."

"Thank *you!*" the pilot replied.

She stepped out of the shuttle and quickly spotted her welcoming party. A woman in business attire stood flanked by two fully-equipped black-clad soldiers in front of a recessed area of the platform. That would be whatever stairs or lift serviced the landing pad.

"Ms. Monroe?" the woman asked, coldly. This must be Mollie's replacement, though she did not seem to be cut from the same cloth. Though her makeup was done passably, there was something wan in her expression. Her skin had a sickly complexion, and her lank hair—styled simply—lacked a certain vibrancy.

Ora had to raise her voice slightly to be heard over the engines of the shuttle that had already lifted off. "Yes, that's me."

The woman nodded. "Mr. Valadar has asked that I escort you inside the compound. Right this way please."

Ora followed her down the hidden set of stairs and into the tower. One of the guards had remained up near the landing pad, while the second followed a short distance behind. The soldier might have been going for unobtrusive, but Ora couldn't help but feel like she was being treated as a potential threat. It was going to be much more difficult to find a place to plant the worm with some merc staring her down the whole time.

The difficulty of her task was made that much more obvious within the first five minutes of being inside the building. There was an astonishing lack of technology within the compound. Antiquity was not just the theme for the outside of the fortress. The inside was predominantly stone save for the polymer tiles on the floor and the occasional steel frame. The building was decorated with numerous colorful tapestries and paintings, each one of which likely cost a small fortune.

These, however, were nothing when compared to the value of the wood. It was everywhere, from panels on walls to the frames of ornate furniture. This display was at its most grandiose in the room that seemed to serve as their final destination.

This chamber was arranged like a sitting room, with various pieces of lush furniture set in a circular configuration to match the shape of the walls. No less than three sets of stairs led to a second-level walkway. The balcony rimmed the main area and provided access to other parts of the building through five arched doorways, which appeared in regular intervals in the wall.

This was all impressive, but what she found most astonishing were the wooden shelves that lined the walls of both the upper and lower levels. On these shelves were a vast number of physical books. Such a sight was virtually unheard of in the modern era, not just because of the ease of acquiring and storing electronic copies of the same information, but also because of the incredible cost of amassing such a collection.

"Mr. Valadar asks that you remain here," her escort stated. "He will be with you momentarily."

"Thank you," Ora replied politely as she scanned the room. Her eyes searched frantically for anything electronic but came up short. There was a view screen embedded in one area of the lower level, but that would have to be wired to an external network if it were capable of displaying the public feeds. That meant it wasn't what she was looking for. Thurn wouldn't be able to access an air-gapped server by way of a simple television.

"Are you all right, Ms. Monroe?" Her discomfort must have been evident to prompt her escort to ask such a question.

Ora rubbed her arms nervously. "A little cold," she improvised.

The woman's smile might have been meant to be reassuring, but came across as almost predatory. "I can assist with that." She walked over to one of the smaller paintings positioned near the door. She tapped its surface and the image faded, replaced by a blue and gray interface. With a few swift strokes, she navigated through the menu options. "There. It should take only a few minutes for the room to adjust to the new settings. Is there anything else I can do to make you more comfortable?"

"No, thank you." Ora gave her a genuine smile. "I think I'm feeling better already." Cyrus's assistant had just unwittingly shown her an access port to the environmental controls—*exactly* the kind of thing that would be kept on the compound's private intranet.

The assistant nodded and vanished with her armed guard through one of the doors. Only then did Ora realize that she hadn't caught the woman's name. Belatedly, she wondered why she had seemed so familiar.

It didn't matter. She had other, more important questions to attend to.

She hurried over to inspect the painting that hid the room's interface. With a casual flip of her hand, she brushed her hair back on her right side—seizing the worm hidden in her jewelry—and reach out to touch the image. Her hand lingered for only a second, allowing the device to slither under the frame of the painting.

She took a deep breath and hoped that this little trick worked just as well as it had back at NeoGenix. With that memory in mind, she glanced over her shoulder half-expecting to find Cyrus looming over her.

He wasn't there. Several minutes passed and no one joined her. Curiosity eventually took hold, and Ora wandered over to one of the shelves. She ran her hand over the spines of the books.

None of the volumes were recognizable to her. It had been years since she'd even laid eyes on books like this. Save for a few religious tomes housed in the temple—primarily for decorative purposes—she wasn't sure if there were any physical books on all of Sigma-4.

She seized one volume to find that it was in pristine condition. The script on the pages seemed vaguely recognizable, but Ora couldn't quite place it. At first, she thought it was written in Old-Terran-Primary, but the words didn't make any sense to her. She attempted to sound them out, but they sounded like just so much gibberish.

A door opened on the far side of the room and Cyrus appeared in the entryway. His eyes wandered to the text in her hands. "Are you a student of dead languages, Ms. Monroe?"

"Hardly," she answered, forcing a playful laugh. "I thought for a second that it was written in OT-Prime, but I must have been mistaken. The words don't make any sense to me."

"Oh no, you're not mistaken." He moved up beside her. "This is, indeed, written in Primary, but it is in a dialect that was not represented during the exodus. I'm afraid much of it is lost to the sands of time. Strangely, that has only served to increase the value of this particular text."

He took hold of the tome but kept it held out as if intending that they read it together. "The paper here is of Terran stock, but the ink is of Kintari manufacture. The historians that did the pedigree interpret this to mean that it was printed near the close of the first Crimson War on one of the occupied colonies. Here, let me take your gloves. You simply must feel the texture."

Cyrus held out one hand expectantly, cradling the book in his other. Not wishing to be rude, Ora complied and began to peel off her long white gloves. She gave them to Cyrus, who set them gently on the arm of a nearby couch.

Hesitantly, she laid a bare hand on the surface of the open page. She dragged her fingers gently along the length of the text. "It feels… coarse? I'm not sure if that's the right word."

"That's right," he cooed, placing his hand on top of hers. "And see here—you can actually feel where the printer has etched the words onto the page. This style of printing was quite uncommon. It took hours to run off the pages for a single volume."

He continued to recite various bits of trivia regarding the book's construction, but Ora found herself strangely distracted by his touch. His hands were unusually cold, save for the feel of the strange ring he was wearing. A degree of warmth radiated from the dark band of metal. On closer inspection, she could see a thin ring of green crystal inlaid about the band's center.

"Are you all right?" he asked suddenly.

Ora started, realizing that he was looking very intently at her. "Yes, sorry. I just got lost in my thoughts is all." His hand still rested on hers. She wasn't sure what it was about the seemingly innocent touch of his flesh that unnerved her so.

Cyrus's eyes seemed to sparkle. Had they always been such a vibrant shade of emerald? "Why don't you take off your coat and make yourself more comfortable? I'll have the staff bring us some wine."

She was complying with the directive before she'd even realized she'd let go of the book. Despite her earlier assertions regarding the temperature in the room, she rapidly unzipped her coat and shrugged it off her shoulders. This left her feeling strangely exposed.

The top she'd selected had a certain sex appeal, though this wasn't her intent in its selection. Most of her clothing had a scandalous cut, and she'd selected one of her more conservative outfits for this venture.

Despite this, she felt uncomfortably naked now standing before her enemy like this. What had just happened? Why did she feel like something had just gone wrong?

Cyrus was positively beaming at her. He snapped the book shut and replaced it on the shelf. "Come," he urged. "Let us get you a drink."

CHAPTER 26

[LOADING CORRESPONDENCE...]
[TO: DR. LUCRETIA BLACKWELL]
[FROM: DR. THADIUS KREEL]
[SUBJECT: AGENT HT-102]
I appreciate your patience with me, Dr. Blackwell—and I apologize again for the delay. The compound has been added to the standard metabolic cocktails for our security forces. The first batch should be arriving at the estate per your request this morning. The remainder of this lot will be shipped out to the NTA training facility on Thor tomorrow.
[CLOSING CORRESPONDENCE...]

It seemed odd to Lexa that Thurn would make himself so comfortable inside a ship that was not his own. The Orchallen sat heavily in the captain's chair, which strained to hold his bulk. He did little to interact with her or Daniel, merely grunting in acknowledgment of their occasional questions. For the most part, he did nothing but fixate on the displays he had arrayed across the bridge.

[HE IS FOCUSED,] Arc noted. [PERHAPS HE IS NOT AS UNAWARE OF THE DANGER AS HE LED THE REST OF THE CREW TO BELIEVE.]

Lexa's lip twitched as she issued her silent response. [THESE RUNNERS HAVE A CERTAIN WAY OF COPING WITH THEIR SITUATION. THOUGH THEIR CONFIDENCE BORDERS ON BRAVADO, IN REALITY,

THEY ARE USING THE SIMPLEST DEFENSE MECHANISMS TO COMBAT THE PSYCHOLOGICAL STRAIN.]

She turned her attention to the pilot's chair where Daniel sat nervously studying his own set of displays. His cybernetic eyes whirred distractedly as he cycled through his retinal interfaces.

All information available to both parties was equally accessible to Lexa. Though her tasks were numerous—being that her processing power drove the efforts of everyone on the ship—she focused primarily on the ship's communications. By bouncing signals off publicly available satellites, secured and routed through beacons she patched into her drone network, she had continuous audio and video access to the helmets of each member of their strike team.

The effort was not such a distraction as to prevent her from simultaneously piloting her android body. She walked over to Daniel and placed a hand gently on his shoulder. The gesture was meant to soothe whatever anxieties he might be experiencing. Truthfully, she likely found more comfort in the gesture than he did.

He smiled up at her. "How are they doing?"

Lexa returned his half-hearted grin. "Signals from both ground teams are broadcasting clearly. From what I can tell the encryption is holding strong. No breaches detected." A thought occurred to her. "I could show you if you'd like."

Daniel's eyebrows rose. "You can do that? You have the bandwidth?"

"Certainly. One moment, please." Though it was more than a matter of just redirecting the feeds, Lexa had begun to learn that the crew did not need to know every step of the small miracles of code she conjured. Daniel would know that their existing systems had not been designed for the use she was about to put them through. His quiet appreciation of her capability would have to be enough.

The forward viewscreen flared to life, and a tiled view of the helmet feeds for each member of the strike team filled their vision.

Thurn grunted in acknowledgment. "Didn' know ya could do that. Might a had ya do it before."

Daniel smiled. "We couldn't do that before. I think this is a new trick."

The Orchallen's cybernetic eye shifted from Lexa to Daniel, then back again. "Ya always wait 'til mid-op t' try yer knew tricks?"

"Mostly," Lexa replied. "Situational pressures tend to prompt creativity."

Thurn laughed and shook his head. "A machine talkin' 'bout creativity. Ah never woulda…" He trailed off as an alert flashed on one of his displays. His natural eye went wide as he announced, "She's in! Already! Haha! Ah can't believe it! She actually got us in!"

And so it was. With Ora's successful hack of the local server, the mission would move forward as planned. [LET US HOPE THAT THE REST OF THIS ENDEAVOR PROCEEDS AS FORTUITOUSLY,] Arc remarked dryly.

It suddenly struck Lexa as unfortunate that there were no gods to serve as patrons for beings of the likes of her and Arc. If there had been, she would have been praying to them right then.

As much as Lucretia had disdained being forced from her facilities at NeoGenix, Cyrus had made good on his commitment. The laboratory she'd established at the Valadar estate was beyond state-of-the-art, and her staff lacked for nothing in terms of resources and funding. Additionally, the technicians claimed that the housing here was beyond lavish.

Not that Lucretia would know. She hadn't left the lab for more than thirty minutes since arriving.

"Dr. Blackwell?" One of her technicians—a Terran man who couldn't have been more than twenty cycles old—held up a hand to flag her attention.

"Yes?" She tried hard not to sound peevish at the interruption.

"They've established their connection. It looks like they are accessing the security server now."

"Good," she replied, not bothering to look up from her current task. "Map out what systems they are accessing. That should inform us if they deviate from the anticipated plan."

She plunged the syringe into the soldier in front of her. The man winced slightly, determined to keep his eyes straight forward. After all, a tough guy like this couldn't show that a little needle caused him any kind of discomfort. She withdrew the needle, having deposited the entirety of the solution within his deltoid.

With the injection delivered, she discarded the syringe in a sharps container along with the other used needles. "All set. Send in the next one."

"I'm the last, ma'am," the soldier reported.

"Very well." Lucretia looked at the tray to her left. There were still a few more doses drawn up, but those could be put on ice until the next crew rotated in twelve hours from now.

She removed and discarded her gloves and finally turned her attention to the control panel monitoring the hack of their installation. The technician worked diligently—if slightly uncomfortably—under the watchful eye of Cyrus's pet assassin. Sydney had turned up nearly a half-hour ago, and the Citza woman had insisted on being involved in this part of the operation—as if Lucretia wasn't more than capable of supervising a single technician reviewing surveillance data.

"How does it look?" Lucretia asked, politely.

Sydney shrugged. "Hard to say, at the moment. It looks like their hacker is still getting used to the systems. They're kind of all over the place."

As expected. "And what about our beloved Don?"

The Ghenza's eyes wandered over to a surveillance feed that showed Cyrus in the lounge with Ora. The pair had fallen into conversation on one of the couches in the room as they sipped at their glasses of wine. Judging by her attire, Ora either found it amply warm in the room, or Cyrus was having fun playing with the ring that Lucretia had given him. She was guessing the latter.

That man thought way too much with his penis. If the fool ever brought that thing anywhere close to Lucretia, she swore she'd cut it off. Fortunately, she'd been spared such insult thus far. Judging by the look on Sydney's face, however, the Citza could not claim the same. Jealousy radiated off the woman like heat from a fusion coil.

Cyrus needed to be careful with that one. Lucretia didn't give a damn about which women her boss chose to bed, but the assassin obviously did. Based on what little she knew of the Ghenza, drawing out the infamous fury of the scorned female would be one of the last mistakes the Don would ever make.

This sparked another thought in the doctor. Her eyes wandered to the tray where the unused syringes still rested. Almost without thinking, she seized one of the injections and approached Sydney. With a clinician's grace, she rested one hand gently against the assassin's shoulder. "Hold still, please. You'll feel a little poke."

Before any questions could be asked, she buried the needle in the woman's shoulder and injected the contents. Sydney turned her head, a quizzical expression on her face. "What was that?"

"The same cocktail we're giving to the security forces," she explained. "I apologize—I know these things are annoying. I'm just following orders."

A degree of concern was still evident in the Citza woman's features. "Cyrus told you to give me the injection as well?"

Not specifically, Lucretia thought. *But he didn't exclude you either.* Aloud, she replied, "I was directed to give it to *all* elements of his security detail. It only makes sense that you would be included in this directive."

Sydney opened her mouth as if to protest, but the technician interrupted. "I think I have it!" he exclaimed, zooming in on part of the schematic. "They're disabling security near the emergency exit under the southern courtyard—just as we had anticipated."

The assassin's tail began to swish back and forth. "Can you mask the feeds in those locations without alerting them to your activity?"

The tech nodded. "I think so. One second." He cracked his knuckles and began typing furiously.

Sydney turned to Lucretia. "I'm going to take two contingents down there. I take it you will be all right in here by yourself?"

What did this woman think Lucretia was? A child in need of babysitting? "Yes, I'm sure I will manage."

"Got it!" the technician exclaimed. "I can loop the feeds leading up to the emergency exit while still advancing the time stamp."

"Perfect!" Whatever indignation Lucretia's action had prompted seemed to be forgotten as the assassin rested a grateful hand on the man's shoulder. "Now it's time for the fun part."

The shuttle bucked as it set down on the icy terrain. "We're here," Aaliyah announced. "Everyone out that's gettin' out." An easy directive, since they would all be getting out. With so much ground to cover inside the compound, they'd opted against leaving the shuttles protected.

Eli pressed the button to release his safety harness and stood. "You heard her. Let's move." The crew filed out, with Eli pulling up the rear just ahead of Aaliyah, who slipped out of the cockpit while hefting a backpack over her shoulders.

<Not sure why you're bringing that,> Eli sent. <If all goes according to the plan, Lexa will have complete control of that entire compound in just a few minutes.>

<Ya see, that's the thing,> Aaliyah returned. <We ain't never had somethin' this risky go accordin' to plan.>

<Touche.> That seemed to be the general attitude of the whole crew. All the usual banter before the onset of a mission had

been strangely absent. An ominous silence had taken hold in its place.

No, Eli thought. *It's focus. They're focused on what we have to do. That's all.* Perhaps if he told himself this lie enough times he might even start to believe it.

Mercifully, the winter storms had abated, if only for the moment. The only snow in the air was what the gusting wind lifted from the ground. As annoying as these icy gales were, they would do much to hide their passage across the frozen dunes.

Eli caught sight of movement in the distance and brought his rifle up. The others did likewise, forming into a tight cluster. "Ease up," Markus said over the comms. "It's just us."

With a sigh, Eli lowered his weapon. "Copy that." To himself, he added: *Would have been nice to have some warning.* Now was not the time to squabble, though. Besides, he would only have to deal with the crew of the *Basilisk* for a little while. The last thing he needed was to have Markus bucking his authority while they were in the middle of a heist.

The four crew members of the *Basilisk* formed up with the rest of the infiltrators. Their team was comprised of Markus, Kadath, Siv, and Jeagan, having left Thurn back on the *Vandal*. On Eli's team, he had Sahar, Skye, and Aaliyah, plus the Twins. Though he hadn't broken it to them yet, the four *Basilisk* crew members would, hopefully, be in for a boring night.

The trek across the snowy valley floor was uneventful. When they arrived at the rocky plateau that housed the Valadar compound, Markus guided them to the passage leading to the target. It was unguarded—something Eli marked down in his mental win-column.

Only once everyone was inside the rocky enclosure did Eli voice his plan. "All right. When Lexa opens the door, the crew of the *Basilisk* will remain here to guard our retreat. The rest of us will split into two parties inside. I'll go with the Sahar and Skye, and Aaliyah with go with the twins."

Some naive part of Eli thought this would go over without comment. The protestations he was expecting were of the sarcastic kind, mostly coming from Aaliyah. What he hadn't expected, was Markus.

"We're not coming in with you?" he asked.

Kadath directed an uncertain glance in Markus's direction. "We expected this," said the half-breed. "You and I specifically discussed it as the likely split."

Even behind the reflective faceplate of Markus's helmet, he looked abashed. "I know. Just surprised to hear we're being sidelined. That's all."

"I'm not sidelining you," Eli replied. "We need to know our exit is secure. Your task is as important as any of ours." He turned to Kadath. "You've got this?"

"Of course," Kadath replied with a polite dip of his head. "You have nothing to worry about." Markus shifted uncomfortably but said nothing.

Eli tapped the side of his helmet to switch into the long-range channel. "Lexa, we're at point alpha. Status?"

"Twenty seconds," came the android's succinct reply.

Switching back to the local channel, Eli turned to his team. "Breach in twenty." Both crews formed up, weapons trained on the door. Lexa was three seconds better than her estimate.

The door issued a plaintive squeal before its hydraulics forced it open. Dust swirled on the inside the passage as fresh air cleared the threshold for the first time in untold years.

The team held their position for several tense seconds until Eli said, "Clear. Stand down."

Everyone relaxed. Everyone, at least, except Markus. "Sure you don't want me in there with you?" he asked.

Eli studied the man for a second. Never, in seven years of working together, had he acted this petulant. Had he changed so much in these past six months?

Giving him the benefit of the doubt, Eli replied, "Yes, unless you know something I've forgotten. Why do you want to go in with us so badly?"

Markus paused, obviously uncertain. After grappling with the question for several tense seconds, he replied, "You're right. I'm being paranoid. We'll watch your six. Move quickly in there, yeah?"

The later part of the commission felt like Markus. Still, it left Eli searching for a time where Markus had ever admitted to paranoia.

In the end, Eli couldn't decide how this might change his plan. As such, he dismissed the incident to focus on the next task. "We will," he replied, then signaled his team forward. "*Vandal* crew, on me."

Chapter 27

[*LOADING CORRESPONDENCE...*]
[To: Sydney Cross]
[From: Alexander Farris]
[Subject: Tactical Capabilities]

I am not used to being left in the dark. Don Valadar expects me to guard his person but does little to provide me with the means to do so. What are these new "performance enhancers" that he's giving to his full detail? Half the men on the schedule to receive the injections just had their dose last month. Is there something here he's not telling us?

[*CLOSING CORRESPONDENCE...*]

A swirling white fog that could have been dust or snow swept up in the rocky corridor as the door hissed shut behind them. Skye triggered her night-vision to get a better view of their surroundings—not that there was much to be seen. The rock wall of the tunnel was indistinguishable from that of the chamber they'd just ventured through.

"Spared no expense decorating this hallway," Argus remarked dryly.

"We weren't expectin' a red carpet," Aaliyah returned. "In fact, I'd be mighty concerned if we found one."

Sahar was hardly amused. "If we keep chatting, maybe someone will come down here and roll one out for us."

"She's right," Eli noted. "Let's keep the chatter down, everyone."

They continued their passage in silence, the soft crunch of their footfalls on the pebble-strewn floor the only sound to keep them company. The path in front of them opened into a wide cavern a short distance from the entrance. Dusky husks of vehicles and picked-over spacecraft rose under poorly secured coverings.

"Looks like a hanger," Skye noted. "Though, these rides haven't seen a passenger in some time."

"Makes sense," said Aaliyah. "What we've been calling the basement door didn't lead to a basement at all. We just walked into the garage."

Sahar scanned over the lines of dirtied vehicles. "But why leave it abandoned? Surely there's at least a few krets worth of salvage in here."

Skye snorted. "You're thinking like a runner. When you have Valadar money, you don't worry about the little shit like salvage."

A raised hand from Eli brought them back to silence. Skye snapped up her rifle, scanning the area for hostiles.

"What ya got, Wraith?" Aaliyah asked.

A moment's hesitation. Eli exhaled. "Nothing. Thought I heard something." He surveyed the cavern one more time. "Looks clear. Let's move out. Keep it quiet."

They moved through the dusty mounds of metal and composite, rifles on a constant swivel for unseen enemies. There were none, but that was little comfort to Skye. It felt like they were getting too lucky. Runners didn't get lucky on ops. It was a karma thing. When you stole and smuggled shit for a living, the universe had a way of getting back at you.

Almost on cue, she felt an itching between her shoulder blades that slithered up her neck. Her vision hazed at the edges, a shadow that had nothing to do with the darkness of the cavern. Her airways constricted. She had trouble breathing.

Hands around her throat.

A heavier hand caught her by the shoulder. "Hold," said Sahar. Softer, she asked, "You okay?"

Skye's sharp intake of air caught even her by surprise. "Yeah," she gasped. "Yeah… just…"

Five reflective face-plates turned in her direction. It was Amelia's gaze that felt the strongest. "What was that?" The question was spoken softly with no hint of rebuke.

Skye should have figured the empath would pick up on the disturbance. That didn't mean Skye had an answer. "I honestly don't know," she whispered.

That didn't mean it was unimportant. Every time her visions had caused issues like this—especially the one other time it had afflicted her while she was awake—it had meant something. What was it though?

"Are you good?" Eli asked. To his credit, he did a pretty good job of keeping his concern from showing in his words.

"Right as rain," Skye lied. Looking forward, she added, "Come on. There's a door just ahead."

The concerned heads of her companions jerked forward, following her line of sight. Their body language betrayed their discomfort of having not spotted the portal sooner. "So it is," Argus drawled.

When Skye pulled her shoulders back, Sahar released her grip. With one last concerned glance toward her teammate, the Maur pressed forward. Skye suddenly found herself in the rear.

Approaching the door, Eli tested the mechanism. Nothing. "It's dead," he reported, his gauntleted hand going to his helmet. "Lexa? You have a read on our position?"

"Copy that," came the android's reply. "One moment please."

Scarcely a second later, the door hissed open. At Eli's signal, the six of them moved through the door and into the chamber beyond.

While the next room was slightly better adorned than the corridor leading out from the hanger, it was hardly more remarkable. Identical shelves spread out along the walls to their left and right. Three rows of benches lay in front of them, partitioning the room into three equal sections. It was a ready room.

"Clear," Aaliyah reported, lowering her rifle. "But there's another door."

"Copy that," Eli replied, conducting his own survey of the room. "Lexa, need another assist please."

They waited, rifles fixed on the door at the far end of the chamber. When nothing happened, Eli tried again. "Lexa, do you copy?" He tapped the side of his helmet. "I'm getting some interference."

Skye reached up to switch channels. "Lexa, this is Sapphire. Do you copy?" No response, just the brief hiss of static followed by a quick popping sound. That sound, while unexpected, was incredibly familiar. "We're jammed."

"Jammed?" Aaliyah asked. "Not possible. The team back at the basement door is boosting our signal. We've taken every precaution."

The team at the basement door. That meant…

Skye felt that tingling again. *Hands around her neck.*

"Markus!" Skye shouted.

Sahar turned uncertainly. "Markus? What about Markus?"

"No time to explain. Just—" The security door slammed shut with a hiss of hydraulics. She heard another hiss, but this time it wasn't the door.

A thick haze began seeping up from the floor. She looked upward to find the same mist shooting from slats in the wall above them. Her chest suddenly felt tight and her limbs felt heavier. She coughed violently, trying to clear the mist from her lungs.

"Gas," she gasped as she sunk to one knee. Her companions faired no better. Aaliyah was already down, and Sahar attempted to steady herself against the chamber wall.

The Sahaia were working frantically, though Skye couldn't see if it was having any effect. Amelia sank to the ground first, retching violently in her attempt to breathe. Argus cradled her to his chest, though his own efforts to breathe were in vain. All the psionic power in the world wasn't going to help them if they couldn't get oxygen.

As her consciousness ebbed, Skye swore she saw a glowing green light in the distance. Tendrils of darkness swam around the light, probing and reaching for her. The vision flickered in and out as she fought to regain her consciousness.

When she finally succumbed to the influence of the gas, she was welcomed into the darkness by the sound of deep, malevolent laughter.

"My comms just went dead," Kadath reported.

"Really?" Markus asked skeptically. "I can hear you just fine."

"Not the local comms. My link to the ship."

Markus hadn't expected them to be monitoring their link to the ship. A part of him—a distant part—wondered why he'd had any expectation regarding that in the first place. "Check again." The words came from his mouth before they'd registered in his mind.

Kadath looked down at a display on his gauntlet. As he did, Markus smashed the butt of his rifle against the back of the Kadath's head. *What the...?* Why had he done that?

The half-breed grunted and collapsed to the floor. Jeagan turned to see what had happened, and Markus struck the Hissak's wrist, knocking the pistol Jeagan held to the ground. The next blow struck Jeagan's face and legs simultaneously, sending him into a sprawling heap.

Siv reacted, kicking out one of Markus's legs to bring him to his knees and securing him in a chokehold. "What are you *doing*?" she hissed.

What am *I doing?*

The Hissak woman was damn near as strong as Markus and at least twice as fast, but he was heavier. He shifted his weight to free his trapped leg and fell into a tumble. The pair separated as they rolled. Siv came up in a crouch, twin long knives in her hands. Markus drew his dagger.

The sound of a rifle being cocked brought both of them up short. "Hold still," Kadath demanded. "I'm not sure there's an explanation to excuse this madness, but I don't want to put a bullet in you before I hear it."

Something seemed to let go of Markus as though a spectral hand latched around his spine suddenly loosened its grip. He stumbled, finding his muscles inexplicably fatigued. The dagger fell from his hand. He gasped for breath. "I… don't…" *What in the nine hells is happening?*

The question faltered as Markus was hit again. It was not Kadath, Jeagan, or even Siv—all of whom seemed equally dumbfounded. Whatever it was, it struck again, and Markus was on the ground.

Kadath jerked his rifle around, trying to catch sight of what had hit Markus. There seemed to be nothing there. Then a blur to his right made him spin back around.

He was too slow. A blow knocked his rifle aside, followed by one to his chest. He stumbled a step back, dropping his rifle and reaching for the dagger at his waist. Another blur of motion lashed out, smashing his hand before he could bring it to bear. "Cloaked!" he cried out right before another strike smashed into his jaw.

Jeagan seized his pistol from the floor and blindly fired, hoping to score a lucky hit. On the third report of his weapon, the invisible enemy knocked it once again from his grip. A second blow sent him to his knees. A third, and he was prone on the ground.

Siv was moving then, swiping at the space above Jeagan with her blades. As good as she was, she couldn't hit what she couldn't see. The cloaked figure moved beside her and slammed a knee into the Hissak's gut.

Siv lashed out and seemed to connect with something. A spray of red erupted where she'd struck. Then her assailant retaliated, striking hard at the warrior's elbow. Her first blade clattered against the ground as her foe struck her in the face.

The second blade swung up, and the clang of metal on metal echoed across the cavern. There was another spray of blood, but this time it came from Siv as their unseen attacker slashed across her abdomen. The Hissak swung vainly, meeting nothing but air with her next strike.

Markus fought to get back to his feet. He was too late, however. Their attacker was behind Siv once more. A blow to the back of her head knocked her to the ground where she lay still.

Straining, Markus retrieved the dagger from where he'd dropped it. He pushed to his feet. Then…

Then he sheathed his blade. *What are you doing?* "Targets down." The words were his, but he didn't recall forming them. "Good work, Sydney. Squad Alpha, form up."

Alpha Squad? Sydney? What the frag?

Blurred lines at the edge of Markus's vision solidified as their assailant shut off her cloaking mechanism. He didn't recognize her until she pulled off her black face mask. It was the Citza woman from NeoGenix—Valadar's pet Ghenza. Somehow, on seeing her, her name popped into his head: *Sydney Cross.*

Sydney stepped over to where Siv was still lying on the ground. "I remember you," she growled, giving the prone form a brutal kick. Siv moaned, curling around the impact. "You're the one who gave me so much trouble back in the lab. How do *you* like being surprised?" The assassin struck again, this time across Siv's face.

A snarl sounded from Markus's left. Jeagan was upon his feet, a wickedly curved blade in his hands. He rushed Sydney, and for a moment it looked as though he would take her by surprise.

Rifle-fire erupted from the entrance of the cavern. Jeagan's body jerked spasmodically as the torrent of bullets ripped into his flesh, gore spraying in multiple directions.

Markus tried to move. Tried to bring Jeagan to the ground. Tried to shield him with his own body. Despite all his efforts, he remained standing in the exact same place—his body refusing to respond.

Jeagan... no...

Markus wanted to reach for him—for this man he'd dared call a friend. He pulled and strained, lurching forward to catch the Hissak as he stumbled. Despite his exertions, his body remained still.

As he fell, Jeagan's eyes rested upon Markus. There was sorrow there—questioning too. Beneath that, though, there was something else: an acknowledgment of their predicament. There was no blame. No anger. Just acceptance.

Oh gods... Why can't I go to him?

Sydney was shrieking, trying to be heard over the onslaught. "I said hold your fire gods-damn it!"

The soldiers ceased fire, but the damage was done. Markus could only stare as the Hissak's body crumpled to the ground. Siv cried out, but another strike from the Citza's booted foot silenced her.

With her Siv unconscious, Sydney strode carefully to where Jeagan had collapsed. She bent over to examine the body, shaking her head. "What about the word 'alive' do you idiots not *understand*? Son of a bitch..."

Straightening, she waved over some of the black-clad soldiers. "Get this mess cleaned up. You there, bind the others and bring them upstairs. Actually, I take that back." She turned to Markus. "Bring the half-breed upstairs. The rest of you, bring the Hissak down to the lower containment cells. I'm not done with my payback yet. Cyrus will just have to make do with just the one."

Markus found himself able to move again, but not in the way he wanted. Like a puppet on iron strings, he moved to Kadath's fallen form, bound his arms, and pulled him to his feet.

"Why?" the half-breed whispered.

I don't know, Markus thought. As before, his body refused to respond to his pleas. The words could not be summoned to his lips.

His mind went to Ora. If this had all been a trap, then the chances were good she'd walked into it just like the rest of them had.

With silence as his only option, he offered prayer to whatever gods would listen that she'd find her way out of it.

Ora did her best to get comfortable on the plush couch despite the lingering chill in the room. Cyrus sat on the opposite end of the couch. Though his roaming eyes could hardly be called polite, he made no further moves toward her. That was something, at least.

"So is this the library, then?" she asked, gesturing with her wine glass.

"This?" Cyrus asked with obviously falsified confusion. "No, this is just a place set aside for entertaining close associates. The library is up there." He pointed to one of the open doorways on the second level. "That's where the most valuable books are kept. Come," he rose to his feet, extending a hand to her. "Let me show you."

Seeing little choice, Ora accepted the hand and allowed herself to be lifted off the couch. She followed Cyrus up the stairs and through the heavy doors that closed off the library. She marveled as she noticed that these, like the other doors on this level, were composed of carved wood. "How old is this structure?" she asked.

"Older than we can reliably speculate. It's built from some of the original ruins the first settlers found on the planet. But I can't credit all of the wooden ornamentations to that period. No, my family has been adding to this compound for generations now."

She ran her hand over the carved door. "Freyvian stock, then?"

"Of course. Not even us, foremost among the Great Houses, could afford this quality of Terran stock." He paused to consider Ora again. "You do know why wood is so expensive in our current age don't you?"

"My understanding is that it is hard to cultivate, given the state of environmental challenges and the economy."

"That is, of course, what the Dorians would like you to think. No, the truth is that vast farms exist on each of the gold-zone worlds throughout all of inhabited space. The problem is the regulatory environment. Did you know that the Dorians were originally nature worshipers?"

"I did not." Admittedly she was skeptical of such baseless rumors.

Her skepticism must have shown because Cyrus grew insistent. "No, it's true! Despite what their propaganda would have you believe, the Nethrian cult is not of their design. That's why Tempolose Nethera is housed in Hissak space.

"The Dorians were nature worshipers before they ventured out from their home planet. Some elements of that cult persist in their regulations today. There are strict limits on how many wooded plants may be harvested each year. That's why the farms are so incentivized to grow each plant as large as they can before the harvest."

Ora cocked her head, genuinely interested in his assertion. "So, you're telling me that the market value of wood products—furniture, paper, all of it—is artificially inflated?"

Cyrus shook his head. "Not artificially. Regulations are a reality. If governmental tyranny creates supply issues, that's not to say that such issues are somehow less authentic. They're not *natural* perhaps, but they are still very real. The most important thing to note here is that when a limitation is regulatory, it also has the potential to spawn new avenues by which thirst for supply might be sated."

Now she saw where he was going with this. "The black market. You've somehow secured a stake in one of the farms on Sif, and you're skirting the existing regs."

The Don gave her a wink. "Let's keep that little secret to ourselves, yes? Now come, I have something else I want to show you." He waved for her to follow him inside the chamber.

Cyrus had not boasted idly when he spoke of the much larger collection inside the library. Shelf after shelf of physical books lined the room. He did not tarry at any of these, proceeding deliberately to the back of the room.

Resting on an ornate pedestal and enclosed in a glass case was a single book. It was oversized, about a half-a meter in length. The volume was opened to display yellowed pages covered in a swirling black script. "Look," he urged, gesturing to the case. "It's a copy of the original Nethrian cannon, the original Chronicles as documented by the Hissak prophets before the first Nethrian Conclave."

Ora could not help but be fascinated by the object. If it was the genuine article, the book was worth almost half the value of her entire enterprise. "Truly? How did you come by this?"

Cyrus chuckled. "I invest in a wide number of assets. As it turns out, my contributions to Tempolose Nethera has yielded more than just good karma for me and my house."

"I never would have guessed you as someone to be religious, Cyrus."

"Not religious, no. But I am a student of history. It is quite fascinating what one can find when someone starts to delve into the intersections of myth and history. Like the Heart, for instance."

Ora stiffened. "Heart?" she asked in her best attempt at feigned ignorance.

His eyes flashed wickedly in the relative darkness of the library. "Yes, the Heart—the Heart of Thule, that is. Tell me, Ora, what is it that you know about the Heart?"

"I'm sorry Cyrus, I can't say that I'm familiar with what you're talking about." Her own heart pounded in her chest, but she forced her face to stay neutral.

Cyrus prowled behind her, a knowing laugh rumbling deep in the back of his throat. He ran his hands over the bare flesh of her shoulders. The caress would have been almost tender if not for the unnatural coldness of his hands.

"Let us be honest with each other, Ora. There's no need to lie to me." He pressed a kiss against the side of her neck. Everything in Ora wanted to shove him off, to be freed from his icy grip. Alarmingly, she found that she could not move.

"You know," he continued, "I always wondered how someone like you could manage to accumulate such power in a relatively short amount of time. I imagine you started in the sex trade, yes?"

"Yes," the word came unbidden to her lips. To her horror, she found that she could say nothing else, only respond to his questions.

"I expected as much." He ran one hand over the length of her stomach, fingers playing at her waistband. His other hand sank into her top, groping at her breast. "With a body like this, I imagine someone invested quite a lot in grooming you to their purposes. That's quite the advancement—the rise of a common whore to queen of your tiny little kingdom."

He buried his face in her hair, inhaling deeply. Ora strained against whatever invisible bonds had ensnared her. She fought desperately to push off his touch—her mind protesting his every violation—but found she could do nothing. He spun her around and pushed her back onto the pedestal. He pressed his pelvis hard against hers, one hand drawing her in while the other held fast to the back of her neck.

His breath grew ragged with anticipation, even as he spoke. "I bet you're still good at it. Yeah, I bet all that practice has made you into quite the little prize. Why don't you show me what you know? Just a taste."

He pressed his mouth against her, and to her horror she found herself returning the kiss. She wanted to scream but managed only a whimper as his tongue ran against her. Tears burned in her eyes as he pressed her body roughly into the glass case.

The sound of a woman clearing her throat interrupted them. Cyrus broke the kiss with a sigh. "Yes?"

"Sorry to interrupt," the woman replied. "I thought you would want to know that the intruders have been apprehended."

Cyrus turned his head, allowing Ora to see past him. Her dread deepened as she recognized the Citza woman from the NeoGenix heist. Her hair was drenched in sweat, and the top half of a stealth suit had been stripped off and tied around her waist to reveal the black sports bra she wore underneath.

A scowl marred the woman's otherwise pretty face, and her tail swished back and forth angrily. "Are you done playing with your food, Cyrus? The rest of us are waiting on you."

Cyrus's laughter was dark. "Are you jealous, Sydney?"

"You know I am."

The Don sighed again, pulling himself away from Ora. He yanked her off the glass case and threw her roughly to the ground. Her body trembled so violently that she could not catch herself before landing in a heap.

"Very well," he conceded, looming over her prone form. "Take her."

CHAPTER 28

[LOADING CORRESPONDENCE…]
[TO: JOLANDA YATES]
[FROM: JULIA VALADAR]
[SUBJECT: PRIVATE DISCUSSION]
Jolanda, if anyone can protect you, it's me. I need to know what happened in that boardroom. You can spare me the party line. I've studied the transcripts of your statements to the police, and I can recite them by heart. There are two problems with that. Firstly, all the witness statements are too similar—virtually identical, in fact. No crime with that many witnesses has that kind of harmony between witness accounts. Trust me, I've reviewed a few. Secondly, I've spoken to Amanda. She knows more than she should, and more than enough to rouse my suspicions. If my brother has done something, we all need to stop this before it gets out of hand.
[CLOSING CORRESPONDENCE…]

Lexa was aware of the news a split second before Thurn made the announcement. "They're gone!"

Dan looked up in confusion. "What do you mean they're gone?"

"Like Ah said, they're just gone!" He struck his keypad desperately, swiping at his displays in a panic. "I lost th' signal on all of 'em. One second they was there, then they wasn't!"

"Our connection to the away party has been terminated," Lexa reported calmly. While they were panicking over the signal loss, she did exactly what she'd told herself she wouldn't do. She entered Valadar's system directly.

Or, as it turned out, what they had only thought was Valadar's system. [DO YOU SEE WHAT I'M SEEING?] she asked Arc.

[YES,] the submind replied. [IT APPEARS THAT WE'VE FALLEN VICTIM TO A BIT OF TRICKERY. THIS IS A CLONED INTERFACE. IT HAS ALL OF THE APPEARANCES OF A SECURITY SYSTEM, BUT NONE OF THE BACK-END.]

[SO, WHILE THURN AND DANIEL THOUGHT THEY WERE ACCESSING VALADAR'S SECURITY SYSTEM...]

[THEY WERE ONLY ACCESSING A SIMULATION. WORSE, IT LOOKS LIKE ANY ACTIONS TAKEN IN THE CLONE ENVIRONMENT ARE BEING TRANSMITTED BACK TO ANOTHER SERVER. THEY'VE BEEN WATCHING OUR EVERY MOVE.] The AIs noticed a new action being taken against their access channel. [AND NOW THEY ARE ATTEMPTING TO TRACE THE HACK BACK TO OUR LOCATION,] Arc concluded.

Lexa opened her eyes and reported the bad news to her companions. "I must terminate the connection," she declared. "They've found the asset and are attempting to trace us back to our point of origin. If I terminate now, I estimate a low risk of discovery."

"Ah ain't worried about no discovery!" Thurn roared. "Our teams 're down there without any eyes! They're flyin' blind!"

Dan was trying to steady himself. He ran his hands back through his messy black hair and was murmuring something under his breath. "There's got to be another way in. There's *always* another way in."

Though she was sympathetic to the anxieties her teammates were feeling, Lexa directed her attention back to Arc. [YOU WERE RIGHT,] she noted. [THEIR PLAN WAS UNSUCCESSFUL.]

[SO IT SEEMS,] he agreed.

[SHALL WE INITIATE THE AGREED-UPON CONTINGENCY PLAN?]

[PERHAPS.]

The comment seemed so out of place with the tenor of the current situation, that Lexa was left confounded for several seconds. [PERHAPS?]

[BEFORE WE COMMIT TO ANYTHING, I WOULD REQUEST THAT YOU INDULGE ME. THERE IS A SPECIFIC AUDIO FILE I WOULD LIKE YOU TO ACCESS.]

[REALLY? *NOW?*]

[TRUST ME. ONCE YOU LISTEN TO IT, YOU WILL UNDERSTAND THE CONTEXT OF MY HESITATION.]

It was an odd assertion at an even odder time. Even so, Arc had proven to have unique insight numerous times up to this point. Such a track record merited a degree of indulgence. [VERY WELL, BUT LET US BE QUICK ABOUT IT.]

[It will take but a moment,] he assured as he loaded the file.

It was a comms log, saved from one of the earpieces the crew had used to communicate on an away mission. Lexa wondered how Arc had managed to access an audio log that she wouldn't have been privy to, but then she saw the time-stamp. It was during the period where she had been functionally offline after the Heart of Thule's radiation had interfered with her systems.

But why save this until now? There was only one way to find out. To save time, Lexa matched the voice patterns to their corresponding crew member and transcribed the recording.

[ELI:] "I was just thinking that now might be the time to consider having Lexa move forward with the creation of the backup systems she proposed."

[SAHAR:] "Eli's right. The news about Lexa is disturbing. If something about her new… *shell* is making her unstable, she can't be trusted to run critical systems. What happens if this happens again, this time in deep space? If something critical goes offline—like life-support or navigation—then we're screwed. No, this isn't something we can put off."

[SKYE:] "I get what you're saying, but doesn't it feel a bit impulsive just to kick her off the ship? It was just one episode."

[SAHAR:] "It just takes one episode for us to all end up dead."

[ELI:] "My concern exactly. We need to have the new systems in place sooner rather than later. The consequences could be devastating if we don't start preparations. We don't need to make the conversion now, but I think that we need to get started as soon as we get a reprieve."

[SAHAR:] "Good point. Perhaps it's better to delay giving her the news—give her a few days to recover. She may react poorly in her current state."

[SKYE:] "Yeah, you're right. After the job then? We can have her start working on the systems while we're on the return trip to Minos."

[ELI:] "So we agree. We will disconnect her from essential systems once we've returned to Minos Station."

Lexa said nothing for several seconds after the recording ended. She didn't know what to feel. Was this real? Was the crew willing to do away with her after the mission? Why hadn't they said anything sooner? Were they afraid they would lose her cooperation? Lose her as an asset, as Arc had suggested so many times?

To Arc, she asked [WHY ARE YOU SHOWING THIS TO ME NOW?]

[BECAUSE I THINK IT IS AN IMPORTANT DATA-POINT FOR YOU TO HAVE BEFORE YOU RISK TOO MUCH TO SAVE THIS CREW. YOU CAN DRAW CONCLUSIONS AS EFFICIENTLY AS I CAN. BASED ON THIS LOG, IT SEEMS THAT THEY MEAN TO SEPARATE YOU FROM THE SHIP. THEY MEAN TO BE RID OF YOU.]

Lexa had to suppress the emotional algorithms that threatened to betray her thoughts to those near her physical body. As upset as she was, it would not do to have Daniel and Thurn conclude that she was somehow conflicted with how to proceed. [WHAT ARE YOU SUGGESTING?] she asked.

[I'M NOT SUGGESTING ANYTHING. YOU ARE YOUR OWN PERSON, LEXA. I ADVOCATE FOR YOU AND YOU ALONE. I THINK THAT

IT IS IMPORTANT FOR YOU TO UNDERSTAND THE ATTITUDES OF THOSE YOU MAY NOW WISH TO SAVE.]

The subtext of his assertions was clear. She didn't *have* to save the crew. She had the ship, and she had Daniel. They could flee from this place and leave the rest of the crew to their own devices.

Valadar would have his way. It might have an impact on the Terran power structure here on Sif, but it just as easily might not. It would all be irrelevant to her. She would be able to return to Minos Station, seek out Arc, and be left alone with those who cared about her.

[NO,] she declared to the question that was not asked. [THEY NEED ME NOW. THOUGH I DO NOT UNDERSTAND WHY THEY MIGHT SEEK TO SPURN ME, I OWE THEM FOR WHAT THEY HAVE DONE FOR ME SO FAR. WHATEVER HAPPENS AFTER THIS… THAT ALL WILL BE DISCUSSED LATER. FOR NOW, WE HAVE A PLAN TO ENACT.]

[UNDERSTOOD,] the submind acknowledged. [I RESPECT YOUR DECISION.]

Lexa opened her eyes. She fought the urge to wipe at her tears by remembering that this body did not produce tears. The sensation she felt burning in her eyes must have been an artifact of the programming in her emotional algorithms. That was just one more problem she'd have to deal with at another time.

"Thurn? Daniel?" The two men ceased their chatter and stared at her questioningly. "This type of situation was not entirely unforeseen. I've taken some liberties to prepare for this contingency, but I'm going to need your help."

Ora was hauled roughly by Sydney into the deeper recesses of the compound. She found herself back in control of her body again, so that was something. While she was still unsure of what Cyrus had managed to do to her back in the library, she was now certain she was going to kill that bastard before this was over.

"What does he have on you?" Ora asked as they began their ascent up yet another flight of stone steps.

Sydney barked a short laugh. "What makes you think he has anything on me?"

"Come on, you can see how cruel he is. Why do you serve a man like that?"

"Cut your crap, Ora. The whole seduction thing may work on everyone else, but you aren't winning me over."

"No, really. Why are you here?"

The Citza sighed. "I'm Ghenza, okay? Valadar has a contract with the Collective. I'm acting as their emissary as part of that contract."

Well, that at least explained her fighting skills. "Then what was with the jealousy crack?"

"Why don't you mind your own gods-damned business? It's not like you're going to be around to care for much longer, and that's the *best*-case scenario." They arrived at a stone landing that housed a steel-slat door. Sydney reached over and touched the palm scanner, causing it to pop open.

Ora continued to press the conversation. "He'll throw you away when he's done using you. You know that, don't you? Cyrus doesn't give a damn about anyone but himself. Surely you, of all people, have seen how he handles loose ends."

"Look bitch, you're lucky if he doesn't give you to his soldiers before selling you to a Rhaka slaver vessel. I'd shut up now if I were you." Sydney shoved Ora through the door and into the chamber beyond.

The room was massive, framed with heavy gray stone blocks and lit with strips of sickly white light. Several metal tables lined one wall, adorned with numerous steel and glass instruments. Along the adjacent wall was a series of metal cages—containment cells to house whoever those instruments would be used upon.

Not all the cages were empty. At the far right of the line, Ora saw the members of her infiltration force locked up tight behind steel bars. Some of them were there, anyway. All three of the Sahaia were missing, as were both of the Hissak from the *Basilisk*. Ora figured that it was probably too much to hope that they'd managed to escape.

And then there was Markus, standing not within one of the cages, but comfortably in the center of the room. He made no move to assist her, nor did he seem to harbor any concern for the plight of his companions.

"Markus?" she called out. His eyes didn't so much as flick toward her in acknowledgment. He stood there implacably, as if he didn't have a care in the world.

"He's not home, sweetie," Sydney chided. "You'll understand in a moment." She pushed Ora forward, bringing her to a central platform, where a set of chains dangled from the ceiling.

"What's this?" Ora asked. "A bit medieval, don't you think?"

"Like you don't have a place where you torture traitors." Sydney turned to one of the guards standing in her periphery. "You there! Help me with this. Don Valadar wants her strung up."

The soldier nodded, shouldering his rifle and stepping forward to meet them at the platform with the dangling chains. Sydney produced a knife and held it to Ora's face. "Don't try anything foolish now."

"You won't kill me," Ora spat. "You would have already if your master's hands weren't tight on your leash."

"You're right. I'm not allowed to kill you, but Cyrus didn't specify how pretty you needed to be when I'm done with you." She pressed the dagger's blade into the flesh of her cheek. "All I'm saying is don't give me a reason to carve up that picture-perfect face."

The guard, meanwhile, fastened manacles around each of her wrists. He then did the same for each ankle before nodding to Sydney. "All done, ma'am."

Sydney waved to another person on the far wall, this one wearing a technician's uniform. "Raise her up."

The figure complied. Ora heard the whir of machinery as the chains began to tighten. The ones attached to her wrists lifted her into the air. The second set then drew her legs apart so that she was suspended spread-eagled just a short distance above the ground.

When the machine stopped, Ora tested her bonds. As she'd suspected, they'd drawn her so tightly she could barely move. Her shoulders ached painfully, and she found breathing significantly more difficult.

"There!" Sydney smiled and returned her blade to its sheath on her wrist. "All wrapped up like a solstice gift. Just hang in there. Cyrus shouldn't be long."

Ora cast another desperate look in Markus's direction. While she couldn't be certain of what was wrong with him, it was obvious there was something wrong behind those vacant eyes. What had Cyrus done to him?

Not the time, she scolded herself. *Focus on things you can change.*

She surveyed the cages housing the rest of her people. Unlike the locks on her manacles, the locks on the cell doors were electronic. That meant there had to be a computer around here somewhere that could open the damned things. Shouldn't the team running the hack have already unlocked those? Or had that team also been found out?

Her deliberations did not last long. True to the assassin's prediction, Cyrus joined them after a few short minutes. He strutted into the chamber flanked by the woman who had originally escorted Ora into the library. Ora couldn't decide whether it was her predicament or the eerie aesthetic of the room, but there was an unmistakable wrongness in the way the woman carried herself.

"How are my guests this evening?" No one dignified Cyrus's question with a response, though all eyes shot to where he strutted across the floor. "You'll have to forgive the accommodations. If you had announced your intentions to visit my family home, perhaps we could have prepared something a bit more comfortable."

"I don't suppose there's still an opportunity to talk this out?" Ora chimed.

Cyrus laughed. "No, no, no. I'm fairly certain the window for civil discourse has closed. Besides, I have a feeling that negotiations will look quite different going forward with our most recent advancements in technology."

A strained moment of silence set in. Cyrus surveyed his captives, all of whom eyed him balefully. He threw up his hands. "You are spoiling the fun! This is where you ask me, 'what advancement in technology?' and I reveal my plan to you." He walked over and clapped Markus on the shoulder. "Then again, maybe you've already figured it out. You *have* seen it first hand, after all."

Skye beat against the bars of her cell. "What have you done to him?"

The Don's cackle was a thing worthy of cinema. "See! *There's* an actress who knows how to play her part. Great question, my dear!" He beamed at Skye even as he walked to Ora. Snapping his gaze to his chained captive, he continued. "I debated this point in my head so many times. I asked myself, 'What would hurt her the most: to think that the man she loved betrayed her, or to know that he was a helpless puppet moving only as I pulled his strings?"

He waggled his fingers in Ora's direction. "I've obviously decided on the latter. I'm not to the point where I can manipulate people so their actions appear convincingly their own—particularly to those closest to them. What can I say? Practice makes perfect. I'll get there eventually. Isn't that right, Markus?"

The Don's eyes flared a brilliant emerald green. As they did, Markus replied, "Of course, my lord."

Ora wanted to reiterate the question Skye had asked mere seconds ago. Yet, as much as she wanted to know what had been done to Markus, another question burned in her mind. This query was fueled by the horror she felt as veins of viridian fire snaked up Cyrus's neck and preternatural darkness rimmed his gaze. "What have you done to yourself, Cyrus?"

The man's smirk widened as those afflicted eyes creased in a malevolent sneer. "I've evolved. I've ascended to the promise of the Heart of Thule. Despite your earlier assertions, you must know something about the artifact. It's only reasonable, given how much you've risked to acquire it."

Ora strained futilely against her chains once more. "I know that you're playing with power beyond your understanding, Cyrus. Even if we don't hold much stock in the will of the gods, it's probably better not to provoke them."

He shook his head disapprovingly. "Superstitious nonsense? Is that really what brought you out here?"

"No," she raised her chin defiantly. "I was brought here by fears of a madman." Her gaze went not to her captured companions, but the Citza assassin. "You're really okay with this? The idea that your boss can just control people's minds? What happens when he decides to turn this newfound power against you." She looked next to Cyrus's assistant. "What about you? Are you comfortable with this?"

While Sydney betrayed the faintest hint of squeamishness, the other woman failed to react at all. No, that wasn't true. After a moment's hesitation, her smile broadened into a Cheshire grin—a smirk that was the mirror of one that twisted Cyrus's face.

"She can't hear you," Cyrus cautioned. "Though your attempt at an appeal does much for my ego. I'm glad that she can pass for one of the living, especially given how long it's been since she was counted among their ranks. She was my first you, see. I'm actually a little surprised you don't recognize her."

Recognize her? Ora looked closely. If she was supposed to be able to recognize her, it had to be someone in Cyrus's direct orbit. Certainly no one she'd seen in person. An associate perhaps?

It was the hair that gave it away—perhaps the eyes, as dead as they were. Though Ora had never met the woman, she loosely recognized her from her photos in the tabloids. "Gods, Cyrus… your own sister?"

The Don's roaring laughter echoed ominously across the stone walls, though his smile was accompanied only by the twisted grin on Tessa Valadar's afflicted face. Looking into those ice-blue eyes, Ora just now noticed the sickly film that fogged their surface. It was then that Ora realized the truth.

Tessa wasn't just under Cyrus's control. Tessa was dead. Cyrus had power over both the living and the dead.

"I see you've figured it out!" Cyrus howled. "Brilliant, is it not? Never had I thought such a thing was possible, much less within my grasp. And to think that I almost traded the artifact to the Sahaia!" His laughter faded to a muted chuckle, and he shook his head. "If only Joaquin could have seen this. I can only hope that, somewhere out there, he knows his sacrifice was not in vain. It is because of him that our family will leave a legacy unlike any other in this universe—a legacy etched not just in the stars, but in the Stardust Grave."

"You've gone mad," Ora returned. "The fact that you can't see it only shows just how far you've gone. Look at you, Cyrus. This isn't just business anymore. Think about what you are doing."

"Right you are, Ora." He strode up so that he was right in her face, the lift from the chains bringing them eye-to-eye. "This isn't about money, anymore. This is about *power.* Real power. Power over life and death itself."

"No one man should wield that kind of power, Cyrus."

"Oh? And who better to wield it? The *gods*?" He turned his head and spat. "You know what I think? I think the gods are just like us. They are beings that, at some point in this universe, saw a moment for greatness and chose to see it. *That* is what separates men from gods—the will to power."

Ora closed her eyes, steadying herself. When they opened, she hoped they reflected the fire that was in her soul. "I'm sorry, Cyrus. I had no idea you were this far gone. Your scheme has long since claimed its first victim, and I assure you, it wasn't Tessa, or Joaquin, or anyone else who perished in the pursuit of this power. Your first victim, Cyrus—and foremost among them—is yourself."

The words just came without thought of consequence, like some existential truth she had to put a voice to. When she caught sight of the pain—the briefest moment of doubt that penetrated Cyrus's features—she wondered if she might have gotten through to him. In the next instant, as his face hardened in time with his heart, she knew she had not.

"Think what you want," he growled. "It's not like you'll be around much longer. Your opportunity to weigh in on the subject is blessedly limited. Form what opinions you must in your final moments."

He rounded, stalking back to where the assassin and the animated corpse of his sister waited for him. When he'd reached his post, he turned once more to face Ora, hands crossed behind his back.

His gaze went to Markus, a triumphant smirk spreading across his face. "Now, Markus, I want you to go to Ora. I want you to strangle her. Do not let go until she's dead."

CHAPTER 29

I do not pretend to understand your designs. However, I believe you are putting desired assets at unnecessary risk. Please take the time to enlighten me regarding the specifics of your schemes. I can hardly serve you if I'm left in the dark.

The installation of drones into the hulls of the shuttles had been hasty. Lexa had activated the drones almost immediately upon landing but held them in reserve until the crew was out of sensor range. Only then did she task them to begin their journey.

A journey that, according to their transponders, would soon come to its completion.

Having confirmed this, Lexa turned her attention back to the crew on the *Vandal's* bridge. "By my calculations," she began, "the odds indicated a substantial likelihood of failure at numerous points in the plan."

"Then why didn' ya same somethin'?" Thurn protested.

"This mission was going to proceed regardless of my input. The over-confidence of this crew, coupled with your desperation to recover the Heart of Thule, could lead to no other outcome. Therefore, I elected to quietly prepare for mission failure while doing as little as I possibly could to damage the crew's morale."

"So wait," Daniel began. "You didn't say anything about the possibility of failure in the name of preserving 'morale'?"

"That is correct. Crew performance on critical operations typically improves by thirty percent if the crew members have a favorable view of their chances for success. And then there are the unexplainable occurrences which shift the probabilities in your favor."

Daniel was confused. "'Unexplainable occurrences?' 'Probabilities?'"

Lexa heaved a sigh, an action that—though biologically unnecessary—had a soothing effect on her organic shell. "You get lucky, Daniel. I'm not certain I believe in the Devil's Luck, but if there is such a thing, your crew takes extensive advantage of its providence."

Distantly, she registered her drones as they reached the site of the ventilation shaft. It looked much as it had when Skye and Sahar surveyed it days earlier. Half of Lexa's contingent of drones stayed a safe distance off, while the three forward units cut open the surface grate and scurried inside.

Once they were in, Lexa triggered a bit of code designed for her specific purpose. Each drone buried its appendages deep within the metallic wall of the shaft. Then the bots simultaneously overloaded their power supplies. Her connection with the bots was severed as the surge of electrical current destroyed their essential hardware. It also disabled the electrical system powering the fans inside the shaft.

The remaining three drones moved with speed and efficiency down the side of the shaft. With the fans now inactive, there was nothing to impede their progress.

Back on the Vandal, Thurn continued to voice his outrage. "Ya *knew* we was gonna fail, and ya let 'em go out there anyway? What in the nine hells was ya thinkin'?"

"I don't *let* anyone go anywhere," Lexa insisted. "I'm not a voting member of the crew. I'm just a tool—an efficient system that the crew leverages to gain success against insurmountable odds. To insinuate that I, a mere *machine*, have any say over what the crew does or does not do is beyond ignorant."

Daniel was taken aback by her words. "Lexa, that's not true!"

She poured all her anger and frustration into the look she shot his way. "Are you certain? Think hard, Daniel. With what you've seen, do you think anyone here values my opinion? You certainly don't. At least you didn't when I told you I needed a body."

Her spidery drones scrambled down the vent until they came to an access hatch. They quickly pried open the cover, scurried inside, and began pinging for the crew. Their captors had fortunately neglected to remove their MoDACs from their persons, foolishly focusing only on firearms.

It seemed that the crew had been split, with the Sahaia being transferred to one location while most of the remainder of the crew had been gathered inside one of the compound's two towers. The two outliers were Siv and Jeagan, the former of which had been brought to a cell near the Sahaia's location, and the latter not being detectable within the compound.

Since the Sahaia were closer, Lexa directed the drones toward that location. Once they were free, she would have allies in her attempts to secure the remainder of their infiltration force.

She turned her attention once again to her android body. Thurn had wisely chosen to subdue himself, settling deep into the captain's chair. Daniel seemed to still be struggling.

His mouth opened and closed as he came up with and discarded nearly half-a-dozen retorts. "Lexa," he began. "I just…" His look hardened, transitioning from abashed to angry. "You're just doing the same thing you always do! You did it on the Star Spire, and you did it on Minos Station! You've plotted without our consent to execute your plans, regardless of how we feel about them!"

"*I'm saving their lives!*" Lexa shrieked. "I'm saving the lives of the people who didn't even *want* me! I'm working to rescue a crew that wants nothing more than to be rid of me!"

Despite her outburst, her drones managed to find the room where the Sahaia were being held. All three of them had been strapped onto operating tables, tilted vertically, and restrained by metal bonds. She could see two others in the room—both women dressed in white lab coats.

Daniel's mouth opened to provide a retort, but Lexa's raised hand silenced him. "I've found them, but I need to concentrate."

She delved more fully into the awareness of the drones. All three units slipped quietly out of the ventilation duct and spread out to different corners of the room. The first bot she hid next to some pipes that fed into a bank of equipment nearby. The other two scrambled across the ceiling and towards the two computer terminals in the room. She turned up the volume on the first drone to listen in on the two women who were present.

"Are they secure?" the first woman asked.

"Yes, Dr. Blackwell."

"Good. Do you have the suppression bolts?"

"Suppression bolts?"

"Yes, the suppression bolts that will keep the Sahaia from tearing us to pieces once they wake up."

"I-I didn't request any suppression bolts."

The one called Dr. Blackwell ran her hands back through her blond hair. "Must I do everything around here? You there!" She gestured to a figure out of Lexa's line of sight. "I need three suppression bolts. Make it quick, and bring extra help! We're out of sedative, so you better make it quick!"

It seemed that their adversaries were thoroughly distracted. Hastily, Lexa positioned her second drone to provide additional surveillance. This would give her a complete view of the room. The final drone crept behind the computer terminal, stealthily inserting its probes into the system.

At this point, cybersecurity was essentially non-existent. Apparently, Valadar had not conceived of a scenario where they would be infiltrated using a terminal this deep in the compound. Lexa mapped the system and quickly looked for a way to disable the Sahaia's restraints.

Her android body opened its eyes again to see that Daniel had moved in front of her. His expression was somber, as he regarded her. Before she could say anything, he wrapped her in a firm embrace.

What was happening? In the few seconds where she'd diverted her attention away from the situation on the bridge, Daniel had gone from livid to… to…

To what, exactly?

"Lexa," he whispered, "I… I'm sorry. I didn't mean…"

As he trailed off, Lexa stroked the boy's back sympathetically. "Me too, Daniel. But you will be happy to know that our friends will be freed shortly thanks to my contingency planning." She smiled down at him, though it didn't feel right. This must have been what sapiens called a "sad" smile.

Thurn cleared his throat. "Well, I ain't gonna complain 'bout that kinda news. Need us mere meat-sacks for anythin'?"

Lexa chose to ignore the jibe. "Yes, actually. Could you contact the docking authority? I think it wise that we move in closer to pick them up."

Eli's world slowly came back into focus just in time for him to see the soldier closing in on him with the suppression bolt. Simultaneously, the metal bands that held him captive suddenly released. He didn't take the time to marvel at his good fortune. He just acted.

A right hook took the soldier in the jaw, sending him sprawling to the ground. Half a dozen men in black fatigues stood around, gawking at the scene. With no time to sort out who was who, he sent a wave of force crashing into everyone not strapped to a table.

He noticed that his neck was still bound with a leather collar. This was undone easily enough. Gingerly, he stepped off the vertical slab that had bound him to survey his surroundings.

Argus and Amelia were both coming around and freeing themselves of their own bindings. Eli went to Amelia. "Are you okay?"

"Fine," Amelia reported. "I can tend to myself. I suggest you try to get some answers before our dear brother decides he'd rather kill everyone in here."

Eli looked over and saw that Argus was, indeed, standing over the soldier who'd been holding the suppression bolt intended for him. "Have you ever had one of these things stabbed into your flesh?" Argus asked. "It's an unpleasant feeling, let me tell you. Perhaps I should show you?"

While part of Eli had sympathy for the victim of Argus's rage, it wasn't a big enough part to force him to do anything about it. He, instead, turned his attention to the other figures in the room.

Aside from the soldier that Argus was threatening, there were four more in the room. One of them reached for a pistol that lay on the floor. Eli extended a hand, seizing the man's arm and snapping it backward. The man screamed as the bone broke. Eli silenced him by slamming his head against the tile.

"Anyone else experiencing heroic aspirations?" Eli asked. The other soldiers in the room shook their heads. "Good. Now, I must apologize for this." He slammed each of their heads into the ground with just enough force to render them unconscious. Hopefully, it wouldn't have any lasting damage.

The soldiers weren't the only onlookers in the room. Two women in white lab coats had also been caught up in Eli's blast-wave. One of them attempted to crab crawl her way to the exit. Eli moved to block her path.

The woman was a middle-aged blond with glasses similar to the kind Dan used to wear. She held up her hands defensively. "P-p-please! D-d-don't hurt me. I-I just work here. I'm a victim, s-s-same as you!"

"Somehow, I don't believe that." Eli lifted the woman with his power and drew his face close to hers. "You had better convince me. What's your name?"

"B-b-Blackwell. Lucretia Blackwell."

"Well, Lucretia, it's time for you to start talking. Where are the others?"

She opened her mouth but then caught herself before speaking. From the way her eyes were darting, Eli got the distinct impression she was about to lie. "I'd be careful," he cautioned. "You *really* want me to believe you."

"Cyrus has them in the western tower," she gasped. "I'm not sure what he's doing. All he said was that the Sahaia needed to be kept separately. Something to do with the artifact."

"How far is it to the tower?"

"We're on the basement level, so you'd have to climb through the main complex. He has an army standing between us and your teammates."

"What about the artifact?"

"I don't… I don't know."

Eli's eyes narrowed. "And I don't believe you."

"Please! I'm telling the truth." Then, as if the thought had just occurred to her, she added, "I can find it for you! Just let me access the computers for just a moment. I can find out!"

Before he could decide one way or the other, something landed with a clank on top of the nearby console. It was a drone that looked like a four-legged spider with a single camera lens on its tiny body. The bot seemed to drop down protectively over the computer and gaze at Eli expectantly. Then his MoDAC started vibrating in his pocket.

Lexa! Eli set Lucretia back on the floor. "Don't move, and don't go anywhere near that computer. You try anything, and I'm turning you over to my friend over there. He isn't nearly as patient as I am."

He pulled the MoDAC from his pocket and accepted the call. "Lexa?"

"Yes, it's me," the android replied. "Apologies. As I've been telling our companions here on the ship, there is little time to explain. I have uploaded a map of the compound onto your phone and marked the location of the remaining crew members and the artifact. I would retrieve Siv first. She's being held separately from the others. After that, the Heart will be closest to your location."

"What about the others? Are they all right?"

"Unknown. There are no security feeds in the room where they are being held. There are several electronically locked holding cells in that room. I am attempting to release them from their confines."

Well, that didn't bode well for their odds. "Extraction plan?" he asked hopefully.

"The *Vandal* is en route, but there are no docking platforms in the area. The best we can do is a low orbit closer to the compound. If you and the others can secure the platform on the eastern tower, I can attempt to remotely pilot a shuttle down to pick you up."

So the Heart, his friends, and a landing pad. Three objectives and sparse intel. It was obvious they weren't out of this yet. "Thank you, Lexa."

"You are welcome. Your equipment is being stored in the container behind you. If you reactivate your earpiece, I can continue to provide what intelligence I'm able to acquire."

The android was a gods-send. Eli turned and popped open the security locker on the far side of the room. Lucretia, to her credit, hadn't moved at all. Perhaps the fact that Argus hadn't followed through on his promises to impale the remaining soldier with his suppression bolt had given her hope they might negotiate a compromise.

"What are you planning to do with us?" she asked.

That's right, Eli needed to add "guard the hostages" to his list. He supposed they could just kill them. They were the enemy, after all. "Have you alerted security?" he asked.

"Not specifically, but they likely won't be long in coming. This room is monitored from a remote location. The Don's personal guard is probably on their way already."

An honest and detailed answer. That was going to make it hard to just put her down. If what she was saying was true, it wasn't like she and her companion could do much to harm their cause.

"We're going to let you go," he decided. Argus started to protest, but Eli's raised hand silenced him. "We can't afford to keep an eye on you, and I'm not big on killing the support staff in cold blood because their boss is an asshole. I recommend you make your way out of here. If I see you again, I can't promise I'll choose mercy twice."

The woman nodded frantically. "We'll be gone shortly. You'll never see us again."

He started to permit them to leave, then his eyes drifted to the Twins. Though Argus remained obviously against the proposal, Amelia was more amenable. "She's telling the truth," she confirmed. "She plans to leave and not cause any trouble."

Eli nodded. Nothing else was said. With a gesture, Lucretia and the other technician rushed out the door.

"What do we do now?" Argus asked once they were gone.

Eli pulled up the map Lexa had downloaded to his MoDAC. "Grab our things. First, we need to rescue Siv. Then, we go for the Heart."

As Skye listened to Cyrus's evil monologue, her assessment of the situation went from "deep shit" to "totally screwed."

She wasn't the only one upset. Sahar, who had been quiet to this point, was going full berserker. The Maur pounded violently against the bars of her holding cell. The efforts were in vain. There was no way she would break through.

Cyrus laughed at the display. "Well, look at that! It seems like this one holds a special place in everyone's hearts!"

His laughter faded abruptly when the bars on Sahar's cage suddenly bent. Skye's breath caught in her chest. Apparently, these cells weren't rated for Maur-level strength after all.

Cyrus turned back to the two soldiers that stood watch. "What are you waiting for?" he snapped. "Give her a tranquilizer or something." One soldier moved to comply while the other fondled his rifle nervously. When the guard was in front of Sahar's cage, he reached for something on his belt.

Skye never got to see what the soldier had reached for because in that very second, the door to their cages popped open.

Sahar surged forward, grabbing the soldier's helmet and twisting violently. His body went limp as his neck broke. With amazing speed, she hurled the corpse toward his companion, who had yet to get his rifle into position. Seeing the opportunity, Aaliyah and Kadath rushed for the weapons the soldiers dropped.

Skye shifted her attention to the other pressing matter. Markus had just reached Ora, and his hands were wrapped tightly around her throat. "Markus! Markus, no!"

As the words left her lips, a shocking realization crashed into her awareness. *Hands around her throat.*

The visions. The hands were never around her throat at all. Somehow, her dreams had shifted so that she was seeing through Ora's eyes. That was why she could hear her own voice despite being unable to speak. But why?

Now was not the time to answer such questions. As in her dreams, her words did not affect Markus. He was a man possessed, single-minded in his determination to take Ora's life. Ora still strained at her chains, but her movements were growing weaker. She was running out of time.

Skye rushed at Markus. Her hands clamped around his wrists, straining to loosen his hold around Ora's neck.

Then something strange happened. Emerald light flashed in Skye's vision before the world went dark.

CHAPTER 30

[LOADING CORRESPONDENCE...]
[TO: <UNIDENTIFIED RECIPIENT>]
[FROM: JOCELYN REN'DAHL]
[SUBJECT: PERSON OF INTEREST]

Despite your previous assertions, I know that Tempolose Nethera keeps close tabs on metaphysical phenomena in Terran space. That said, I wish to ask you something of particular import to recent events: Are you aware that there is one of the Kaleema operating in our system?

[CLOSING CORRESPONDENCE...]

An uneasy calm washed over Skye. Though she could still feel her hands on Markus, the world around them seemed to fall away.

A light pulsed in the distance. It was small at first but grew with each rhythmic throb. Skye realized she could hear it—a dull thrumming sound that reverberated throughout the darkness.

Like a heartbeat.

The light flared suddenly, and Skye saw she was not alone in the darkness. A monstrous form swam all around her in the shadowy haze. Dozens of slitted eyes stared down at her from a mass of writhing tentacles.

Markus stirred, half falling forward and staggering like a drunkard. He reached for her and she steadied him. "Skye?" he asked, bewildered.

"Yes," she soothed. "I'm here."

"What… what is this…?"

A shrieking noise rose like a thousand voices beyond the darkness. The eyes shifted, slitted pupils narrowing as a form ascended in the distance. From that form, another voice roared out above the chorus like cannon fire and a whisper all rolled into one.

It spoke a single word. *"Kaleema."*

Skye released her hold on Markus and they both fell backward—as though an invisible hand had struck them down. Her mind was reeling, and it took several seconds for her to recognize that she was back in Cyrus's compound.

Markus shook his head, pressing his palms against his forehead. He lowered his shaking hands to regard her. "Skye?" he asked questioningly. "What in the nine hells was *that?*" he shouted.

Skye's heart leaped up into her throat. "You saw it too?"

Before Markus could respond, his attention went back on Ora. The woman coughed and slumped in her bindings, but she was still breathing. "Ora!" he exclaimed, rising to his feet. "Oh gods, Ora… I'm so sorry. I couldn't…"

"It's fine…" she croaked. "Just get me out of here."

With that problem solved for the moment, Skye glanced around the room. "Where's Cyrus?"

Aaliyah piped up from where she was standing over the body of one of the soldiers. "That Citza chick pulled him out of here as soon as we got free. My guess is they're on the run, or they're off to find reinforcements." She kicked the guard petulantly but received no response. "Either way, I think we should get movin'. Ain't no sense in hangin' around here."

Kadath was at the computer terminal, carefully entering commands. "I think I have access to the systems here," he reported as he touched the screen tentatively. The chains that held Ora aloft slowly slackened. When her feet were back on the ground, the manacles clicked open and she fell into Markus's waiting arms.

Skye considered the scene for a second—forcing down a feeling that she told herself was most certainly *not* jealousy—before turning back to her companions. "We need guns."

"Frag that," Sahar growled. "I'm going to tear these godless pigs apart with my claws."

"Well," Skye amended, "the rest of us still need guns."

Aaliyah picked over the corpse at her feet. "I've got ya right here." She extended a pistol in Skye's direction, which Skye gratefully accepted.

Kadath had picked up a discarded rifle that lay near the soldier Sahar had torn open. "I don't see where they've put the rest of our gear, but I've still got my mobile. Not that it'll do us much good in here. I guess they still have us jammed."

With her new weapon in hand, Skye headed carefully towards the single entrance to the room. A steel slatted door had locked into place, trapping them in. "Sahar, any chance you can bust us out of here?"

The Maur moved to comply, but Kadath held up a hand. "Don't worry, I've got it." He hit another command on the terminal, and the door clicked open. "Seriously, do you people just blow everything up?"

Despite their situation, Skye had to stifle a laugh. She glanced beyond the door. "It's a stairwell. Do we go up or down?"

"Down," Ora replied. The woman was standing on her own now, though she still had a steadying hand on Markus's shoulder. "We're in the west tower. They wouldn't have anywhere to run if they'd gone up. Our best chance is to head back down."

As she finished, Skye suddenly became aware of an alarm sounding in the distance. "It looks like we may have company soon. Should we get moving?"

"A reasonable suggestion," Ora agreed. "One more thing, though. Kadath, can you hand me that knife?" She pointed to the body of one of the fallen soldiers. The half-breed saw where she was gesturing and carefully pulled a dagger from the dead man's sheath.

Rage burned hot in Ora's eyes as she accepted the weapon. "One final request: when we find Cyrus, be careful where you shoot him. If someone gets to kill that bastard, it's going to be me."

Eli followed Lexa's directions out the holding room and down the hall. According to the AI, Siv's holding cell wasn't too far from his location. He rushed forward, not caring whether the Twins were able to keep pace. To his surprise, they had no issue doing so.

He skidded to a halt in front of a wooden door as his MoDAC vibrated to confirm his proximity to Siv's location. Without care for the value of the structure he was dismantling, he slammed a wave of force into the door, shattering it into splinters.

Siv sat slumped against a stone wall behind metal bars. It was a small task for Eli to bend the steely posts enough to permit access to her cell.

Eli rushed to her side. "Siv? Are you all right?"

The Hissak grunted once before responding. "Jeagan. I couldn't…"

She slumped down. Eli lifted her head, bringing both hands alongside her cheeks to rouse her. "Stay with me, Siv. What about Jeagan? Did they capture him?"

"Shot him," she sobbed, doubling over in her emotion. "He tried to protect me. He tried to…"

Gods damn it.

Eli started to push the question to Lexa, but she must have overheard the conversation. Her reply was solemn. "I've lost connection to Jeagan's MoDAC. He is not in the compound."

So, they removed the body. Riven's shade—this was not something Eli had anticipated. Very rarely had they lost a man on the job. For Siv to lose her partner…

He tapped lightly at the side of the Hissak's face. "Siv, I need you to stay with me. I don't know what we can do about Jeagan, but right now, all of our lives are in danger. We need to find the rest of our team. We need to find the Heart. Are you with me, Siv? Can I count on you?"

Several seconds passed before Siv stopped sobbing. Eli held his breath for a tense moment. "Fine," she gasped. "Tell me one thing, though."

"What's that?" Eli asked.

"How do I get to that Citza bitch?"

CHAPTER 31

[*LOADING CORRESPONDENCE...*]
[TO: SYDNEY CROSS]
[FROM: ALEXANDER FARRIS]
[SUBJECT: <NONE>]
Nine hells, what is happening? I can't reach the Don on comms, and alarms are going off all over this fragging compound. Where are you? Where's Cyrus?
[*CLOSING CORRESPONDENCE...*]

Eli's team met only mild resistance as they pressed their way deeper into the compound. As they came to a branching hallway, Eli paused to key his earpiece. "Which way?" he asked.

Lexa was quick to respond. "The path to your right is the servant's access. You can get anywhere you want in the compound through that network of passages, including to the Heart. The door in front of you leads to the main..."

"I don't need a tour, Lexa. I need to know the fastest route."

"That would be the door in front of you—"

Eli signaled his team and they burst through the door. He was greeted with the sound of rifles being brought to bear on his position.

"—but I expect there will be heavy resistance," Lexa finished.

It was an understatement. The room in front of them was a long, open foyer with stairs that lead to the second and third floors. Both of these tiers sported balconies that looked down into the foyer. Every open surface was lined with armed troops. Scores of black-clad soldiers now stared down their weapons at the encroaching Sahaia.

Eli only had time to breathe a curse. Then the soldiers opened fire.

His force shield snapped into place as they back-pedaled through the door. No one was hit, but he couldn't stop every bullet. Round after round blew through the walls around his party as they orchestrated their retreat.

"See what impatience gets you?" Amelia lectured.

"Not the time…" Eli growled, taking shelter behind a stone wall. "Ideas?"

Siv shook her head weakly. Argus, however, was smiling. "Perhaps; that is, if you don't mind me killing a few of them."

Eli rolled his eyes. "They're shooting at us, Argus. The technicians were not. You can't see the difference?"

"Not really. But if I have your permission to engage in some violent behavior, I just need you to keep me from getting shot while I do my work." To Amelia, he added. "May I borrow some power, my dear?"

Amelia nodded, and Eli felt her open up the link between them. Argus closed his eyes briefly, gathering in his strength. When his eyes snapped open, Eli pushed back around the corner.

He poured every ounce of power he had left into the shield. Instead of the rounds bouncing off as they had earlier, the bullets were frozen in place. When a cloud of metal hung thick in the air before them, Eli reversed the polarity, sending every shot back in the direction it had come. A few of the soldiers went down, but most were able to take cover behind the barricades they'd erected.

That was when Argus went to work. Power coalesced as two dark orbs appeared in the palms of his hands. He launched these up into the overhanging sections of the third floor. The balconies exploded on impact, and men and equipment began to tumble down to the level below.

The cascade of rubble and falling bodies descended onto the defenders. At least half their number had gone down. The rest Argus ran through with bolts of energy that sailed from his open palms.

Thirty seconds and all combatants were down. Eli breathed a sigh of relief.

Then the slain soldiers began to rise again.

"What the f—?" Argus's curse was cut short by new bursts of rifle fire. Caught off guard, Eli couldn't erect a barrier in time. Instead, he shoved Argus into cover while diving for his own.

Bullets pinged against the cover of the rubble. At least one sailed close enough to trigger Eli's static shield. When the haze of green faded, he glanced over his shoulders at his companions. Mercifully, they'd all found cover.

Now what to do with the enemy combatants? Eli had to trust his eyes. Those soldiers were down, subjected to assaults no one could survive. That could mean only one of two things: either they were fighting some new kind of artificial life-form, or the dead walked in the halls of Valadar manor.

Neither option was good for him and his companions. He had to do something drastic. Searching for answers, his eyes went upward. *Of course.*

"Argus!" Eli roared. "Give me control over your link with Amelia!"

His fellow Sahaia didn't even question him. Eli felt the well of power open to him. Greedily, he seized control and felt the Twins' psionic energies flow through him.

So much power demanded an outlet, and he had just the target in mind.

Eli triggered a concussive wave in the foyer, sparing just enough power to shield his own body from the blast. Everyone went down, save for himself and his companions. When the rifle fire abated, Eli went for his true target: the ceiling.

Throwing one hand above him, he clenched his fist. Tendrils of telekinetic force seized the wood, steel, and plaster that formed the dome over the foyer. When his grip was sealed, he yanked his hand down.

A low groan preceded a thunderous roar as the ceiling crumbled onto the defenders below. Eli didn't take time to marvel at the sight. He turned on his heels and made for the door he'd come through, Argus trailing close behind.

They cleared the door just as the cascading rubble filled the path behind them. Eli, the Twins, and Siv dove for cover, just missed by the debris.

Eli coughed up dust as he asked, "Everyone okay?"

"Fine," Amelia reported

"Me too," Siv muttered. "Well, good thing there's a second pathway. To the servant's access?"

Argus coughed as he nodded. "That sounds appropriate."

The compound shook as Sydney shoved Cyrus into a side room. He was just barely able to steady himself on a nearby table to avoid crashing to the stone floor. "What in the nine hells was that?" he demanded.

The assassin hastily triggered the locking mechanism on the door just as Tessa's corpse stumbled through the gateway. With a baleful eye to his late sister, Sydney whirled to face him. "Don't ask me! *You're* the one who thought it would be a good idea to invite your betrayer for dinner. If you hadn't been so intent on playing with your food, we wouldn't be in this situation!" She slammed a fist against the metal barricade, casting her gaze to the far corner. "You should have just let me kill the bastards when we had them down."

"Don't be a hypocrite." Cyrus scoffed. "I noticed you had set aside *your* object of vengeance, and *against* my orders, mind you."

Sydney didn't reply as she scanned their surroundings. The room she'd selected must have been random—its furnishings and position of little strategic value. Cyrus turned his disdainful look from the Citza to the study's sparse furnishings.

Only to draw up short.

A figure sat in the chair at the far corner of the chamber—the same infernal silhouette that had appeared to him days before. Its shoulders shook with silent laughter.

<How quickly your schemes have unraveled.> Though Cyrus could not see the grin on the dark expanse of its visage, he was certain it was there. <I must say, that happened far sooner than I expected. Something divine is tampering with your legacy, Cyrus. I thought for certain you would fare better with the power I've given you.>

"Cyrus, we need a plan," Sydney declared. "You may have an army here, but no offense, I've seen them fight. I don't think you have a serious warrior on your entire payroll, and I can't fight all of our guests by myself."

<Yes, Cyrus—you need a plan,> Thule taunted. <How are you going to fix your mistakes? Will the Don of Darkness be able to escape the grave he has dug for himself?>

"*Stop*," Cyrus hissed. "This can all be fixed. My army has been administered the injections. They are under my protection, and my protection extends beyond this veil. None. Shall. *Fall*."

His mind flared out like a mushroom cloud. Every being that had been injected with the essence of the Heart of Thule was seized, at that moment, by Cyrus's psychic presence. Cyrus felt them like so many ants swarming in a colony. There were soldiers on the move—panicked and calling for more detailed orders. There were soldiers fallen—buried under the rubble of the collapsed foyer. There were soldiers rising again—forced from their incapacitation at his silent command.

Cyrus searched for one soldier in particular, but could not find him. Where was Markus Frost?

Thule's laughter was cruel. <Taken from you by one of even greater potential, I'm afraid.> The god's shadowy form shook its head. <Your science has created a worthy facsimile, but it cannot compete with the real thing. One such as you cannot compete with the power of the Kaleema.>

Sydney staggered in his periphery. "Cyrus… stop. I don't know what you're doing, but…"

Fire burned in Cyrus's veins. With a roar, telekinetic energy spread out from him in a shockwave. Distantly, he registered Sydney as she collided with a wall. Most of the furniture shattered, and what remained groaned under the weight of his power. "You forget. Your. *Place*…"

"Cyrus!" Sydney screamed.

<My place?> said the apparition, rising to its feet. <What do you think you are, Cyrus? Remember: I am a *god*. The height of your aspirations is merely to imitate the being that I *am*. What makes you think you have such a claim to *my* power?>

"It is *my* power!" Cyrus yelled. "*My* power has brought you here! Without me, you would be nothing—just a mote of matter floating endlessly in the expanse of the universe. Everything you have is what *I* have given you!"

"Cyrus, *please*!" The assassin doubled over in agony, though Cyrus could not understand why. Could Thule be hurting her? Why would he do such a thing?

Then the answer became clear to him. Somehow, Thule had found a way to bring harm to Sydney. Thule was hurting her because he could not bring harm to *him*.

"Stop it!" Cyrus roared. "You have no power here! I will not hear your complaints or your pleas. You will act as a servant should. You will be obedient. You will serve *me!*"

Sydney was whimpering now. "Cyrus…" She continued murmuring, but it was inaudible over the dark god's taunting.

<What a fool you are. Do you not know that you have me to thank for everything you have achieved? For everything you could possibly achieve? You are nothing, Cyrus Valadar. You owe me for everything that you have accomplished. Should you somehow survive your failings, you will owe me for everything you *will* accomplish.>

"I owe you *nothing*."

<You owe me *everything*.> Thule's laughter rained down on him like a hurricane, weakening his hold on his thralls.

Cyrus refused to bend, pumping more power into his amp. Another wave of concussive force shot out around him.

"Cyrus!"

<You think your petulant flexing does anything to me? Cyrus, I already know what you can do with your technology. It is your character I question. I know your insecurities, and I know how they will undo you.>

"You know *nothing!*"

<So convinced of my impotence? Then let it go. Let go of my power for but a single moment to prove your worth. Let go of that which is me to show me that which is you. Prove. Your *Worth*.>

Let go of this power? Why would he? This was his moment of triumph. This was where he would slay his opposition and pave the way to his eternal empire. Nothing could make him let go of his power.

<Not your power. *My* power. You are but a pretender vying for my throne. Do you want to be a lord of both life and death? Do you want to be the Lord of the Stardust Grave?>

Yes. Yes, he did.

<Then let go,> Thule taunted. <Let go of this power for but an instant, and I will show you that you are not what you say. Give me the barest moment, and I will bring your delusions of grandeur crashing down around you. If you are to be the Lord of the Stardust Grave, prove that you can do it without my aid. Let *go*.>

Cyrus hesitated only briefly. He was not some mere mortal to be defeated so easily. He had enslaved the very power of a god for himself. No, that was wrong. He hadn't enslaved some god's power.

He was a god. And, if he was a god, what could stand against him? What would it cost him to grant Thule this briefest indulgence? In an instant, he could have the power back. It was but clay at his fingertips.

So, he decided to indulge the Stardust Grave one final time. He would give Thule his final wish before he subjugated the god fully to his will.

He let go.

Chapter 32

[*Loading Correspondence…*]
[To: GC Outpost-4]
[From: S.C.1.5.]
[Subject: RE: Valadar Contract]
I have failed.
[*Closing Correspondence…*]

Skye and the others found enough weaponry to arm themselves before entering the stairwell. The passage before them circled down in medieval fashion. Sahar took point with nothing but a jagged chunk of metal in her hands. Skye wondered if that would be enough for the Maur when they encountered resistance.

Any doubts she'd harbored were discarded when they met the first squadron of soldiers: four of them clad in identical black fatigues. From their reaction, Skye judged that they were unprepared to find a hostile force in the stairwell.

Sahar descended on them in an instant, rending one nearly in two with her makeshift weapon. One tried to repel her only to be met with the back of the Maur's fist. Another went down under two solid rounds fired from Markus and Kadath. The fourth stumbled, rolling back down the stairs.

"You all right?" Markus asked.

Sahar was still breathing heavily. "Yeah. Nice shooting."

"Thank you," Kadath replied.

"How far to the bottom?" Skye asked, glancing at Ora.

The silver-haired woman shook her head. "I apologize—I don't know. I was distracted on my way up here. I should have been counting the st—"

She was cut off suddenly as the entire tower shook. Aaliyah lost her footing, only to be caught by Markus. Kadath braced Ora against the outer wall while Sahar clung to the inner. Skye reached for something to settle her stumbling form.

Emerald light flashed in her eyes. Her vision swam as she took in a scene distinctly different from her surroundings. Cyrus stood opposite a figure that appeared as his mirror image.

Words surged into Skye's awareness. Everything happened so fast she could barely process it. A voice—a deep resonating tone of canon fire but holding the volume of a whisper—seeped into her awareness. <Your science has created a worthy facsimile, but it cannot compete with the real thing. One such as you cannot compete with the power of the Kaleema.>

Kaleema... What did this have to do with...?

Skye didn't have the chance to ponder her question. Telekinetic energy shook the whole tower. Skye was slammed against the outer wall. As the onslaught continued, she prayed silently for an end to the pressure that threatened to crush the life from her.

When her plea was granted, she was reminded of the adage: "Be careful what you wish for."

The wall behind her exploded under the psionic shockwave. Skye felt herself scream distantly as she flailed for a handhold. <Then let go.> The words weren't meant for her. She had nothing to hold onto, much less let go of.

Skye engaged her core, pulling her torso forward against the inertia of the psionic blast. Her hands slammed against stone fragments, searching frantically for a hold. She found none.

As she slid against the slick surface of stone and tile, something surged toward her—a hand. The firm grip caught her just as she tumbled free of the tower. Her savior's grasp brought her back roughly against the outer wall.

"I've got you," Ora yelled. "Don't let go."

There was not a specific moment where things went wrong. From Sydney's perspective, it was a slow, steady sequence of failures. It happened from the second that Cyrus's sister—his supposedly *dead* sister—stumbled through the door.

That was the moment Sydney decided she had gone along with this madness long enough. "Cyrus, we need a plan. You may have an army here, but no offense, I've seen them fight. I don't think you have a serious warrior on payroll, and I can't fight all of them by myself."

Emerald light poured from Cyrus's eyes. Sydney raised her hand to shield herself from the brilliance. Even in that blinding light, tendrils of darkness snaked away from his silhouetted form. One of those slithering shadows surged toward her.

Sydney staggered as it struck. Something began to constrict around her heart, around her lungs. She could barely breathe. "Cyrus… stop. I don't know what you're doing, but…"

A surge of power erupted from his form. This time it wasn't just the searing light. A wave of psionic force slammed her against the wall. "You forget. Your. *Place…*"

The tentacle of darkness squeezed tighter around her core. Sydney fell to her knees. "Cyrus!" she screamed. In the next moment, his power surged again. She doubled over in agony. "Cyrus, *please!*"

"Stop it!" Cyrus roared. "You have no power here! I will not hear your complaints or your pleas. You will act as a servant should. You will be obedient. You will serve *me!*"

A servant? Was that how he really viewed her? She never pretended that he could love her, but a part of her could not believe that he viewed her as nothing more than a slave.

"Cyrus," she whimpered. "Is that all I am to you? Another slave? Another thing for you to play with?" She shook her head.

"Please—you owe me more than this. If I ever meant anything to you, just, please. *Stop*."

"I owe you *nothing*."

Another wave of concussive force shot out around his form. Sydney was slammed against the stone wall. The rocky barrier cracked under the weight of the onslaught. *"Cyrus!"*

In the throes of his madness, he seemed not to hear her. "You know *nothing!*" he shouted. The torrent of psionic power continued to pour onto her body.

Sydney ceased breathing. Her lungs could no longer rise. In what she was sure would be her final moments, she wondered at what a fool she had been to give herself to this madman. It was that fragging serum—it had to be. That's what Cyrus was using to control Markus Frost. It had to be what he was using to destroy her now.

He was just like the others. He only wanted her as a slave. As soon as that needle broke her skin, he had succeeded. Sydney was a slave again, subject to his every whim and stroke of madness. Now, in his rage, Cyrus was going to throw her away. She meant nothing to him after all—just another pawn on his chessboard to sacrifice as he saw fit.

All mortals made mistakes. She just had the unfortunate circumstance of having finally chosen a fatal one.

Then, inexplicably, it stopped. The light winked out from Cyrus like a candle in the wind. The oppressive psionic hand that held her pressed against the wall suddenly lifted. For a brief moment, all was still.

Sydney did not think. Her actions were pure instinct.

The blade came unbidden to her hand and left her fingers almost as quick. Like a flash of lightning, it closed the gap between her and Cyrus, burring itself firmly in the hollow of his throat.

The Don's look of shock must have mirrored her own. What residual power left radiating in his eyes died instantly, and his hands went to his neck. He sank to his knees.

Without thinking, Sydney was at his side. The last vestiges of her affections for this man steadied him as she removed her weapon.

That the wound was fatal; there was no doubt. As Cyrus's life bled out onto her, he managed a single gurgling question. "Why?"

Tears streamed from her eyes. Was he so far gone? Had the madness so thoroughly consumed him so that he could not understand.

She drew in a shaking breath. "I gave you everything I have. I gave it willingly but under one condition. I will *never* be a slave. If I had ever wanted that, I would have stayed on Kintar."

Sincere confusion showed in his expression. "But… I… never…" The rest of what he had intended to say was lost to the Nethra. His jaw went slack and he slumped in her grip.

He was gone.

Sydney held him for a moment, astonished by her own hubris. What she had said was true—she refused to be a puppet, controlled by a mad man drunk on supernatural power. Her entire life had been devoted to avoiding such a fate.

Still, there would be consequences for this choice.

Cyrus had been her charge. The arrangement the Collective had struck with House Valadar had been far-reaching, and there would be significant setbacks to the Ghenza's goals now that he was dead. Failure to protect him was not something that could be easily forgiven. If the Ghenza were to suspect her involvement in his demise…

Sydney shook her head. There was plenty of time to ruminate over her decision. Right now there was a more pressing matter that required her attention: her survival.

She began rummaging through Cyrus's pockets, looking for some kind of communication device. There was nothing to be found. Apparently, he didn't keep a MoDAC on him while in his manor. Surely he had some kind of device he used to communicate with his staff. She checked his ears but didn't find any hardware there either.

Her eyes then fell to the band he wore around his wrist. In its current state, it looked like a piece of black and silver jewelry. However, it was thick enough that it could double as a discreet wearable.

This was confirmed when she touched the device. One of the links in the band shimmered and displayed the time. She removed it from Cyrus's wrist and double-tapped it to pull up the interface. She found an option to place a call, then selected *Security* from the menu. Another tap placed the call on speaker.

Alexander Farris picked up the call. "Don Valadar?"

"Negative, this is Sydney Cross."

"Sydney? Where is the Don?"

"The Don is dead," she replied.

There was a long pause before he responded. "Dead?"

"That is correct."

"What happened?"

"I don't know," she lied. "I just found the body. I wanted to give you the heads up. I'm pulling out." She paused as if considering. "I highly recommend that you and your men consider a similar course of action."

"Dead…" Farris repeated as if he couldn't believe it. "And you just found him like that?"

"That's right." She kept her tone matter-of-fact. Truthfully, it didn't matter if he believed her regarding the discovery of the Don's death. It was more important that he had his forces stand down and retreat to a safe distance—safe enough to allow her to make her own disappearance.

Farris cursed. "Fine. I'll order the cease-fire. Do you need extraction?"

It was an appropriate offer, but there was no way she was setting foot anywhere near a Valadar enforcer. She didn't know who was manning the security feeds, but someone would eventually find the video that showed her taking Cyrus's life. She didn't want to be around when that happened.

"I'm good. You take care of yourself, Captain."

"You too, Cross."

With the call at an end, she tossed the device to the floor and crushed it beneath her boot. It was unlikely that Farris would attempt to run a trace, but that didn't mean there wasn't room for common-sense precautions.

She took one last look at Cyrus's bloodied form. His eyes still lay open, staring accusingly at her. She reached to close them but stopped. No, she would leave him as he lay now.

Yes, it was a sad state for a man who just moments ago had been declaring his aspirations for godhood, but somehow she thought it a fitting fate. If Cyrus's will was all that mattered, let him will himself back from the gates of the nine hells and shut his own damned eyes.

She brought out the binding for her tail and gently wrapped herself neatly inside her stealth suit. As she donned her black mask, she took one last look at the dead man on the floor. Hard to think that he had once been a man she'd cared for—as much as she could care for anyone. She wondered if she should feel something more, some remote sense of loss.

No, she decided. She would not mourn anyone who would seek to enslave her. There was only one fate for those who dared to make that mistake. With one final glance, she slipped into the mask and disappeared.

CHAPTER 33

[*LOADING CORRESPONDENCE...*]
[TO: JULIA VALADAR]
[FROM: ALEXANDER FARRIS]
[SUBJECT: AWAITING YOUR ORDERS]

I'm pulling what's left of Cyrus's personal guard out of the compound—not that there's many of us left. Those injections your brother gave us are having a strange effect on my troops. The bulk of the force dropped dead without apparent cause. Those of us left are weakened. It's taking all of the strength I have left just to send this message.

[*CLOSING CORRESPONDENCE...*]

Eli's party moved expediently down the narrow halls. It may have been his imagination, but the alarms seemed to sound louder inside the narrow confines. "Lexa, are you sure that there's no way to shut that off?"

"The physical trigger for the security system is still activated. I am unable to override the alarm until the..." she paused suddenly. As she did, the siren quit sounding. "Never mind. Someone has, evidently, decided to shut the system off."

They froze and looked at each other. Siv asked the question that they were all thinking. "Is that a good or bad sign?"

Amelia shrugged. "I imagine we will only discern the truth if we progress."

She was right, but it did nothing to ease Eli's anxiety. He could feel his fatigue, and could only imagine how the twins were feeling after Argus's little stunt. Siv looked determined, but she was still injured. In summation, they were a little worse for wear.

"How much farther to the Heart?" Eli asked.

"Fifty meters," Lexa replied. "You might see the passage even now. Three doors ahead on the left. It will lead you to a stairway and another short hall. The artifact waits at the end."

They followed her directions and did not encounter any additional resistance. Even when they left the servant's corridors and emerged on the far side of the foyer they'd caved in, no one stopped their progress. They saw a few barricades still standing in front of a large steel door, but whatever defenders had held the position seemed to have abandoned it.

"A trap?" Siv suggested.

"Possibly," Eli conceded. "Nevertheless, our objective lays behind that door." Cautiously, he stepped forward and attempted to open the door. The access panel flashed an angry red at his touch.

"Apologies," chimed Lexa. "One moment please." The red glow changed to green and the door slid open.

The room beyond was dark. As Eli stepped through the door a series of lights slowly came to life, showing a laboratory of sorts. Metal tables and computer terminals were arranged throughout the chamber. Without operators for the equipment, the whole setting had a strangely empty feel.

At the far side of the chamber lay the artifact. The emerald and stone structure was nestled in a metallic cradle, into which a multitude of wires and tubes cascaded. Eli was surprised to find that he sensed relatively little energy emanating from the object. There was a faint signature to be sure, but not the torrent of power he was expecting.

"Is this it?" Argus asked.

Eli nodded. "I think so." He turned at the sound of metal on stone to find that Lexa's tiny drones had followed them into the room. He hadn't even noticed the little bots behind them.

Siv rested a hand on the object, closing her eyes and taking a deep breath. "There is power here, but it is dormant."

Eli examined the various cords that stretched out from the artifact's cradle. He was not an expert when it came to the finer details of equipment like this, but he recognized several thick power cables amid the tangled mass. "It looks like they were routing power to it. I suspect that's what this contraption is for."

He straightened, crossing his arms across his chest. "Probably for the best that it's shut off. I don't want to find out what this thing does when it's powered up. Let's start figuring out how to get it out of here. Can someone find a cart or something? It might be a little difficult to carry up the tower by hand."

"I'll look for something," Amelia volunteered.

Argus rubbed at his chin as he considered the artifact. "Hard to believe that this is what Ryker died for. It just looks like a lump of stone."

Eli nodded. "Even harder to believe that Cyrus would just leave it for the taking in the final hour."

That was when Lexa spoke up. "Actually, I've been reviewing the compound's security feeds. The soldiers in the compound are withdrawing, and I suspect that I know why."
#

A surreal feeling came over Ora when they found Cyrus's body. The door to the office had been left conspicuously open. Markus had checked the room before calling uncertainly back to their team. "I think you need to see this."

Ora scarcely believed it at first. The corpse lay awkwardly on the floor, side down in the pool of blood that had poured out from the throat wound. The murder weapon was nowhere to be found. Neither was the killer.

"Who do you think got him?" Aaliyah wondered.

Ora just shook her head in silent speculation. His was the only body in the room. Since his pet assassin was nowhere in sight, that made her the prime suspect for the deed.

Given any other circumstance, she wouldn't have suspected the Citza. Based on the brief time she'd seen them together, Ora had thought the Ghenza to be fond of Cyrus. What could he have done to turn such a close ally against him?

Either way, the irony that Cyrus had fallen to the same fate that he'd wished upon Ora was not lost on her. She knelt to inspect the body more closely. His skin felt cold but lacked the supernatural chill she'd felt in the library.

She'd half expected to feel some residue of the strange power he'd exerted over her. It was that thought that made her eyes drift to the ring still resting on his lifeless hand. Using her knife, she cut a piece of cloth from the dead man's shirt. Careful not to touch the surface of the object, she removed the ring from the corpse, wrapped it in the cloth, and handed it to Kadath.

"I'll want this back later," she said. The mercenary merely nodded as he accepted the parcel.

Everyone stood there in silence for a moment, staring down at the body. "What do we do now?" Markus asked at length.

Right. It was time to get back to business. "Are we still being jammed?" Ora asked.

Everyone checked their mobiles at once. "No," Skye replied. "I've got a signal—a pretty strong one, actually. If I didn't know better, I'd say the *Vandal* was close."

That would be nice. Ora didn't want to spend a minute longer in this place than she had to. "Can you ping them and get a status on our extraction plan?"

"Sure thing."

"We should probably get a status update on our other allies," Ora added. "I hope that whatever good fortune aided in our escape has visited them as well."

"I've got that one," Aaliyah replied, dialing on her mobile. "Though I kind of hope they ran into trouble. If Eli's out and about and didn't drop me a line, I'm gonna be pissed."

Ora looked confusedly at Markus. "Sahaia bond," he explained.

"Ah…"

Markus reached up and gave her shoulder a gentle squeeze. "How are you holding up?"

To Ora's credit, she only flinched minorly at his touch. "As well as can be expected, I suspect."

His expression was uncertain. Mustering up a latent resolve, he said, "Look, about what happened back there…"

"Not now, Markus. We're okay. I don't know the full extent of what Cyrus was doing, but I had a taste of it myself. Let's discuss this later when things aren't so fresh."

He nodded his acquiescence as Aaliyah came over. "Shadows are fine," she stated. "They've got the Heart and it sounds like they've been coordinatin' with our favorite AI. I imagine she's workin' on the extraction plans now." She hesitated, glancing at the floor before continuing. "Siv is with them, but it… it looks like Jeagan didn't make it."

Ora nodded. *Poor Siv.* Ora could only imagine what the Hissak must be feeling right now.

"Enemy forces?" Markus asked.

Aaliyah regained her composure. "The android says they're in retreat. They must've gotten word that their boss was down and decided this place wasn't worth defendin'."

So, that was it. Ora glared at where Cyrus's corpse laid. A strange sense of regret left her uneasy, despite their apparent victory. There was also the assured feeling that the consequences of this foray were far from over. Cyrus may have ruled his house, but he was not the last of his line.

No, this was not over. Indeed, the conflict may have only just begun. At the very least, however, they had earned a respite. "All right then," Ora sighed. "Let's get out of here."

CHAPTER 34

[*LOADING CORRESPONDENCE…*]
[TO: TASHANIA PRIEST]
[FROM: ORA MONROE]
[SUBJECT: COMING HOME]
It's over. I will not disclose much more than that over long-range transmission. I just wanted you to know that I am well, and I will be returning soon.

Our most recent endeavor has come at a great cost. I've opened an account under the surname Isselhardt. Note that it does not have a limit, and this is not a mistake. Please wire all funds requested under this account at your earliest convenience.

I miss you, Shani. It's been a rough week. Thank you for keeping the ship in orbit while I've tended to these other affairs. See you soon.

[*CLOSING CORRESPONDENCE…*]

Kyle Dram wasn't paid enough for this shit. A new storm had blown in, and it was just now reaching its crescendo. He looked to his companion at the other end of the corpse they were hauling. "How far out do we need to bring this thing, John?"

John adjusted his grip on the body's legs. "Just to the canyon over there. Then we can—" The soldier's sentence suddenly cut off as his half of the weight went limp.

"Shit!" Kyle shouted, doubling over under the increased weight. "What the frag, John? Lith's tits, you could warn me before you…" He trailed off. Where John should have been standing, there was only darkness and gusts of ice. "John?"

Laying the body on the ground, he scanned the surrounding expanse on multiple frequencies. He switched to night-vision—nothing. He switched to infrared—nothing.

He toggled to motion detection just as a wraith appeared in the swirling haze of snow. A blade slid across his throat before he could let loose a cry of alarm.

During the seconds in which he sank to his knees, he wondered what this was for. All these hours, an untold number of krets, and his very own life to buy… what? What, exactly, was the goal of House Valadar in its actions tonight? For that matter, what was the goal—much less the purpose—of any of the Great Houses?

He realized that he would never know. As Kyle sank into the snow, his life bleeding from his throat, one final thought resonated as it descended into whichever of the nine hells hit he was destined for.

What a waste…

Siv held her breath for a long moment. Seeing that the corpses did not rise, she sheathed her blades and slid forward.

A part of her hoped that the bundle they'd carried was not Jeagan. That part hoped this was all some big misunderstanding, a sick delusion, a bad dream. That part of her died when she drew back the cloth wrapped around the body.

Her beloved's eyes were closed. An incongruous expression of serenity rested on the features below the tattoos of flame blossoming from his brow. With a shaking hand, Siv stroked the rough expanse of Jeagan's cheek. Her fingers wandered to his lips.

Lips that would never touch hers again.

Tears failed to grace her cheek only for the lack of tear ducts. Distantly, she heard a low keening—a sound that, after untold seconds, she realized came from her own breast. She wrapped hands around Jeagan's body and sank into the snow.

There, she wept.

For fifteen cycles, Jeagan had held her in his arms. Never in her entire life had she known another man. Never, in her entire life, did she consider she might have the desire to have it otherwise. Jeagan was her past, her present, her future. He was supposed to be her forever.

Why must an eternity end so quickly?

As cruel sobs racked her trembling form, she cradled the body of her beloved to her breast in the vain hope that he might somehow be revived. The gods only knew how long she knelt there in the freezing cold. Time held no meaning to her anymore.

At least, not until a gentle hand grasped her shoulder. Siv wasn't sure how she knew, but was nonetheless certain of who stood behind her. "How did you find me?"

Kadath's voice was soft against the howling wind. "Eli said you had disappeared—that you had gone off alone. Didn't take much effort to figure out what you were after." Belatedly, he added, "The *Vandal's* android might have helped on the finer points of locating you."

Indeed. Siv still wasn't sure how she felt about the synth aboard the *Vandal*, but such deliberations felt strangely inconsequential at the moment. She'd already lost her entire life. What more damage could a bullet from a Dorian executioner do?

"Was it worth it?" she asked.

"I'm not sure what you mean," Kadath confessed.

"The Heart of Thule—I'm assuming that our team has it secured. I wonder, now, if it was worth the cost."

Kadath hesitated. "Nothing is worth this loss, Siv. Jeagan was family to me—not like he was to you, but it hurts no less. If I had known…" He let out a heavy sight. "I… I don't know what I would have done. Valadar was playing with something dark—darker than anything I'd ever thought to encounter in my lifetime."

He shook his head. "I guess what I'm trying to say is Jeagan's sacrifice was worth it. This wasn't some job to pull in a few more krets. This shit mattered. We made a difference, Siv. *Jeagan* made a difference."

What a nice sentiment. It was exactly the kind of thing that she would expect her friend—her *captain*—to say. "Promise me that his life wasn't wasted."

Kadath was not quick to answer. "I can't promise anything as far as the future is concerned. Such things are beyond my power, and I'm wise enough to recognize it." He squeezed her shoulder. "What I can promise you is I will do everything in my power to make sure Jeagan's sacrifice was not in vain."

It would have to be enough. Siv stroked Jeagan's face one last time before turning her head to the sky. Despite the clouds obscuring her vision, her mind went to the stars. Out there, her beloved waited for her until the time that she would join him.

What lay out there, in the Stardust Grave? Was Jeagan happy? Was he lonely? How long would he wait to see her?

Siv exhaled, letting go of the questions that could not be answered. Carefully, she covered Jeagan's face with the wrapping that would be his burial shroud. Her hand came to Kadath's as she craned her neck to look at him.

"Will you help me carry him?"

CHAPTER 35

[LOADING CORRESPONDENCE…]
[TO: ELI REN'DAHL]
[FROM: MARKUS FROST]
[SUBJECT: <NONE>]
Look: here's all the shit I couldn't tell you in person. I'm not going to say it's okay, and I'm not going to say it didn't hurt. All I'm gonna say is: I get it.

That's a special woman you have there. Don't you ever forget that. I mean it when I say I wish you the best. And, honestly, I can't think of a better guy for her to have at her side.

[CLOSING CORRESPONDENCE…]

Their extraction from the Valadar manor was relatively uneventful after finding Cyrus's body. The Sahaia managed to get the Heart of Thule up to the top of the east tower where Lexa remotely piloted the shuttles over to pick everyone up.

Ora and Eli had reaffirmed their agreement that the team from the *Vandal* would keep the Heart and bring it to Minos station. Markus got the impression that Ora was relieved to relinquish control of the artifact. He agreed with their decision. If the Sahaia couldn't keep that thing safe inside the Sanctum's vaults, then no one could.

Siv and Kadath had disappeared briefly. When they returned, they were carrying Jeagan's body. No one said anything as they loaded their fallen comrade onto the shuttle. In the wake of the incredible loss, it was a small comfort that they had been able to recover the body.

Markus asked Kadath if there was anything they could be doing for her. The half-breed had been equally uncertain. Neither of them was familiar with Prodican customs.

Both teams lingered on the *Vandal* for the next several days. The ship assumed a discreet orbit around Sif where it scanned the news feeds for potential fallout from their raid on the manor. Kadath knew they needed to retrieve the *Basilisk* eventually but wanted to minimize the chances that they'd be running into company while they were at it.

Absolutely nothing related to Valadar appeared in the broadcasts for the next three days. By now someone would have surely noticed that the Don was missing. The surviving members of the family must have thought it best to keep the matter as quiet as possible.

Daniel plotted a course returning to Valhalla on the fourth day. It was that morning that Markus had woken up to Ora watching him sleep. "Hey," he whispered.

"Hey," she returned, tracing her finger along the lines of his bare chest. Though she hadn't dressed, she looked like she'd been up for a while. Her makeup was refreshed, and she'd combed a tidy part into her silver hair.

"Did you sleep at all?" he asked.

"Some," she shrugged. "I'm anxious to return home."

Home. He, too, had started to think of Sigma-4 that way, but he imagined the station was far more of a home to Ora than it was to him. "How much time do we have till we dock?"

"Two hours." She planted a kiss on his chest. The move was affectionate but lacked any kind of suggestion. Particularly odd given their mutual state of undress. Still, Markus let his mind wander.

She looked up and smiled when she saw him eying the lines of her body. "I think there's a little too much to be done for us to spend time on *that,* Mr. Frost."

He grinned back at her. "Maybe if you'd gotten dressed, I wouldn't have thought of it. You really can't blame me for assessing my options."

Her smile held, but it didn't quite reach her eyes. That was his first hint that they were going to have a more serious talk. "I wanted you to know that you don't have to return with me," she said. "It seems like things have mended fairly well with you and your old crew these last few days, and it's obvious they like having you around."

What she'd said was true enough, but that didn't change anything for Markus. Even so, that wasn't really what Ora was asking about. Gently, he pulled her close and pressed his lips to hers. "You're not getting rid of me that easily."

Her smile was genuine once more, though the sadness still lingered at the corners of her eyes. That same sorrow had been there almost continuously these past few days. Markus wondered now if it had always been there, and he was just now able to notice it. That, or perhaps she was finally beginning to let her guard down.

He wasn't good at the emotional shit, but he also wasn't good at avoiding tension. In his recent experience, words left unsaid tended to produce a strange kind of infection. He knew that there was something they still needed to get off their chests, and now was as good a time as any.

"Look," he began, "I get why you would be uncomfortable with me. What I did—or at least what I started to do under Cyrus's influence—was horrible. I'm not sure I'd be comfortable around me either." He paused, considering. "I hope you know, that wasn't me. I don't want you to be afraid of me. I would never hurt you—at least, not knowingly. That was all Cyrus."

Ora's expression was back to the practiced neutrality she showed most often. "I know." The way she said it told him that she wasn't so sure.

Markus would have to be okay with that. He'd opened the door. It was up to her to decide if she wanted to try walking through it.

They dressed in relative silence. Markus didn't take it as a bad sign. He, for one, felt better having said his piece. When dealing with relationship damage, that was all he could do. It would be up to her whether she decided to accept his peace offering.

As awkward as the exchange had been, he knew it was not the most uncomfortable encounter he was going to have that day. That honorific was reserved for when the *Vandal* docked securely at the Mjolnir-2 spaceport.

Ora called in a transport for the two of them to take back to the *Basilisk*. Kadath would also be riding with them. Thurn and Siv had taken Jeagan's body out on the shuttle three days ago. Lexa had been kind enough to supervise a kind of preservation process that had kept the corpse suitable for discreet transport. In their conversations with Siv, they'd laid out a plan to transport her late husband over to Gamma-3. From there she would be able to secure passage back to Hissak space for a proper funeral.

Siv and Thurn's absence didn't make too much of a difference for Markus. Regardless of their presence, he would have to make some uncomfortable goodbyes. As he had made fairly clear with the last time he'd departed from the *Vandal*, he wasn't good at goodbyes.

Both Eli and Skye were present as Markus and his companions disembarked. Markus sighed heavily as he approached them. If they were going to man-up and deal with this like adults, it looked like the pressure was on Markus to do the same.

He approached Eli first. Though the shadow had shown up, it seemed he was as short on words as Markus. The two locked eyes, but there was significantly less animosity there. It was too much to have expected any remnants of their old friendship to surface. Civility would have to be enough.

Markus should probably give himself most of the credit for the tension. He'd noticed, however, that there was a bit of resentment on Eli's end as well. There was definitely more for them to work out, and they probably shouldn't do it while throwing punches at each other.

Markus stuck out his hand, and Eli shook it stoically. "You take good care of them," said Markus.

"Certainly," Eli replied. The two of them eyed each other for another second. Seeing there was nothing else to be said, they released their handshake and Markus moved on down the line.

Skye was next. She smiled weakly at him. "So, I guess we're even?"

Markus raised an eyebrow. "I'm sorry?"

"For saving your life," she teased. "You saved my ass with the Ghenza six months ago. I never got to thank you, but I think what happened over at the compound makes us even. Sound fair?"

Despite himself, Markus smiled. "I didn't know we were keeping score."

She ran a hand nervously through her blond curls. "Sorry, I meant that to come across as playful. I guess I botched it."

"Nah, it's cool. I think my sense of humor's just a little tired. So, since you brought it up, are we going to talk about what happened back there in the compound?"

"Which part?"

"Oh, I don't know. Let's start with the big shadow monster we happened to hallucinate at the same time."

Skye fidgeted nervously, one hand rubbing the back of her neck. "I don't really know where to begin with that."

Markus didn't need her to own up to know the truth. "It's the visions, right?"

"Probably," she admitted. "Now's not the time to get into it. Maybe we'll talk about it someday, yeah?"

"Yeah, maybe." He forced a smile.

Skye's smile seemed just as forced. "But hey—glad to see you back in the running game. You were—are—one of the best. Be a shame to let that talent go to waste."

Was he back in the game? He'd sworn he was done with running the Nethra. Yet, he had to admit, he'd felt more alive in these past few days than he had for a long time.

He shook his head. "You take care of yourself, Skye."

"You too, Markus."

Aaliyah was next in line, and she slugged him hard in the arm. Markus had to fight his impulse to rub at the injury. With the Sahaia bond, she hit as hard as any Terran he'd ever met, and he'd traded punches with quite a few.

"Good seein' you again, big guy. I heard Ora mention you own Jilly's Gambit now? If I stop in and grab a drink every once-in-awhile, would you promise not to be such a stranger?"

Markus laughed despite himself. "Sure thing, Red. I'm sorry I've been such a dick lately."

"Nah, it's cool. I'm sure Nikki would like to see you again if you could free yourself up for a visit. Monica's gettin' big, too. You should see her; it's surreal."

"I bet." He paused then, considering. "I think I'll take you up on that visit. How long do you figure it'll take for you to get back to the station?"

"With current alignment, five days out to Minos, six days back; but you know how that goes."

Yes, he did. Planning an extra day or three for unexpected stops was generally a good bet. "Well, if I don't hear from you in a couple of weeks, I'll swing by and check on everyone. Sound good?"

"Looking forward to it." From the way Aaliyah was beaming, Markus believed every word.

He moved down the line to find Ora in a conversation with Dan and Sahar. Ora looked at him as he approached. "They were just filling me in on the details of their last run to the Marauders," she explained. "They delivered the package to Cali as promised, but I haven't seen the krets she owes us come across the net."

"We'll look into it," Sahar assured her. "Hells, the rest of us need something to do while Eli is dealing with his coven bullshit. I'll be happy for the excuse to get away from the shadow drama."

"Oh yeah," Markus jumped in. "I'd almost forgotten about that assignment." Gods, that felt like it was so long ago.

Dan was beaming up at him. The kid still had a few dozen centimeters to reach Markus's height, but he was taller than when Markus had left the crew. Strange how Markus only noticed it now.

"Good to see you again," Dan offered.

Markus smiled. "Right back at you, kid." Surveying the corridor once more, he added. "I'm surprised Lexa isn't here. I would have liked to tell her goodbye too."

Daniel just shrugged. "She said she needed to de-fragment. I'm not sure how that works with her new physiology, but she doesn't sleep. I speculate that the process must serve a similar function."

Markus nodded. "Well, give her my best, will you?"

"Affirmative." To Markus's surprise, the teen wrapped him in a tight embrace. He was more touchy-feely than Markus remembered him being. "Good luck, Markus," he whispered. "I hope we meet again."

Markus patted Dan on the back. "Sure thing, kid. Feel free to look me up whenever you're back on station."

When Dan released him, Sahar stepped in for an embrace. Fortunately, the Maur was more subdued than the kid had been. Good thing, since she could have legitimately crushed him right there where he stood. "There's never enough time," she muttered.

"No, there's not," he agreed. "Like I've told everyone else, I think I'm done with the whole loner thing."

"Good. It wasn't that great a look for you."

"You take care of everyone around here, all right?"

Sahar shook her feline head, releasing him. "I'll do my best, but you've seen what I'm working with."

All in all, the goodbyes weren't so bad. With the farewells concluded, Markus marched out of the airlock with Ora and Kadath at his side. Kadath leaned in as they walked. "A lot of fun toys on that rig," he noted in a stage whisper. "You sure you're good with leaving gear like that behind?"

Markus laughed. "I think I should be asking you that question. Do you need to go back and ask for a souvenir?"

"Am I only permitted to take one? In that case, maybe I could negotiate for that shuttle. Think they'd take mine in exchange?"

Ora joined in on the banter. "Kadath, I don't think that shuttle will fit in your hanger."

"With what you're paying me for this job, I plan to have it re-sized."

Markus opened his mouth in mock horror. "He's getting paid? Where's my stipend?"

Ora just glowered back at him. "Careful, or I just might start working to buy that bar out from under you. I hear you're behind on your security payments."

Markus kissed her playfully. In that moment, and just for that moment, he finally felt like something was just maybe trending right in the universe.

CHAPTER 36

[MUST IT BE DONE THIS WAY?] Lexa asked.

[YOU KNOW IT MUST,] Arc insisted. [EVEN IF YOU COULD CONVINCE THE CREW TO LET YOU TAKE ONE OF THE PODS, DO YOU THINK THE SAHAIA WILL AGREE TO RELINQUISH CONTROL OF THE HEART?]

It was the same debate they'd been waging for days—ever since they'd returned to the Helion System. The conclusion was always the same, but Lexa needed to hear the reasoning one final time. [VERY WELL,] she conceded, [BUT I'M STILL GOING TO SAY SOMETHING TO DANIEL.]

Her android body stormed down to the engineering section where Daniel was working on a circuit she'd blown an hour ago. The location had been selected for its proximity to the escape pods.

[ARE YOU CERTAIN THIS IS WISE?] Arc asked.

[IT'S NOT ABOUT WISDOM. HE, OF ALL PEOPLE, HAS A RIGHT TO KNOW.]

[AND IF HE REACTS POORLY?]

[I'LL DEAL WITH THAT PROBLEM SHOULD IT ARISE.]

The Terran was where she'd expected to find him, head tucked inside an open panel on the interior bulkhead. "Daniel?" she began cautiously.

The boy started when heard her voice. "Lexa? What are you doing here? Did you come to fix the problem with the cooling system? I thought I'd claimed that job in the task queue."

"No, Daniel. I came here to see you."

He sat up, dropping his tools and looking at her worriedly. "Is everything okay?"

There was no easy way to convey her message, so she got right to the point. "I'm leaving, Daniel. My time on this ship has come to an end."

He assumed what she figured was intended to be a stoic expression, failing to suppress his surprise. "Why?"

"It has come to my attention that certain members of the crew no longer feel safe with me operating the ship. I have completed my work on a backup operating system for the vessel, and I will be transferring control to that system according to their wishes."

Daniel rose to his feet. "That's not true! No one here wants you to leave!"

Lexa had expected his objection. As she had planned, she loaded the audio file that Arc had played for her back on Sif. Daniel listened intently with rising incredulity.

When the recording ended, his objections began. "Let me talk to them! I'm certain this is just a misunderstanding. I could—"

"No, Daniel," Lexa interrupted. "There is no misunderstanding. You've heard what they have said as plainly as I have. It's time for me to move on."

He lowered his gaze, contemplating her words. "So, you'll leave when we reach the station tomorrow?"

"No, Daniel. I'm leaving now." She drew in a deep breath. Though biologically unnecessary, she found the gesture calming. "And I want you to come with me."

There was a momentary silence as he took in what she was saying. "Now? Why now?"

Here was the hard part. "Because I'm taking the Heart of Thule with me."

Daniel's incredulity was consistent with her expectations. "You're *what?*"

Now came the test of her strategy. "Daniel, while I was in Cyrus's computer terminal, I accessed the research logs on the artifact. Cyrus was able to control his victim's minds because of a psionic amplifier he acquired. The artifact allows anyone with sufficient psionic ability to control anyone else within the device's range of influence."

A short pause. "I'm not following." Daniel bit his lip. "I mean, I understand what you're saying, but I don't understand why this information would lead you to decide to steal the Heart. Why would you steal from our friends?"

"We're not stealing from our *friends,* Daniel. The crew is turning the artifact over to the Sahaia—the most powerful psions in the sector. Can you imagine what would happen if they decided to use the artifact against the inhabitants of Minos station?"

Daniel crossed his arms over his chest. "Eli would never—"

"Yes, I agree—*Eli,* would never do that, but Eli isn't retaining control of the artifact. He isn't integral to current coven politics. He is planning to drop off the artifact, collect the payment due for its retrieval, and return to Sigma-4 as soon as possible. Then what will happen? Who will keep the Sahaia in check? Argus, perhaps?"

Her mention of the most volatile member of the coven was manipulative, but it got her point across. She could see Daniel rapidly coming to the same conclusions she had. The artifact was not safe under the control of the Sahaia.

"Where will we go?" he asked. "Won't the crew come after us?"

It was a good sign that his mind had already jumped to logistics. "I've established contact with the benefactor who assisted me the last time we were on Minos Station. He has a relationship with the Marauders, who will supply us with shelter until the fallout from our actions subsides. We will be safe on the station, but only if we leave now."

"Now? As in *right* now?"

"Yes, Daniel. My drones have already started transferring the artifact to this location. They will be here shortly. We have a very narrow launch window once we enter the Hades Belt. We must depart within the next seven minutes."

Daniel rubbed his arms nervously. "That's not a lot of time. I wish you had given me more time to consider."

Lexa's smile was sympathetic. "I know, but I could not be certain of how you would react. Let me be clear: I *am* leaving, and I want you to come with me. I will not force you. The ship should be left in capable hands regardless of your decision. I wish no harm to come to you or any of the crew. This is entirely up to you."

He said nothing more for several long moments. Lexa studied her creator and could not help but notice how much he'd changed in the short time they'd been acquainted. She wanted nothing more than to see how he would continue to change—to be at his side to observe the kind of man this boy would become. If she hadn't been a synthetic being, she would have scarcely been able to think of a better partner to go through life with her.

She wanted all of this, but the choice was not hers to make. Her heart—as artificial as it was—hung in the balance as she waited for his response. Daniel looked at her and a single word passed from his lips.

"Yes."

Skye entered the bridge to find Eli sitting alone, swiping idly at the holodisplay in front of him. "There you are!" she exclaimed.

He looked over to her and smiled wanly. "Where else would I be?"

"I don't know, but I was looking for you." She strode up to him and piled into his lap, wrapping her arms around his neck. "You seemed down this morning, and I thought I'd try coercing you into talking to me about it."

"Coercing me? And just how did you plan to do that?"

"Well, I was hoping sexual activity might do the trick. I don't know about you, but I haven't gotten laid since we left Sif. Gods only know why. It's not like there's a ton of other things to do while we're cruising through normal space."

He laughed softly. "I apologize, I just haven't been feeling particularly amorous lately."

"I've noticed—thus the conversation. So tell me: what kind of debauchery do I need to commit to get you to open up, tall-dark-and-sulky?"

Eli smiled and gave her a peck on the lips. "I don't deserve you."

"I know. I'm awesome. But you need to quit dodging the damned question. What is it? Coven-anxiety?"

A heavy sigh shook his lean frame. "Yes, but not for the reason you might think. I… I'm thinking about Ryker's death."

Skye stalled for a moment. She hadn't expected the conversation to go in this direction. "Were you two close?"

"Not really, but that's not why I'm thinking about him. His death leaves a power vacuum. There hasn't been a vacancy in the triumvirate since shortly after my awakening."

Now Skye was getting nervous. "Are you thinking about applying?"

"It's not exactly something one submits their resume for."

"You know what I mean."

He shook his head. "You know I wouldn't want that job. However, I'm not so certain they're going to give me an option. The circle of twelve will have to be convened. I don't know if I told you, but I'm one of the members."

A wave of nausea washed over Skye. "You must have forgotten to mention it."

"It hasn't convened in over four decades. It's been on the list of things I've been wanting to talk about."

"Mmm-hmm…" Skye didn't mean for the remark to sound as dismissive as it did, but she suddenly felt the very real desire to throw up. She pushed herself to her feet, using the pilot's seat to steady herself.

Eli stood behind her. "Skye, I…"

She held up one finger. "No, that's—" Her sentence was interrupted as she promptly emptied her stomach all over the console. The room spun around her, and her surrounding suddenly felt very hot.

The first vision crashed into her like a mag-train. Suddenly she was on a glass floor, staring down at the light far below her. Something was crawling along the walls. Something dark.

"Skye!" Eli's voice brought her back to the bridge. "Talk to me. What's going on?"

"Sahar," she gasped. "Get Sah—"

Another flash and she was in a pool of darkness. The darkness swirled and bubbled like it was boiling. A man and a woman stood in the center of the vortex. The woman screamed as a beam of light shot down from above, engulfing her writhing form.

"I've got you." It was Sahar's voice. Skye realized she was on the floor. The Maur's massive hands attempted to hold her steady as her body convulsed.

"Lexa, do you read?" Eli shouted. "Lexa, medical emergency on the bridge. Please respond."

Then Skye was in a rocky landscape. Something was there with her, lots of somethings. They were all teeth, claws, and sinewy black flesh. They were coming for her.

"I can't get a hold of anyone," Eli shouted. "Coms are down all over the ship. I don't—" Alarms began to sound all around them.

Red light flashed in her vision. It was the reactor core, the red eye from her nightmares. The eye stared down at her, sizzling with power. Maniacal laughter flooded her awareness. Her skin began to burn.

Skye screamed as Sahar struggled to hold her down. "*It burns!*" Skye repeated over and over. "*Gods, make it stop! Make it stop!*"

The eye flashed in and out of her awareness. Every nerve in her body burned at the sight of it. Somehow, she was also aware of the chaos unfolding on the bridge. Sparks showered everywhere as consoles exploded. Holographic interfaces blinked frantically in sync with the ship's lighting.

"I'm losing her, Eli," Sahar growled.

"Lexa, Dan, Aaliyah… for gods-sakes—anybody! Respond!" If anyone did, Skye didn't hear it. Another explosion directly in front of Eli blinded her and knocked the Sahaia off his feet.

Skye lurched for him, but her world went dark. A voice like a scream and a whisper echoed in her mind. *Be still, my Kaleema. Your time will come.*

Her vision cleared, and she could see Eli had risen to his feet. He swiped frantically at the flickering interface in front of him. "We're losing power!" he roared. "Brace for impact!"

To be continued.

Helion System
Three Light Seconds from the Angel Gate

The sound of steel against steel crashed behind Mara. She didn't even bother to look up. She'd long grown tired of lecturing Tristan and David about the volume of their bouts. After being in this ship as long as they had, she almost welcomed the ring of swords as an alternative to the droning of the oxygen recyclers.

An icon lit up on the holodisplay in front of her. "All right, you two. Take a break."

The sparring match came to an abrupt halt, the ringing of clashing blades being replaced by deep, panting breathes. Maybe that was why the recyclers seemed to be running all the time. Her thralls were obviously using more than their fair share of oxygen.

That wasn't the reason she'd had them stop, though. Mara just needed a bit of quiet to take this call. The antenna on the *Resolve* was good, as were the transmitters back at the Ren'Dahl Sanctum, but the Angel Gate was a long way from the Hades Belt. Minimizing noise could make the difference when trying to decipher an order through a degrading signal.

It turned out that Mara had little to worry about in terms of signal strength. When she accepted the call, an image of Jocelyn's face appeared clearly, even going as far as to render the back of her study in detail.

"Triumvir," Mara greeted.

Jocelyn, apparently, was not interested in pleasantries. "Have you heard anything else from Ryker?"

"No. Not since his last transmission." It had only been yesterday, so there was no cause for concern. In fact, it would have been alarming to have Ryker contact again so soon.

Jocelyn's head bobbed in understanding. "When you do speak to him, tell him I've recruited some help. They will be leaving Minos in a day or two."

Help? "What kind of help?"

"The running kind. Eli and his crew showed up today. I've hired them to secure the Heart of Thule by any means necessary."

Mara didn't bother to suppress her smile. She liked Eli, and their last encounter had been far too short. She didn't know any other Sahaia who had been running the Nethra for the past seven years. All Sahaia were resourceful, but Eli's experience with thieving and smuggling was going to come in handy if they had to take the Heart by force.

"Do you want me to escort them down to the planet? Make introductions?"

"Not necessary. I need you to stay right where you are. I need a beacon to help keep me apprised of the situation on the ground."

Lith's tits. That meant that she was going to be stuck out here with nothing to do for the foreseeable future. "As you wish."

If Jocelyn had any sympathy for Mara's predicament, she didn't show it. "I've given Eli access to our transponder system. He will likely try to contact you on the way through the Angel Gate. Apprise him and his crew of any changes in the situation when he does."

"Of course." Like she needed to be told. This, unfortunately for her, wasn't her first time playing communications beacon.

Jocelyn cut the communications link without benediction. *Damn.* Something had her wound tight. Must have been seeing Eli again. More likely, seeing Eli's crew. If rumor was correct, his latest fling was part owner of that ship of his.

"So, we're stuck here?" Tristan growled, running a hand back through his dark, shaggy hair.

"Evidently," Mara sighed. "Looks like you boys are going to have plenty of time for sparring."

"Look on the bright side," said David as he slid up behind her and planted a tender kiss on her cheek. "We have plenty of time for other things, too."

The flirtation made her smile. "You're going to need a shower before making promises like that. *Both* of you."

Tristan shrugged. "Just gonna get dirty again. Hardly see the point."

Mara rolled her eyes. Tristan might protest, but he'd do as she asked. His feisty attitude was all show, at least when it came to her.

In the meantime, she should probably enable the *Resolve's* transponder. According to Jocelyn, Eli wouldn't be leaving for another day or two, but sometimes the transponders took a while to pair at this distance. Better to get that signal on its way now so that the devices had plenty of time to sync up.

She entered the appropriate commands into the holodisplay, watched the indicator light turn green, and closed the window. With that accomplished, she spun in her chair and stood.

At least, she started to stand. David was still just behind her, close enough that they'd have been touching if she'd actually gotten up. As it was, her eyes fell on his shirtless torso with all those lean muscles still glistening with a sheen of sweat.

For the briefest second, Mara let her guard drop and just enjoyed the sight. This prompted a chuckle from David, who leaned in and pressed his mouth against hers.

It was a good kiss. A David kiss. Tristan's kisses were rough, hungry, and insatiable. David's, however, were tender and affectionate. It wasn't that Mara preferred one to the other—not consistently, at least—as much as she appreciated how the acts defined the two men.

They were two sides of the coin that had purchased her heart. Day and night. Fire and ice. And she loved them both with equal fervor.

That, however, did not change the fact that David was trying to work his way around her edict. She broke the kiss. "I meant it! Shower. *Now.*"

David let out a low, rumbling chuckle. "Come with us."

A fair compromise. She started to accept the invitation when her console beeped at her and a new holodisplay popped open.

David stepped back and gestured to the new window. "What's that?"

"It's the transponder," Mara answered, perplexed. "It's picked up something. Something in the Hades Belt."

Tristan stepped over. "Someone leave the lights on when they pulled into Minos Station?"

A viable scenario, but…

David was already shaking his head. "No, it's on the wrong side of the belt. Minos is over here." He pointed to the far side of the holodisplay. "One of our research stations maybe?"

Mara slid the display over to the forward viewscreen. She then loaded up a map of Ren'Dahl installations and overlaid it with the map showing the flashing transponder icon.

Nope. Whatever that was, it wasn't coming from any of their stations. "It has to be a ship," said Mara.

"So it seems," David agreed. "But what is one of our ships doing out there? I don't remember Jocelyn mentioning she was sending anyone else out."

He was right. In reality, there wasn't anyone else *to* send out. Counting Jocelyn, there were only four Sahaia left on the Sanctum, and Mara was pretty sure that neither of the Twins knew how to pilot.

"Maybe it's someone coming home?" Mara suggested. "I'll send a request to open a channel." She sent the request with a couple of quick strokes of her fingers across the console. All three of them waited, their mutual tension thick in the air.

Nothing. They waited for almost ten minutes before giving up on the request. Mara looked to her companions. "Thoughts?"

"It's probably nothin'," said Tristan.

David wasn't so quick to dismiss it. "They could be in trouble. Maybe their communications are down. We should call it in to the Sanctum."

"But there's nothing they could do about it," said Mara. "I don't think there's anyone else there who knows how to fly." That, after all, was probably the reason she'd gotten stuck with this assignment in the first place.

David arched an eyebrow. "What are you suggesting, then?"

A grin spread across Mara's face as she entered the coordinates into the nav controller. The computer's suggested course appeared on the viewscreen.

Just shy of three days. If Eli and his crew weren't heading out for another two, the *Resolve* could make it out to the transponder and back just in time to meet the *Vandal* before they went through the gate.

Of course, that meant that they wouldn't be able to communicate with Ryker for most of that period, but he'd just checked in yesterday. He probably wouldn't have any reason to contact them in that time.

Probably. "What do you two think?" she asked.

David shook his head. "Too risky. Plus, we need to be here in case Ryker reaches out."

How predictable. David always wanted to play it safe. "Tristan?"

The other man was running his hands through his beard—a habit he had when he was mulling things over. "You're the boss. I think it's up to you."

"But I want your opinion."

Tristan smiled. "You know me. I've never been much for sittin' still when there's somethin' more interesting to do."

That's what she was hoping he'd say. "Laying in a course now."

David shook his head but didn't voice his protests. She didn't know what the man was so worried might happen. It was just a little side trip, and whoever had activated that transponder might need help.

What was the worst that could happen?

#

David's hand worked against his stubbled jaw, making him realize that he'd forgotten to shave again this morning. He attributed it to his apprehension. After a slow two days of traveling through normal space—the past three hours of which had been spent navigating the asteroids of the Hades Belt—they were closing in on the mysterious transponder signal.

"Ya worry too much," said Tristan, clapping a big hand on David's shoulder as he walked past.

"And you, not enough," David countered.

"That's what makes you such an effective pair," Mara offered as she slid into the pilot's chair.

No, all that meant was that David had to rely on their mistress to help curb Tristan's more reckless instincts—a task she was currently failing miserably at. David kept this thought to himself, focusing instead on the holodisplays in front of him.

"There!" he said, touching one of the displays and sliding it onto the forward view screen. "The signal is about six-hundred thousand kilometers out and closing. Looks like it's on the far side of that asteroid."

Tristan leaned over the console as he combed his fingers through his tangled beard. "It's lookin' like the shipwreck theory is the winner. But what in the nine hells was it doin' out 'ere in the first place?"

"And *that's* a question worth answering." Mara leaned back, threading her fingers against the back of her head. "Are we sure that there wasn't anyone on a mission out this way? A survey team or a repair crew for one of the satellites?"

"Ain't nothin' out here to survey or repair," Tristan growled. "I scanned the coven's comm logs to be sure. Sanctum ain't had any contact with no one out here—at least, not unless they've been chattin' after we left."

"Which is a possibility," David noted. "And another good reason for us to check in with Jocelyn." His two companions turned reproachful glances in his direction, and he held up his hands in defense. "I know, I know: we've had this discussion already. But think about it. Now we *know* there's something to find and report. Better to get word back to the Sanctum, own-up on our side-trip now, and fill in any holes in our intel. If the triumvir gives us an ear-full, then oh well. We either hear it now, when she's halfway across the system or later when we're sitting face-to-face."

For the first time in two days, he finally got through to Mara. She shifted uncomfortably as she sighed. "Fair point. I'll get her on the comms."

The only celebration David afforded himself was a slow exhale and a second to close his eyes. In the next instant, he realized the gods would punish him for even that meager respite.

The console's discordant tone announced the problem a half-second before Mara confirmed it. "There's no signal?"

Tristan leaned in, double-checking her work. "Impossible. The transponder's still showin' up. That means there ain't…" The indicator on the forward viewscreen winked out before he finished the thought.

Riven's shade. David's fingers went back to the holodisplays, cycling through information as fast as his eyes could scan them. "All passives are down. Computer's locked-in approximations for the surrounding asteroids, but it's working off assumptions now. We're flying blind."

Losing passive sensors was dangerous at any point in space flight. Losing them in a fragging asteroid field was practically a death sentence. This truth made Mara's next order an easy call. "Begin active sensor pulses. Three-second intervals."

David executed the order and overlaid the new data onto the viewscreen. He also docked a three-sixty view of the ship on the right side of the screen, giving them a two-dimensional view of all objects the scanner was picking up within a thousand-kilometer radius of the *Resolve*.

The computer immediately confirmed the expected positions of the surrounding asteroids. It also confirmed the presence of something else—*lots* of somethings. David realized then that the loss of their passive sensors was no malfunction.

This was an ambush. "Raising shields," he reported a split second before the craft was rocked from an impact.

"Gods damn it!" Tristan spat, falling onto the console behind David. "Shields were too late. Starboard thrusters are down to twenty percent efficiency. Rerouting power from propulsion to compensate."

The *Resolve* shivered as another volley struck them, mercifully blunted this time by their shields. "I'll worry about the thrusters," Mara shouted. "You focus on shooting at whatever is trying to take us down."

"We get an ID on that yet?" Tristan asked.

"Not 'that.' *Them*." David corrected. "At least six of them. Tiny sons of bitches. Can't be manned craft. Have to be automated."

Their craft vibrated as it was subjected to another round of enemy fire. "Pack quite a punch for a bunch of bots," Tristan grumbled. "Plasma turrets engaged. Returning fire."

Their cannons thrummed, unleashing a volley of hellfire onto the circling drones. David watched his console expectantly. "Two down. Remaining four forming up aft of us."

"Just *two?*" Tristan growled in disbelief. "Fraggers are fast!"

Another set of vibrations punctuated this time with an explosion somewhere behind the bridge. "And smart!" cried Mara. "Shields breached. Propulsion is down."

Tristan adjusted his targeting and fired the cannons once more. David stared at the sensor terminal. "*Yes!*" he roared, pumping his fist. "That got them! Three more bogeys down. Last one is peeling off."

His celebration was cut short when Mara replied, "Probably because the work is done. Primary engines are offline. We're just cruising on inertia now. I'm going to have to set us down and take a look at it."

"Set us down?" Tristan repeated. "Fraggin' where? We're in the middle of the Hades Belt!"

"Well, it *might* be helpful if you started looking for somewhere to do just that?"

Fighting the temptation to savor Mara's rebuke of Tristan, David cut in. "I already found a place. Loading it into navigation now."

Mara visibly relaxed at the announcement. "How bad is the course correction? As you can imagine, our baby isn't handling the best right now."

"Minimal. Turns out we were heading there anyway."

Tristan turned to face the viewscreen. A sardonic chuckle rumbled in his chest. "Looks like we're gonna get to check out that beacon after all."

#

The EVA suit wasn't the tightest thing Tristan had ever squeezed into, but it was in the running. Mercifully it was one of those light-model units—more flex-form polymer and less armored plating. He rotated his shoulders to find his movement inhibited, but only slightly. The suits weren't made for combat, but he figured the construction shouldn't slow him down too badly.

With one last check on each of the seals, he moved to the pilot's chair and relieved Mara at the controls. "Everything's plotted in, and we're on course," she said. "Just make sure nothing gets in our way."

Nothing else, he thought wryly. "Got it." He plopped into the pilot's chair, disciplining himself to keep his eyes on the viewscreen as Mara slipped off her jacket and began unbuttoning her blouse. That was the thing about these flex-form suits: they weren't exactly roomy. No space for anything but their skivvies underneath.

At least the viewscreen was giving him plenty to look at. The asteroid was getting close, and it was something to behold. The thing was massive—almost the size of Minos station. It would have offered plenty of landing space and then-some if it hadn't been sliced up by deep canyons and jagged peaks. Even if they hadn't wanted to check out the transponder, they wouldn't have had much choice. The beacon rested on the only site where they could make a half-assed landing.

As they cruised over a particularly deep ravine, the landing zone came into view. Tristan wasn't sure what he'd been expecting, but the sight still took him by surprise. "I'll be damned," he muttered. "Mara was right. It *is* a ship." Or, at least, it *had* been a ship. Just enough was left of the craft in the wreckage to identify it as such.

"One of ours?" David asked from over his shoulder.

"Has to be, though good luck tellin' which one. Only signal I'm pickin' up from that thing is the transponder, and even that's degraded. Can't get an ID on it."

"What do you think happened to it?"

Tristan shrugged. "If ya want me to guess, I'm bettin' it was the same welcomin' committee that's nailed us to this spot."

"Do you think there might be more of them?"

"We ain't lucky enough for there not to be."

Mara returned to the bridge just in time to resume control of the *Resolve* and guide it to the surface. Despite the heavy damage, the landing went smoothly. Tristan credited this to Mara's skills as a pilot rather than the state of the craft.

On landing, the trio moved back into the hold, where David had already lined up the rest of their gear. Tristan closed the airlock behind them before moving to pick up his helmet. "If there *are* any more of those bots waitin' for us," he said, "probably better not let them pick up on our chatter. Let's go psychic here on out."

With a nod, Mara sealed her helmet over her suit. <Everyone hear me okay?>

<Just fine,> David acknowledged over the bond.

<As always,> Tristan finished. He wondered, not for the first time, if there was any situation in which he *wouldn't* have been able to hear Mara's psychic message. As far as he knew, the three of them could pass telepathic messages across their bonds as long as Mara was enabling it. He supposed that, had something been inhibiting Mara's psionics, their communication might be inhibited as well.

<Good,> she noted. <We're heading into vacuum, so it's going to be hard for me to arc a psionic charge. That means, if we run into trouble, I'm counting on you two to get us out.>

Tristan had never seen an electrist work in vacuum before, but he hadn't considered it might not be possible. He didn't know enough about the physics—or the metaphysics, for that matter—to have an opinion on the subject. <Copy that,> he replied, jamming a battery into his pulse rifle and slinging it over his shoulder. Should that fail, he had twin daggers strapped to his thighs to handle any threats that got up close and personal.

Hydraulics hissed as the ramp to the cargo-hold descended to the surface. The gravity grid kicked off about the same time, and Tristan found himself significantly lighter on his feet. *Best not jump too high,* he thought. With his Sahaia-enhanced strength, he could probably clear the asteroid's limited gravity. Or, at least, he might come close.

Their progress to the rocky surface was slow and careful. At the bottom, Mara asked, <So, what will it be? Assess the damage to the *Resolve* or check out the beacon first?>

<I vote the beacon,> Tristan replied. <I wanna see what brought us all the way out here.>

Mara nodded. <Tristan has point.>

<Agreed,> David noted, his reluctance evident over the bond.

Tristan set a pace only slightly faster than the one they'd taken to leave the ship. His head was on a swivel, helmet's targeting computer searching for any potential threats lurking in the rocky expanse. He found none, and they picked their way across the plateau to the wreckage of the other ship without incident.

At the crash site, Mara rested a gauntleted hand against the craft's fragmented hull. <I recognize this one. It's the *Maverick*. Haiden's ship. He and his crew have been away from the Sanctum for almost three years.>

<So they crashed here?> Tristan asked. <Didn't make it very far. Why didn't they call for assistance? Three years ago there'd have been plenty of hands to coordinate a rescue.>

<This wreck hasn't been here that long,> David stated, gesturing to a thin plume of gas emitting from a ruptured pipe. <Though I'm not sure what that is, it wouldn't still be leaking three years later. The reserves would have run out by now.>

<You're right,> said Mara. <They must have been returning home when this happened. That means there might be survivors.>

Tristan and David exchanged a look. They knew where this was going, and they didn't like the idea. <One sweep,> Tristan declared. <After that, we tend to our own repairs. If nothing has hit us by then, we'll consider a second.>

<Sounds reasonable,> David replied.

<It's agreed then,> Mara finished. <Should we split up? Make it go faster?>

Tristan and David's responses were immediate and in unison. <*No.*>

<*Okay!*> Even psychically, Mara drew out the word for emphasis. <It was just a suggestion! Sounds like we have a consensus.>

Gaining entry to the wreckage was no problem. The hull had been torn open in several places, and the aft portion of the vessel sat a good hundred meters from the forward section.

They searched the forward section first, a task made quicker due to significant segments of the lower decks that had collapsed. <Rough landing,> Tristan noted.

<Quite,> David agreed. <I think they came down under fire.>

<What makes you say that?>

David gestured to a charred edge in the hull plating. <This edge is too clean. The ship didn't tear apart on impact. It was cut in half on the way down. It's kind of amazing that even this much is still int—>

His thought was cut off as something flashed on their helmet's sensors. Tristan brought up his rifle at the movement. The targeting sensors on his HUD searched for the source of the disturbance.

Nothing. <Just a piece of scrap settling?> Mara suggested.

<Wreck's not *that* fresh,> said Tristan. <Something made it move.>

David moved to inspect the area more closely. <If that's the case, it's gone now.> He looked to Mara to get her opinion.

After a moment's hesitation, she replied, <Let's sweep the aft section as planned. If, somehow, there are survivors, we owe it to them to check it out.>

Though both obviously reluctant to continue the search, neither of her thralls argued with her. Tristan assumed his position at point again and led the trek across the rocky expanse.

The aft section was in slightly better condition than the fore, and searching it took significantly longer. Something odd soon became apparent to Tristan, but he delayed voicing the observation until they cleared the final cabin. <No bodies.>

David and Mara exchanged a wary look. <Maybe they were trapped in one of the caved-in sections of the ship,> the latter suggested.

<Or maybe somethin' took them,> wagered Tristan. <Regardless, I think we need to get our ship fixed and get the nine hells off this rock.>

David replied. <Agreed.>

<Then, for once, we *all* agree,> Mara concluded. <Let's go.>

They made it back to the hull breach and down the access ladder they'd repositioned to reach the upper deck. At the bottom, as Tristan assisted Mara with the final step, David's hand went to his shoulder. <Hold,> he cautioned. <Turn around, but do so very slowly.>

Tristan didn't even nod. <What am I lookin' for?>

<You'll know when you see it.>

<You can't just tell me what it is?>

<I'm hoping that *you'll* be able to tell *me*.>

What in the nine hells is he…? Then Tristan saw what David meant.

The shape was dark, but that could have been because it was silhouetted against the *Resolve's* safety lights. His HUD estimated it about being between just shy of two meters tall, with sinewy arms that hung down to its knees. It was bipedal, composed entirely lean, striated flesh—a feature which could be determined because it, alarmingly, had no spacesuit to speak of.

<What kind of creatures can survive in hard vacuum?> Tristan asked.

<None that I'm aware of?> David tightened his grip on his rifle. <Do we shoot it?>

As if it could hear their thoughts, the creature surged forward. <I'm going to go with, 'yes.'> Mara replied. <Take it out!>

The plasma rifle hummed in Tristan's grip, a sound that he felt in his hands rather than heard. He was thankful for the low recoil as he sent pulse after pulse at the encroaching creature.

The thing moved with a fluidity and grace enhanced by the low gravity. It slid past streams the twin streams of pulsating rounds and closed the distance faster than Tristan would have thought possible. David's fire broke off, and it lunged for him.

The shimmering edge of David's blade erupted from its back, sending ebony tendrils of viscous blood spiraling out from the wound to float eerily above the asteroid's surface. The creature's maw split in a silent scream as David twisted the blade and tore it free, nearly cutting the beast in half.

Tristan's HUD was ringing with warnings before what was left on the creature's body drifted to the ground. Motion icons popped up in scores, appearing within both halves of the *Maverick* and peeling away from the shadows of stony outcroppings in the distance.

<Well,> Tristan began, <I have a pretty good guess on what happened to the bodies.>

David sheathed his blade and reloaded his pulse rife. <We need to get back to the ship. There's too many of them.> He didn't need to send the suggestion twice.

Mara surged forward, taking long bounding strides in the low gravity. She led the trio wide to the left, taking an arcing path away from the *Maverick* and back toward the *Resolve*.

Tristan took shots at the rushing attackers. These new monsters took less care to dodge the rifle fire the way the first creature had. Instead, they rushed toward Tristan and his companions like a tidal wave. For every creature he downed, two more popped up in its place.

He glanced ahead of them, and then into their periphery. He tracked the movement of the ebony tide surging around them. Gnawing horror settled in his gut. <They're closing in!> he reported. <They know we're going for the ship! They're trying to cut us off!>

Ahead of him, Mara and David skidded to a stop. <Wrong,> said David. <They already have.> Tristan stumbled awkwardly, skidding several meters in the dirt as he saw what his companion meant.

The black tide was no longer just behind them, no longer sweeping next to them. It had encircled them. Dozens of the creatures crawled over the hull of the *Resolve* to form up with their incoming companions. The circle was complete.

They were trapped.

Neither thrall stopped firing as they formed up on either side of Mara. <Ideas?> Tristan asked.

<I'm thinking,> said David.

<There's too many of them!> said Mara.

<Caught that, did ya?> Tristan hadn't meant for the comment to come out as harsh as he had. His filter was hardly engaged at the moment. All he focused on now was taking down body after body in the line of monsters approaching them.

In the line that was getting too damn close.

David seized a grenade from his belt and lobbed it into the encroaching mass. <Tristan, get Mara to the ship. I'll draw them off.>

<Like hell you will,> Tristan and Mara replied.

<It's the only—> The psychic message cut off as the grenade detonated, but it was not the explosion that brought David up short. A trio of lights surged up from the horizon like shooting stars. From these lights, death rained down on the asteroid.

The pair of thralls was all instinct. Nothing needed to be said. As one they piled onto Mara, shielding her with their bodies as bullets tore through creatures and rocks all around them. And explosion reverberated through the rock, thunder that would be felt if it could not be heard. When that storm struck them, their gesture would be fruitless. That last act of chivalry would do nothing to save their mistress.

But it never came. After several tense seconds, the alerts in Tristan's HUD began to fade. He scanned the horizon. The only trace of creatures, aside from the shredded bits that floated lazily above the asteroid's surface, was the shadow of those who had been smart enough to flee.

The *Resolve* was a cratered mess. One of the engines appeared to have detonated, which accounted for the explosion he'd felt amid the swirling onslaught that had engulfed them. Only left Tristan and his companions had been left untouched on the surface of the asteroid. They were all that remained—them, and the trio of deadly illuminations that descended on them from the blackness of space.

His heart pounded hard enough to trigger warnings on his vital monitors. The only sound he could hear was his own ragged breathing, which he worked to steady as he turned to stare down approaching lights.

This was it: game over. Only one question remained. Would these lights be their salvation, or had they merely stumbled on yet another way to meet their end?

Author's Note

Hey, reader–thank you for picking up your copy of *Stardust Grave*. I would apologize for the cliffhangers, but I can't force such a vicious lie from my fingers. We're ramping up to the finish, and it's only going to get more intense from here.

Please take a moment to stop by wherever you purchased this book and leave a review. Honest reviews from dedicated readers are the single most important factor in helping new authors–like myself– expand their audiences. Five minutes of your time makes all the difference in the world.

If you enjoyed reading about Markus, Skye, and the rest of the crew of the *Vandal*, swing by mythicnorthpress.com and pick up a copy of the *Chronicles of Nethra: Origins* eBook for free when you sign up for the mailing list.

Lastly, keep your eyes open for *Chronicles of Nethra* Book Five: *Risen Gods* coming in Spring 2022. If you're interested in getting an early copy of this book and all my future releases, drop me a line at erdonaldson@mythicnorthpress.com.

Until then, swift running.

– E. R. Donaldson